AN EVIE BLACKWELL COLD CASE

TRACES OF GUILT

DEE HENDERSON

THORNDIKE PRESS

A part of Gale, Cengage Learning

GALE
CENGAGE Learning·

Farmington Hills, Mich • San Francisco • New York • Waterville, Maine
Meriden, Conn • Mason, Ohio • Chicago

GALE
CENGAGE Learning·

LIBRARY OF CONGRESS CATALOGING-IN-PUBLICATION DATA

Names: Henderson, Dee, author.
Title: Traces of guilt : an Evie Blackwell cold case / Dee Henderson.
Description: Waterville, Maine : Thorndike Press, 2016. | © 2016 | Series: An Evie Blackwell cold case ; 1 | Series: Thorndike Press large print Christian fiction
Identifiers: LCCN 2016012565 | ISBN 9781410490612 (hardback) | ISBN 1410490610 (hardcover)
Subjects: LCSH: Cold cases (Criminal investigation)—Fiction. | Missing persons—Investigation—Fiction. | BISAC: FICTION / Christian / Romance. | GSAFD: Mystery fiction. | Christian fiction.
Classification: LCC PS3558.E4829 T73 2016 | DDC 813/.54—dc23
LC record available at http://lccn.loc.gov/2016012565

Published in 2016 by arrangement with Bethany House Publishing, a division of Baker Publishing Group

Printed in the United States of America
1 2 3 4 5 6 7 20 19 18 17 16

TRACES OF GUILT

ONE

Joshua Thane

"Catch anything this morning?"

Josh Thane turned at a woman's friendly call, smiled as he stood, and promptly decided to leave the fishing gear in the boat for later. "Hey, friend. It's good to see you." He stepped onto the dock holding his bucket and a stringer with two fish. "I'd give you a hug, but you don't want to smell like me."

Ann Falcon laughed. "Appreciate your thoughtfulness."

"Paul with you?" he asked as he moved toward her.

"He's tied up in meetings, so today it's just me. I flew down from Chicago with some case files for a state cop, have plans to take her aloft to see the area this afternoon. I'll fly back tomorrow after I touch base with a few friends."

"Then what do you say to fresh fish for a

7

late breakfast? A hot grill, some lemon slices, and a nice plate in front of you in about thirty minutes."

"I'd say wonderful."

Pleased, Josh nodded and stopped beside her. "You get prettier every year, you know. Marriage suits you."

Ann smiled. "It's got nice benefits. I haven't been this relaxed about life for as long as I can remember. How about you? Seeing anyone in particular these days?"

"Can't say there's anybody specific, though Will seems to have settled on a girl since you were last down."

"I heard. Karen Joy Lewis. She's one of those friends I'm stopping by to visit."

"Oh, really?" Josh mentally recalibrated just who Karen might actually be. "I did hear she's from Chicago. What are the odds, you two being friends, that she just happens to end up in the small town of Carin . . . ?"

"Well," Ann said, grinning, "I might have mentioned she would like this town when she was considering a move."

Josh had been around Ann long enough to know the top layer of that answer was only the beginning, but he'd leave it for his brother Will to sort through the details. Will and Karen's dates over the last year had morphed into a pretty sizable crush on his

8

brother's part. Given Ann's comment about her relocating, Josh idly wondered if Karen Lewis was actually her real name.

Ann had worked mostly homicides before she retired as a cop, but she'd had her hands in a lot of different matters since then. The fact she was a pilot had her on call for just about any kind of situation needing to move people quickly out of trouble . . . or toward it. Josh had been out on several ground searches with her over the years, his two dogs being part of the statewide K-9 responders. He couldn't say walking fields looking for a buried body was anything but grim, yet the hours spent walking with Ann had cemented a good friendship.

Ann followed as he went to the cleaning station and with deft strokes filleted the two bass, tossing the remains down the sluice chute into the lake. The gulls would have the scraps picked clean before the meal was ready.

"You do that with such skill."

"A lot of practice." Josh finished rinsing his knife and returned it to its holder. "It's easier to clean a fish than dress out a deer. I'll leave the hunting to others in the family."

"What's the latest on sightings of wildlife around here?"

Josh loved the question. Carin Lake and its surrounding woods covered enough territory to attract a broad array of creatures to this central Illinois area. "There's a cougar I hear occasionally, one ranging wolf — big, beautiful silver-gray pelt. We've got some fox, a lot of deer, wild turkeys, rabbits, birds of all kinds. Hawks are thriving, and four nesting pairs of eagles at the north end of the lake soar this way most days."

Josh led the way from the pier across the parking area to the trail back to his place, a comfortable five-minute walk.

"I see you've added on the study you've been talking about," Ann noted, taking in the house as they approached. His multilevel home fit into the landscape, showcasing the skilled touch of a good designer who understood nature.

"I'm threatening to now actually write that book I've been talking about — *Photos and Stories of Carin Lake* as told by its most distinguished fisherman."

Ann didn't chuckle at his offhand remark. She swiveled half a step to view his face, then nodded to herself, looking pleased.

He knew that look. "What?"

"You're settling down."

"Bite your tongue," he shot back.

She laughed. "It's a fact, Josh. The youngest of you Thane brothers is no longer darting hither and yon — you have a business, a boat, a house, and now an interesting project in mind that will require time, thought, and reflection."

"Ann," he said, shaking his head, "I'm not that guy. Gabriel can settle down — he's the Carin County sheriff — with a need to be the calm, settled rock around here for the long haul. And Will might do something similar now that he's back home. Give him something that needs tending and he's fine. He'd probably like a bunch of kids, spend his days patching up scrapes and settling disputes and teaching them to care for the animals he's healing or raising. I'm the bait shop guy, with the boats, thirty miles of lake and inlets — the more time on the water, the better life is for me. Settling down to marriage and a family is impossible for me to fathom."

"There speaks a man who hasn't met the right woman yet."

Josh smiled, but didn't correct Ann's casual rejoinder. Actually, he'd met the right girl already. He'd grown up with Grace Arnett on the periphery of his youth. She'd moved away when she was fourteen, abruptly gone from his life. But that first passion, one serious enough even his broth-

11

ers hadn't kidded him about it, had roots. His mom had wisely let him grieve his loss for a long while before gently prodding him to ask another girl to the community dance, getting him back on the path toward living. He had moved on, though he hadn't forgotten Grace. Yeah, he'd found his "right one" a very long time ago.

Josh unlocked his front door and led the way inside to the parts and pieces of his life — the books, the cameras, the outdoor gear spread about but in a fairly orderly way. Though he lived alone, he lived neat. This was home, and he kept it comfortable for himself and those of his family and friends who dropped by.

Ann perched on a stool in the kitchen and watched while he put together the makings of a meal that would land on the outdoor grill. He paused to get them both cold root beers, not bothering to ask her drink of choice. She'd been forever swiping his extra bottle of the locally made root beer, one of the better exports of Carin County.

Once the fish was searing on the grill outside, he pulled out a medley of fresh vegetables, also for the grill, selected a sharp knife, and deftly began cutting the pieces.

"I'm in need of a favor, Josh."

He nodded, slicing mushrooms thin.

"Thought as much."

"Am I that transparent?" She raised an eyebrow.

"Only to old friends. You're worried." He tapped a finger against his forehead. "If somebody knows your face well, you've got a little giveaway that's easy to catch. It's not Paul, or you would have already said something. Not Karen, or you wouldn't have laid that hint on me about her, then casually moved on. Probably not my brother Gabriel — if you knew of trouble at that level, you wouldn't be here. You'd be talking with the deputy sheriff or with Will about protecting Gabriel's back from whatever it is." He paused, tilted his head as he considered her. "So . . . process of elimination, you're worried about something, and I'm the guy who might be able to help you solve a problem. Spill it. Let's see what I can do."

"I love the fact you know me so well, Josh. Just saying."

"Have you ever added up how many hours we've walked and talked about life while trailing dogs on the search for gravesites? Kind of like Will and his army buddies. With hours to talk, you get to really know someone. You and I, we got past surface stuff years ago. If you weren't too old for me," he added with a grin, "I would've been testing

13

the idea of Paul being your right guy."

She laughed. "Easy on the age references, pal. I don't qualify as your mother."

Josh simply smiled again.

"I have a friend who's going to ask you for a favor. If you can accommodate her, I'd like you to say yes. It's mostly going to involve a lot of your time."

Josh considered that, nodded. "You aren't normally so cryptic."

"She's not ready for what she's decided to do, and I can't talk her out of it," Ann replied, shook her head. "I'm a bit frustrated and worried and annoyed with myself. I should have seen this coming. If she changes her mind — and I still hope to be persuasive — I don't want those details in your head too. I'm mostly here to see if you're in a position to agree. I'll direct her elsewhere if you're taking off for a vacation or starting your book or —"

Josh lifted his hand to stop her, having already decided his answer. "I won't turn her away if what she asks is something I can do."

"I appreciate that, Josh, more than you can know." Ann went to brooding as she turned her root beer bottle back and forth between her palms. She eventually looked directly at him, and he stopped slicing green

14

peppers to meet her gaze. "It's someone you know, Josh. It's Grace Arnett."

He went absolutely still. A thousand questions whirled through his mind. He finally asked, "How long have you known each other?"

"Since she moved away from here . . . within a year or two. She's been living in Chicago the last dozen years."

"You didn't say anything."

"Sometimes I keep secrets, especially when I'm asked."

Her serious expression reflected what he was now feeling. Josh hadn't seen this side of Ann so directly before, though he was aware it existed — the ability to close the door on things she wouldn't talk about. She did keep people's secrets, had a reputation for it. If Ann felt the need to now run interference for Grace, the favor Grace was coming to ask wouldn't be a casual one.

He looked at the cutting board and the peppers, then back at her, thoughtfully nodded. "I can handle it, Ann."

She gave him a small smile. "Grace needs a safe guy, and you're the first name of a few on my list. It's going to help that you were childhood friends." She looked away for a moment at the call of a hawk outdoors. "Or that assumption may be my biggest

15

miscalculation yet. She remembers you, Josh." Ann sighed, then said, "I've never mentioned Grace around here because she asked me not to do so, for reasons that make sense to me also. You'll learn those details if this goes forward, and when you do and have questions, bring them to me. Grace is dealing with too much already, and the answers aren't easy ones."

Josh wasn't accustomed to being on the serious side of trouble, and that's what this felt like. Ann was back in her former day-job mode — being a cop, carrying the weight of serious matters, and doing her best to prep him on how to handle it. "Okay." He'd deal with it. He went back to chopping vegetables.

"She'll probably be in the area in a few days. I'll call if that changes."

"If that happens, then we can talk more about Grace." He scooped the vegetables into a grill mesh. "Trust me, Ann. Your friend is safe with me. I knew her long before you did and still care about her." He headed outside to the grill.

She followed with their drinks, silverware, and napkins. "Be yourself with her, Josh," she advised as she set the outdoor table. "She'll need that — just try to keep everything at a slow speed. You'll understand

16

what I mean when you see her." She pulled out a chair. "I've given you enough surprises for one morning. What do you say we eat and talk about the weather?"

He sprinkled olive oil and parmesan cheese over the veggies, spread them out in their holder to brown and crisp. "It's beautiful out now and going to rain later," he noted, glancing at the horizon. "November has been mild thus far, and the leaves are taking their time to drop off the branches. That covers the weather." He slid a slice of fish onto a plate and placed it in front of her. "We'll eat in courses. Why don't we talk about you and Paul? Any truth to the rumors he's heading to Washington, DC?"

"I've heard the rumors too," she agreed easily. "He likes running the Chicago FBI office. I wouldn't mind the transition if he wants deputy director. I can fly back to Illinois in a few hours, and I can do my writing anywhere. But for now, he's not looking for that move." She motioned with her fork. "Great fish, by the way. Done just right." She reached for her drink. "Paul's more likely to be offered a position he can't refuse — be asked to step in after someone resigns in scandal, or the like — an emergency overnight promotion. He has the management skills, field experience, and a deft hand

17

at navigating political problems. He's a heavyweight in the bureau — every year that becomes more apparent to me. It's inevitable he's going to end up in DC one day, which is probably why the rumor's going around."

"Did you expect that when you married him?"

She shrugged. "He's a good cop. One of the pleasures of my being retired is I can flow with whatever his work life is. If he needs to be in DC someday, I'll adapt. There's always work that needs to be done somewhere. I'm still working cases that interest me — either cold ones with Paul on our own time or helping out wherever and whenever asked."

Josh scooped the vegetables into two bowls and set one beside each plate. "You mentioned you were bringing case files for a state cop?"

"Yes, helping out a friend." Ann stabbed a mushroom slice, nibbled cautiously around it for the heat, and nodded her approval. "It's good." She stabbed another one. "Governor-elect Bliss wants a task force to take another look at unsolved missing-persons cases across the state — understandable given his family's personal history with his sister, Shannon. The task force is going to be small, maybe four to six cops, and won't officially start work until after the inauguration in January. Sharon Noble, a cop with the Riverside PD — that's a suburb just outside of Chicago — will be leading it. She's decided they will work county by county, first taking a look at cases five to fifteen years old. Carin County has two that fit: the missing six-year-old Dayton girl, and the Florist family disappearance that you probably remember. A state cop is here to take a look at the two cases, do a trial run of sorts for what the task force will tackle next year. I brought down what the FBI has on the two cases for her."

"You're helping out? Not just transportation, but working the cases?"

Ann nodded. "Paul and I will both be involved. He's providing FBI resources to the task force, data searches, lab work, that kind of thing, when needed. I'll be co-ordinating things with him. Mostly I'm involved because it sounds like interesting work, and I'm between book projects at the moment."

"Dad was sheriff during both those cases, spoke of them often," Josh said. "I've lived with them for a lot of years — all the Thane brothers have. You need some info, observa-

19

tions, when you get into the details, find us."

"Thanks. That's helpful. The state cop is named Evie Blackwell. You'll like her. She and I are similar, only she's got a sunnier personality."

Josh laughed at the remark.

"She's good at solving puzzles," Ann added.

Josh smiled. "So are you."

"Let's hope that holds true again." Ann glanced at the horizon. "And that the weather cooperates. I'm meeting Evie at two to take her up for an overview of the county. You see a plane flying low and slow across this lake shortly after that, wave. I'll toggle wings back."

"I'll be watching." Josh put down his fork, then touched her arm, pointed. "An eagle. The other in the pair should show up soon."

"Wow!" she exclaimed as she watched its powerful yet graceful climb. It came soaring back toward them, the mate not far behind.

Josh was pleased at Ann's reaction, for this was one of his favorite moments, living in this place. They finished the meal while watching the two eagles circle above the lake.

Ann pushed back her plate. "Thanks for a great meal, Josh. I could spend hours sitting here enjoying the view, although the lake from the air is going to look spectacular too. I'm sorry the flight might disrupt the eagles."

"Not much bothers them. I'm glad you came by. And I deeply appreciate the news about Grace." Josh set their dishes inside, grabbed his phone and keys, and walked Ann down the path to the bait shop and her rental.

"Looks like you've got steady customers," she noted, eyeing several vehicles besides hers in the parking area. "You must be pleased with the business."

"I am. It helps that I've got a captive market, and fishing has been the best on the lake in years." He held the car door for her. "Drive careful. Fly even more careful."

"Always." She waved goodbye and pulled out of the lot. Josh pushed his hands into his jeans pockets, considered going back to unload his boat or joining his two employees at the bait shop, and instead turned and walked back toward home. He wanted to sit for a while, simply think . . . remember.

Grace Arnett is coming back. He settled on his front porch, still watching the eagles, a cold soda in his hand. Ann couldn't have rocked his world harder than she just did. He felt relieved, edging toward overjoyed.

And at the same time he was wary about what had Ann so worried. She'd handled scores of homicide cases. She didn't get nervous; she sized up the problem and dealt with matters. *What is the favor Grace wants?* He'd no doubt spend a couple of days wondering until she showed up and asked him.

He made one decision in advance. Whatever the favor was, he'd handle with care in how he reacted, and he'd say yes if there was any way he could do it. It wasn't often a guy got to go back to the best days of his youth. *Grace Arnett.* Josh smiled, shook his head. He probably still had a school notebook or two tucked away with her name and his encircled by a heart. If she was inclined to take a trip down memory lane, he had some nice ones. The innocence of first love didn't get more beautiful than Grace. It was saying something that no girl since had come even close.

Two

Gabriel Thane

Gabriel Thane liked being sheriff, but there were days he wished he wasn't tethered to the phone and the job. Last night's date had ended abruptly so he could go break up a bar fight. And now, a Saturday, his grass had to be mowed and gutters cleared before the rain came in, yet he wasn't making much headway. He killed the mower as his cellphone rang yet again, tugged out his phone, and tried to sound polite as he said, "Sheriff Thane."

"Got yourself a problem, Son, out on County Road 62 near the old bridge. Lady hit herself a deer. Only she isn't here at the wreck. I've got a blood trail that seems to indicate she's walking toward town."

"How bad is it, Dad?" He left the mower mid-strip in the backyard, headed to the garage, the phone tucked against his shoulder. He grabbed the red medical backpack

23

and a blue one of general supplies out of the old refrigerator, and a jacket from the mudroom.

"Big buck came through the windshield," his father was saying, "airbags deployed, she put the car into a tree. Found her busted phone on the passenger side floorboard, along with a spilled purse. That's how come I know it's a she. Driver's license reads Evie Blackwell, thirty-six, a Springfield address."

"I'll head that way from here. Call the Tanners, Delaines, see if she knocked on a door."

"Those are the next calls. Bring your med kit. The blood already feels tacky. An hour ago, I'm thinking."

Gabe clicked off, headed to his sheriff-issue truck, tossed the gear in, reversed out of the drive, and turned north.

His street became County Road 62, and the bridge his dad mentioned was within half a mile of the turnoff to his brother Josh's place. Had she walked north rather than toward town, she would have had help within minutes. She was looking at six miles of asphalt road and not much traffic since the new bridge and highway extension had been completed. Now he felt irritated with himself for being irritated at the interruptions. This was the job, and he liked to think

24

he was as good at being sheriff as his father had been before him.

He gave it a couple minutes and hit redial. "Anything, Dad?"

"No one's seen her. They'll walk down their lanes to the road."

"Not good. She passes Delaine's, there's nothing until town." He turned on his flashers, added speed to close the distance to the crash. "Describe the blood trail."

"I'm thinking she's got pressure on a pretty serious cut. I've got multiple drops with every pace. She's walking reasonably straight, no weave to her steps, heading south to town."

"An hour, she could be at two miles or four." Gabe thought she'd probably sat down, woozy from the impact and the walking, putting her somewhere on the side of this road, hopefully still conscious.

"I'm now driving south," his father said. "Aaron's coming out to haul in the vehicle, and Henry's going to deal with the buck."

"Good." He caught the turn and shifted rapidly to brakes. He said into the phone, "Found her, Dad! Just east of Kimble's land. It looks like a pint of blood dumped down her front. I'll need your help here. She's got dogs. Two of them."

The German shepherds, both anxious,

were pacing around her as she took each unsteady step. Five-foot-three, short brown hair, charcoal dress slacks and matching casual jacket, a red blouse, bloodstains now a much darker red. A holstered handgun on her right hip, just visible under the jacket.

She looked as startled to see his truck as he was to see her. He quickly pulled to the side of the road, out of the way of any traffic in the turn but angled out some to protect her — the shoulder here wasn't that wide. He stepped out, but wary of the dogs, not walking forward. "Ma'am. We've been looking for you. It looks like you need some help."

"I don't hunt deer. I think it's nature's joke that I take one out that size at the start of my vacation."

He let himself smile a bit. "Yes, ma'am. I'm told he was huge." He reached for the backpacks, the jacket, moving slow because the dogs were now standing between him and her. "The reason you are armed, ma'am?"

"Illinois State Police. Evie Blackwell. My badge is in my pocket . . . I think, maybe." She tried to concentrate. "Yeah, jacket pocket. I need to sit down." She did so where she was, and the two dogs whined and crowded her.

"Want to tell your dogs to relax for me? I've got a first-aid kit. I need them to let me near."

"You look familiar. You're somebody I'm supposed to know. Boy, I have one nice-size headache."

"Reassure the dogs, Evie."

She said something, and the two dogs both dropped to a watching rest, their attention on him. He wondered how hurt the dogs might be. Likely in the backseat of the car, they would have been flung around during the crash. He wished Will was here right now. His brother wasn't a vet, but he knew enough animal husbandry that the town vet often called him when the creature needing treatment was wild. Will was good with anxious animals.

"Anything else hurting besides the headache?" Gabriel carried the backpacks and jacket over with him.

"Everything, but nothing feels serious."

She shook her head at his offer of the warmer jacket, then quickly lifted her hand to her forehead at the pain of the movement. He opened a water bottle from the supply pack, handed it to her, opened another, then dumped out the case holding flares to use as a drinking bowl for the dogs. Between them, the dogs drank down two more water bottles.

The blood had done a good job of dripping down the shirt. Gabriel studied the hand towel she was pressing against the side of her face. He wanted his dad here before he moved it. If the towel stuck on drying blood and she cried out, the dogs were liable to snap at him — or worse. He listened for his dad's truck with its distinctive old motor.

"You're on vacation, Evie?" he asked, trying to get her to focus on him so he could see her eyes. The idea of getting her back on her feet before help arrived struck him as a bad idea in case she passed out. The dogs would be a very serious issue then.

"A working vacation." Her brows furrowed and she straightened a bit. "You're Sheriff Thane."

"Yes."

"Ann said to find you."

"Ann?"

"Falcon."

"You know Ann and Paul Falcon?"

"Yes. Sorry." She pressed her hand again to her head. "This headache is like eating ice cream fast, times a zillion." She turned her face upward to see him. "A case. We're working a case in Carin County. Two." She was mildly slurring her words as she said,

"She'd better tell you. I'm fumbling."

"You're doing fine." She had startlingly green eyes, still focusing, if rather damp with earlier tears. He heard his father's truck. "When the doc stitches that cut, they'll also give you something for the headache."

Her eyes filled with a touch of panic. "This is like the vacation from hell."

Oh, he could sympathize. "We'll do what we can to turn that around so it ends nicer. Think your dogs will go with my father?"

She hadn't noticed the truck, but the dogs had. His dad parked on the opposite side of the road, stepped out, and Will pulled in right behind him. Both dogs surged to their feet, and the men wisely stopped where they were.

Will crouched down where he was, studied the animals. "Evie, what're their names?"

"Apollo. Zeus."

"War dogs?"

She gave a little nod, looking surprised.

He whistled softly, and both dogs whined in reply.

"Tell them to relax, Evie," Gabriel instructed. The smell of blood obviously had them knowing they needed to defend her, but they were anxious about how. She spoke to both, the words sounding foreign to his ears, and the dogs dropped down once more into a watching rest.

Will, a retired combat medic, should be the one dealing with this cut, but calming and checking out the dogs was also his domain. Gabriel wanted a look at the cut to know what they were dealing with, and then he'd get her to his truck and the doctor, see that it was properly stitched.

He waited until the dogs had accepted Will's presence and allowed him to carefully look them over for injuries, then turned back to Evie with some wet paper towels. "Ease off the towel, Evie, and let me see."

He didn't allow what he discovered show in his face. He carefully used the damp towels to soak away the crusted blood around the long gash by her eye. She blinked fast as it stung, pulled in a breath. He knew it was painful, and fresh blood began to trickle.

She'd needed stitches an hour ago, but the gash was clotting over, and he could butterfly it closed. He got it clean, then used gauze and pressure, a hand behind her head to brace her as he stopped the last of the bleeding. She didn't resist, but she held her breath against the pain.

She did have rather distinctive green eyes, now wet with more tears. He pulled the cut closed with thin butterfly bandages, opened fresh gauze, placed it over the wound, took her hand and instructed her to hold the bandage against her head while he tore tape strips. She pulled in an easier breath, no doubt relieved he was about done. "This will hold until the doctor can do a proper job."

She tipped her head back to look at his father. "You look like him."

"Caleb Thane, ma'am," the man said, hunkering down in front of her. "Father of these two."

"I know your name also . . . I think. I have a question for you about . . . Oh, brother, I can't remember right now."

"I suspect that headache makes a lot of things hard to remember," Caleb reassured her.

"My dogs?"

"Will is going to take good care of them," Caleb promised.

"Evie, were the dogs trained in Dutch?" Will asked.

"Yes."

"I thought so. I'll get them settled for you." Will walked toward his truck and called the dogs. They whined and looked at Evie, who rubbed fur, stroked ears, reassured them, and then gave them an encouraging command to go. They left her, reluctantly looking back as they trotted over to Will. He opened the back passenger door on his extended cab truck, and the dogs jumped in with ease.

Gabriel thought this was the best he would get for now — the dogs calm, Evie patched together. "I want you to stand, Evie," he said, reaching for her arm. "Let's walk over to my truck." She nodded. His father helped from the other side, and they lifted her up. She blanched.

"Easy!" Gabriel got a chest full of bloody shirt and weaving woman.

"Back stiffened up," she managed to say. Her hand curled tight into his shirt. "Ouch!"

"Walk it off. We'll help." Ten steps and he could put her into his truck, get her settled.

She gingerly stepped forward, her hand began to relax its grip, took another step, nodded, and they walked slowly to his truck. Gabriel removed her firearm, passed it to his father, then lifted her onto the passenger seat, used his jacket to cover her, pulled the seat belt across. He covered her hand with his and squeezed gently. *A lousy opening day for a vacation.* He wasn't going to let it end that way. "Dad, the crash scene, can you make sure anything personal is recovered before her car gets hauled in?"

Caleb nodded as he handed back the holstered firearm, and Gabriel tucked it behind her seat. "Will do, Son. Clinic or the hospital?"

"Hospital. She's got a nice concussion under that headache."

"I suspect you're right. I'll see you there. Drive slow."

Gabriel climbed into the cab, looked over at Evie. Her eyes were closed, the bruising and swelling around the gauze distinct. He started the truck, reached over and killed the radio, made a three-point turn, and headed back into town.

"I smell of sweat and blood," she said.

He smiled at the soft complaint. "After the doctor, there's a hot shower in your future."

"Excellent." She was quiet a moment. "I probably shouldn't have left the crash site, stayed with the car —"

"Actually, I would have done the same thing. Not much traffic, houses a ways off. Walking didn't help your wound, but we'll have you fixed up soon."

She lapsed into silence. He made himself relax.

"The Florist family . . ." she said quietly. "That's what I wanted to ask your dad about."

Just the mention of the case caused his muscles to tighten. "I know it. A deputy disappears, his wife and eleven-year-old son — it's never gone inactive."

She carefully turned her head his way. "I remember now. I've got two weeks' vacation, plus weekends on either end, so sixteen days, enough time to see what might be there. Ann's going to help me."

Evie's here to look at an unsolved case? Ann Falcon's coming down to help her? It raised a lot of questions. Gabriel looked over, met her gaze. Not so clear and focused now. "Evie? Hey, look at me." Her eyes cleared some. "We'll talk about work after the doctor is done. Where are you staying? Did you check into a hotel?"

"Umm, rented a house."

"Yeah? Where?"

She looked confused. "I don't . . . I'm not sure."

"Will Ann know?"

"Yes."

"Close your eyes. Just let the next hour or two pass. It's going to get better."

"Promise?"

He didn't think it could get much worse. "I can promise that."

Gabriel walked through the rather large ER

in their small-town hospital. Carin County, with its major lake surrounded by state parks and private campgrounds, had an economy built mostly around vacationers and tourists, with family farms spread across the rest of the county, interspersed among a dozen more small towns and villages. This hospital was the center of the area's medical care. Severe sunburns, bad sprains, broken bones, asthma attacks, beestings, poison ivy, the occasional heart attack, all kept this place hopping during the summer months, and farm accidents added intense adrenaline spikes year-round. The most serious injuries were airlifted to the regional trauma center in the state's capital, Springfield, yet the majority of patients were treated right here.

He stepped around the ER curtain for number sixteen. Evie's eyes opened, and she looked his direction, nearly focused this time. "You're looking more awake," Gabriel commented, pleased.

"What did they give me?" she asked.

"Tylenol with codeine. Your body just needed some rapid rest, and out you went as soon as it got an excuse."

She lifted a hand briefly to the bandage. "How many . . . ?" Her voice drifted off.

"Twelve stitches." He'd answered that a

couple of times already, but he thought this time she'd probably remember. "Getting hungry?"

"Want out of here."

"Another hour after the doctor comes by, he'll spring you," he reassured.

"Hey, Evie" came from the other side of the bed.

She turned her head. "Ann . . . how long have you been sitting there?"

Ann simply smiled. "I saw a photo of the deer."

"Yeah. A shame. What a way for him to go and for me to begin a vacation." Her voice became more animated. "Pretty scenery, heavy trees, some sunlight filtering through, a glimpse, and then *wham*" — she struck the mattress to illustrate — "he comes right across the hood and smashes into the windshield. Huge buck. The car collided with some trees, and I about killed my dogs. Tossed them forward like tumbling socks in a dryer." She looked at Gabriel. "How are they?"

Each of Evie's reports was getting more detailed as her brain became clearer. She hadn't mentioned the sunlight coming through the trees before or provided the sound effects. A few hours, the doctor assured them, and most of the impact symptoms would pass.

Gabriel pulled out his phone, scrolled to a picture, turned it toward Evie. "That would be my brother Will's porch they are guarding so faithfully, along with two of his lambs. Maybe their sheepherding genes? He fed the dogs the steak I was supposed to be sharing with him for dinner, so they're being nicely pampered."

She smiled at the photo.

"Will says they've got some painful bruises," he said more seriously. "They'll need a few days' rest, but they survived the crash fine."

"Oh, I hope so. I totaled my car, didn't I?"

Gabriel considered it possible, but he only said, "I haven't heard the official answer yet. New radiator, new windshield, some bodywork — maybe you get it back."

"Yeah . . ." She closed her eyes with a sigh. "You promised a shower."

"It's still coming." The bloody shirt was gone, replaced with a clean one Ann had brought in from her luggage, but Evie's hair was matted, and he knew she wasn't going to feel normal again until she could get that hot shower, soak out the aches. They could cover the bandage with waterproof tape. He glanced at the woman also watching Evie.

"Ann, you want to get some coffee?"

"Yes. Evie, rest for now. We'll be just down the hall and back shortly."

"I didn't get to go flying with you today," she murmured, eyes closed.

Ann covered Evie's hand with hers, smiled. "Consider it rescheduled. The week will be filled with other gorgeous days."

"Promise?"

"That's an easy one. We're going up as soon as Doc says yes."

"I feel like a dropped ice cream cone — *splat* and busted."

Ann chuckled. "Get some rest, Evie."

Gabriel handed Ann a coffee, poured one for himself. "You don't come this way often, but when you do, it tends to be memorable. Sorry I missed your arrival. There was a note at the office that you'd been by. And Josh said you were out to visit him this morning."

"Evie wanted to introduce herself to you first, present the task-force mandate, ask about the cases. We were planning on treating you to dinner this evening to discuss the details."

"I've filtered pieces of it together now. But for clarity's sake, tell me what Evie would have said had she not met that deer."

"Our governor-elect wants a task force to take another look at unsolved missing-persons cases across the state — not surprising given his family's history. And Evie's boss wants her on it next year when it officially begins work. Sharon Noble out of Riverside PD is going to lead it. Noble's decided working county by county, looking at open cases five to fifteen years back, would be the place to begin.

"Carin County has two cases that fit that profile — the missing six-year-old Dayton girl who was the focus of an AMBER Alert, and the Florist family disappearance. Evie planned to use her vacation to do a trial run of sorts, dig into the files, see if this approach could work. She's rented a house here in town to avoid a poor hotel housekeeper getting startled by a wall of crime-scene photos. Evie was going to ask you for assistance, copies of your case files. I brought down duplicates of the FBI files with me, and she's arranged for the state files to be sent over."

Gabriel nodded at the summary but with a frown. "I'm surprised she didn't call weeks ago to get this request in the works."

"She wasn't certain when this vacation window would open up. She's Lieutenant Evie Blackwell, Illinois State Police, Bureau of Investigations. Her job can be as disruptive to schedules as yours. Don't let first impressions fool you, Gabriel. She's very good. Paul figures she'll head up the BOI one day."

"I saw resolve today, courage, and stubbornness — trying to walk to town with her dogs after that kind of injury."

Ann smiled. "Okay, that description would be on target. Add curious and it's a decent sketch. Evie didn't call you in advance because she didn't want to get a no. You might have felt obliged to let family in the area know, and they might have convinced you to rescind your cooperation and give it a thumbs down. That's a big downside for merely saving some hours of copying time."

Gabriel considered that, tipped his cup slightly in Ann's direction to acknowledge her point. "You know how significant the Florist family case is to this community, to my department. I don't want to see the case reopened on a whim. I don't want family members having to deal with the questions, have their hopes raised, if it doesn't make sense — unless there's something new to work."

"That's one of the reasons why I offered to bring the FBI files down myself," Ann replied. "To reassure the Florist family this isn't being done for form's sake. To reassure you and your father that this isn't going to be an exercise repeating what has been done before, where everyone says, 'Good investigation, sorry it's not solved,' and it's all boxed away again. We're going to rethink the case, figure out why it hasn't been solved, and solve it, Gabe. Evie's the right person. I've seen her work."

Gabriel sighed, sipped at the coffee. "You don't often put yourself that far out on a limb, Ann. We seriously want this case solved, but it hasn't cracked despite intense efforts. I don't need expectations raised like that. I appreciate the sentiment, but I know the case." He considered her. "You're going to be around helping Evie if we do this?"

"Yes. I'll be in and out over the next two weeks — it's a quick flight down. And with Paul providing FBI data searches, research, lab work as needed, we'll have the tools required. We'll also take a hard look at the Dayton girl's disappearance. Governor Bliss wants to know if the investment of a core group of experienced, focused detectives can clear unsolved missing-persons cases, and I'm committed to showing him that it can. Carin County is a test case. I want a win here, Gabriel. For its potential and also for your sake."

Gabriel recognized the sales job she was doing, and Ann acknowledged this with a small smile of her own. "Seriously, Gabe, that's why I suggested they start here. Two cases, with a lot riding on what can be done. Evie believes in this enough to give up her vacation to get a head start on the work. I believe in it enough to be down here helping. We just need you to say yes."

The second case Evie was interested in, the missing Dayton girl, would be easier to give her, as it didn't have a strong local connection, at least in the known facts. A vacationing family from Florida, traveling to Chicago, had stopped at a hotel just off the Interstate for the night when their six-year-old daughter was snatched. An AMBER Alert was issued across several states on the assumption it was an abduction of opportunity by someone also traveling. Gabe and his father both had substantial time working the case, but he'd always known both the victim and her abductor were likely long gone from their county, even the state. The Florist family, however, remained an intensely local and emotional matter.

Gabriel realized saying no wasn't going to fly in these circumstances and so shifted to the implications of his saying yes. "I want to be in on the work. I was there at the Florist house after the disappearance. My father about put himself into an early grave working it. I want us in the middle of it, day one."

"We'll need you," Ann agreed, accepting the condition.

The Florist case mattered for both personal and professional reasons. It wasn't his personal white whale, didn't keep him awake nights, but it certainly bothered him. And he knew it still haunted his father. Gabriel wouldn't let his hopes rise. He'd concluded after the last review that it was going to take a significant break, like the discovery of bones, to solve the case. And if Evie and Ann wanted to look deeper, he'd certainly support them and be right there with them every step of the way. He'd be able to satisfy himself as well as tell the community there was nothing else that could be done unless and until new evidence turned up.

"Evie's probably told you she's rented a house — 47 Kearns Road," Ann mentioned. "We can set up there. Or we can work downtown if you prefer."

"For this," Gabriel decided, "the old post-office building might be best. It's been stripped down to a large open room, and there are tables still set up from last month's flea market. I can put a retired deputy on security while the case files are laid out. If you want to speak to deputies who've worked the cases, they can walk over from the sheriff's office for a conversation. You'll be having quite a few of those, I imagine. Evie can take what she wishes back to the house — I know she'll be working all hours on this if she wants to get through it in just sixteen days. I know the place; it's one of Trina's. She owns most of the block around her home, rents them out to tourists and families. Evie will be more than comfortable there."

Ann nodded her agreement with that plan, but then hesitated. "Gabriel, don't miss the tree for the forest," she advised. "Solving this case requires finding one right idea, not comprehending everything that has been done on the case to date. When Evie locates that answer, it will be on a specific hour of a specific day. Sixteen days can be enough for that to happen."

"Got it." Gabriel forced a smile. "If nothing else, the next two weeks will not be boring." He refilled his coffee. Ann declined. "What were you out talking with Josh about?" he asked. "He said something about Grace Arnett coming back to town."

"Grace doesn't want it widely known, but

she'll be in the area in a few days. Josh is going to help her out with something. He'll explain after she's here."

"It will be good to see her, Ann. She's been missed."

Ann looked troubled. "I've got some serious reservations about her coming back, but I haven't been able to talk her out of doing so." She glanced over, caught his gaze. "We'll need to discuss those concerns, Gabriel, probably fairly soon."

He lifted an eyebrow. "Something else to fit into our otherwise normal, uneventful day?"

She chuckled. "If I didn't show up and create a commotion occasionally, you'd become a bored small-town sheriff," she joked. "When are you getting married anyway? I heard via Iris you were out on a date with Joanne Liffe last night."

He winced. "Please protect me from gossiping staff. Joanne's a lawyer in Decatur, nice enough woman, works in Springfield when the legislature is in session. I have a feeling I'm a little too rough-and-tumble for her taste. She thought 'sheriff' meant some glamour to go along with the authority. The date ended when I got a call to take care of a bar fight. I'm not brokenhearted about it, though. This date was mostly to quiet down

Mom, who's been asking me if I've been on one lately. I'm not looking to catch someone."

"Hmm," Ann murmured. "Marie's got three sons, none of whom have found 'the one' yet. That has to be a trial for her."

"So she tells us. Rather often, I might add."

Ann chuckled, offered an apology that he waved off.

Gabriel understood his mother's point of view — she wanted to know each of her sons had found someone to love, and she wanted grandchildren. That he'd found someone years ago, loved her only to lose her, underlined his mom's concern that he wouldn't try again. He accepted the fact he wasn't in a hurry to do so.

But it wasn't just his mom interested in the subject. He happened to be the sole remaining bachelor in the Carin County sheriff's office now that Henry Gonzales had remarried his ex-wife. Law-enforcement jobs were notoriously hard on relationships. Being the only single guy around the office was a rare happenstance — a divorce or death of a spouse was inevitable, but for now he was the center of some unwelcome attention. Knowing they were well-intentioned, he tried to be polite with the "helpful" introductions coming his way. He knew he would choose a lady one day. He considered himself marriage-minded, just not in a hurry. The job and its demands, the time and energy a good marriage required, took some finessing. He wasn't sure he wanted to take on that complicated equation right now.

He'd been surprised, in fact, when Ann had married Paul. She'd always had similar reservations about how to make a marriage work when one was a cop. She'd ended up marrying a cop and immediately retiring, so they didn't have quite so many competing pressures on the marriage. It seemed to be working for them. Ann and Paul were in the marriage-success column of friends he knew well. But he didn't think that step was for him, at least for now.

"I'm thinking Will and Karen might be the first to tie the knot," he mentioned to Ann. "My brother is smitten." He smiled as he said it, liking the word. It did a nice job of describing his otherwise rather quiet brother. Karen had arrived in town just over a year ago, taken a job as a cook at the Fast Café, rented half a house, and become part of the community. His brother had spotted her early and staked a claim, much to the frustration of other single guys who would have liked a chance.

"That's another conversation we should have, Gabriel," Ann said quietly, and the way she said it had him snapping a hard glance her way.

"Karen? What's the story there?"

She glanced around. "A long one, and not for public ears."

"Now I'm just going to worry myself into knots until we have the conversation."

"Once Evie is settled for the night, I'll come find you for some ice cream, fill you in. Karen's got history Will is going to need to know — you as well — if the relationship is going somewhere. It's another reason I'm here. Karen wants to discuss how and what to tell Will, or if I think it best she say nothing, which has been my advice up until now."

"Come on over tonight. You've got my number and address. I'll pick up the ice cream, we'll talk."

"Deal." She rested a hand lightly on his arm. "We'll talk about Karen, about Grace. I'll dump those problems off my plate onto yours, then I'll help Evie start to dig into the two cases. It will be a typical week for us."

Gabriel had to laugh. "Been there, done that, haven't we? Just don't give me another dead body, Ann, like the last time you dropped by. It's been quiet — I'd really like it to stay that way."

"I'm retired."

"Sure you are," he said with a wry smile. "The governor-elect merely has your phone number, and anytime the FBI has something sensitive, Paul sends you out in advance to give us a heads up. You're retired only in the sense you now pick and choose what you *want* to do."

Her eyes glinted with humor. "The perfect definition."

They saw Evie's doctor coming down the hall, and their conversation shifted.

"Do you want to drive Evie over to the house or have me do it?" Gabriel asked Ann.

"Why don't you drive her and I'll follow you. I've got her things your father brought in my rental, along with the FBI case files I brought down. I'll take the files by the old post office after she's settled, if you can arrange for me to have keys."

"I'll do that. Just to satisfy my curiosity, where are the state files?"

"Still loaded in a van over in Springfield, I think. She was going to call once she was at the house and have them delivered. I'll get that done for her, have them brought to the post-office building."

"I'll get our case files copied tonight. The staff will appreciate the overtime."

"Thanks, Gabriel."

"If we're going to do this, let's do it right."

"We're in agreement there." Ann headed toward ER, slot sixteen, Gabriel following. Evie was going through the coordination tests with the doctor again. They seemed simple — he'd hold up a finger and ask her to touch it with hers, instruct her to hold out her arms and bring her index fingers together, drop a rubber ball from one hand and catch it in the other. She hadn't been able to do the exercises when she first arrived. She was anticipating each one now and cruising through them. The vision tests and memory tests were not as easy for her, but she mostly passed the questions. She was still struggling to hold on to a set of three words at the beginning of a conversation and repeat them back when asked.

"I can go?" Evie asked the doctor.

"You're going to need to be cautious about that headache for a couple days. Don't drive until it eases up, alternate ice and heat for the stiff muscles, and come see me if your vision or balance changes at all. But otherwise, you're sprung."

The doctor swept aside the curtain as Evie said, "Oh, I could hug you, but I'll settle for saying a big thanks. Can you do the paper-work fast?" She swung her feet around to sit up on the side of the bed. Gabriel saw her clench her teeth for an instant at the movement, but he could tell she was deter-mined to leave.

The doctor signed off on the electronic chart. "I'll have the nurse bring in the discharge paperwork and get you prescrip-tion samples for the pain-killers so you don't have to find a pharmacy tonight."

"Great. Thanks. Ann, do you remember where they put my jacket, my shoes?"

Gabriel caught Ann's attention, held up his keys, and pointed to the lobby. He'd bring his truck to the pickup lane for Evie. Ann nodded, and he headed out. One problem in this day was nearly resolved.

He had the impression Evie Blackwell would be an interesting woman to get to know. Probably not as interesting as Ann had been in those early days when first mak-ing her acquaintance, but worth consider-ing. He wanted to see Evie without that headache scrambling her thinking. *Curious.* That was the word Ann had used to describe Evie. He'd add *pretty.* She was easy to look at, mostly those green eyes and that smile he'd caught only a glimmer of so far. It was not going to be a dull few weeks, and that was fine with him.

He started the truck and moved it into place, let it idle. He figured he had a couple of minutes. He picked up his phone and found a number, made a call. "Sheriff Gabriel Thane for Paul Falcon, please."

"One moment, Sheriff." Paul's longtime secretary must have his name on a short list — he always got through immediately.

"Yes, Gabe."

"Ann is safely here in Carin, which I'm sure you already know. I need a read on an Evie Blackwell. A guy's read. I'm told you know her."

"I do. Solid cop, good investigator. Cracks me up with her jokes. Left a shamrock glacier behind in the freezer when she last stayed over as our guest — a painted rock with frozen layers of water coating it. You probably had to be here to appreciate its humor. It was St. Patrick's Day, the Chicago River was green."

Gabriel smiled. "I can see it. She had a car accident today, hit a deer, got her brains rattled a bit. I'm trying to get a sense of what normal would look like."

"She okay?" Paul asked, instantly serious.

"Will be. The doc is doing the release paperwork now. Ann's with her, so I'd say Evie is in good hands."

" 'Normal' for Evie . . . Curious. Funny. Not too serious about anything."

"Not words you hear associated with a cop very often."

"She doesn't see a need to be serious. She figures crimes are serious enough. She prefers to enjoy the day and the work and solve the puzzle so there's justice again. She likes everything there is about being an investigator, even the paperwork.

"She's a sunny-mood kind of lady by nature, likes to laugh, and uses that to her advantage. Ann always carried the weight of a grim bloodstained scene home with her. Evie doesn't. She lets herself put it aside, like a gift of grace to herself. She's got the rare ability to be a lifer in the job and not burn out. Don't underestimate her. But to your immediate question, when she's laughing again, she's probably edging back to normal."

"Thanks. That's helpful. The one thing I haven't heard today is laughter."

There was a slight pause. Then Paul said, his tone offhand, "She's seeing someone, I think, a guy by the name of Rob Turney, if that would be useful information to have."

So much for being subtle about why he called. "Yeah. Figures. The interesting ones tend to be seeing someone."

"He's not there, and she is, for the next couple of weeks at least."

"I'm not one to poach," Gabriel replied, unwilling to ignore that line even for an interesting woman. "Odd, isn't it," he said casually, signaling a shift in the conversation, "how I'm the last one to know there's interest in our little county up at the governor's level?"

"Comes with the territory — having friends among those whom the governor calls. I like the guy. I voted for him. But a word of advice to tuck away? Bliss is persuasive at getting you to say yes to what you didn't intend to do when you arrived at the meeting. I don't think Ann had in mind spending Thanksgiving and Christmas helping get a task force organized so the group could be formally announced in January. Ann's invested in it now, owns it, but you've got our next governor to thank for that. He rolled her up neatly in a bow, made it so it became her idea to volunteer. Then he looked at me, and without having to say more than 'You'll help her out?' had the FBI's assistance, coming out of my budget."

Gabriel chuckled. "Nice to know you two can occasionally get snookered like that. Seriously, I'll send Ann safely back your way tomorrow. I appreciate her being here today.

It's been helpful to hear her point of view. And her help with the aftermath of Evie's accident was invaluable."

"She was glad to come."

"Oh, and, Paul, before I let you go — Karen Joy Lewis. Anything you might like to say?"

"Bravest woman I know. Talk to Ann."

"Intriguing redirect. Thanks."

"Gabe, don't forget. You still owe me one decent game of darts and a case of that local root beer."

"Come down with Ann one evening, you can collect." Gabriel hung up with a chuckle, lifted a hand to the attendant pushing Evie out in a wheelchair. Ann had married a good man. He enjoyed watching the dynamics between the two of them, considered both of them his friends now. He thought Evie might join that circle over the next couple of weeks. Ann liked her, and that said a lot. He got out and circled the truck to open the door for his passenger.

Rather than taking the shortcut, Gabriel drove down Main Street so that Evie could get a sense of the town. He kept an eye on Ann following behind, slowing when she got caught at one of the town's few traffic lights, then crossing the railroad tracks. If there was a rich and poor side, they were now on the monied side. He turned onto Kearns Road, drove three blocks, parked on the right side of the driveway, leaving room for Ann to pull in beside him.

Evie hadn't gone for a small apartment with a few rooms. She'd rented a two-story Victorian on a corner lot, with four bedrooms upstairs and high-ceilinged spacious rooms downstairs. A wide back deck had been added more recently, and a fenced backyard completed the property. Gabriel had been inside the house for several parties over the years. He watched Evie studying it with satisfaction.

"You're vacationing in style," he said.

"Eating out, staying in a nice place — there should be some perks to a vacation besides fresh deer."

Remembering Paul's comments about her, he appreciated the touch of humor. He came around the truck, opened the passenger door. She sat for a moment, and he could see her considering the stepping-down problem. She gave a half-amused smile. "I need to do this for myself, but it might take a while." She put a hand on his shoulder, took a deep breath and stepped down, then unclenched her jaw and blew out.

"The stiffness has to show up before it can fade," Gabe commiserated.

"Yeah. Got that."

"You've got keys?"

"Trina mailed me a set."

"Then lead the way."

She studied the walk and carefully took a step. He kept a hand near Evie's elbow just in case she needed help, though he knew the only way past this was to stretch those tight muscles. He gave her serious points for the focused way she went about it. Her back was bothering her, he knew, but it was to be expected at this point. She took the six porch steps with a firm grip on his arm and her other hand on the railing.

She unlocked the house. It truly was a beautiful historic home, with hardwood floors and a polished banister, long formal drapes highlighting tall multi-pane windows. The furnishings were both formal and modern: long sofas, high-back chairs, book-cases for both books and pottery, cabinetry with clean lines, and fresh flowers every-where. He looked around with appreciation. "Trina puts out a nice welcome."

"She called it her summer-house-style package, with food and drink stocked."

"You chose well, Evie. I'm glad you'll be enjoying this place. It's one of the nicer homes in town."

"Thanks. An added benefit is that Ann won't fuss about staying with me when she's here. The dogs will be okay with your brother? I hate to impose any longer —"

"They'll be fine," he assured her. "Rest is going to help."

"Yeah," she said with a small yawn. Then she looked at the staircase.

"Sorry, there's no elevator."

She gave him a glance and half smile. "I'll manage." She took in the stairs again. "I hope."

"The couch is long enough and looks comfortable."

"Don't tempt me. I want that hot shower." She resolutely started up the stairs.

Ann joined him, watching her progress.

"I'll bring in Evie's luggage," he said.

Ann offered keys. "The two black cases in the trunk are hers, and if you could also manage my blue bag, I'd appreciate it."

He nodded and went to get them.

Evie had disappeared by the time he returned. Ann took one of Evie's bags and indicated he could leave the other two by the bottom step.

"Anything else I can do, Ann?"

"We're good. I'll be by your place this evening."

"Thank you. We need to have that conversation today, even though we'd both no doubt be better off crashing like Evie."

"I may catch a brief nap once she's settled. You?"

"A yard half-mowed is calling my name."

"Life doesn't stop just because things get complicated."

He shared a smile. "How very true. It is good to have you in town, Ann." He nodded goodbye and headed back to his truck. He looked to the horizon where rain was coming in. It fit the way this day had been going. But, strangely, he found himself kind of pumped. It hadn't been a boring day. *Now, getting that mowing done before the rain hits . . .* he'd need to hustle.

Ann Falcon

Ann was fixing tea when she heard a knock on the front door, figured Gabriel had forgotten something, or maybe Trina was stopping over to see that all was comfortable for Evie. Out of habit, Ann glanced through the side window first and instinctively moved her jacket over her side arm when she saw who it was. She opened the door wide. "Mrs. Thane," she greeted the woman with a smile.

"Marie, please, Ann. The other makes me

sound old." The two women laughed. "Caleb told me what happened, and I thought some supplies were in order — ice packs, my chicken soup, bread out of the oven an hour ago." She carried a full picnic basket.

"Evie will appreciate every bit of it, as will I." Ann invited her inside and accepted the basket. "This also saves me a trip your direction. I was planning on coming out to talk with you soon. Do you have a few minutes?"

"Of course."

"I'm back here in the kitchen," she explained, motioning her guest toward the room. "Evie wanted a shower and a nap, then dinner, so this is well timed. I was just looking through the items in the refrigerator for meal options, so your basket will do nicely. Would you join me for tea?"

"Please."

Ann emptied the picnic basket, fixed tea for them both, got out cookies Trina had supplied, and joined Marie at the kitchen table. She considered what to say first, how to say it, and finally just went to the heart of the matter. "I'm going to disrupt the lives of your sons, and probably yours too, and I thought it only fair to give you a heads up."

Marie smiled. "A bit of disruption every once in a while can be a good thing to my

60

way of thinking. You're working on the Florist matter with Evie, my husband tells me, so that would be Gabriel's disruption."

"Yes," Ann said. "Grace Arnett is coming back to town to ask a favor of Josh. And I have some history with Karen that's going to involve Will."

Marie nodded thoughtfully. "It sounds like all three of our sons are going to have an interesting month."

Ann finished one of the cookies. "You're one of the strongest women of prayer I know."

Marie looked a little surprised.

"I've got two good friends in Grace and Karen, neither of whom believes in God. That's not unusual, but there are moments in people's lives when the topic comes back to the surface, and this is one of those times for both of them. I'm floundering, Marie. I'm not ready for what is coming. Would you please pray for me? And them?"

The woman's expression softened. "You know I will, Ann. I understand the weight you feel. I've got two sons who believe and one who does not. I love all three, but I admit a special place in my heart for Will and his struggle with faith."

Ann hesitated. "Would you mind if Will married someone who also didn't believe?"

"If you're talking about Karen, the answer is no. I'd have two people to pray for then. He softens when she's around, and that's a good thing. God loves my son, and He loves Karen. I've come to accept the fact that God understands better than I ever will how to seek and save Will. Getting married would be good for him — I have no hesitation on that."

"Things are going to get difficult in the coming days — for him, for all your sons," Ann said, choosing her words with care. "Will is going to find himself in some deep waters. And Josh is going to be asked to carry a very hard thing. They'll need family during this time."

Marie smiled. "A nice way to say they're going to need their mother."

"I wish I could explain further right now, but it's not my place. I just wanted you to know the need was going to be there, and to let you know how much I would appreciate and covet your prayers these next few days. For me and for them."

Marie nodded. "Karen matters to Will today. I can also say that Grace matters to Josh; that might be mostly in the past, but it will hold for the present too."

Ann appreciated Marie's calm and confidence. "I'm grateful for your prayers. It's been a lot of years since I carried something so heavy as these matters. I don't want your family to be hurt with what unfolds."

Marie's hand covered hers. "You know us well enough to realize we're tight as a family, thus your desire to speak with me. Let go of some of that concern you're carrying, Ann. You'll do with care what you've come here to deal with. I recognize a cop doing her job. You might be retired, but it's still part of you. I've had a sheriff as a husband, now a sheriff as a son, and a soldier who's come back from multiple tours and not ready to discuss matters. I'm the glue of the Thane family for a reason. My sons will be fine."

"I'm glad they have you."

Marie laughed softly. "You'll come to Thanksgiving dinner should you be in town, you and your husband. You'll join the family for the day. We'd be delighted to have you."

"Should we be here, Marie, we'd be honored to join you. Paul would certainly appreciate your cooking over mine."

Marie laughed again as she rose. "You just haven't cared with a passion about food the way you do about people. Now quit fretting, Ann. You've done the important first part. You've told me enough that I can pray.

God and I have plenty of history regarding praying for my sons and the women — or lack of them — in their lives. You'll tell me should there be specifics you want mentioned, and I'll make sure God hears it from me that you need extra strength and wisdom for what is coming."

Ann rose too and hugged the woman. "Thank you," she whispered. There was comfort just in talking with the lady she had come to think of as one of her spiritual mothers.

Marie studied her face. "Close your eyes for a moment, Ann."

She did as asked and then felt Marie's hands come up to cradle her face. Marie said softly, "Jesus, no one understands a heavy load better than you. No one has ever borne heavier. Bear up under this one with Ann, so she will know her only purpose here is to help others, love expansively, and be your hands and feet, your words of advice and wisdom when opportunities present themselves for her to help Grace and Karen. And yes, Josh and Will and Gabriel. Do whatever is necessary for Ann's success in the days ahead. Show your love to my friend and comfort her by your Spirit. Amen."

Ann didn't bother to wipe her eyes. "The Thane sons have a really great mom," she said shakily.

"Thank you. Enjoy that soup and the bread with Evie. You'll be fine, Ann. In the days ahead, my sons are going to come looking for my counsel, and I'll pray over them and tell them the same as I've told you. It's the mother in me."

Ann walked with Marie to the door and said goodbye, lighter in heart than she'd been for a while. The Thane sons were in good hands — their mother's and the Heavenly Father's.

"God, give me so much of your wisdom it leaks out of me," she whispered. Will and Josh would have difficult weeks ahead, but it was Gabriel she worried about the most. She would do what had to be done — a lifetime of history for her as a cop had her accepting this. But the reality of what that meant never got easier.

THREE

Gabriel Thane

Gabriel finished his mowing in the rain, came inside shaking water off his jacket, resigned to the fact that if the rain turned heavy it would overflow the gutters he hadn't had time to clear. He turned on the kitchen television, settling on ESPN's Saturday-night football game for diversion as he put together a simple meal and sat down at the table to eat. November's on-again off-again weather would last a few weeks, then December's grip of winter and blast of arctic air would arrive with a vengeance. Any of his job outdoors would get rather miserable for a few months.

The fireplace, opening both to the kitchen and living room, had been sufficient to warm the main level the night before. Gabriel stirred the remaining wood, added kindling, new logs, and set a match to it in preparation for Ann's visit. He had stopped

66

to pick up chocolate chip ice cream, her favorite. He started coffee brewing and sorted through the mail while he waited. He also mentally shuffled work schedules for the coming week to free up time to help on the two cold cases. He was finishing up invoice payments when he heard a car pulling into the drive. He met Ann at the front door. "Evie asleep?" he asked.

"She's settled and grateful for the pain pills," Ann replied as she stepped inside. "I doubt she moves before morning, and even then I'll encourage her to sleep in. She asked me to pick up saltine crackers, 7-Up, and more Tylenol, so she's already thinking about dealing with day-after aches and pains — it's not the first time she's had a day like this."

"I can handle those items with what I've got around here. She's been banged up before?"

"She took a bad fall a few years back. While chasing a suspect into a tear-down, the floor gave way and dropped her into the basement. And a few years before that, she walked away from a helicopter crash."

He winced at the images. "Well, I guess this one gets on the list as another close call." Gabriel motioned back to the kitchen. "You want to join me for some coffee or would you prefer hot chocolate?"

"Coffee is fine."

Ann settled into a chair at the kitchen table, holding her hands near the fire. He fixed a mug for her, filled his own, took a seat on the other side.

"A long day," she said over the mug's rim.

He nodded. "I'm thinking we're both going to have longer ones over the next weeks. This morning my plans were to mow, clean the gutters, have dinner with Will, look at blueprints for his new barn. One phone call and it all turned into something very different. But I already like your Evie Blackwell. In principle I even like the idea for the new task force. The honor of being the first county chosen, though . . . I would have been more comfortable being fourth or fifth."

"I suggested this one be first for personal reasons," Ann confessed. "Evie was planning on going north for her vacation and starting with Bridgewood County, just outside Chicago, with its five cases that fit the profile. But Evie's got a guy up that way, and he's in the 'What do you think about marriage?' stage of the relationship. She's not on that page and needed a break from the drama. So we came south instead."

"Rob Turney. Paul mentioned the name."

"Yeah. Banker type. I keep telling Evie if she moves on, this is not going to be the last guy interested in her. Evie outclasses him."

"Odd you'd have such a strong opinion," Gabriel mentioned, amused, though he had to admit Ann rarely voiced such a firm one.

"The day after Flight 174 crashed," Ann said, turning serious, "Evie did this impromptu puppet thing with the kids at church, a brilliant teaching moment about life after death. And Rob sat in the back of the room, listening politely, then smirked as she finished. I had violent thoughts."

"That would do it," Gabriel said. "And Evie's point was . . . ?"

"She said something like . . ." Ann closed her eyes, recalling. " 'People die. But when they love Jesus, they don't stay dead. They are raised to life again so they can be with Jesus. And for all eternity, for years and years and years of forever, they never have to think about death. It will never be something that will happen again. They will always and forever be alive, in heaven.' "

Gabriel waited until Ann opened her eyes. "Agreed. He's a jerk."

Ann slapped her hand on the table. "Thank you! I knew I wasn't overreacting to that arrogant smirk. The kids got the point, and that was the reason it mattered. Rob didn't see that. He just reacted to the 'years and years and years of forever' way she chose to phrase it."

Gabriel smiled. "I once explained it not quite so eloquently as: Death is similar to a sneeze — you can feel it coming, but then you sneeze and it's over. You can tell people you sneezed, but you can never do that same one again even if you wanted to . . ."

He stopped as Ann started laughing. "You know I'm going to tell that to Paul," she said between chuckles, "and he's going to mention it to Bryce, and a few weeks from now Bryce is going to write on a chalkboard in front of a thousand people, *Death is a sneeze,* and have them in stitches. So, tell me, how much attribution would you like? I'll go with your initials if you want to save yourself some humorous fame."

"Anonymous might be best," Gabriel replied with a grin. He turned his mug in his hand as he enjoyed her humor, then finished the thought. "We think about death, you and I, cops in general, more than most people. It helps to tame that monster down to size occasionally. I'm going to enjoy heaven. The weight on my shoulders that I'll die in a work-related tragedy will one day be gone forever. That's enough reason for faith right there. Alive forever with Jesus, death never again being something you have to think about . . ."

"I couldn't agree more," Ann said, getting up to pour herself more coffee and topping off his too. "When Evie talks about death, she's remembering a lot of crime scenes. You can hear that reality in her voice. Similarly, when she says Jesus loves everyone, she's got faces in mind — both those who have done horrific crimes and those of innocent victims. Her faith is part of her life. Evie's an optimist about justice and life and things working out. Rob doesn't seem to connect with that. He says the right words, but that's all it is — words."

"You sound worried."

Ann lifted a shoulder. "I have a lot of friends, but female cop friends are a special lot. I like her personally. Professionally she's simply a solid cop." She stopped to smile. "No, let me rephrase that. She's a solid detective. Evie doesn't like being a cop in its broad definition. She doesn't want to be the officer someone calls when the couple next door are fighting, or there's a car crash, or someone is shooting up a store. She wants to be the one called when a car is stolen or someone is dead in an alley. She does the cop part when necessary so she

71

can have the part she loves — being a detective."

"She would hate being a sheriff. It's ninety percent cop, ten percent detective."

"Precisely," Ann said. "What she enjoys is solving real-life puzzles."

"Why are you telling me all this?" Gabe's hands circled his mug. "I'm enjoying the conversation, but you rarely take a turn like this by accident."

"You're going to be around Evie for a couple weeks," Ann replied. "I want you to have a sense of her, and I want her to get a sense of you. You're a cop and good in that role. If she marries Rob, leaves state investigations because of its travel demands, takes a job at the local police department, she's going to get squeezed back into that cop role. I want her to be sure. If she quits entirely — Rob would prefer that, I'm sure — I don't know what Evie does. In my case, I quit because I knew writing was as powerful a passion for me as being a detective, and there was a transition already in place. Evie doesn't have that in mind, at least not yet."

Gabriel drank the last of his coffee, thoughtful. "You worry Rob's going to do a Christmas-party proposal in front of family and friends, and Evie's going to say yes

72

because she's got a tender heart, didn't say no before it reached that point, and doesn't want to embarrass him or others present."

"I am. Call it intuition, whatever. I can see a problem coming, and as her friend, I'm worried. I don't want that to be the decision point for her, that path of least resistance. I want her to have a future with the right man, like I have with Paul." She smiled. "Rob might turn out to be a fine husband, and I think anyone getting Evie will have a very good wife, so it's not doom-and-gloom ahead. I'm just concerned about something less than I would hope for her."

"I kind of doubt Evie gets pushed into something this big unless she wants that direction." He turned to stir the logs in the fireplace, added another one. "Though this topic does make me curious — did you ever consider declining Paul's proposal?"

Ann didn't answer for a long moment. "I thought seriously about declining, yes."

"I wouldn't have guessed that from this vantage point."

"My caution wasn't about Paul, but about the necessary accommodations — on both sides — that being married would require. I've always functioned best with significant blocks of solitude. Paul loves me enough to still give me that time. The hours alone in the plane for the flight here today, the flight home tomorrow, are as important to our marriage as the fact I shared an early breakfast with Paul before I left this morning, and will be back to have dinner with him tomorrow evening."

"You are at your best, Ann, when you are alone with God. That's probably true of every Christian to one degree or another."

She nodded her appreciation of the simple but profound truth. "It's a fundamental fact about me. Had Paul not seen it, understood, and accepted what it meant, our marriage wouldn't have been able to flourish. I don't draw energy from being married, I draw energy from being alone, which I can then feed into my marriage. Cut the solitude out of my routine and I'm in trouble. It's not the same degree with everyone, but for me it was core." Ann paused for a moment. "That's what I worry about when I look at Evie, that Rob hasn't grasped the critical few things that make her who she is. She's going to marry him, then struggle to make life work. I don't want that for her, Gabe."

He got up and lifted the gallon of ice cream out of the refrigerator, scooped generously, set two bowls on the table, and slid the container back in the freezer. He sat back into his chair before he answered. "I rather doubt Evie's blind to the concerns you've mentioned, Ann. And if she hasn't seen all the ways a marriage can go wrong, she's no doubt seen the majority of them during her first years being a uniform cop on patrol. Trust her judgment, is my advice. I doubt she got to this point in her career without being willing to do hard things. I'm sure she'll tell Rob no to a marriage proposal if that's what she decides is best."

"I hope that's the case."

Gabriel studied his friend as he dug into his ice cream. "A final comment and then we'll leave the topic of Evie. When she's wearing an engagement ring, but before the wedding ring, tell her your concerns once more. Until then, you're writing the future. That's something you're gifted at doing, but it's not real yet. So let it set."

"Let it set," Ann repeated, scooping up another spoonful from her bowl. "Okay. Letting it set."

Gabriel considered her a moment, smiled. "You'll figure this out, Ann. There's a reason God brought the two of you together to be friends."

"Thanks for that."

He ate more ice cream, his thoughts shifting to why she'd come over this evening. "All right, now tell me about Karen Lewis."

"Before I do, is it your opinion the relationship between your brother and Karen is serious on Will's part, and a good thing for him?"

Gabriel didn't have to reflect on his answer. "Yes to both."

"Then I'm going to tell you a story tonight, because Karen and I have talked at length today, and we're in agreement that your opinion would be useful to have. But what's said here stays with me, with Karen, possibly with Paul — no one else — until Karen comes to a decision about the situation. If a circumstance develops where security is a concern, if it's an imminent safety issue, you tell anyone you feel is crucial for need-to-know."

Gabriel studied her expression, having seen it on rare occasions in the past. Ann was about to give up one of her secret people, and she only did so with a great deal of reluctance. "Agreed."

"Her name isn't Karen Joy Lewis. It's Karen Josephine Spencer. Three and a half years ago she was a line chef at a neighborhood restaurant in Chicago, one with a really good reputation for Italian cuisine. The couple who ran the business were killed after closing hours . . . stabbed to death. Karen saw the tail end of the murders, saw the man who did it, gave the police a sketch, picked him out of a lineup, testified at the trial. The jury didn't believe her; they returned a verdict of *not guilty.* He walked away from a double murder, is now walking the streets a free man."

Gabriel instantly knew where this was going and felt his stomach clench. Very few things bothered a cop more than the situation she just described. But he didn't comment, choosing to let Ann give him the rest of the details first.

"His name is Tom Lander. He blames Karen for the loss of his reputation, his marriage, his business. At the time, he managed money for private clients, who promptly, wisely, moved their funds away from him. He's a very dangerous man. He walked free on a double murder and he's felt pretty invincible ever since. He found it amusing to set out to destroy Karen's life, and he nearly succeeded. Saying he scared her doesn't do justice to what happened. Paul and I got her out of Chicago, gave her a new name, a new age, for that matter — because it was only a matter of time before he would take her life. Since that trial he's also killed his ex-wife. There's no arrest yet on that stabbing, but it isn't for lack of Chicago PD's efforts to make the case."

Not just a guilty man going free, but a violent one with a taste for payback. Gabriel had gotten to know Karen since she'd moved to Carin, and his opinion of her was rising with every word Ann said. She was young to have faced this, strong to have weathered it, war-toughened just as his brother had been, even though her fight had not been on a battlefield. No wonder Will found something in Karen that intensely attracted him. She was a realist with a strong backbone and a willingness to do what had to be done. Will would instinctively be drawn to that. It also was no doubt why Karen understood the combat-medic side of his brother.

"Lander's still in Chicago," Ann continued. "A friend keeps an eye on him for us. So far he has no idea where Karen has gone. Her family members and friends have had their homes broken into, laptops, phones, and phone records stolen, so we know he's hiring people to find a lead."

"That's pretty aggressive on his part."

"Very." Ann shifted in her chair, her worry about the situation apparent. "Karen didn't want to leave Illinois, so I chose Carin. It's close enough that Paul and I can keep tabs, and if she needs to leave quickly, I've got the airport close by. She's been able to relax here, to breathe again, and she's not looking over her shoulder. Here she's coming back from a deep, black hole. Having Will's attention, the normalcy of a guy being nice to her, has literally helped save her. With Karen having to leave behind everyone she knew, cut ties to everything in her past, Will has given her something in the present to hold on to and rebuild around, which has been a lifesaver.

"The jury's not-guilty verdict shredded something inside her, Gabriel. She told the truth, and she wasn't believed. Add that on top of the horror of seeing the murders, and this young woman took the hardest hit I've seen a civilian take in recent years. When he walked free, it was like 'Hell, Part Two' closing in on her. She couldn't turn around without him being there, watching her, following her, worse — walking up to her friends and introducing himself. He was toying with her, and we were going to get a call that she'd been stabbed to death."

"You were right to get her out of there."

Ann nodded. "Moving Karen was a drastic but necessary solution. This is behind Karen so long as Tom Lander doesn't locate her. And if Karen one day marries Will, it buries her under another layer of name changes and public records. But if Lander finds her, it becomes a problem with its own dimensions. He's not the type to move on, to forget a perceived wrong. He won't let up if he locates her. He will harass her, spook her, terrify her in creative and insidious ways, and then do her physical harm, probably kill her. And I think I know your brother well enough to predict that Will moving away from here, starting over somewhere else with a new name for himself and his wife, is a lot less likely than Will finding a way to permanently stop Tom Lander from ever terrorizing his wife again. He's got the training, the know-how."

"And then we'd have another murder to deal with." Gabriel shook his head, leaned forward to steeple his hands in front of him. "From Will's perspective, the guy found her once, he'll find her again, so end the problem for good," he finished softy.

"Exactly," Ann said. "Staying hidden for a year is different from staying hidden for five years, or ten. Something's going to give this sanctuary away. Karen's going to want to go back to Chicago to visit a family member in hospice care, attend a funeral or a wedding. She'll eventually make contact with Chicago and leave a trail. Or Lander is going to get creative on how to find her, launch one of those social media campaigns, 'help me find this woman,' posting Karen's last-known photo, and someone's going to want the money and send a response, 'I saw her yesterday in Carin, Illinois.' "

Ann's expression turned more troubled. "There is no way to protect Karen from ever being found again. The only protection is to move her if she's discovered. Maybe it's next year, or five years from now, but the day will come when for her own safety and the safety of those around her, Karen needs to leave here and cut all her ties to Carin County. And if she's married to Will, what's the answer to that dilemma? What if she has a two-year-old daughter . . . ?" Ann didn't try to finish the thought.

Gabriel was already there. "I'm running that story thread into the future, seeing those collisions too."

"Karen wants a future with Will, she wants to be free of this, but there's no answer that gives her that," Ann said. "Until Tom Lander is in jail or dead, Karen and everyone she cares about is at risk."

Gabriel absorbed that. "What does Karen need to hear from me, Ann?"

"Her question is simple. If she tells Will this story, says she doesn't want to marry him because of it, will he accept that decision?" She hesitated, then added, "My read

81

of it — she's not going to marry him and take the risk that trouble could find her again and touch her new family. That's her bottom line. Maybe she sees it differently in three years, five, but I don't know. She's not the first person I know to face this catch-22, and it has no real solution. For right now, she wants to stay here in Carin with Will as a friend, if she can do that without having to carry the burden of knowing he's put his life on hold for her."

"Okay." Gabriel said it quietly, mentally getting his arms around the problem. "Okay," he breathed again. He'd been a cop a long time. He had lost his naïveté about the world years ago. Ann was right that there was no solution — at least no good one — to this problem. Tom Lander would do what he could, and Karen would have to respond in whatever way she could. Not pulling someone else into her problem was instinctive on her part. To the extent she could keep Will at arm's length, a friend but no romantic entanglement, she could protect him should she need to again cut ties and drop out of sight. Gabriel understood how Karen had reached this point.

But he also knew Will was not a man easily shifted off his own course of thinking. Will hadn't mentioned marriage in his casual conversations yet, he hadn't changed direction in his plans for the next year, but it was clear to any who knew him well that he was carving out room in his life for Karen. When she walked into a room, his face would light up, and he'd often say softly, "There's my girl." His affection for her, his demeanor in public, was clearly staking a claim. It was clear to family and friends the relationship was deeply serious on his part.

Gabriel's opinion of the two as a couple hadn't changed with Ann's news and the insights it gave. He'd thought last night Karen was right for his brother, and he still thought the same tonight. But how they could get past the implications of this was an enormous hurdle.

Ann rose to pour them the last of the coffee. "That's the story, Gabriel, at least the highlights. I apologize that it got this complicated, that your family got pulled in, before I told you this. I was walking a narrow line on what was best for Karen. She needed this last year to heal, and I watched that happen in large part because of Will. I haven't wanted to take her away from that. But it has reached a decision point. It may well be that the better course is not to tell Will. Instead, she simply tells him she's not interested in pursuing the relationship further and he should look for someone else to date."

Gabriel grimaced at that suggestion, shook his head. "That's not going to fly." He couldn't fault Ann's reasoning that the tightest security was no one knowing Karen's situation. But now there was Will . . .

Gabriel gestured with his coffee mug. "If Will helped save Karen's life, as you put it, you need to understand she's done something similar for him. I haven't seen Will as content, as at peace since he came back from the war. This relationship has been helping them both in equal measure. Will cares about Karen more than any other woman he's ever dated, going back to high school. She's inside the circle of people Will considers his to protect. He's going to take care of her, Ann, romance or not."

Gabriel paused, thinking about his brother. "Will's tied to this place, this land — by history, by family. Karen's correct about that, and I'm glad she appreciates it. But she may not be seeing the broader picture. Will was away at war for six years, hasn't said much about where he was, what was going on, but he stayed in touch with family, he stayed connected all through it. If Will had to change names and take Karen five states away, spend a decade there to keep her safe, he could do it and see it as a temporary necessity, much like going on deployment. I see him able to segment life away from here for a while. So leaving Carin might be an acceptable fallback plan in Will's view of this. The day in the future when Lander is no longer a threat is the day they would return."

"That could be a very long wait," Ann cautioned.

Gabriel's phone rang. He seriously considered ignoring it, but at this time of night didn't have that luxury. "Hold that thought." He got it from his pocket and rose. "Sheriff Thane."

He listened to his dispatcher. "Patch the call through," he replied, then covered the phone. "This is going to take a few minutes, Ann. Get some more ice cream, make more coffee —"

"I'm fine. Go do what you need to do."

He nodded and headed into his home office while a call from the deputy in the next county transferred to him.

Gabriel found Ann in the living room, settled in one of the comfortable leather chairs by the fireplace, paging through a book she'd picked up from his side table. He mentally shifted from the rash of vandalized cars his caller wanted help on back to their conversation about Karen and Will. He took a seat near hers. "Karen needs to tell Will the story, tell him all of it, then give him some room to think. Tom Lander is a nasty problem, one I don't underestimate, but there are options that might let a relationship between Will and Karen work. Don't bet against Will, Ann. That's what a lifetime as his brother has taught me."

Ann set aside the book and gave a thoughtful nod. "I'll tell Karen your perspective. If she agrees, she tells Will the details, I do, or you do. I think I'd prefer to be the one — an initial angry reaction at not having been told about this already is not only likely, it's to be expected. Karen is sensitive to even a hint of anger right now. She would flinch and blame herself for having not told him, even though she was following my advice. It wouldn't be a good setup for the rest of the conversation they need to have. I'll take the blame for Karen's silence, give it time for things to settle before Will and Karen talk."

"Will would handle it with some care if she told him herself. But see if she's comfortable with you and I having the conversation with him."

"I'll talk with her tonight, let you know,"

86

Ann agreed.

It was a plan. Gabriel leaned back in his chair, crossed his ankles, and gave a small smile. "That leaves Grace."

Ann simply closed her eyes and dropped her head back.

"That bad, huh?"

Ann sighed and shifted in the chair to look over at him. "Will and Karen are the knot you can see. You can work with it to try to find a solution, even though you know the cleanest way to undo the knot is to cut it. Take that kind of problem, square it, square it again, and you'll begin to get a sense of what's going on with Grace Arnett."

"It's become a night for hard things. Lay it on me, Ann."

She smiled at his attempted humor. "Oh, I wish I could share the weight of this, Gabriel, because it's crushing me."

She took a deep breath and eased into it. "I've known Grace since she was sixteen. I met her shortly after she moved away from Carin. She's become a good friend. If I had a younger sister, this relationship would be it. She's told me some things over the years, and I've told her some things — it's definitely not a card-at-Christmastime bond. She's one of the few I let inside my life. And she's chosen to let me into hers. That

87

underlies what I'm going to tell you, Gabe."

Ann went quiet, absorbed in her own thoughts before she continued. "Grace is planning to ask Josh for a favor, and if she does, I'm encouraging him to say yes. He'll do whatever he can to help her — I know that about Josh. But Grace isn't ready for what she's decided to do. I've got an inkling of what's coming, and I know it will be more than she can manage, and yet I can't talk her out of it." Ann gave a small shrug. "I don't mind painful truths coming out — that's the way people come to healing, the way justice finally gets done. But there is a season, a time, for that truth. I know what Grace is already dealing with. I'm afraid the truth she wants to find isn't going to be that simple. She'll break, and it will be a crippling wound, difficult to heal, and will forever leave its mark."

"Ann, you're being cryptic."

"And deliberately so."

"What's Grace coming back to do?"

Ann shook her head. "If I can persuade her to wait — and I haven't given up on that — I'd rather you not have those details yet. If she does go ahead and ask Josh, he'll tell you, and you and I will have, without question, a rather intense conversation then."

"Is there a security concern?"

"No, there's nothing like that in her situation. I'm simply a friend wishing I could get her to delay the course she's set herself on."

"A good friend, Ann." He wasn't going to get anything more at this point, and he accepted that. "You think Grace is coming this way in the next few days?"

"Tuesday would be my guess. If the task force hadn't decided to focus on Carin County, I would have found another reason to be in the area. I'm not letting Grace do this without a friend around."

He nodded. "I'll help her, and help you too, however I can. Just let me know what you need."

Ann nodded back. "I appreciate that, Gabriel, more than you can know. If Paul's not able to be here, you're going to get my initial reaction. Which could be ugly because I can't afford to show those emotions to Grace." She picked up the coffee mug she'd brought into the living room and stood. "Despite appearances, I really didn't set out to complicate your life with this visit. It's just . . . well, you know me, enough stuff happens that weeks like this are inevitable once in a while."

He smiled. He did indeed know her.

"Paul's coming down?" he asked as he stood too.

"Yeah. We're going to be doing some back-and-forth flights. I'll have those hours in the air to talk with him, he can be here for half a day, adding his perspective to what's happening, and I can have him back in the FBI office the next day. It works for us."

"I've watched it work." Gabe started heading toward the kitchen. "Let's get those things for Evie before you leave. You look tired, Ann, and this hasn't even begun yet. Evie digging into the two cases, Karen and Will sorting things out, Grace coming back . . . you'd better catch some rest yourself along with Evie."

"I'm going that way next. Thanks for the visit."

"What are friends for?"

She smiled. "I've been blessed with having two of the Thane brothers in that role for years." Ann followed him into the kitchen and set her coffee mug in the sink.

Gabriel got out an empty grocery sack, retrieved two 7-Up bottles from the refrigerator, a bottle of Tylenol he kept in the spice cabinet, then opened the drawer next to the silverware. Every chili and soup order he called in came with cracker packages, and he added a handful to the sack. "I think I've

90

remembered everything on Evie's list."

Ann accepted the sack. "She'll appreciate this. Thanks."

He walked with her to the front door. "Call Paul."

"We've got a phone date in" — she glanced at her watch — "forty minutes."

"I like that about the two of you." He held her jacket as she slipped it on.

"Thanks again." Ann tugged keys out of her pocket. "If by tomorrow Evie's headache has eased off, she's going to eat lunch and then want to get to work, so I figure we'll be at the post-office building during the afternoon. I plan to leave for Chicago around four p.m. I'll be back Tuesday, early morning."

Gabriel made a mental note of the schedule. "I'll make a point to stop by the post office before you leave. The case files she needs should be there by the time you come in." He leaned against the doorframe as she walked out to her car. "Take care, Ann."

She lifted a hand in farewell. Gabriel pushed his hands into his pockets as he watched her pull out of the drive. His brothers had a hard week coming at them: Will hearing the truth about Karen, and Josh helping Grace . . . with what, he didn't know yet. The Florist case would make it an equally rough week for him. "God, help me be ready for whatever's coming," he whispered.

Being sheriff of Carin County meant carrying heavy truths about those who lived here. Name a crime and he could pretty much identify someone around Carin who had committed it, either in the distant or recent past.

Karen had been hiding in plain sight. He had to admire that about her. She'd concealed her connection to Chicago and the murder trial with such skill, he had never had cause to wonder what she was hiding, and he was a man whose second nature was to listen for those false notes in someone's story. Ann had done a superb job coaching her on how to handle it all.

He was sure there were other buried secrets, dark skeletons or worse in his county . . . maybe even a living monster around. Ann's concern about Grace suggested there was another story he didn't know about. *Yet,* he thought. The truth was going to come into the light as it always did. He'd deal with it because that went with the job.

Gabriel shut off the porch light and walked through the house, banked the fire and closed the doors on it, set the house alarm, and headed upstairs. He sincerely hoped the phone would not ring again during the night.

Ann Falcon

Ann nudged off her shoes inside the front door of Evie's vacation rental, walked upstairs, heard the radio playing faintly in Evie's bedroom. She eased open the door, confirmed Evie was comfortably sleeping, her back and neck elevated with pillows, and quietly closed the door again. Ann walked to the third of the four bedrooms and sank into the soft mountain of pillows. She got out her phone, hit the speed dial.

Paul answered on the first ring. She could see on her phone's screen that he was home in their shared office, the artwork behind him one of her favorite pieces.

"Hello, darling."

Her eyes filled at his simple greeting.

Paul shut down his laptop. "Rough day?"

"Just long. Gabriel and I talked for close to two hours."

"Did you tell him?"

She shook her head, whispered, "No, not yet. Only about Karen."

She read the quiet empathy in his eyes. "Okay."

"I should have."

Paul shook his head. "If you couldn't tell him tonight, it was because it wasn't ready to be said. Grace is going to get through this," Paul reassured. "You'll be there for her. Josh will help her. I'll be around. Rachel will come if needed. Her doctor will be on call. Grace will have people she trusts to help her — she won't face this alone."

"Just get me to next weekend and I'll be able to believe it." There was nothing else she could do tonight, so Ann forced herself to change the subject, looking for something lighter to think about. "How did your Saturday go?"

"We had to arrest a state congressman for leaving lewd messages in women's public restrooms, canceled a 10K race because of bomb threats — called it a permit problem — and finally managed to catch the guy who has been tossing rotten eggs at FBI cars leaving the parking garage. That gets me to about three p.m. when I thankfully came home. The world didn't stop going crazy, though. I just decided it could wait until Monday. I shared a late lunch with the dog — we had BLTs — then we played in the park and went to visit Jasmine. Black is a happy boy." Paul tilted the camera. "Say hi to Mom."

The dog swished his tail on the floor but

94

didn't bother to roll over. He had four feet in the air and was comfortably napping upside down whenever food or conversation was not directed his way.

"Hey, Black." Ann laughed at the dog's body language. She had seen him in that pose many times. Every time she was away, she regretted the trip. "I wish I was home."

"Tomorrow night you sleep in your own bed, can snuggle with your favorite guy — that would be me. Favorite guy number two will happily welcome you home by snoring to break the silence."

Ann laughed. "Oh, yeah, that's home. That sounds nice."

"We both miss you too, Ann. One of us even more than the other."

"Paul, next time our new governor calls, I'm going to say no."

He simply smiled. "You only said yes because you wanted to get Evie established in the group, and to prove to yourself your skills haven't gotten rusty in the last couple years. By inauguration day I predict the task force will be ready to officially get to work, and you'll be ready to dive into another writing project."

"I'm already close. The task force will get to work as soon as Bliss is inaugurated and signs the paperwork."

"You're efficient and effective, which is why he wanted you involved. Solve the two cases in Carin and put a bow around the task-force announcement."

"That would be ideal. It's going to be good to have you down here occasionally."

He smiled at his wife. "I'll bring my special kind of FBI super-agent magic, dazzle everyone with some truly geeky lab reports. They changed the letterhead again. It actually says *Geeky Lab Report* on our internal docs."

"You know that's part of the fun, figuring out how long it takes the boss to notice and what he's going to do about it."

"Well, Agent Top Dog — get it? — sent in a Blackie paw print with a request to ID the thief who just ate someone's paycheck."

Ann laughed so hard, she had to wipe her eyes. "And now I'm supposed to sleep for a few hours?"

"It's called levity, minor humor, 'I miss you, so let me make you laugh,' with the hope of banishing that haunted look in your eyes as only your beloved husband can do."

"As only you can do," Ann agreed softly.

"Go to early church, help Evie get started, then fly home. Black and I will take care of you once you're here."

"That sounds like a wonderful deal. Good

night, Paul."

"Sleep well, Ann."

She put down the phone, only to lift it again to send Charlotte Bishop a text: *Could you sketch me an "Agent Top Dog" logo? I need a whimsical Christmas present for Paul. I'll forward a photo of Black to base it on. Let me know. Thanks.*

Ann set her phone on the bedside table, knowing Paul would call first thing in the morning to say good morning. She set her clock so she could make the early service at the Thanes' church, then turned in for the night, grateful to have the day done.

FOUR

Evie Blackwell

Evie taped another piece of white easel paper on the wall as high as she could reach. "I made a fool of myself, didn't I? I'm trying to remember what I said from the time Sheriff Thane found me on the roadside until they let me out of the ER, and it's an embarrassing amount of blur and sentence fragments. I must have sounded like an idiot, Ann, or maybe even drunk. I'm surprised he's letting me access the files."

She glanced over at her friend, but Ann simply smiled and offered another large sheet of paper. Evie moved down the wall and taped it in place. The wall was marked up with nail holes and peeling paint chips, yet it was smooth and would hold the paper. "And how many times did I say the equivalent of 'you promise?' to either you or Gabriel? I've counted five of them. I'd blush if I wasn't so mortified."

"You're a happy child when you're concussed, Evie."

"Ouch. Even the teasing makes me want to wince."

Ann laughed. "Relax. You made a first impression, and now you'll make a second one. You're good at this work. Don't try to correct things by over-apologizing. Instead, give Gabriel something to contrast it with — the real you, without a brain-rattling crack to the head. You don't want to swing from 'slightly out of it' to appearing as if you're anxious to impress. Just settle for being Evie Blackwell and you'll be fine."

Evie sighed. "My aching sense of pride will take your advice. At least I know it will be hard to make that first impression any worse." She stepped back and considered the taped sheets. It would work as an improvised crime board. She looked at the opposite wall she'd papered first. "I think we're good. Nothing's falling down . . . yet."

The post office had interesting décor with its high ceilings, faded paint, and scratched concrete floor. But the long walls, good lighting, and tables made it a better place for laying out two cases than her original intention of trying to set it all up back at the house.

"Where do you want me to start?" Ann

asked as she surveyed the boxes.

"Boxes on that wall are the Dayton girl; boxes here will be the Florist case. I'm thinking timelines first, and any photos."

"Works for me," Ann said. She opened the first box on the Dayton abduction. Evie dug into the Florist files.

The sheriff would walk in at some point this afternoon, probably with his father and a deputy or two, and Evie would like to have something on the walls so she could avoid eye contact with Gabriel. She would need his help — no one knew these cases better than the local cops — but she still wished she'd been able to say a normal hello to the man before she'd wrecked her car and became a babbling idiot.

This experiment of looking at cold cases needed to go smoothly, hopefully be successful. She sincerely hoped the way she'd arrived on scene was not a precursor to the rest of her time in Carin.

The next few weeks would set the tone for her place on the task force, and she wanted to bring something positive to the table when it officially launched in January. Sharon Noble was recruiting good, experienced cops. Theodore Lincoln from Chicago and Taylor Aims from St. Louis were already definites. Rumor had it David Marshal was coming back from New York just for this. If Ann continued helping out next year, there wouldn't be a stronger list of names for the assignments ahead.

Evie wanted to play a useful role in that group, learn from them, get the experience that only working with great cops could give. She knew the task force on her résumé could cement the rest of her career, be the reason she might make head of the state Bureau of Investigations one day. She wanted a success here so badly it worried her. Normally solving a case was motivation enough. Having her emotions personally tangled in an outcome just made for stupid mistakes. She'd jinx it herself by trying too hard, or caring too much about the impression she was making, miss something because her mind was distracted. "Ann?"

"Yeah?"

"Tell me to shut up. I'm thinking too hard."

Ann laughed. "The case?"

"Haven't even gotten that far yet. I'm still wandering around in task-force stuff. How did I end up getting picked for this? To represent the State Police? Did you put forward my name?"

"Your boss likely looked around for someone young enough not to care about the long hours without extra pay, tough cases with incomplete records, relentless reporters and public scrutiny, someone who could face explaining to the governor why a case isn't solved. I'd say your name was likely one of two he considered."

"Oh. Why are *you* doing it?"

"Because I want to. Why did you say yes?"

"Because I want it."

Ann grinned. "See? We're *simpatico,* you and I. Do you want to talk through the Florist case today or the Dayton girl?"

"I was thinking we'd look at the Dayton case when you get back Tuesday. For now I'd like to take advantage of the initial curiosity about what's going on to get people talking about the Florist case. Most of the deputies worked the original disappearance, or at least one of the subsequent reviews of the case."

Ann nodded. "That makes sense."

Evie taped up photos of the Florist family. Scott and Susan Florist, their young son, Joe. A deputy, his wife, and their boy, all three missing. Scott was a good-looking man, his wife's smile reflected in her eyes, and she looked happy. The boy had a grin full of mischief.

Evie's hand traced across the three photos. If she felt her mind wandering to the task

102

force again, to her place on it, she had only to look at the photos to bring herself back to what really mattered. She wanted to find out what had happened to these three people. There was extended family in this town who needed answers. She took a deep breath and felt herself settle in for the duration. This was what she was good at, right here, working a case.

She found a marker and to the left of the photos drew a long line across the length of the wall. Midpoint she scored the line and wrote down the date of the disappearance. She didn't know if the answers to the case would be found in the information before or after that date. The trigger for why a crime happened often rested days or weeks before it occurred. The actions of the guilty party after a crime were often just as revealing. Sometimes it was a combination of both that helped her figure out the puzzle.

She gingerly picked up the first box, her stiff back complaining, and carried it over to a table, took a seat, and began to sort out the contents, looking for information and facts she wanted to highlight on the timeline.

"Evie," Ann called over, "the list of open questions — do you want them first thing on the wall as people come and go, or do you want them deeper in the room so someone has to walk past all the gathered facts before they get to the questions being asked?"

"Deep in the room would be best. I don't want to have to explain to curious deputy George or family member Flo how come I want the alibi for the sheriff the night the Florist family disappeared."

"Ouch."

"Too tough?"

"Nope. Work it hard and work it deep."

Evie nodded, kept turning pages in the file. She fully intended to do just that.

Half an hour later, Evie turned away from adding a date to the timeline, saw the sheriff through the glass just before he pulled open the door, and made a point of sitting back down at the table and pulling over some paperwork, giving it her attention.

"Hey, Ann," Gabriel said as the door closed behind him. "I recognize the Dayton case. That wall is already looking useful."

"It's getting there. It's a simple case for the most part. She was a beautiful child."

"That she was."

"We need more office supplies — Post-it notes, yellow pads of paper, pens, tape, markers. Where do you recommend I get them?"

"Tell Iris. Shopping for office supplies makes her day."

Ann laughed. "I may tag along with her. A good color variety stack of Post-it notes makes my day too."

Evie heard Gabriel crossing the room in her direction and glanced up. He was in uniform, carrying a folder, very much the sheriff with similar appeal today as when she was a young girl thinking uniforms made the man.

"Hello, Evie." His opening was friendly, and she heard not a trace of humor about her post-accident demeanor, a point in his favor. He leaned against the table beside her. "How's the headache?"

Her head was still painful, and the stitches pulled — not what she wanted to admit. "It's not aching like it was," she answered with some caution.

He smiled, no doubt recognizing the dodge. "We're bringing in a big cooler that we'll keep stocked with ice and soda. Consider it a perk of the job and help yourself. The root beer is local and excellent, but if you get tired of it and prefer other types of soda, we won't razz you that much."

She relaxed a touch more, appreciating the one-of-the-guys tone more than she would like to admit. "Thanks for the heads up."

"You and I have some business to complete." He placed papers beside her. "The police report on the deer you hit for your insurance company."

She flipped pages, saw photos, winced. "I didn't remember it being this bad."

"You were fortunate to have been able to walk away from it," he commented, his tone now serious. "Give it a read and sign the last page. You can hand it back when you next see me. You've got a nice buck you earned the hard way if you're interested in venison. Henry hauled it in to be butchered."

"Thanks, but I'll pass. I don't mind barbecued venison steaks, yet under the circumstances it doesn't seem quite appropriate. Henry's welcome to the buck in exchange for his time dealing with it."

"I'll let him know," Gabriel said. "Your car is at Aaron's Auto Shop. He can arrange to ship it to the garage of your choice, or he can work with Thomas over at Crane's Body Shop and get the work done here. I'll vouch for the fact they know what they're doing."

"If they can fix it within the next two weeks, I'd just as soon get the work done locally. I can get by with a rental."

"Aaron thinks about a week plus — I'll tell him to get started. The place next to Aaron's is a used-car dealer. Ben will give you a week-by-week rental if only to be able to tell the next customer, 'It's been driven for the last week without the engine having a problem.' I wouldn't buy from him because most have been in prior wrecks — he likes to buy very cheap and mark up double, but he's honest about it. You could pay more at a name-brand rental company if you like, get something without the history, or take a chance with Ben."

"You're steering me towards him."

"Well, he'd be a first cousin to the missing Detective Scott Florist."

"Ah, then Ben it is."

"Thought you might agree." He held up a set of keys. "For the yellow convertible parked outside. I figured you wouldn't mind the flash." She walked over to the window to look at the car. "Consider it another perk for the vacation," he said behind her. "It didn't leak oil on the way over here, which is a good sign. Stop by and sign the paperwork with Ben sometime before the end of the week. You'll be able to angle the conversation over to the case while you're there."

She blinked, laughed. "Thanks. That's an excellent-looking car."

"Sure is. Just FYI — knowing the sheriff isn't going to get you out of a speeding ticket. We need every fifty bucks we can get for the town's budget."

She pocketed the keys he offered. "I'll try to remember."

"City and county maps," he said as she returned to the table. He laid them beside the accident paperwork. "Don't get lost. There's a GPS in the car, but I wouldn't trust it for the back county roads."

"Okay."

"Your dogs are fine with Will. He'd like to keep them another few days, if that works for you, to make sure their bruises are fully healed. I marked his place on the map."

"I spoke with him earlier today. I'm grateful to him. I just hope they haven't already changed loyalties."

He chuckled. "Will likes to tend things." He pulled a phone out of his shirt pocket. "I brought you a spare office phone. We'll spot you some minutes in return for your time on our cases. It's GPS-tagged so I can always find you. It will get you through until you can get yours replaced."

She turned the phone over, saw the number taped on the back. "Very useful. I've been borrowing Ann's."

He set another sheet of paper on the table.

"Phone numbers you might need. Local stuff, Florist family relatives. Speed Dial One gets you me. Two is Josh. Three for Will. If we can't answer a question for you, we'll know who around here can."

"Why are you being so helpful?"

"I've decided I like you," he said lightly. "Maybe it's the green eyes."

She didn't reply. He spun car keys around his finger and turned toward the door. "I'll be back in about an hour. You want to start by talking through the Florist case?"

"Yes."

"Honey cashew chicken for dinner or beef fried rice?"

"Both."

"I'll bring enough to feed Dad too should he wander in. Let him know." He disappeared out the door.

Evie picked up the last thing he had left on the table. A roll of sweet-tarts. She thoughtfully opened the end of the roll and slipped one out.

"And you were worried about first impressions because . . . ?"

"Shut up, Ann."

Ann laughed and settled on the chair across from her, held out her hand. Evie passed over the candy. "Was that normal Gabriel Thane?"

"Pretty much."

"I think I can turn down the heat in this place. He must have been born flirting with his nurses."

"He does have that effect," Ann agreed.

"Think he killed the Florist family?"

"I think you can mark him off the list. I wouldn't assume the same for his deputies."

Evie looked across at Ann. "Ouch."

"Look hard and look deep," Ann repeated.

"Yeah." Evie slipped another sweet-tart from the roll. "I see why you like the Thane brothers. Josh is the one I haven't met yet, but from what you've said, he sounds like a nice guy too."

"He's more laid-back than Gabriel and Will, probably goes with being the youngest." Ann glanced at the time. "I'm going to head back to Chicago earlier than planned if you think you'll be all right on your own here."

Evie smiled. "I'll be fine — thanks for all the help, Ann, getting me this far."

"No problem. I'll be here early Tuesday morning. If you solve either case while I'm gone, I'll buy the hot fudge sundae."

Evie nodded in appreciation of the subtle encouragement. "An excellent motivator. Call me when you land so I know you're safely home."

"Will do."

Ann collected her jacket and briefcase and headed out.

Evie had the post-office building to herself. She tapped her foot on the cement floor and heard the echo. She wrote *radio* at the top of her to-do list.

She walked over and locked the door, then turned to the mostly blank crime wall she was filling and looked at the neatly stacked boxes waiting for her. "Okay, Florist family. What do you have to tell me?" She carried another box over to the table, pulled out her chair, and opened the top folder.

She finally felt as though the chaos of her arrival was ending and life was getting back to normal. She had a case to work. That felt really, really good.

FIVE

Gabriel Thane

The post office lights were on, but Ann's rental car was gone. The yellow convertible still sat on the street where Gabriel had parked it. He tapped on the door glass, pleased to see Evie had locked herself in.

Evie came over to unlock the door. "Dinner," he said by way of a casual greeting, nodding to the two sacks he carried. "Sorry I'm later than I intended."

"No problem. How about over there?" She pointed to a free table.

"Ann get away okay?"

"Yes. She'll call when she's home."

He unpacked the disposable plates and utensils he'd brought and set out the meal. Ann's wall was mostly as he had seen it earlier, while Evie's wall had grown considerably in details. "You've been busy."

"First day game plan — get set up."

"What's day two?"

"Shove case details in my mind until they leak out."

Gabriel smiled at Evie's description. He began to walk through the Florist crime wall, reviewing the photos, the timeline. He paused at the end to review her list of questions. "I don't know whether to be insulted or impressed," he said, "that you want my alibi for the night they went missing." *She's not messing around.*

"Someone in the department. Someone in the county. Maybe job-related — a person Florist arrested. Or it was a family thing."

Gabriel knew he was a good cop, thought of himself that way, but she said it so casually. *Someone in the department . . . Or it was a family thing.* It felt hard to breathe.

He turned toward her and found her watching him steadily. He pushed his hands into his back pockets. "You're right. But those aren't casual categories."

"Going to get protective, Gabriel?"

He thought about the missing deputy, his wife and son. He let out a huff of air. "No. You ask your questions. That's why you're here."

"Was he having an affair? Was she?"

Gabriel simply grimaced. "I'd say no, but we'll check it again. You don't mince words."

"I don't like wasting time. If this was a

113

typical case, it would have been solved by now. In order to discover what someone else didn't see, I've got to come at it from as many hard angles as I can find."

This wasn't going to be a casual look at the case, a simple review of what others had done, but cutting through that work to discover what others had missed. "Evie, I think you're going to wear the department out over these next couple of weeks."

Her eyes glinted with humor. "You'll all survive me, Gabriel." She turned back to the table. "Let's eat."

Gabriel dished out fried rice onto his plate, sampled it, added extra soy sauce. Evie, digging into the honey cashew chicken, asked, "Tell me about the Florist case."

He glanced over and was glad to see she'd found her appetite. He gave her the summary from his point of view: "Twelve years ago, the Florist family left their home on a Thursday evening in August for a three-day camping trip with friends. They never arrived. Vanished somewhere between here and the campground located at the north end of Carin Lake, a distance of about thirty miles. Their friends notified the police just after seven o'clock Friday morning when they still hadn't arrived and calls went unanswered. Police found nothing at the house, found no sign of the truck they were driving or the camper they were towing along the possible routes they might have taken. They simply disappeared — a deputy, his wife, and their eleven-year-old son. A massive search and parallel investigation began, with hundreds of officers involved. It generated no answers to the mystery."

"That's what interests me the most, Gabriel. Three people vanish, and the case remains unsolved. It's got me more than curious."

"Having known them, the words I'd use are *sad, mad . . .*"

"Point taken."

Gabriel set down his fork, shook his head. "Your objectivity will be an asset, Evie, and I shouldn't knock it. Most who have worked this case over the years come to it with perspectives of having known one or all three of them, or they know their family members in the area."

"I can appreciate this case is personal for all of you," Evie replied. "I truly don't mean to sound distant or cold about them. Talk to me about the family. I'd like to know how you remember them."

From the years of thinking about this case, Gabriel could recall them as clearly today as when he'd last seen them twelve years ago. "Susan May Florist was a part-time bank teller. She also worked a day a week at the local bakery icing cakes. I'd see her at department picnics, baseball games. She had a nice laugh and a kind heart. She always made a point of asking about the Thanes." He sipped at his soda, glanced over at the photos on the wall.

"Their son was into baseball. Joseph Patrick Florist — everyone called him Joe — was a good kid, polite, curious, fascinated by what his dad did, still young enough to hold a bit of hero worship for his father. I tossed around a ball with him, took him fishing a couple of times. I knew him enough to like him.

"Scott Simon Florist worked a civilian job at the courthouse for several years before deciding he wanted to join our police force. He entered the academy older than most, joined the PD as a patrol officer, wanted to become a detective and put in the work to get there. He was a smart man, a good cop. I didn't work directly with him, since he mostly partnered with Phil Peters, but our paths would cross in the break room, at training classes, sometimes at the firing range. He had a reputation for being careful with the details. And he was good with kids.

A fifteen-year-old got picked up for vandalism, Scott would take the case, nail down the details, and figure out if there was something going on at school or home before he wrote up the report. He'd take the extra time. I respected the guy.

"Susan and Scott were married for fourteen years. That was one of the saddest parts of the investigation. Looking at who might have wanted to cause them problems, going through their personal lives, talking with friends and family, seeing what a strong marriage they had, knowing they could have been one of those rare 'married for fifty happy years' newspaper profiles one day. Instead, they became a case number."

"What do you think happened to them?" Evie asked, propping her elbows on the table.

He shook his head rather than try to answer. "I've stopped trying to guess."

"My experience Saturday with the deer," she said, "makes me wonder if they had a similar experience. Did they hit a deer? Need to stop for repairs because the vehicle or camper got banged up? It takes them off the route they're traveling to deal with repairs, it's the middle of the night, maybe they pull into the wrong place at the wrong time and encounter trouble."

117

"I don't remember a theory of them hitting a deer ever being addressed. It's a place to start," Gabriel agreed, interested in the idea if only because it was a new avenue. She'd been thinking about that possibility, while the idea hadn't even crossed his mind, despite his having been there to help after her accident. He mentally chalked up a point for Evie. She was doing the job better than he at the moment. He planned to catch up.

"Fresh ideas, Gabriel. New ways to look at what's here. I'll do what I can to find things we should consider." She nodded toward the boxes. "You've been through these files many times. Give me the highlights."

She likes working cases, Gabriel thought, seeing how she'd relaxed. She was engaged, working on something that mattered, and comfortable with the job. "Let's start at the core of it," he began. "Since the day the Florist family disappeared, there's been no activity on their credit cards, bank accounts, savings or checking. No one at the time it happened tried to get money out of their accounts before we realized there was a problem. The credit cards didn't expire for four years, and the accounts were deliberately left open. No one came across a wallet or purse and tried to use the cards later.

"Since the day they disappeared, there has been no contact with family members or friends. The Florist family had strong ties to the larger community. Things were stable financially, marriage solid, no hidden vices surfaced such as alcohol, drugs, or gambling. They left behind all they owned, along with two pets — a dog and a cat, which they had arranged for a neighbor to look after. These aren't the type of people to try to skip out on unpaid debts, for example, or to get clear of a family dispute." He hesitated. "Combined, those facts suggest they were murdered," he concluded. "Questions so far?"

Evie shook her head. "Go on."

"The bodies of three people are hard to hide well enough they don't eventually get found. If you leave all three in a vehicle, park it somewhere, the bodies are going to be found. Maybe they end up in a landfill in the first couple days, but that doesn't happen as often as the TV shows imply, and three of them disposed of that way unnoticed is tough to fathom. Maybe in a body of water, but it would need to be one not churned up frequently, not often fished, otherwise something gets brought to the surface.

"A burial is likely in the countryside, but not crop land — they would have been discovered as the ground was tilled and replanted, the soil turned over. We're looking for wooded land that doesn't have terrain torn up that often by floodwaters. And the graves would have taken some time to dig in order to be deep enough so that wildlife wouldn't dig up the remains. Hunters would have found bones had the graves been disturbed. We've had some extremely wet and dry years over the last decade and that breaks up the ground surface."

He shook his head. "Other possibilities: access to a funeral home, a crematorium. But the more likely answer is land you control, land in which you buried the bodies, hiding the evidence of your crimes on your own property. But should ownership change, the bodies are there, ready to point right at you.

"It's equally time-consuming and difficult to make vehicles disappear. No one's tried to get insurance on their truck's VIN number, so the truck probably wasn't found by a third party or sold to anyone. An abandoned camper of the make and model of theirs hasn't turned up either. Someone could have stripped the vehicles down to parts and done so out of sight. Or they found a way to dispose of them — a junk-yard crusher, a body of water, an abandoned gravel pit. Or they're still sitting undiscovered in a barn somewhere under a tarp, most likely on land owned and controlled by the one who did the crime.

"So," Gabriel said, taking a deep breath, "that means we have no crime scene. We don't know where whatever happened occurred. At the start of their journey, at their home, during their travels on one of the roads or at a stop along the way, or if it happened near or at their destination.

"The reason for the crime is also unknown. We don't know if this was personal — if the deputy and his family were targeted and the camping excursion was an opportunity to act. We don't know if the focus was the vehicles more than the people or if one of them was the target. We don't know of related crimes in progress, where grabbing this family might have been a part of an ongoing escape." Just saying all this out loud left a hollow feeling inside him. Gabriel forced himself to finish. "We know some things that did *not* occur, rather than much, if anything, about what did happen. It's a painful position to be in."

Evie shook her head, her expression showing strong disagreement with his last statement. "You've spent twelve years eliminating things, Gabriel, and that's progress. What's left, however improbable, is going to be the answer."

All he saw was a case that had gone cold — it needed a new discovery like bones to move it forward again. But maybe she could see something he didn't. "I don't know where a person even begins on something like this, Evie."

"The map you brought me." She pointed to the wall where she'd taped it. "I'll fly over the area with Ann this week so it's better fixed in my mind. They were driving from their home at the south end of Carin Lake to the state park thirty miles north. The lake inlets fork there, where the eagles have nested. That campground is still in Carin County?"

"It is."

"Then let's assume for now that the person who did whatever this is also lives in Carin County."

"Okay."

"You concluded in the summary you just recounted that the family was murdered."

"Yes."

"Murder is a violent act, the killing of a child even more horrendous than an adult murder. Let's start by looking for the person who could do such a thing."

He was startled by that definitive statement. "How?"

"You know who lives here. I want a list of the people you would consider violent. Then I want you to cross off those who are unlikely to be the one to kill a child. How many people in Carin County could murder three people, one of them a child? A hundred? Fifty? Less? I bet you know this person.

"Who did you think was a violent adult when you were a boy growing up here? Who do you still think today is violent? Who on that list has moved away? A domestic disturbance call, a drug arrest, a bar fight, an assault complaint that involved someone on your list. Cops have bumped into the violent ones who live in Carin. Because the case is twelve years ago, you'll need your father to contribute a list too. Violence often runs in families — the father may be on his list, the son on yours."

Gabriel nodded at the reasoning behind her request. "It will take some time, but I can do that. After we get our lists together, we'll see which ones have alibis for that Thursday evening, Friday morning."

"We could do that. But I was thinking

more along the lines of asking those people who they think is capable of killing the Florist family. If you want to find a particular kind of violent man, Gabriel, you ask violent ones who know him. This person could appear controlled but have that snap to his fury. People around him will know that about him. It won't necessarily be the hothead your deputy might have worried about on sight, though it might be someone who's related. The person we want is violent, likely told someone a detail or two, or had a partner. There's a rumor out there. Someone knows something useful. I'd like you to focus on finding that rumor or name. That's your strong suit. You know this county and its residents. Start there."

Gabriel could see merit to that strategy. "Okay, while I focus on violent citizens around Carin County, what's your target?"

"Motive. Were the deputy and family a chance encounter or were they targeted? If it's random, there's nothing for me to find. But if it's this family specifically, either one or all three of them, then something happened that made the person we're looking for say, 'I'm going to harm the Florist family.' I want to find the trigger event. You find the person who could do this. I'll find the reason he did."

Gabriel looked over the boxes stacked behind her, filled with interviews, reports, notes. She was trying to recreate something fresh from the information, a new way of looking at the data. "I understand where you're coming from — if you find a motive, it moves this case a leap forward. But you've given yourself a hard assignment." He glanced at the crime wall, the questions listed there. "What about the idea they hit a deer?"

She shrugged. "I'll multitask. I assume someone in the county picks up dead animals by the side of the road. A deer is probably going to get a mention in a daily report. You have an archive of that kind of paperwork?"

"We throw stuff away only when we run out of room to store it, so yes, that paperwork is probably still buried in the archives. Stop by the office and I'll point you in the right direction."

"Thanks. If there's a violent man who works nights at a garage on the route they would have traveled, put a red circle around him."

Gabriel smiled. "You really think there's a way to reexamine this case, put it together differently, and find an answer?"

"Yes. I do. It's all about context, Gabriel.

How many cases actually remain unsolved because of lack of evidence? You said it yourself — the bodies could be buried on land the person owns, the vehicles under a tarp in a barn on the property. I think the evidence no one has found thus far — the vehicles, the bodies — is still sitting out there and waiting to be discovered.

"Give me names of violent people in Carin County capable of murdering three people, one a kid, and give me who on that list owns property. If they killed twelve years ago, it's probable they killed someone else in the years before or after that. Think about the person who could have done this and see if their behavior over the last dozen years raises flags. Cases solve when you can get a thumbnail under a corner of the answer and peel it back."

"Optimism is your middle name, Evie."

She nodded. "Gabriel, think about this. You see these intervening years as an obstacle to solving the case. I see it as an opportunity. The person who did the crime has had all this time to show us his true colors. Maybe it wasn't obvious at the time, but now, looking at him today? I bet it's obvious he's got a violent streak. There's that Bible verse about things in the dark not staying hidden. A person's true colors show over time. Take advantage of the extra information the last twelve years have created. His friends back then are probably not his friends anymore. Someone knows him, can tell us, 'I think Jerry did it.' The more years pass, the more some people get annoyed with each other, drift apart, find old tensions simmering. The former friend who will now give him up is a powerful investigative tool."

She tilted her head slightly. "It's not simply this crime, you know — you can find him by a general pattern he leaves in his wake. Violence rarely limits itself to a single type of assault. Who was showing up at school with bruises? What woman has shown up at the hospital or clinic with signs of being hit? Who was self-medicating with alcohol? If he's in the community, others are brushing up against him every day. Who were people afraid of back then? Who are people afraid of today? Sometimes that question points to the right direction."

Gabriel found himself making mental notes as he listened to Evie, not so much about the case itself but about how she was thinking. He let himself relax. Maybe they would end up after these weeks with no results, but she was right. They could work on the ones around the person they wanted to identify. "Thanks for the fresh perspective. It's useful. I'll look for a name of someone who might have done this. You look for a motive. One of us might get lucky."

"Luck is mostly perspiration." She nodded again at the boxes. "As helpful as those files will be, it's not likely going to be enough to find my motive. I'm going to need some time in the archives. I want to understand what was happening in the town and around the county in the weeks and months leading up to the family's disappearance."

"You're not a woman of small ambitions. Or maybe it's better stated you're a small woman of large ambitions?"

She grinned. "I like either one. I could use that stenciled on a sign in my office. Seriously, Gabriel, if this wasn't random, then something happened before their disappearance to trigger a decision to harm the Florist family. I'm not going to find that something in the notes about the search, though maybe an item in an interview will point back to it. More likely it's in a separate police report filed in the months or even years before the family disappeared."

"You're welcome to browse through the archives," he repeated. He nodded to her left. "Hand me that pad of paper. I can start listing names of violent people from memory. Would a phone call bother you? I'd like to give my father a call and have him start doing the same."

"Go ahead. For the rest of this evening I'm reading until I can't see straight."

He glanced at the other wall. "You want to talk about the Dayton girl's disappearance?"

"Tuesday will be soon enough, when Ann is back in town."

He nodded and dialed a number. "Dad, I have a question for you." He pushed away from the table and walked across the room as he explained what he needed.

Evie Blackwell
Gabriel got called away by dispatch, and shortly thereafter two deputies came over carrying more boxes. Evie got up to let them in, pointed where to stack them. "Could I ask you a question?" she asked when they'd made their deliveries.

"Sure," the nearest deputy replied.

"You know what's in the boxes. What do you think about the State Police coming in to look into the Florist case?"

"Meaning you, ma'am?" He looked at the wall, the timeline she was creating of the crime, then at his partner, then back at her. "Way we heard it from Marissa, who heard it from Iris, the boss decided to say okay, told them to pull out the boxes, copy every piece of paper, including any dust bunnies that might be hiding in a box corner. He wanted you to have it all, so I'm guessing he's going to join in on that review himself and help you out. Only way it can be gone through in a reasonable amount of time."

"Last time we worked it," said his partner, "he pulled it all into a conference room, and one of us was always working that room until there were simply no more questions we could think to ask. No offense, but we've been at this case for twelve years and it's not going to yield. To tell you the truth, we're glad it's not going to be us this time."

"Have you any personal theories about what happened?"

"A truck hauling a camper, it's a gas guzzler," said the first cop. "They stopped to fill up, someone saw money in the form of that new tricked-out truck. A gun to the boy's head and tell the dad to drive, what's he going to do? The truck and camper were likely sold to a chop shop a state away before their friends even called to report the family didn't arrive. Makes me churned-up angry, but it's what's logical. There's a plot of ground with three bodies a state away that will eventually turn up."

She nodded thoughtfully. She turned to the other deputy. "And you? A personal theory?"

"Variation on the theme. They were carjacked and ended up near Canada or Mexico. Convenient cover for someone who needed to stay under the radar, then killed once they weren't needed. Why else risk taking three people if not primarily for their vehicle? You have your offenders who like children, your guys who want to grab a pretty woman, and a subset who just hate cops, but to take all three? It's not logical if one was the preference. There are much easier targets than three people who would have been tight with each other, tuned in to where each other was, at whatever stop they made for gas or food. Someone needed the truck, and liked the idea of the camper as it gave a nice cover."

"It was one of those hard-sided Airstream travel trailers," the other officer added, "not the type where the roof cranks up that has canvas sides. It could move contraband easy enough. A guy with a gun in the trailer with the boy, another in the truck with the husband and wife, who's going to look twice or think something's wrong?"

Evie found it an interesting premise. "You think they crossed with someone who got control via the boy or maybe the wife, and under duress they drove far away in the first few hours, were outside the search zone from the very beginning?"

They both nodded. "You can't find the truck or camper, you can't find the bodies, which after some point in a search means they aren't there to find," the second one continued. "This area has been searched hard, and it's still searched every spring and fall when the ground shifts from freeze and thaws and rains by friends and family who go out hiking, hunting, and looking for clues. The woods around here are being systematically covered. It's the respectful thing you do — 'I think I'll go out and look for the Florists' when it's a nice evening and you have an extra few hours. There are grid maps of what has been searched, what's next to cover. The deputy's cousin kept that map updated at first, then later it went to his nephew to update. They keep current copies of it available at the library's entry-way brochure rack, so you can pick one up and go to an unsearched grid if you're inclined to help."

"That's very useful to know. Thank you, officers. I appreciate the insights."

"We wish you luck, ma'am."

After they left, Evie flipped the lock on the door while considering what the officers just told her. A local guy would know where a search had been done, where people were heading next. It would be easy enough to move something you didn't want found into an area already searched. But a lot of people wandering around . . . the officers were right. If there was something nearby to find, in twelve years someone would have stumbled on it.

But that gave her another thought. Had there been any homicides in the last dozen years that might be the death of someone who had discovered a detail about the Florist family's disappearance? Someone killed before they could report what they found? If the killer was still local, it made sense that he'd been doing what he could to keep the crime under wraps.

It was worth putting on the wall. Evie went and picked up a marker and wrote *Other homicides over the last decade,* adding to her list. She could sense actual progress. Small maybe, but progress just the same.

Gabriel Thane

Gabriel laid down the pages of names on the table, including suggestions from his father. There were more violent people in the county than he initially estimated, but it was still a manageable number. He glanced over at Evie. She was right — the sheriff's office had interacted with most on more than one occasion. While his deputies might be able to add a few more to the list, it was mostly complete. He got up to open the cooler, get out cold drinks. Without comment, Gabriel set two Tylenol tablets on the table beside Evie, a soda beside the pills.

She looked at the time, reached for the pain relievers. "No wonder the headache is coming back with a vengeance. I should have taken something an hour ago."

"It might also have something to do with all the reading. We both need a break. Come, take a walk with me."

She conceded his point, pushed her chair back, and rose. He locked the building behind them, called George to cover on-site security until they got back. "Let's walk to the bakery and see what's left. Everything goes for half price in the evening." He nodded that direction and set out at an easy pace, so she could work the stiffness out of her back.

He could tell the stitches were bothering her by the way she'd occasionally run her finger along the edge of the gauze. "Tell me something I wouldn't know about you. Easy stuff qualifies at this point. Where do you live? Cubs fan, Cardinals? Like big cities, visit downtown Chicago occasionally, or avoid it at all costs?"

She glanced over at him, apparently decided he was mostly making conversation and letting her choose the topics, and nodded before casually replying, "I rent a house in Springfield, near the State Police headquarters, and tend to fill it with garage-sale finds. I'm only a Cardinals fan, but camouflage it with a Cubs hat if I happen to be north of Interstate 72. Let's see . . . what else? I mostly work alone, as we're short-staffed at state investigations. I seriously miss having a partner. I like to drive and think about cases. I stay as far away from the madness of crowds as I can, though I love the ethnic food, the music diversity, and the art you can only find in a big city. Mostly the food. If I could transport that out, I'd be thrilled. Moroccan food, Indian, Thai. You could talk me into about any road trip if there were meals like that as part of the journey."

He liked the mix she'd given. "An interesting set of answers."

"I can add a few more: I enjoy cooking but am not a very good chef. I'm a lover of comedies, old movies, romances, have a building tolerance for watching sports. Oh, and I hate the smell of gunpowder. Seeing as how I'm a cop, that might be worth mentioning."

That remark diverted him from her personal life for a moment. "Ever pull your weapon on the job?"

"Twice, both backups of another officer in a tight situation, but it's been a long time. I like the Bureau of Investigations, which is mostly paperwork, talking with people. I'm a good shot, steady, calm, decisive. You have to be in this business for the sake of the cop beside you, but because I don't like shooting, I'm probably more serious than most about my time on the practice range. I shoot a hundred rounds three times a week, after the workday is done, as it's important to be accurate when tired. If I don't like the results, I shoot another hundred rounds. The discipline isn't the problem. I just don't like guns and the smell. I tolerate carrying a firearm because it's a job requirement."

Gabriel didn't say anything for a long moment, wondering if he had cops like her on the county payroll. Being averse to the smell of gunpowder was probably a bit unusual. He had his share of those who'd pulled their guns on the job and bore the scar of that memory, often no longer enjoying shooting deer or wild pheasant. "You're not into hunting, I take it."

"Never have been. And after hitting that deer, I can't say I would ever be. Taking a huge animal's life just for the sake of sport or meat you probably don't need seems like an overall loss. Such beautiful animals — majestic and powerful and free. I'd be in the camp that says take a picture, don't kill them."

Evie half turned to consider him as they walked. "You're a dozen questions ahead. Fill in some blanks of your own."

The fascinating thing about an interesting woman was the journey to discover those unique items that made her . . . well, interesting. Only this one had another guy in her life, which put a rather tight box around the moment.

As far as understanding him, she mostly had to know his family, and that seemed an innocuous direction for this conversation.

"The dam that made Carin Lake was built in 1962. My parents own what is now called the Southern Woods — basically the south end of Carin Lake, land given to them by the state to compensate for what the lake had put underwater. They've added on to it over the years with purchased pieces. I mention it because I spent the first eighteen years of my life either in those woods, on the water, or trailing my father around on his job. Came to love nature, that water, and always admired my dad.

"I never thought of becoming anything but a cop," he continued. "I like people, I like when things are peaceful in a community, between neighbors. I like being the one called when a crisis hits, able to respond and help them out. I'd have probably become an EMT if Dad hadn't been the sheriff. He insisted on college, and that was fine with me. I enjoy school and I used it to broaden what I knew about the law and this job. Because Thanes have been here so long, we know the people of this county. It was a natural step to run for sheriff after Dad's retirement.

"It's interesting being the oldest son. Josh, the youngest, put his roots down in a place beside the lake. A bait shop, boats for rent, part interest in a campground. His business thrives and grows as large as he wants it to. He spends time on the water most days.

"Will went overseas as a combat medic, came back and settled on the opposite side of the lake from Josh, but more in the country. He's a mechanic now, small-engine repair. If it's got a motor, call Will. He's very good at putting things back together, whether people, animals, or machines.

"Like I said, being a small-town, small-county sheriff fits who I am. I do the state conferences, spend more time taking classes on law enforcement and forensics than I would care to add up. But the degrees aren't the goal. I'm not looking to make a name for myself elsewhere. I have a place here, a job that needs doing with excellence. I care about the people of Carin County who voted for me. I'm not a particularly ambitious man."

"Hmm . . ." Evie cocked her head. "Sure you are, Gabriel. Your ambitions are focused here, in this place, in this role. You've spent your whole life dreaming and planning and working to get right where you are today. You want to live up to your expectations of yourself, deliver on what you know being a good sheriff means. Your ambitions have brought you to your goal. You want to live it now, so enjoy the moment."

He was impressed with how much she'd captured from his brief description. "True enough. This job is a big piece of my day-to-day life, and I like it that way."

He slowed their pace a bit, shifted to lighter subjects. "I like watching baseball, soccer, football, but prefer to watch them live at the high school or the park sports diamonds. I like being around the families who come out for the games. I like the hot dogs and popcorn and sitting on a folded blanket to cushion the hard bleachers." They both laughed at his description.

"I'm a theater movie fan and enjoy the big-screen experience, those few hours when I don't think about police matters. I don't usually go to see police procedurals — they get so much so wrong." More laughter. "I enjoy fishing, the peacefulness of it, but mostly the time with whichever family member or friend I talked into going out with me for the hour."

"You focus on people in both your work and play."

He nodded. "I like talking with others. And I like to think I'm on good terms even with those I have to occasionally arrest."

They had arrived. She looked in the bakery window. "Do they have sourdough bread? I'm hoping for something fresh from the oven I can take back sliced and have for sandwiches."

Gabriel held open the door for her. "You'll find that and more here."

They made their selections and started back, Evie eating a soft pretzel she'd bought along with a loaf of bread. As they approached the post office, she said, "I'm ready to call it a day."

Gabriel, eating a bagel loaded with cream cheese, nodded. "Good. If you want to work until midnight, you should wait till after your body has another day or two to recover."

"I'm getting there. It's mostly sore muscles now. I'm going to soak in a hot tub for an hour and enjoy some music, then find a movie to watch on TV."

"A nice plan. I'll lock up for the night. I'll be tied up most of tomorrow morning, but I'll be by in the afternoon or maybe I'll run into you around town."

"That works." Evie took out the car keys and moved to the convertible. She slid inside and shifted the seat to her preference, turned the key in the ignition, and grinned at the engine's powerful hum. "I'm glad it isn't so cool tonight I have to put the top up," she told him.

He stood back, considering her. "You and the car look happy together. Good to drive?"

"I'm fine. I appreciate the selection."

"See you tomorrow, Evie." His phone rang, and he got it out as she drove off. *A nice first day with her,* he thought. She was a woman with some good ideas on how to work a case. *And nice to have around,* he added as he said "Sheriff Thane" into the phone and mentally shifted gears back to the car-vandalism problem.

Six

Evie Blackwell

Evie knew she was ambitious, had given up trying not to be. She was unlocking the post office before five the next morning. There was somebody out there, living free and thinking he . . . or she . . . had gotten away with murdering a whole family. She was in competition with that person, looking for the truth, looking for the culprit. She wanted justice — for the Florists, for their extended family, for the law. And she wanted to win.

She put down the loaf of sourdough and package of cheese she'd brought with her from the house, along with a thermos of coffee. She walked over to the dozen photos of the family now on the wall and moved them around in a different order, a habit that let her see them in other contexts, look again at the details, see the people afresh at the center of the puzzle.

143

She stepped back, studying the photos, the timeline, the facts on the crime wall, pulling it back into her memory. By doing so many cases, she had learned how to work them, to pack the details down into her subconscious, then wait for that *eureka* moment, the one pivot that would connect things together, point to a question, a fact, and she'd have it. Like seeing the end of a chess match when there were still a dozen moves to be played. She could solve this case. Twelve years of collected evidence and interviews was a gold mine, and all she needed was to put her finger on the *one thing*. She was convinced it was here. She could find it. God had created her with the skill set uniquely suited for such work. She solved crime puzzles, and this one desperately needed solving.

She opened the next box of files and dug into the work. It wasn't personal to her, and that distance helped her perspective — she didn't have assumptions about the victims or others around them clouding her view.

She no longer apologized for liking her job, even though she was careful about saying aloud something of that sort. This family was missing and likely dead. That reality fueled her motivation to solve what happened, why, and who did it. But she couldn't help but enjoy the hunt, the puzzle of it, the search to locate the key to solving the disappearance. She wanted to find a thread before the day was over, something that might lead to another "something."

She poured her first cup of coffee and started reading, making notes.

Gabriel Thane

Gabriel slowed as he drove by the post office, seeing the lights, Evie's rental parked at the curb. He glanced at the time. *Early even for a dedicated cop.* He doubted it was inability to sleep that got her up before dawn. She was in Carin to work, to solve these cases before her vacation leave was over.

Once Evie finished with the two cold cases, he reminded himself, she would be on to the next assignment. *And back to what's-his-name,* he thought a bit ruefully. She'd give a friendly wave and smile, a *how're you doing?* if she crossed paths with him at a conference, but she'd likely not be back in this county for a few years or more. He'd do well to remember that reality.

He had work waiting for him, deep enough to swallow his Monday morning — and the reason he also was rolling into work so early. If he wanted to help Evie this afternoon, he had to move a whole day's worth of work this morning.

He glanced one last time at the lights in the windows and had to smile. He appreciated that she was focused on the job. He'd noticed the same thing about Ann on their first meeting. That friendship had become something rich and deep over the years, but it had begun because the way Ann focused on her work was not to be missed. Evie was showing him the first hints of something similar. *Maybe a good friendship is something I can look forward to.*

Several hours into his morning, Gabriel looked up at a tap on his office door. The woman who had lingered in the background of his thoughts while he worked was standing there. She wore dress slacks and a blue-and white-striped shirt, a jacket over her arm.

"Hey, Evie." He noted the fresh bandage over the stitches showed the fading edges of bruising. Other than that, she looked fit, alert.

"Mind if I look through the archives?" she asked.

"Sure." He dug out keys from his desk drawer and motioned toward the hallway. "Third door on the left marked *Records.* You want the side room labeled *Archives.*"

He handed over the two keys she'd need. "Thanks."

He gave it an hour, then wandered back with some coffee. She'd made herself comfortable at a worktable in the middle of the filing cabinets. "What are you hoping to find?"

"I'll know it when I see it. Anything interesting, helpful . . ."

He noticed the files spread out on the table, saw she was reading reports from the animal-control officer.

"No dead deer were picked up on the days in question, to my disappointment," she said, shaking her head. "Two dead skunks, a dead fox, too many smashed squirrels for him to bother counting, just a check on many species — the daily reports are like that. He'd been on the job for six years at this point, liked his work, liked keeping tallies. He even sketched on the back of the report the roadways he cleared that day, where he found remains."

"He was probably aggregating that data to find animal trails most in use," Gabriel explained, "so he could follow them back through the woods during hunting season, have a leg up on his fellow hunters."

"Okay . . . that's helpful. I wouldn't have thought of that answer, as I don't hunt."

He read the tabs on the files she hadn't yet opened. "You're looking at murders in Carin County?"

"As many as I can. Even solved ones, before or after the family disappeared, could be useful to me. Would you be able to get someone to generate a list? Murders in the county over, say, the last thirty years? Maybe another of particularly violent crimes, assaults?"

"What are you looking for?"

"You don't start killing with a family of three. You start with one, and it's probably an accident or due to temper. You don't start on a deputy who has his family right there to protect. So if the person we're looking for is from around here, where are his first kills?"

"That sounds depressing, Evie. And you can say it so calmly."

"But do you think I'm right?"

"I think I'll get you the lists. You're going to need a bigger wall for your timeline."

"I'm thinking the same thing. I don't know what's relevant. But once I see it, the timeline is likely going to be the key to understanding this case." She looked over a file she was holding. "How's that other list, the violent ones, coming?"

"With some deputies' input, we've got the

names. I'll get you a copy. I'm heading out to talk to some on the list, see if I can find out who else should be on it."

"You sound kind of doubtful."

He shook his head. "No, I think it's a solid way to approach the problem. But I'm thinking we won't see the right name without something else to point us there."

Evie nodded to her notes. "That's where my side of this comes in. I have to find you a motive, something that would pull a name on your list to the top. We still need a trigger, a reason to carry out the crime. The one thing I'm confident of is the motive isn't going to be something trivial. If this doesn't turn out to be a random crime, the motive of the person who went after Deputy Florist and his wife and son is going to be huge. If motive is there, I'll find it."

Gabriel smiled at her confidence. "I'll send you in some lunch. Anything you don't like?"

She shrugged. "Raw onions. Sushi."

"I'll come up with something without getting near those. Don't read too long without a break or your headache is going to return."

"How do you know it's gone?"

He reached over and lightly touched her forehead. "You've got a tell when it's there — the headache's gone, but you've still got

149

the ache around the stitches."

"It feels like I've got fishing line knit through my skin," she complained.

He chuckled. "It's probably close to the truth. I'll see you later. Call if you need anything."

"Sure."

Evie Blackwell

Evie watched Gabriel leave, looked at what he'd left behind on the table. Another roll of sweet-tarts. *A bit of magician on his part,* she thought, since she hadn't seen him put it there.

She slipped one out and with new determination turned her attention back to the files. Gabriel had the list of names. She needed to find that *why.* She liked Gabriel's smile — find something useful and she'd get another of them. Not that she was working the case for his smiles, but still, it was a nice side benefit.

So far, nothing in the files included the names of Florist's wife or son. Was that a simple courtesy to the deputy if his son had been in on something that caught an officer's attention, maybe vandalism at the school or petty thefts involving kids in Joe's circle of friends? She'd begun compiling a list of names to investigate further. It would

150

be hard to find a motive directly involving an eleven-year-old who, from everything she'd seen up until now, seemed to be a good boy.

Susan Florist had been a clerk at a bank. There'd been a heart-attack death there — a disgruntled customer denied a loan extension. Also a series of threatening letters related to the bank's foreclosure on farmland. Since Susan was a part-time employee, nothing in the bank's actions likely would have drawn attention to her. Evie hadn't come across any reports of an attempted bank robbery, or a bank employee embezzling funds, or someone acting inappropriately toward female staff.

Evie moved her shoulders around to loosen them, started to think about missing Deputy Scott Florist, but then stopped and circled back to his wife, Susan. The bank was a hub of the community. She would know people's financial business as a teller handling deposits, working a customer-service desk. Things like bank balances, bounced checks, church contributions, those behind on paying back a loan, those spending more than they could afford, child-support payments. Financial matters were always emotional flash points when there was trouble. Susan would be in a position to see and hear a lot of personal information about people in the community.

Evie thumbed through the case files she'd brought with her, looking for the write-up on Susan and her work history, took her time reading through it. Susan had handled opening accounts, provided access to the safe-deposit box area, and worked the front counter taking deposits and processing withdrawals. She hadn't been involved with loans or business accounts or reconciliation of problems. But the general tasks she routinely handled would have been enough to learn personal information about the bank's clients.

Evie circled Susan's name on her notes, circled the bank, and wrote out a simple statement: *You know my secrets, and I think you told someone, maybe your husband.*

Evie tapped her pen against the notepad, intrigued by the places that possibility could take her. A couple had a joint checking account, but the wife kept a secret account as a just-in-case cache? One with statements going to another address for privacy? Someone worried about a violent streak in her husband? Maybe someone withdrawing a bunch of cash, cleaning out an account in preparation for bolting, and Susan was the person who assisted in the withdrawal. . . .

Yes. There might be something here. Whether it led to the family's disappearance was a different question. But Susan would have known at least some of the community's secrets, and someone could naturally conclude she'd told her husband some of those secrets. *A good line to tug,* Evie thought as she put a Carin Lake fishing spin on it — she was throwing out a line for ideas and had just hooked something that felt big.

Should she mention the idea to Gabriel? No. Not yet. Ideas were fragile things. There would be any number that didn't get into her net before she found something worth sharing with him. She'd pursue this one on her own and see where it went. The fact she'd come up with one possibility told her she'd find more.

Back in the post office after a quick stop to buy a radio, Evie returned to the timeline. The music helped the place feel friendlier, echoing down the long room like a concert hall. Evie found herself moving in step to the rhythm as she moved back and forth between the files and the wall.

Susan Florist had been an organized woman. Evie fully appreciated that as she taped more calendar pages up. Susan had used a month-at-a-glance layout, one or two

153

words capturing the daily schedule. Doctor. Baseball practice/Joe. Spanish class. Haircut/ Scott. The woman had laid out the Florist family's life in neat orderly boxes and archived the expired pages. Evie started with the month the family disappeared and went back in time. She fit almost two years' worth of the calendar pages in towering columns on the wall. Finished, Evie pulled out a chair, put her feet up on another one, and carefully studied the results.

Susan Florist, tell me something interesting about yourself. I know it's here, buried in these dates. Your son's life. Your husband's. Yours. What do I need to see?

She reached over for the roll of sweettarts, peeled off another. She scanned and absorbed month after month of the Florists' lives. She wasn't looking for any particular item. She was simply reviewing the routines, the interruptions. Car in for maintenance, the dishwasher breaking, a visit to the vet, the places someone would interact with Susan more often than Scott, and vice versa. A birthday party invitation for Joe, scout meetings, youth group, or places with just Susan and Joe, without Scott.

New notations appearing . . . Joe at Mike's, Yates/dinner here, some coffee/10 a.m. reminders. The Yates had moved into the community? A new couple who also had a son, Susan is making time to get to know the wife, the boys are in school together, have them over for a meal to introduce them to her husband? That might be a useful thread — new people in town. A look at school records could give her a sense of who had arrived the year or two before the Florist family disappeared. You might tell new people something about your lives, what's going on, invite them to your home. Sometimes disguised monsters came to visit —

"Evie."

Her elbow popped against the edge of the chair, and her feet slid off the second chair and smacked on the floor.

Gabe smiled apologetically. "Sorry," he said.

She rubbed her elbow. "Sure you are."

"Look at the bright side. Maybe it will take attention away from the other aches and pains." He laughed at the look she gave him. "I am sorry. Listen, I'm heading out to do more interviews. Want to come along?"

He'd interrupted a train of thought that was going somewhere, and she had to push down irritation at his reasonable question. She shook her head. "Thanks, I'm good."

"Okay. You spook easy — that's interesting to know. I'll whistle my way in next time."

"Fine. Good. I hope an interview goes somewhere."

He chuckled and disappeared out the door.

She walked over to make sure the door was locked, fixed herself a sandwich while she was up, and returned to rescue the second chair, get settled again. She shook her head to clear the interruption, looked at the calendar pages, and pulled the schedule information back into place piece by piece.

New people coming into their lives, showing up in their schedule . . . someone new who has a dark and dangerous side. Would he maybe come in via Joe? A new coach for Little League, a new dad of a teammate? It seemed most likely through Joe. Or through Susan via a woman, a wife, a girlfriend. Not directly through Scott, not stepping into their personal lives. The door would open through Joe or Susan. *Unless it was a new guy at work . . .* She paused on that thought. Yeah. A nice cover. Scott brought someone new into their lives, someone new on the job. If it's a cop, they think he's safe and have no hesitation about letting the person into their lives.

Evie could feel when the moment of

concentration peaked and the idea began to fade. She tried to get the feeling back, but it wouldn't form. It didn't mesh with the calendar, she realized. New people coming in via Susan and Joe were there, but not Scott. No fishing dates, no golf outing, no guy stuff — little markers that should be there. Evie wrote herself a note to check school records on the possibility of a new couple showing up with a boy Joe's age, but the rest of the what-if wasn't holding together.

She stretched, ate another sweet-tart, went to the last calendar month of their disappearance, month by month in reverse order, and looked for another possibility. Something else was here somewhere.

Evie heard the post-office door open, knew it was Gabriel, and didn't look up. He was whistling the same tune as when he'd come in with an update on his interviews and when he brought in dinner. She didn't mind the whistling, but the song fragment looping in her head was annoying.

"It's eight o'clock. You need to call it a night."

"Yeah," she answered absently, just to acknowledge the remark, no particular inclination to follow his advice. She was just glad he spoke so he stopped whistling.

"What're you doing now?"

Over the course of the day she'd been reviewing the contents of the various boxes collected from the Florist home. She read letters, flipped through notebooks, scanned a diary of Susan's, looked at saved Christmas cards, found restaurant coupons and school flyers — the normal clutter a family collected over time and eventually discarded. At the moment she was deep in their financial, insurance, and medical paperwork, tracing where they sent checks, looking for signs of secrets, an affair, child-support payments, bailing out a family member who kept getting into debt, something. Even the boy had an account for his allowance and interesting purchases to his name. She condensed the last hours into a single word: "Finances."

"Evie. Pause long enough to look at me."

She glanced up. Gabriel was wearing a bright pink Hawaiian shirt and holding two glasses of crushed ice and something red with straws stuck in them. He handed one of them to her. "Sip it slowly."

She complied, and smiled. Tart and fruity.

"Don't ask what's in it. It's safe for cops to drink on duty, contains no alcohol, although it's probably got a dozen other things — including a touch of lime juice and part of a can of cherry pie filling — from what I saw land in the blender."

"You were at a party?"

"Good one too. A coming-home party for vacationing friends, three weeks in Hawaii. We didn't want them to feel so much culture shock coming back to Illinois. Come on, take a break. You can drop in on the last half of the party with me."

"Where is it?"

"Two blocks east, above the pizza place."

Okay, meeting the town's residents would be a decent use of her time, and she could use a break . . . and more of this punch. She pushed back her chair, tucked the phone he gave her into her pocket with her keys, picked up her drink.

"How many people were interviewed today?" she asked as they walked toward the door. "You told me earlier about yours, but were there others?"

"Between Dad, myself, and deputies who had the time, we interviewed thirty-eight. We added another six to the list based on feedback — people we all agree we should have thought of ourselves. How'd you do?"

She glanced back at the tables. "I've got some ideas." She really wanted to pursue a couple of them for another hour or so . . .

He reached over and pulled her through the doorway. "It'll still be here tomorrow. You'll think better if you clear it out of your mind for a bit."

She waited while he locked the place up, nodded to the retired deputy coming their way. Gabriel must have been confident he would get her to take a break.

"You need a warmer jacket," he pointed out. "We can ride —"

"No, I'm fine for a few blocks. Come winter, I live bundled in layers that make me look like the Michelin Man. I'm stubborn about giving in to winter."

He smiled. "A cute image. Tell me something else I wouldn't know about you."

She gave him a considering glance. "Okay, but I answer one, you answer one. Sure you want to go any further? I already gave you the easy answers."

"Yes."

She sipped at the drink and decided to make it interesting just to see how he would respond. "Let's see, I build a snowman every February just to force away my increasing annoyance with winter. I vacation comfortably — land somewhere, rent a house, eat out, take a stack of books and movies, pretend I live there, and decide if I would like the area as someplace to retire

160

one day. I'm trying to get up the nerve to take flying lessons so I can travel around as easily as Ann does. I like to run with my dogs, play Frisbee with them, enjoy tug-of-war with their ropes. I used to go to the gym to stay in shape, but now the dogs help me accomplish that and with a lot more fun. I'm single, never married, though I've been close enough a few times it would take a sharp knife to shave the difference. I take my birthday off. I sleep in, then put a hundred dollars in my pocket and go shopping for whatever catches my eye, write down a list of what I want most, and hand it to God as my birthday wish, have a special meal — steak, baked potato, asparagus, a richly iced cupcake — curl up on the couch to watch a good movie or reread a favorite book to top off the day." She looked over and found him watching her. "Birthdays aren't celebrated enough as they should be," she finished, feeling a bit defensive.

"Define 'almost married.' "

Trust him to catch that one. She blew out a breath. "Let's see . . . not in any particular order. One got called off by the groom a few days before the wedding. Another, I returned the engagement ring. The third" — she grinned, cocked her head — "we'll call it career-goal differences, but in reality his mom didn't like me, and we mutually concluded she never would. That gets me to age twenty-six. I've since become wiser and stopped letting guys ask me the question."

He was silent for a long moment. "I'm not sure what to say. That's an . . . unusual history. Allow me a tactless question — how old are you now?"

"I'll admit to thirty-five with a year of fudge. When I'm forty it'll be three years of wiggle room, and I'll work my way up from there."

"Dad had told me, but I wanted it from you. Word is you're seeing a guy by the name of Rob Turney."

"That's the word, is it? Accurate enough, I guess."

"Don't take this the wrong way, Evie, but that almost-married list is sad."

She liked that he was willing to say such a thing. She agreed with him. With a shrug, she replied, "I was looking for something I thought a guy could give me, with the added edge of being a bit commitment shy. They were good guys with solid jobs, I wasn't going to be marrying lazy bums, and any one of them would have made a fine husband. But I didn't fight very hard to keep a wedding in view once things in the relationship began to go south. I've grown out of it, that need for a guy to fill the voids, make me complete. I grew up." She shook off the memories and offered a smile. "And that constitutes my list of personal crashes." She could tell he wasn't sure what to say, and she was of a mind to let him off the hook. "Are we at the party? I see Hawaiian shirts in the windows above us."

Diverted, he glanced up. "Yes." He opened the door in front of them. "Stairs to the second floor, then take the door on the right. Hosting us are Glenda and James Fitzgerald. You'll want to ask about their son, Mark, and their cat Sophia."

"Got it."

"The Florists' extended family is mostly here. I counted six of them," he mentioned as they topped the stairs.

She shot him a look. "You should have told me earlier. I need a Hawaiian shirt too."

"In this crowd, someone is going to spill that punch on you — you'll be nicely colorful. Hang around with me for a bit. I'll introduce you to folks or you can peel off and see if you can corner a lady who likes to gossip. Either is going to make for a fun evening, maybe even productive."

He opened the door, and the volume promptly spiked. Between music and conversations, it sounded as though the entire town had gathered in what could be at most a three-bedroom apartment. Gabriel stepped in first, drew her into the room behind him.

"Gabriel! You brought a date. How nice! Come in, come in. I see you've already gotten her a drink. What's your name, dear? I'm Linda the librarian, but most people just call me the town crier. Come on, let's get you a plate and some food, and you can tell me where Gabriel has been hiding you."

Evie cast Gabriel a wicked look, and he grinned his reply. Linda was cutting a path for her toward the kitchen. This was going to be an interesting evening, even if it didn't turn productive.

"Learn anything useful?"

Evie glanced up at Gabriel on the step above her. She was sitting on the stairway they had climbed two-plus hours earlier, edged over to the side so people still leaving could get around her. She sniffed the drink Gabriel put into her hand before tasting it. "I've got a headache again."

"It's the music. Most of their friends must have hearing aids they can turn off," he quipped as he sat down beside her.

"I learned that the Florists' relatives know more about me than anyone other than my mother." She took another sip of the punch.

"The small-town rumor mill can be very efficient when stirred up by something this dramatic," Gabriel said.

"I'm guessing the banker in the family ran a credit check, probably even looked at my recently canceled checks, since I keep an account with the same state bank."

"Want me to go slap him on the wrist?"

She considered it briefly, then shook her head. "No. If I get in a bind and need to know details about someone, he now owes me a favor."

Gabriel's shoulder pressed against hers as another person passed. "They mean no real harm. They're just protective."

"Don't they understand I'm trying to find their missing family members?"

"You're State Police, a not-so-favorite badge around these parts."

Evie thought she could understand that. She went back to his original question. "I think they were in marriage counseling over in Decatur — Scott and Susan Florist. It wasn't all a happy family, going back about two years before they disappeared. The aunt kind of confirmed it for me. And money is missing out of their family assets. Mr. Florist-family-banker didn't realize what he confirmed as he complained about the

165

problems of maintaining, then settling an estate when the State Police won't rule it a homicide and the courts won't issue death certificates for seven years. If you ask the right question and sound like you know more than you actually do, that guy can talk himself into some useful tangents."

Gabriel took the drink out of her hand. "Trust you to have made that kind of progress. Okay, this isn't the place for this kind of conversation." He pulled her to her feet, steadied her so she wouldn't fall, led her down the stairs and out the door.

"You seem bothered I've gotten answers from the Florist family."

He shook his head, kept her hand in his, and moved briskly down the sidewalk. "Lower your voice, please. Take a look around."

Groups of friends were saying lingering goodbyes around a few cars on the street. She shut up. Gabriel strolled along, gave her hand a friendly swing as he said, "Pretend you're having fun."

Evie caught a few smiles directed their way, indicating they thought it nice the sheriff had a date, and found it interesting she didn't mind the assumption. "I *am* having fun."

Gabriel finally slowed. "Okay. You can

safely say whatever you would like now."

"Give me back the drink. This version is the best so far."

He handed her the glass. She sipped at it and nodded. Her throat was dry from having talked quite a lot. "I want the recipe for this, if you can pry it out of the blender guy. Anyway, it was easier to talk about the case than duck questions about being your date. And most everyone I met brought up the subject of the Florist family. So I went with it."

"Which is why I pulled you over to the party — well, one reason." He unlocked the post office, guided her inside. "You've got some thoughts running around your head."

She was grateful to step into the heated building after her brave words earlier about nixing the car. "They were in marriage counseling, probably over in Decatur, and there's between forty and eighty thousand dollars missing from what their banker relative expected to find in the estate." She walked over and set her drink on the table, pulled her phone out to check for messages. "I'm not sure where they were siphoning away cash that smoothly from their accounts. I maybe had a whiff of something being off in their finances before you pulled me away to the party, but I haven't pinpointed it. I need to get my head back into those numbers."

She started to move toward the open files, and he reached over to put a finger lightly under her chin. "Not tonight," he said firmly, turning her to face him. "That's a task for tomorrow. You're sure on the marriage counseling?"

"Sort of. Sure of the location — Decatur — and that it was a standing Wednesday evening appointment for both of them. Pretty sure it started about two years before they disappeared."

"Why didn't *we* have this?" He looked puzzled and extremely frustrated, a combination that was rather appealing. She had known she would get his attention with this idea, so she hadn't mentioned it until she was reasonably confident.

She patted his arm in sympathy. "Because it's not really there, Gabriel. Not in their schedule books, not in what they told their family and friends, not in their finances — no checks have a memo line saying 'marriage counseling.' It wasn't only Susan keeping something covert, or just Scott — it was both of them. They worked together to keep it under wraps."

She studied the crime wall and the month-at-a-glance calendar pages. She'd found

168

something new, and she wasn't above admitting to herself it felt really good. "The aunt knew something. I think they were using her to cover up what they were really doing. A friend says, 'I called you Wednesday evening, but didn't get an answer.' And they would say, 'Sorry about that, we were over at my aunt's, and cell reception isn't good at her place.' Like that. They'd stop by the woman's place for ten minutes, use the stop to cover a three-hour gap in their evening."

Gabriel pulled out a chair, draped his arms across the back of another one. "Tell me what you're seeing to get to that conclusion."

Evie thought about where to begin, decided to simply walk him through it. She made herself comfortable in her chair and propped her feet on the next one over. "I've been looking for motive to harm the family, digging for something that would be a trigger, trying to track their movements, what happened in their lives. I've been looking at any schedule or calendar I can find, anything with dates on it. You've collected a lot of paper on this family, Gabriel. Name the subject, and an officer put together a file on it. That's proved very helpful when I have a feeling something is there but hiding beneath the surface. I've been into the guts of those boxes today." She looked around at the stacks.

"I found that Susan suddenly developed an interest in speaking Spanish. That's what I first noticed. She audited classes over in Decatur at the junior college. Spanish I, then Spanish II, Advanced Spanish — two years' worth of Spanish classes. Always on a Wednesday night. No grades, no exams, but merely auditing the courses. She started about three weeks into the semester, so it wasn't something she planned and began at the term's start — she just abruptly joined that first class. I figured they were planning a vacation to Mexico when I first noticed it, but that much Spanish over that length of time didn't make sense. And I checked — she had four years of Spanish in high school and another year in college. She could have skipped all the classwork and simply bought a refresher set of audios to brush up.

"I figured maybe there was an affair on the side, with a standing appointment on Wednesday evenings when she knows her husband is at work. If she gets asked about the Spanish classes, she can rattle off a sentence and say how fun it is.

"I looked up Scott's schedule to confirm he was regularly working Wednesday nights. What I found was the opposite. Scott never drew a paycheck for work on a Wednesday night. If he was scheduled to work that night, he'd arrange to swap with someone. Or he would work a double the day before and flex the time off the rotation. In the two years before they disappeared, Scott was never paid for work done on a Wednesday night. That's just weird, isn't it?" She paused and looked at Gabriel, and he nodded his agreement.

"So then it was like, *huh,* both doing something on Wednesday evenings. Are they taking tango lessons, then a room at a hotel, and don't want humorous digs from family? They tuck Joe in with a friend or relative, have an evening away on their own, a date — they're married, why not?"

She glanced again at Gabriel, but he simply signaled that she should keep going. She looked back at the crime wall. "Joe's schedule, such as they had for him, says baseball coach, Decatur, on Wednesday nights. To work on his hitting, throwing, and field work? I'm thinking, wow, I wish my parents had sprung for private coaching when I was learning to hit a ball. So I looked at Joe's game records — he kept information like that for himself. His performance over the two years in his actual league goes *down,* even with a weekly

171

coaching session. Joe's running a bluff, same as the parents."

"They were covering up family counseling, or counseling for Joe. It fits better than marriage counseling," Gabriel suggested.

Evie nodded. "That's what I thought at first, but it doesn't track. Counseling for a kid is triggered by something, and his school reports are fine. Good attendance, good grades, a rather popular boy. I checked his medical records. Precautionary X-rays after a bad fall and tumble on his bike are in file. The kid has fewer broken bones than I do, less stitches than I have right now. I checked for changes in his behavior the last two years — disruptive, grades changing, fights with a classmate — nope, it's all good, the boy is cruising through life on a happy arc. There's no sign of a trauma — walked in on a crime, got molested or did some molesting, walking in his sleep, developed a serious disease. The last one kind of made sense, actually. The kid is sick, got a childhood cancer or something, get him counseling to help along with the doctors.

"So I went looking at medical claims against Scott's insurance, Susan's. There's nothing for doctors of any kind for Joe beyond normal checkups and shots for school and league play. There are single

172

prescriptions written to Susan for anxiety, Joe for sleeping pills, issued once and not refilled. Issued two years before they disappeared, by a doctor in Decatur, a private practice, same date on the prescriptions. So I tracked down the prescribing doctor." She pulled over her laptop and opened it.

"Some interesting things about Dr. Richard Wales," she said as she typed his name into the search box. "He's a psychiatrist, works with cops who have discharged a weapon in the line of duty or had to take a life in the line of duty. He does the general 'you're fit for duty' psych eval most cops have to pass before they're hired. One of the other things he's known for is counseling couples after they have lost a child due to a tragic accident or a miscarriage." She turned the screen so he could see the doctor's web page.

"Deputy Florist never fired his gun on the job that I can find. But he no doubt got cleared by Wales before he was hired here. Dr. Wales's business card is probably tacked on your employee human-resource board. Susan Florist is holding down her job, her friends see her as happy, the photos show a contented woman. Maybe they lost a child to a miscarriage. It hurt, made them sad, but it wasn't crippling. They hadn't told family yet that she was pregnant again.

"They want some counseling. Maybe they were trying to decide if they would try for another child, or adopt, and the decision was making the marriage a bit rocky, they wanted some help sorting matters out. But *two years*? It's either a lot of small things or the issue has some size to it. Friends aren't seeing problems in the marriage, neither Scott nor Susan are talking about troubles, neither expresses a worry about Joe. But these two are keeping Wednesday in Decatur on their schedule and hiding the fact they are both going over there."

"Why do they take Joe along with them to Decatur if they're the ones getting counseling?" Gabriel asked as he turned the laptop back to her. "Where is he during those hours? For two years, Joe doesn't say anything about his parents seeing a therapist every week? That doesn't fit any kid I know. A kid has a secret, eventually he has to tell at least one of his friends."

Evie reached for the sweet-tarts roll, took one, gave the last to Gabriel. "I think Joe's there at the office with them. Maybe they didn't feel comfortable leaving a then-nine-year-old with friends, didn't want to explain where they were going or why." Evie pulled another folder out of the stack, thumbed through the photos inside, slid several over to him. "From the photos of his room, Joe had several well-thumbed books about how to play and win DDM. It's a multiplayer online video game that charges users by the hour, the kind a young boy would relish playing. In one of the boy's notebooks, there are pages diagramming levels and moves and ideas for how to proceed. But he doesn't have the computer hardware to run the video-intense game, and there are no charges on his parents' credit cards for game time. He's playing the game somewhere. I think he's playing it at the doctor's office."

"Interesting . . ." Gabriel said.

"Yeah. I think the kid was getting to play video games for two hours if he would keep his mouth shut about what the family was doing on Wednesday nights. A decent trade-off. If asked, say you were practicing baseball. Some weeks, one or the other parent might actually take him to that coaching session. Other weeks he's at the doctor's office playing video games while the parents talk with the doctor."

"All right, we need to talk with this doctor," Gabriel decided. "And I need to find out if anyone around the sheriff's office had any suspicion this was going on. I sure didn't. But others worked with him more closely."

Evie nodded. "I've already called the doctor. We're on his schedule for Wednesday lunch, the first decent-length interval he had open. I don't want a ten-minute 'I can't say anything because of client privilege' round robin with him. We need him to confirm the appointments were going on for that length of time and who in the family the sessions were with. It may tell us absolutely nothing about the crime, but if it tells us more about the family, that itself might point to something useful. What was it that caused them to begin going to counseling? I want to know that detail."

Gabriel nodded. "This is big, Evie. We didn't have this." He leaned back, arms linked behind his neck as he looked over at her. "Nice job finding it."

She appreciated the compliment but did her best to shrug it off. "If I can't find something, I'm not looking hard enough. We see if and where this leads, then we decide how frustrated you should be at not having discovered it before."

He looked from the crime wall back to her. "You've been searching for a day and you're finding things. The cop in me is both impressed at that and bothered I didn't have these results before. Seriously, thanks." He nodded to the finance paperwork. "This will still be here tomorrow. It's late. You need to get out of here and get some sleep."

"I know. Ann will be here in the morning. We're going to put a pause on this one and shift over to the Dayton girl's disappearance."

"That won't slow things down much. I've got names on my list to finish interviewing, and I want to talk with officers in the department about what you've found here. Wednesday lunch, you said, to interview the doctor?"

"Noon. For an hour."

Gabriel smiled. "I'll make sure it's cleared on my schedule."

"Let's hope it's worth the time."

"It will be, one way or another."

Evie got to her feet when Gabriel did. He was right — it was time to call it a day. She needed some downtime.

He locked up the building behind her, nodded to the security officer on his way over, and escorted her to the yellow convertible. "Drive careful, Evie."

"Always do." Evie settled in the driver's seat. "I really like the car."

Gabriel grinned. "I'm glad. It's cold enough you should raise the roof tonight."

"The heater is like a blast furnace. I'd put up the top, but what's the fun in that?" She started the engine, lifted a hand in farewell, and headed back toward the house.

A good, productive day, she decided. She could feel this new lead had substance. It would tell them something, and hopefully that would point them in the right direction.

A few more days like this one and she'd be looking at solving the case. She smiled at the thought. She'd take it.

Seven

Joshua Thane

Josh found himself on full alert, anticipating Grace's appearance. He figured she would come by the bait shop, as Ann had, rather than call, so he found reasons to stay around the dock rather than go out on the lake as he normally did. At dawn Tuesday, he went into Carin for groceries, his dogs with him, and then came back to his shop, which wouldn't open for another hour. Those who needed bait before hours helped themselves from the outdoor cooler, leaving cash in the honor box.

He pulled around to the pier side of the parking lot. A slender woman with shoulder-length light-brown hair was perched on one of the picnic tables, feet dangling, hands tucked in the pockets of a down jacket against the cool morning. He took a breath, stepped out of the truck, and let his dogs out. The two Labradors rolled on the grass and then ran to the docks to explore. He turned toward his visitor.

She looked at him. "I'm —"

"Grace Arnett," he finished with a smile as he approached. "I remember you, Grace. I made you a valentine in the sixth grade." He thought the small, blond, blue-eyed girl she'd been back then the most beautiful person in the world. Two years behind him, she'd been in the fourth grade, and he had ridden his bike in circles, waiting for her class to dismiss so he could give her the valentine before she got on the bus. He could still remember her surprise and pretty blush, the dropped gaze, when he handed it to her. Her thank-you was soft and sweet and had lingered in his mind for a long time.

"I still have it," Grace told him with that still-familiar smile, "tucked away in a box of childhood keepsakes."

"Nice, Grace. I don't have a box, but I do keep the memories."

Her eyes held a sadness. The years had knocked the naïveté out of him, and he recognized what it was. He now knew a victim when he saw one. He didn't let his smile fade, for he was glad to see her, no matter the circumstances. He got them cold drinks from the cooler. "Ann mentioned you might stop by. Are you passing through town or staying awhile?"

She pushed away a strand of hair blowing across her face. "That depends a bit on you," she said, her voice low. "No one in town knows I'm here, and I'd like to leave it that way for now."

"Sure thing. But now you've got me curious."

"You know my history."

Puzzled, he nodded, but answered what she seemed to be asking. "Your parents went missing when you were two, your uncle became your legal guardian and raised you here. He was killed in a hunting accident when you were fourteen. I know child services moved you away, but I don't know details from there. I do know I missed you. A lot."

She smiled. "Thanks for that. I went to Trevor House in Chicago, lived there while I finished high school. Ann has friends with history there."

"Since then?"

"Odd jobs mostly. Bookkeeping, inventory, office temp work. That kind of thing."

"Still draw those cartoons?"

She seemed surprised he remembered. "I've published a few, have a monthly gig for a magazine now, mostly providing the better ones I've already done. But occasionally I have a new idea worth the time to sketch out."

"Good for you — congratulations."

She dipped her head in thanks, nodded toward the shop and the boats. "I can see you're thriving on your lake."

He chuckled. "Yeah, I've always been a bit possessive about Carin Lake." He took a seat on the other end of the picnic table. "Business is winding down for the year now that November is rolling by."

He drank more of his soda and without staring tried to get a good picture in his mind of her at twenty-seven. The last mental images he had of her, she was fourteen going on fifteen. She'd turned into a graceful woman, if a nervous one, he noticed, as she turned the bottle between her hands.

"I need a favor," she said, averting her eyes.

"Ann said you might ask. You'll find a receptive ear."

"I'm told your two dogs are used by the cops in searches, that they're trained as . . . what is it, cadaver dogs?"

"They are. Ann pass on that nugget to you?"

"Paul did."

So she knew both Ann and Paul well enough to be comfortable on a first-name basis. That was good to know. "What's the favor?"

"I want you to help me search my uncle's property." She looked over at him. "For human remains."

He opened his mouth, then quickly shut it, gave himself a moment for her words to sink in. "You think your uncle killed your parents?" he finally asked, shocked by the thought of it but determined to hold his tone even.

Grace looked away again. "He had money troubles, then suddenly he had none. The property is two hundred acres, forty of it lake-inlet water and mature forest. I know it's hard to make a car and two people disappear. He could have, though."

He thought about her conclusion, the painful implications that would have arisen for Grace even to be thinking such a question. No wonder Ann was stressed about this.

Grace looked over at him. "Will you help me search?"

Josh felt slightly sick. "Yes, I'll help you, Grace. But when we search, and likely find nothing, what then?"

"I'll sell the land knowing I at least looked. The farmland already has a buyer, the woods and access road will attract somebody who likes to hunt."

"You've let the property sit for years, the land leased out to be farmed. Why sell now? Has something changed recently?"

"It's simply time. I don't like facing old ghosts, but it needs to be done." She stood, placed the bottle in the recycle bin. "I've rented a motor home and will be staying at the campground down the road — slot twenty-nine. I was thinking we could go over to the property, look around, decide how best to do the search, then plan a schedule that works for you. I'll help however you direct. Hopefully I won't be in your way."

"Well, it takes two people to do a search and record the terrain covered so there's no doubling back over grids." He stayed at the table, studying her. She looked tired, tense, but otherwise in good health, so she could probably handle a tough four-hour walk, turn around and repeat it again after a break. Adding volunteers wouldn't help really; more than two people would just impede the dogs' work. And he doubted Grace wanted word to get around about what they were doing.

But he much preferred that she stay at the campground while he did the search with one of his brothers instead. She didn't need the cruel reality of what might be found. "I'd rather someone else help me, Grace," he said. "Searching for remains this old can be done, but it requires near perfect conditions for the dogs to pick up a scent. The ground around the gravesite had to be firm enough that an air cavity formed, trapping the decay, but loose enough now the odors can rise." He kept his voice neutral as he deliberately gave her some of the gruesome details, watching to see if she got shaky. She'd turned to face him, had paled, but then simply sat and waited.

"The dogs will inevitably alert on animal remains, even though they try to distinguish the difference. There are going to be numerous false positives that will have to be dug up and checked. Someone else will be working behind me with a shovel. It's going to be long, hard days pushing through underbrush and crossing rough terrain, looking for something I really doubt we'll find after this much time."

"Josh," she said, her voice low, "I've lived with this for twenty-five years, wondering where my parents are. The rawness of this reality . . . a search to find them? At least I'm looking. I want to be — need to be — out there. I'll handle it."

He slid off the table. "Then we'll give it

our best effort, Grace. If the ground reaches the freeze point or we get the first snow, this all will have to wait until spring."

She nodded, stood, and pushed her hands back into her pockets. "I'm sorry, I should have told you already, but I'm not expecting this to be free. I'll pay for your time and your dogs' effort. You've got a business and a life, and it's a big request."

"If we find something, you can make a donation to the K-9 fund. My time's my own to give, Grace. Don't worry about it."

She studied him, then nodded. "You can tell your brothers and your parents about this, if necessary. Please limit it to that. I'm not ready to deal with a reporter or curious neighbors."

"Understood. Get yourself settled in at the campground. Once the bait shop is open, I'll drive down and join you. We'll go over to the property and take a look, make a plan. We've got good weather today, and we'll take advantage of it."

"I appreciate it, Josh."

"I'm glad you came back. No matter how this unfolds, it's nice to see you again."

Grace nodded her thanks, and Josh watched her walk to her car.

She wants to find her parents. Her murdered parents . . . What had Ann let him walk into?

186

He knew Ann was flying in today and so he sent her a text: *Grace asked her favor. Call me when you have privacy to talk.*

Evie Blackwell

"Ann, you wanted to talk about the Dayton case this morning?" Evie asked, finishing a donut and reaching for her coffee. They were getting an early start at the post office and that suited her, as Day Four of her vacation needed to cover a lot of ground.

"Yes."

"Where do you want to begin?"

Gabriel, who had brought the glazed donuts and coffee with him, took another and slid the box down to his father. Caleb pulled out a chocolate long john for himself. Evie shook her head when Caleb silently asked if she wanted the box back. She was getting spoiled with how the Thane men fed her. She liked Gabriel's dad. He was a salt-of-the-earth type guy who said a lot with few words.

"Summary first." Ann took a last bite, stretched her legs out, looking relaxed. She already told Evie that she had flown out of Chicago before dawn, had been thinking about this case all the way to Carin. She now spoke from memory. "The Daytons are an upper-middle-class family. An executive father, stay-at-home mom, one child, trying to have a second child — a good marriage by all accounts. They transferred to Florida with his job, but still have family in Chicago.

"Thirteen years ago they were traveling by car from Florida to Chicago on vacation, stopping at small antique stores, showing their daughter the mountains in Tennessee, horses in Kentucky, farms and cows in Ohio, generally aiming toward Chicago but not on any particular schedule. On the night of Friday, July 24, they stopped at the All Suites Hotel here in Carin County, just off I-42. Six-year-old Ashley Dayton was abducted from the hotel just after nine p.m.

"Her father, Elliot Dayton, was bringing luggage from the car to their third-floor room via the elevator. Her mother, Arlene Dayton, was getting sodas and snacks from the vending machines on their floor, and their daughter, eager to help, took the ice bucket to the ice machine farther down the hall. The mom got back to the room, the father did, the girl did not. The father found the ice bucket on the floor by the ice machine — their room number was on it — but no sign of Ashley. She hadn't cried out, and neither parent had seen another person on their floor. Elliot rushed down the stairwell to the parking lot while his wife called 911.

"Cops had an AMBER Alert active on the highways and area roads within twenty minutes. Both Carin and State Police swept the hotel, checking rooms and interviewing guests. No one reported seeing the child in the parking lot with anyone other than her parents. No one heard or saw a child struggling. Ashley Dayton, a blue-eyed, blond six-year-old with a pretty smile and outgoing personality, would smile and say hi to a stranger, but had a good security sense about her, knew to stay in sight of her mom and dad. She was grabbed that night, hustled down the stairs, probably out to the back parking lot, and driven away before anyone saw the abduction." Ann looked over to Gabriel's father, sheriff at the time of the abduction. "A decent summary?"

Caleb nodded. "They had filled up the car with gas before checking into the hotel, but otherwise hadn't stopped in Illinois before they arrived here. It's unlikely they were targeted by someone who knew the family. This was a crime of opportunity by someone at the hotel or someone who saw them at the gas station, which is located across the street from the hotel. Checks of vehicles at the hotel, those who filled up a vehicle at the station during the hour in question, didn't generate a name we could fit to this. A couple of locals remembered seeing the family at the station, one remembered saying hi to the girl, yet no one observed anyone take an unusual interest in the family."

Evie made notes as Ann and Caleb talked. She could visualize the scene. By nine that summer night, it would be dark but still warm, people inside in air-conditioned rooms, or outside, heading with purpose to where they needed to go without rushing about it in the heat. Travelers, mostly friendly with each other, sharing a glance at other cars packed like theirs with luggage and kids going somewhere. The hotel would be the same — tourists staying overnight, leaving for another destination at first light. Families rather than business people, Evie thought, as the single business traveler would try to make it home before the weekend.

Truckers, taking advantage of the cooler night hours and the slack in traffic, would be moving their cargo at a good pace, keeping their fill-up times short. Overnight-delivery folks would be starting to refill vending machines and counter snack displays. People would have been out for a meal. At nine o'clock, it would not have been a deserted area. Had the girl been able to break away from her abductor inside the hotel, or at least outside the hotel, someone would have likely heard her crying or seen her running.

A trucker is interesting, Evie thought, someone who saw the girl, had one of those big extended-cab sleeper berths inside the truck, a place to put a child, bound, mouth taped, while he cruised down the highway passing cops. He'd still be on schedule for his deliveries, since the snatch was probably at most thirty minutes from the sighting of the girl at the gas station to her disappearance from the third floor of the hotel. The father would have moved the car to the closest entrance door before hauling in the luggage. Finding the right floor, their assigned room, would have taken only minutes.

Evie felt her heart squeeze with emotion as she could see the sequence play out. Pull around back of the hotel. Use the stairs or the service elevator, glance down hallways, spot the family coming and going. And there she is, coming right to you without her parents, compliments of the ice machine. Scoop her up and you're gone. Maybe in a delivery uniform, maybe even having stayed at the hotel before or parked behind it to grab a few hours of shut-eye.

Hand across her mouth, out the back door, into the cab of the truck, close the door and you've got your prize. Pull out, watch the speed, you're gone before the parents' cry of alarm alerts people to look around.

Someone who knew the area well enough to make a snap decision and get away with it. Confident. Quick. Maybe he'd gotten another child in the same area before. Evie felt a surge of interest at that idea . . . not the first time he'd grabbed a child, not the first time from a hotel along the Interstate. Maybe if they looked at those towns within driving distance of the hotel, going back a few years, they might find another footprint pointing to this same perp.

She wrote, *Not the first abduction from a hotel along this Interstate for this guy. Where else? When?* She underlined the idea so hard, her pen nearly went through the paper. Had someone pursued this possibility or was it a fresh idea? Maybe they had given it only a cursory glance, not gone far enough back in time. Forward in time would be worth checking too, she realized. He successfully snatches this girl and feels lucky, so then after a few years, why not take another one along the same stretch of freeway? Maybe the piece of the puzzle she was looking for was more in the present, in the years since the girl went missing.

Evie tuned back into the conversation. Gabriel was saying, ". . . a lot of calls came in. She's a pretty child, there were numerous sightings on interstates all around the Midwest, but none panned out as Ashley Dayton. Without a lead on a vehicle, all the police activity on the roads couldn't stop this guy from slipping through and away. To cover the bases we did a systematic search of every campground and state park in the county, to see if her abductor sat tight, waiting for the police and public interest to fade before he moved on, but we didn't find any leads.

"What else?" Gabriel said, more to himself than the room. "This case was highlighted on the 'help us solve this crime' TV shows during the second and third years, and that generated more leads on blue-eyed blondes, but again, not this child. The parents still live in Florida. They have two other daughters now. They call every year on the anniversary of Ashley's abduction to see if there's anything new, but they mostly gave up hope after about three years."

"In abduction cases," Ann mentioned, her voice grim, "most often the child is dead within a day. An alarming number are dead within four hours."

Evie had heard that stat before, but it always caused a pang to hear it again.

Gabriel studied the crime wall. "So how do we approach it, Ann? Go back to those we can place at the hotel, the gas station? One of them is most likely the abductor or saw who was. But we've focused there before without success."

Evie was studying the photos on the wall. "Maybe it was someone eating at a restaurant nearby," she said before Ann could reply. She pointed at a photo. "There's a Denny's and a Pizza Hut and what looks like an Italian restaurant. They would still be open that time of night. Someone eating at a restaurant or walking across a parking lot could have looked over at the station — it's well-lit — and seen the girl."

Gabriel slid forward in his chair. "An interesting idea," he said, and Evie could tell by his tone that he liked it. "I know video was collected from any business in the area that had security cameras, but I don't think receipts were pulled."

"It's going to be hard to track down names without credit-card receipts," Evie agreed, "but some diners inevitably would go over to see what was going on at the hotel, check out the gathered cop cars. Locals would remember who else was in the restaurant that night. It's the kind of excitement you remember even a dozen years later. You've talked about it with friends, speculated on the crime, followed the news. Locate a few spectators' names from cop notebooks, and we can push out from there, see what people remember."

Gabriel nodded. "Make a note, and let's pursue it."

Evie picked up her pen and did so.

A phone beeped a text alert, and Evie glanced at hers, not sure whose it was. Ann scanned hers, typed a quick reply, and pocketed her phone again. "Is the door locked?" she asked.

Evie glanced at the door, surprised by the question. "Yes."

"It's a good idea, Evie," Ann said quietly. "But it won't be necessary." She opened her briefcase, removed a manila envelope, picked up a roll of tape and walked over to the crime wall. She visibly took a deep breath, let it out, then tore a piece of tape from the roll.

Ann taped a picture of Grace Arnett, age six, beside the photo of Ashley Dayton, also age six. "Any questions?"

The similarities were heart-stopping, though after a second look, clearly two different girls. Evie was so startled that for a

195

moment she stopped breathing. She saw both Gabriel and Caleb go still. The silence in the room was palpable.

Ann wiped the heel of a hand across her eyes. She turned and held Gabriel's gaze first, then looked at Caleb. Evie felt herself prepared when Ann looked at her. She understood now why Ann had arranged for Carin County to be the first county, why this case was one of those being worked, why Ann had made sure she was here for Grace.

Ann taped up another photo. "Grace's uncle, Kevin Arnett, was an age-and-gender-specific pedophile who likely killed Grace's parents to gain legal guardianship of her. Grace was a blue-eyed, blond two-year-old when he first saw her. Her parents disappeared three days later. Kevin molested Grace from age six to twelve. When she hit puberty and wasn't as attractive to him anymore, he grabbed Ashley Dayton to recreate his six-year-old perfect princess. It's probable he killed Ashley that same day. The child is likely buried on the uncle's land."

Evie agreed with the whispered word from Caleb. She looked over at Gabriel, his face now gray with shock. Grace would have been at school with the Thane brothers, likely attended the same church. This was a girl they all knew well.

"Ann," Gabriel said softly, "when . . . ?" He didn't need to finish the question.

Ann was visibly in pain when she sighed and said, "Grace told me the specifics of the abuse two years ago. I knew as soon as she described what had happened to her that this Dayton case had its answer.

"Grace doesn't know about this child, and it's too soon for her to learn of this. She's still coping with her own history. Knowing her uncle abducted, raped, and killed a child because he didn't want Grace anymore — something she was relieved about at the time because her abuse was over — is going to devastate her all over again. She's not ready to deal with this child's death. She'll blame herself."

Evie had met Grace once at Ann's, remembered a woman in her twenties with a quiet poise, knew the friendship with her went back years. The fine line Ann had been walking was the kind of thing any friend would struggle with, but an officer of the law more than most, with the needs of the living and the dead colliding. Ann could no longer help the child who was gone, couldn't arrest the uncle who was dead, and so she'd done what she could to help the living victim.

Evie watched the silent communication between Gabriel and Ann, their attention locked in a rich conversation without words. She felt a faint envy at the many years and shared experiences underlying that friendship. Ann would need his support, and Gabriel was offering it.

"Why has Grace come back?" Gabriel asked Ann.

"She doesn't know about this missing child, but Grace is trying to deal with what she *does* suspect. She just asked Josh to help her search her uncle's property for human remains. She's looking for her parents."

Gabriel winced and closed his eyes briefly.

Ann let that statement stand for a moment before she continued. "The odds Josh can find those remains after so many years is admittedly low, but he'll be walking the property to find whatever can be discovered. If Ashley Dayton is buried on the uncle's land, Josh and his dogs will find her. We let Josh do his work, and we'll support Grace however we can if there are discoveries out there."

She paused, sighed, and added, "If we do find the child's remains, we'll help Grace to face this. If we can't find the child, we keep this probable answer to the Dayton case to ourselves and her parents. What we tell them needs to stay pretty high level unless we can formally close the case. I don't want them seeking out Grace. If we can't find Ashley's remains, we don't tell Grace about the case."

"We're not going to cause further pain to a living victim, Ann," Gabriel agreed, speaking for the group. "Not when it's Grace Arnett."

Ann nodded at his reassurance.

Even though Evie didn't personally know Grace or the uncle who'd done this, she could imagine what others in this room were dealing with. She shook her head, trying to get her concentration back, to see what had to be done first to work the case now laid out in an entirely new pattern. She studied the map on the wall. "Can someone describe the property? What are we dealing with here?" Evie asked.

"About two hundred acres," Caleb replied, getting up and moving over to circle the area with a marker. "Most of the land is leased out and planted with corn and beans, but Carin Lake cuts into it on the west side. The shoreline and woods here" — he indicated the spot with the marker — "are on the property. There's good hunting in these thick woods. Probably twenty acres or better of timber are going to have to be searched. The house here," he said, using the marker again, "is set back from the road a distance. I remember there being a barn or two. The estate trustee kept the house together enough that the roof didn't leak and the windows were still solid, but it hasn't been lived in since Grace moved away. I don't know what Grace has done with it since she reached eighteen and the property was distributed to her."

"It's the same," Ann said. "The house is basically as it was and still unoccupied. Any evidence that remained out there, we'll find and collect. When we're done, Grace plans to demolish the house and barns, turn the acreage back into tillable land, and sell the place. She's got an offer from the man now leasing the farmland. She'll make a separate arrangement for the wooded acres and the access road with one of the hunting groups in the area. She doesn't plan to come back here again once this is done."

Evie thought Grace's plan to return it to farmland, cut any connection to the place, was the best decision she could make, given the history there.

Ann rubbed the back of her neck, walked over to the crime wall, took down the two photos, and returned them to her briefcase. Evie watched her lock it, understood the gesture.

"I'm convinced Kevin killed Grace's parents to gain legal guardianship of her," Ann said as she straightened, turned to the group. "Whether we can prove that and find a way to close the cold case on her parents' disappearance is difficult to say at this point. But they came to Carin to visit family, vanished from their hotel on a Friday night — a car and two adults — leaving their daughter with a cousin who was babysitting while they went out to eat. They wouldn't leave a child they loved. They were murdered that night. It's likely the uncle concealed it all by hiding the evidence on the land he owned. Now, twenty-five years later, we're going to try to find that proof. And in the process hopefully locate Ashley Dayton as well.

"We need to make sure the search doesn't leak. Nothing gets written down, entered into a computer, formalized. We leave the initial work to Josh, reevaluate once he's done. And we keep news of the missing child away from Grace for as long as we can."

"Ann, does Josh know the full picture?" Gabriel asked.

She shook her head. "Not yet."

"He's going to have to know." At Ann's nod of agreement, Gabriel pulled out his phone and walked to the other side of the room to make a call to Josh.

Evie knew Josh couldn't walk beside Grace on that property and not know they might locate the remains of a child, not know the farmhouse was a place that haunted Grace with the memories it stirred. She watched Gabriel as he spoke with his brother. His father had been sheriff while this was happening, Gabriel was the sheriff now. Evie didn't think any of the Thanes would be the same after today. A child had been abused on the periphery of their lives for years, and they hadn't seen it.

Looking spent, Ann came back to the table and sat down. Evie refilled Ann's coffee, would have put her phone in her hand and told her to call Paul if she thought Ann would step aside for a few minutes right now. Evie got a brief look of thanks and knew Ann was at her limit.

Evie realized she was the only one in the room not getting personally whipsawed by the revelations and mentally stepped in to take over, started making notes on what had to be done next. There was a high probability before the next two weeks were over that the Dayton girl's disappearance would be closed with the discovery of her remains. It wouldn't be a celebration when they closed the case. They would have a success, but at a very heavy price for those who knew the whole truth.

"We need to take another look at her uncle's hunting accident," Caleb said.

"Yes," Ann agreed, sipping at the cup of coffee.

"Arnett's death looked like a hunting accident," Caleb went on. "He was shot from an angle indicating the bullet came from above, from the deer blind. He wasn't wearing anything reflective or bright. Someone mistook him for an animal and fired, then ran from the scene. At the time it didn't play any other way. An anonymous call came in of a shooting accident. We couldn't trace cellphones as well back then, but it seems likely it was called in from a road out that way — once whoever did it was away from the scene. What prints could be recovered from the blind were people you'd expect to have used it, and those folks had reasonable alibis for the time in question."

"Grace didn't kill him," Ann said quietly. "I'd lay money on that. It probably was just what it appeared, a hunting accident."

Caleb gave Ann a reassuring nod. "Actually, Grace was with Josh when her uncle was killed — riding their bikes over by the ice cream shop and then to the library. Grace was the one girl Josh didn't mind knowing that his affection for books ran as deep as hers. A deputy met up with them at the library so we could keep Grace away from the scene." Caleb sighed. "This hurts, Ann. Hurts really bad. It surely takes a lot of courage for her to come back. How is she?"

"Still in deep pain. Quiet. Facing that past. Dealing with it. Moving too fast through the memories, in my estimation. I'd say she needed another year before taking this step. But I haven't been able to shift her from this course. She's facing it, trying to get through it, get it done and behind her."

"I never saw it." Caleb shook his head. "Not in her uncle, not in her. I noticed Grace around town most weeks. Growing up without a mom or dad. The sadness was in her eyes most of the time. She was a quiet girl. But I took it as that. I never once suspected this, and no one told me anything even in confidence that they had questions. I would have acted, Ann. God is my witness, I would have believed her."

"I know, Caleb. I know."

"If my boys had seen anything, if she had said anything —"

"She didn't, Dad," Gabriel said, rejoining them. "We would have gotten a clue from something she said, I promise you that. We all liked her, Josh most of all. Grace didn't let us in, not to this secret. Not to this darkness."

"Josh coming in?"

"He's with Grace now, on the way over to the property to have a look around, lay out a search plan. I didn't tell him much. He'll come by here afterwards, and we'll tell him."

"How's he sound?"

"Determined."

"He's a good man when it comes to doing what has to be done," Caleb said. "Did she choose Josh, Ann, or did you?"

"When it became apparent I couldn't change Grace's mind about coming back, I suggested Josh and his dogs as the next step. I figured Josh being a friend would help matters."

"Good thinking. Whatever we can do for Grace now, we're going to do," Caleb said firmly, nodding at each of them around the circle.

Gabriel sat down by his dad. *He's in pain,* Evie thought, *coping, dealing, but in emotional pain.*

"Who else in the county was a victim?" Gabriel asked. "It's unlikely Grace was his first."

Caleb looked ill at the remark. "We're going to have to figure that out now, Son, however painful it is to ask the questions," Caleb replied.

Ann shook her head. "Grace, then Ashley, may have been his first near home. Kevin Arnett was a careful man. He hid what he was, and did it well if it turns out no one in the community ever suspected him. He spent four years grooming Grace before this started so he could ensure she wouldn't talk. I'm thinking there may be signs early in his life, before he was eighteen, but after he became a man . . . I think he was carefully hiding who he was. You're going to find his other crimes away from the area, not in this county."

"I hope you're right, if only so I have one less weight to grieve over tonight," Caleb said. "It's bad enough it was Grace." He looked over at Gabriel. "Depending on how things go, you'll need to alert the adjacent counties in case they have their own unsolved cases. . . ."

His voice drifted to a stop, and Gabriel said, sounding thoughtful, "There was a felon in our county, a registered sex offender who disappeared abruptly. His body turned up about eighteen months later, behind the truck stop off Highway 19. Wasn't that roughly about the time Grace's uncle was killed in the hunting accident?"

Caleb thought back and nodded. "Guy named Frank Ash. He worked with scrap metal at the junkyard. His focus was on young boys, liked to pull them in via their curiosity about sex.

"He didn't show up at work for a week, on the run before we got a call, toward the end of May. His cabin had the feel of someone gone a while — belongings still there, trash gone bad, milk spoiled. We worked it as a probable murder, but couldn't find his body, couldn't nail down where he'd been. We did turn up two boys who admitted he'd molested them after his prison release. We looked hard at their families and figured that was where our answer was, but couldn't prove it with what we had."

"Frank Ash disappeared in May. The next year, July, the Dayton girl was abducted," Caleb said. "Grace's uncle got killed that fall. Frank's remains turned up behind the truck stop the following year. I remember we had guys still working that scene when the Florist family disappeared, so it would have been the same week in August. It was a busy few years. The entire department practically lived on overtime."

Evie carefully listened to the overlap of crimes, got up and went to the timeline on the wall, picked up a marker. *Frank Ash gets out of jail,* she wrote, *molests two boys, disappears and is presumed murdered. Ashley Dayton is abducted, Grace's uncle killed in hunting accident. Frank Ash's body is found, Florist family disappears.*

Evie turned to face Caleb. "Frank's body . . . when it was found, he'd been dead a couple of years?"

Caleb thought over her question, and she saw his eyes widen. "Dead a couple years, likely back to the May when he disappeared. Shot in the chest three times. Are you thinking — ?"

"No way did Deputy Florist kill Frank Ash and Kevin Arnett." Gabriel's hand moved to rest on his father's shoulder.

Evie heard the certainty in Gabriel's statement, faced him and said, "You've got two dead child molesters in Carin County and a deputy who abruptly disappears the week a murdered body turns up —"

"Evie," Ann interrupted. Evie looked her way and saw Ann shake her head slightly. Not, Evie saw, that she didn't agree with her, but there was a time for everything and this wasn't the right time. Evie set down the marker and stepped away from the crime wall. The sequence on the board was what it was, and to her it looked like one long crime.

"I'm not saying we don't look," Gabriel said, his hand on the table fisted with stress. "But we know Scott Florist. This isn't him. Not shooting a man and dumping his body behind a truck stop. Not shooting a man from a deer blind. Scott's the guy most likely to have been trusted by the boys, to have heard about Ash, the one most likely to go arrest the man and toss him back in jail. If anything, I could see it going the other way. If Frank Ash wasn't dead, I'd have him at the top of the list to have killed Deputy Florist and his family."

"No, Gabe, Evie's right to wonder," Caleb said to his son. "She's just off on the core question. We've got two sex offenders in Carin County during those years. Did we have a third?" He looked back at the time-line, then again at Gabriel.

"Think about it," he went on, walking over to the crime wall. "Someone in the county is afraid Frank Ash is going to get arrested and say to the cops, 'I'll give you someone else who likes kids.' Someone in the county knows Arnett is molesting his niece, he's worried when it's going to become known, and neighbors are going to start looking sideways at each other. Every child is going to get asked by their parents if anyone's touching them. A third guy is out there and wishing the other two weren't stirring up questions.

"Deputy Florist worked in the schools, he coached Little League, he was good with kids. Somebody got worried Deputy Florist was the one most likely to figure this out. So kill Frank Ash, Kevin Arnett, then kill Florist and his family to make sure he's covered his tracks."

Ann got to her feet and began pacing the room.

Evie wanted to accept Caleb's summary. One killer simplified everything. "A sex offender hides his behavior, but kills if he must," she said slowly, thinking it through. "This is too many murders. He would have tried to leave the area before it reached this point." She studied the sequence again. "Another idea. If it wasn't Deputy Florist being a vigilante, killing the two people abusing kids and then leaving town abruptly with his family, what if that idea of a vigilante is correct? Someone in the community, maybe a victim of Frank Ash who's grown up? Kill Frank Ash out of vengeance, realize Grace is being abused, and kill the uncle to help her. He thinks Deputy Florist is getting too close to seeing the truth. One person in the community who took out two bad people in vigilante killings and then had to kill the deputy and his family to stay under the radar."

Evie looked between Caleb and Gabriel as they considered that possibility. Gabriel slowly nodded. "A victim carries a lot of anger around. Murder isn't a stretch. But a panic murder of a deputy and his family? I don't see it, Evie."

Ann walked back to rejoin them. "I'm not saying don't explore down that road, Evie, but step back for a moment and look at something." Ann picked up a marker and moved to an open sheet of paper. "We've got a dead offender who likes older boys, a hunting accident that kills one who likes younger girls, a deputy and his family who disappear. Each crime a year apart. We want them linked because it simplifies matters, but look at the facts. They are different victim sets, different MOs. We've most likely got three years of random crimes, not one linked event.

"Unless you see Deputy Florist as the instigator, you have to bring in a new person

211

to link the three cases. I'm not ready to go that way. And I'm not willing to see a good cop as a killer without a strong piece of evidence pointing us in that direction. The Florist family did a total disappearance. They left behind bank accounts, everything they owned, their pets. The case file reads that they were murdered. The facts indicate these are different crimes."

Ann tapped the board. "Frank Ash was killed by one of his victims or by a family member of one of his victims. That person is likely still in the community. They wouldn't feel much guilt over what they'd done; they'd more likely feel satisfaction.

"Grace's uncle was a hunting accident. Whoever did it probably moved away from the community or died an early death of a heart attack. It's hard to live with accidentally shooting and killing a man, then stay put in the community around his friends for a dozen years. We know *now* that Kevin Arnett was a monster, but at the time of his death, he was thought to be an upstanding member of the community.

"The Florist family murders were most likely someone who hated the deputy, who seized the opportunity to kill him and his family. It was probably someone linked to him via the job. Or it was a random crime.

Maybe a carjacking en route to the campground. Someone needed that truck and camper and took it by force. With either, the person responsible is likely long gone from this area." Ann laid the marker down. "Different victim sets, different MOs, across three years. We're better off to work the cases separately. If and when they cross, then we follow that thread."

Evie accepted Ann's point. If they were linked crimes, it was going to show up as they pursued them individually. One approach didn't preclude the other. She needed to dig further into who Scott Florist had arrested over the years he'd been a cop.

"Back to Grace," Ann said. "Josh looks for the remains of Grace's parents, for the child Ashley Dayton. I'm going to spend as much time with Grace as I can, will try to convince her to trade off with me so I'm out searching with Josh. But we mostly stay out of Josh's way and let him work. So while that's going on, we shift directions and look at the Florist case once again. Where were you on ideas for it, Evie, before this quagmire opened up?"

Evie had to mentally regroup even to follow the question. The Florist case seemed like ages ago, rather than just yesterday. "Umm, let's see, Gabriel was looking for people in the community violent enough to kill a family of three, to kill a child. I was looking for a trigger for them to have done so. We've found a doctor the couple may have been seeing for counseling. We have a meeting with him scheduled for tomorrow."

"Yeah? That's great news," Ann said, pleased. "Stay with that for now. It will be interesting to hear what the doctor has to say. The list Gabriel is putting together sounds like a good candidate pool for the crime."

"Ann," Gabriel said, "going back to Grace and her uncle's land. We need to get forensics to go through the buildings on the property."

Ann nodded. "I'm thinking later this week, once Grace and Josh have established a routine. We can arrange forensics to go out when Grace will not be there. I don't want to crowd her."

"It's going to take long days over a couple of weeks or more to search that much land, and that's if the weather cooperates," Gabriel noted. "Will she accept more of us going out to help?"

"The Thane family, I think, but she doesn't want this known in the community. She's not going to be comfortable with deputies out there," Ann cautioned.

"Ann," Evie said, "where should Grace stay tonight? There's plenty of room at the house."

"I'll see if she'll come into town. If she won't, you and I will go her direction. She's rented a motor home and is staying at the campground near Josh's place." Ann looked around the group. "Anything else we need to talk over?"

"It's a hard thing, what you brought us today, Ann," Caleb said. "A hard thing. Not easy on you, not easy for Grace. But we had to know."

Ann held his gaze, nodded. "I'm sorry it's here, Caleb."

"Criminals like this have a way of weaving their way into a community. Let's fully root this one out. Whatever Grace needs from us, you let us know."

"I will, Caleb."

"Ann." Gabriel waited until she looked his direction. "You and I need to talk later tonight."

Ann gave a slight smile. "Same place, same time?"

"Works for me."

Evie saw their unspoken conversation and once more wished she had a something like that. She didn't have anything like it with Rob at present. Gabriel turned to her and said, "Evie, why don't you ride with me? We'll go out to the uncle's land, meet up with Josh and Grace. She can ride with us back to her camper while Josh comes in to talk with Ann and Dad. Josh will need some time after he hears this."

"Sure." Evie went to get her jacket and several water bottles, glad for the reason not to be here any longer. She wasn't sure she could manage watching Joshua Thane learn the truth about Grace Arnett's childhood. Some things ripped a person's heart out. She paused before she left to rest her hand on Ann's shoulder, share a look in sympathy as well as comfort. Ann would need to be the one to tell Josh. Evie wished for her friend's sake that the day would soon be over.

Evie didn't know what to say to Gabriel as he drove out of Carin. She could see he was anywhere but in the present, his knuckles white on the steering wheel. This cut personal and deep with him, and she could practically feel the guilt rolling off him. Not saying anything didn't suit Evie, but what to say was a mystery. All the Thanes were protective, and Evie was beginning to pick up on just how deep that characteristic ran. She deliberately interrupted his train of thought. "You and Ann. That friendship goes back a lot of years."

He glanced over at her. "Yes, it does."

"The two of you seem close — like a brother and sister with lots of shared history."

Gabriel smiled, put his attention back on the road. "An interesting way to put it. We are very good friends."

"It's never been romantic?" Evie kept on, because it forced Gabriel off what this day had been.

He shrugged. "She was the Midwest Homicide Investigator when I met her, working around the clock to solve a homicide in the next county that spilled over this way. A mom and two girls shot to death in their bedrooms. Ann figured out it was a revenge killing, but not the ex-husband, not a boyfriend. They arrested a guy who thought the mother was responsible for the death of his daughter. The mom, her girls, his daughter had gotten pinned down in the middle of a holdup at a mall store. His daughter got killed, they survived. So he killed her and the daughters. You get to know someone when you're working a case that many hours. She'd sleep in the car between interviews, but otherwise didn't stop until it was solved."

Evie tried to picture that intensity. She knew Ann, she had worked cases with her, but this picture was new. "I haven't seen that side of Ann. She's mellowed some?"

"Some. Mostly she retired. There was the pace of the MHI job — she'd finish helping with one homicide case, then get called to another. I insisted we talk about something personal over meals just so we wouldn't have the crime scene images to deal with while we ate. That started the friendship. That and the fact she wasn't trying to impress me or get my attention — she was just doing her job. She made a serious impression that summer. When she got married, Paul also became a good friend.

"Josh knew her better than me initially. He and his dogs had started with the state's K-9 group. He'd mention Ann occasionally, what she was working on. I started carving out some time when she was in this area to help her out or I'd track her down at a conference. You can't touch on a subject and not find Ann has an interesting opinion to offer."

"How often do you get together?"

"In person? Maybe a couple of times a year. Either Ann or Paul, or both. It depends on what's going on. I probably talk to Paul more often." He paused to point through the windshield. "Up ahead on the right. That's the Arnett place."

Evie turned her head. It looked like a typical farm, with neatly planted rows of crops in the surrounding fields, a faded-red barn, in the distance a thick line of trees. *The lake inlet would be that direction,* she thought. The house wasn't in view yet. Gabriel turned off the road. The drive in was pitted with deep potholes, and a spreading layer of weeds had pushed up through the crushed-rock surface.

Gabriel parked behind the truck by the gate. They could see Josh and Grace walking on the far side of the overgrown pasture just at the tree line. The house was up ahead on the right, a traditional two-story country home probably built in the '50s, with a steep roof and wraparound porch. It was desperately in need of paint, but otherwise still standing tall. "Do we wait here or go join them?" Evie asked.

"I think wait here," Gabriel replied. "We'll want a look at that house later when Grace is not here, so we have a sense of how much time has decayed what's inside. Sun-rotted fabrics is hopefully the worst of it, along with resident spiders and mice. If water has been kept at bay, the structure itself should still be in good shape."

Evie got out of the truck, leaned against it with her arms crossed to ward off the chill of the November day. She tried to imagine growing up on this farm — barn cats, chickens, maybe a goat or two, maybe pigs, certainly cattle. The way the gates were configured, she didn't see any sign that there had been horses. "Grace would take the bus to school from here?"

Gabriel leaned against the truck beside her. "The school bus came by this area just after seven a.m. She'd ride it to school in the morning, have breakfast there, finish classes, come back on the bus in the afternoon. She'd be here unless her uncle brought her into town for something in the evening. He did that frequently, as I remember — they weren't that secluded out here. It was part of his charm, and he was well-liked around the community. A social man, having to raise a young girl. More than a few ladies in town were thinking he would marry once he became her guardian, but he never chose to do so. Obvious now . . ." His voice drifted off. He shook his head. "Back then," he continued, "he was focusing on the farm, raising his niece, and pushing the cops to figure out what had happened to his brother and wife. When Grace got older, come summer she'd ride to town on her

220

bike, hang out at the lake or the library. Her uncle treated her well in my memory of things, and that's what's so painful now. If she wanted to be in town, he'd bring her, she'd go shopping with other girls, go to the ice cream shop with friends. People thought he was an okay guy, doing a decent job as a replacement father."

Evie glanced over at Gabriel, could hear the hard emotion in his voice. "You know as well as I do," she said quietly, "that many people are excellent liars and can hide well who they are and what they do. You were only a teenager back then. You saw what he wanted you to see. And Carin worked to his advantage. This farm and town were the extent of her world, and he controlled it, all its parameters. By taking away her parents, he made sure he had absolute ownership of that girl's life — from toddler to teen."

Gabriel kicked at the dirt, jammed his hands in his pockets. "You sound so calm. I haven't felt this much rage in decades."

"I won't try to touch the emotion of this, it would eat me alive. But I'll do whatever I can to help Grace get her answers, and maybe find a measure of peace."

"Paul said you don't mentally carry a case home with you, that you do that as a gift to yourself."

"It sounds cold, but yes, he's right. I won't let this inside. I'll be eternally grateful I didn't endure that kind of childhood, empathize with Grace's pain, then do my level best not to let it get any further. I can't do my job if I can't walk away from it. These cases will always keep coming. I can't carry the load, so I try very hard not to attempt it."

"I'm not going to say you're wrong in that approach. Not today."

Evie looked over the pastureland, at the line of thick woods, then at the smaller yard around the house. Finding Grace's parents would close a lot of questions. The obvious hiding place would be out in those woods, buried deep, undisturbed for as long as the man had owned the land. "Do you think her parents are buried here?"

"If the uncle killed them, it makes sense. But he knew this county as well as anyone. He could have buried them, demolished the car in a hundred different places. For her own reasons, Grace must believe it to be here. I'm not inclined to ask her why she thinks that, to ask if the uncle said something one day that got her wondering. Her asking to do the search is enough for me."

Evie nodded. She tried to make out the features of the two walking across the pasture in their direction. "Regarding Grace, I've met her only once, Gabriel. She's a friend of Ann's, but she's not going to know me very well, if at all."

"Sometimes that's better, Evie. She'll see you as just another cop, and that will make it easier to let you help her with this. With me, there are childhood memories to complicate things."

"She's going to realize fairly soon that Ann's told us about her past."

"I'm sure Ann will let Grace know who's in the loop," Gabriel said. "That's how relationships with friends stay together. It's going to be healing, in a way, for Grace to be with people who aren't treating her with kid gloves or keeping her at a distance. That said, Evie, a piece of advice?"

"Sure."

"Grace has survived by hiding. So that's where she thinks her security rests. I wouldn't mention something to her she doesn't bring up first."

"That makes sense." She looked over at him. "Gabriel? An observation of my own. You're going to do fine with her, all the Thanes will. You care too much not to."

"Thanks for that."

They watched Josh and Grace coming toward them. Evie thought she looked

223

stressed, maybe a bit thin, but mostly the woman she remembered. Evie saw Josh take hold of Grace's hand as they drew near. Grace didn't pull away, something Evie was thankful to see.

Gabriel went to meet them. "Hello, Grace."

"Gabriel." She smiled. "It's been a long time. I heard from Josh you're sheriff now. Guess I better behave myself." They chuckled, and Evie was impressed at the woman's effort to remain relaxed.

"Taking after Dad." Gabriel gestured back toward the truck. "You remember meeting Evie Blackwell, a friend of Ann's?"

"Yes. Hello, Evie."

Evie smiled as she walked over, held out her hand. "Hello, Grace."

Gabriel shifted his stance, resting back on his heels, hands tucked into his pockets — clearly trying to find the right words. "Ann's told us you're searching for your parents, Grace. We're going to do everything we can to help you out with that, get you whatever answers are here to find. Ann wants to come walk it with Josh at times, as I will, and my father too, so we can cover as much ground as we can while the weather is decent. It's going to be taxing for you to be out here every day."

"I appreciate that, Gabriel. I do. But for some of this, most of it really, I simply need to do this."

Gabriel nodded and looked to Josh. "You've got a plan in mind now that you've seen the property?"

"I think the dogs can clear the pastureland and the area around the house rather quickly. We'll flag whatever the dogs find and leave it to someone else to check out. There will be false-positives, animal bones and the like, given it's a farm and good hunting land. My focus is to keep the dogs moving."

"Sounds good," Gabriel replied, clearly relieved they wouldn't be stopping to check out every location themselves. "Let me, Dad, and Will do the shovel work. There's a lot of land to cover here."

Josh nodded. "That's my thinking also. We walked back to the lake to get a sense of it. The shoreline has turned into steep bluffs, undercut by the rising water in the spring and fall. So we're not looking to search the shoreline itself, other than from a boat.

"There are numerous animal trails in the woods. The deer blinds have been set up on the obvious ones, the underbrush cut back so that a vehicle can get through and close to the blinds. I think we'll check those spots next, let the dogs search the animal trails. After that we'll start a systematic search — from one point in the pasture straight through the trees to the water, then back to the pasture. Like a checkerboard, moving west to east. We'll work daylight hours, with a break as often as the dogs need to stop, until we're done. Probably two or three weeks, depending on the weather and how the dogs handle it as we push through the woods."

Evie could tell Josh was providing a lot of details, not for their sakes but for Grace, who would do best with more information rather than less.

Josh opened his truck's tailgate, pulled over a cooler, offered Grace a water bottle and opened one for himself. "I need to run into town, pick up a couple of GPS readers, marking flags, get the topology map for this place enlarged by sections, put together water, jerky, doggie treats, that kind of thing, then pick up the dogs. We'll do a few hours yet today while the light is still good. See if we can't clear the area by the house."

Gabriel nodded. "Grace, how about we give you a lift to the campground while Josh goes into town? Josh can pick you up there after he collects the dogs."

"That's a good idea, Grace," Josh concurred. "You had an early morning. Get yourself a nap while you can. I'll come your way about three. We won't stay till dark, but we'll get a start at least."

Grace considered the group, nodded. "I'll take your advice as this unfolds, Josh. Ann says you've done more of these searches than anyone around."

"Today will mostly be training on how to mark the maps, and you'll get a feel for how the dogs work. Why don't you pack some snacks for us — whatever's handy. We'll get a decent meal once we're done tonight."

"I can do that," Grace said.

"I'll call if the time changes."

Evie motioned toward Gabriel's truck, and Grace walked over to it. As Evie followed, she heard Gabriel mention, "Josh, you'll probably find Ann and Dad at the old post-office building."

"I'll find them," Josh said.

Evie chose the backseat in the extended cab so Grace could sit up front with Gabriel, hoping a conversation with him would break the rather cautious politeness among them.

Gabriel settled in the driver's seat, and Grace said, "I appreciate you doing this."

"It's no problem. I'd say it's the job, but

it's a lot more personal for us than that. All the Thanes would like to see this settled for you, Grace."

Grace nodded and looked out her window. They drove mostly in silence to the campground.

What is there to say? Evie mulled over in her mind. *I'm sorry your parents were murdered, it has to be hard looking for their bodies, and by the way, we know what happened to you here?* There weren't words to bridge those kinds of realities, and she didn't think it wise to try. At least not yet. She caught Gabriel's glance in the rearview mirror and gave him a brief shake of her head. There would be better moments than this one for a conversation over the next couple of weeks.

Gabriel Thane
Gabriel slowed as he read lot numbers, pulled to a stop at Lot 29. "Nice campsite, Grace. You've got a good view here," he said, looking for something — anything — to say.

Grace stepped from the truck, paused to smile back at him. "Lovely view and I like the camper. It has a microwave and a TV, shower and queen-size bed. I'll be comfortable. Thanks for the lift, Gabriel."

"You'll call if there's anything you need, right?"

"You know I will."

She raised a hand in farewell and walked to the motor home, unlocked it. Gabriel watched her step inside, waited as Evie shifted to the front seat.

"I'll drive the long route into town," he said, "show you the turnoff to Will's place when you want to pick up your dogs. That will give Josh time to hear the full story from Ann and Caleb before I bring you back to the post office."

"Want me to help with the shoveling?"

Gabriel shook his head. "You've got two cases to pursue during this working vacation of yours. The only thing left to do on the Dayton case is to find the burial site, and it's likely where Josh is looking. It's going to be many hours patiently waiting for the dogs to indicate something, digging up animal remains to clear those flags, before we find the little girl's body. We'll get it done, but there's no use in taking up your time on the search here when there's another case needing your focus."

He glanced over, saw a look he couldn't interpret. "Feeling left out of the action?"

"No. Nothing like that. Just struggling to get back momentum for what I was working on yesterday."

"Ann's bombshell still has aftershocks, and it's going to take more than a few days to absorb them," Gabriel agreed. He thought about yesterday, the sense of breakthrough he'd felt when Evie posited the idea that Scott and Susan had been seeing a marriage counselor, the sense that finally some progress was being made on the case.

"Evie, you need to know that for this community, the Florist case is even more significant than the Dayton one. A family disappears, a deputy . . . besides their relatives, no one in Carin County would be more pleased to see it resolved than the cops who work here. You'd be doing us a big favor to stay focused on it. You'd be doing *me* that favor."

She offered a small smile. "I understand. Thanks. Want to come by the post office for a while?"

"I'd like to, but Dad and I need to talk, and Will needs to hear from me what's going on. While Grace is in the area, it's going to be a Thane family matter. Anything you need from me?"

"Not at present. Keep in mind lunch tomorrow, the interview with the doctor. I'd like your impressions of him."

Gabriel nodded. "I'll make sure the time

stays open."

He pointed out the turnoff for Will's, then turned back to town through the forest where Evie had originally met up with the deer. He slowed so she could see the spot.

"No warning he was coming, just a glimpse before the collision," Evie said, turning to see the gash in the tree. "Makes me wonder if there haven't been a lot of such accidents on this road."

"Between county deputies and the state highway patrol, we work a lot of car and animal collisions around the lake," Gabriel said. "You want me to stop to pick up something to eat?"

"Sure. Something I can carry in for Ann and me. That Italian place you mentioned — is spaghetti-to-go an option there?"

"Definitely. Let's make it for three."

Gabriel stopped at the restaurant, and Evie stepped out of the truck. "I'll get the order started. It shouldn't take long."

Gabriel texted Will and then called his father, learning he was on the way home. That set his plan for the next few hours. Stop at the office, confirm all was quiet there, go visit with his father, go talk to Will, then out to the farm with a shovel. He'd leave Evie out of that part, at least for now.

Evie came back with three lunch sacks,

set his in the back. Gabriel felt her look. She said, "You're shutting me out, aren't you?" She pulled a breadstick out of a bag, broke it in half, handed him a piece. "Too many moving parts, this one doesn't need Evie, so start segmenting the people and figure out what needs managing next."

"It's not that." He took a bite of the breadstick. "Nice addition to the lunch, and it's hot."

"I'm not complaining, Gabriel," she said around her own bite, "just noting your body language."

"It's called triage," he said with a comfortable shrug. "Sheriffs do it all the time."

"Understood. Take me to the post office so I can huddle with Ann, and go do whatever's next on your list. You can mark Evie off that list of yours. I'm good."

He smiled at her tone. "I might keep you on the list simply as the one not in trouble — or making trouble. You haven't told me a joke today. I'm told you're good at them."

Evie considered the request for a moment. "Okay. A guy passes a homeless man on the street, holding a sign asking for lunch money," she began. "He stops, pulls a twenty out of his wallet, but says, 'First, I'd like to ask you some questions. Are you going to use this twenty to buy a drink?

Cigarettes? Bet on a pony?' The homeless man replies, 'No, sir. I gave up all those things years ago.' The guy puts the twenty back in his wallet and says, 'Come home with me, have a shower, I'll find you a change of clothes, my wife will fix us a good home-cooked meal.' Startled, the homeless man answers, 'You're sure, sir?' Guy smiles, says, 'I want my wife to meet someone who doesn't drink, smoke, or gamble.' "

It took a second, but then Gabriel laughed. "Going to try to improve your husband one day, Evie?"

"I plan to marry well, so he'll mostly be a livable type of guy right off the bat."

Gabriel laughed again as he came to a stop in front of the building. Evie swung out of the truck. "Stop long enough to eat, Gabriel."

"I will, Mom."

She waved and headed inside.

He needed that light moment. He scanned the street and didn't see Josh's truck. Gabriel felt his smile fade, wondering where his brother may have gone. Somewhere to do some painful grieving, he suspected, before he had to get back to Grace and present a calm face. It was going to be that kind of day. He hoped he was up to doing the same.

Gabriel parked in the front drive at his parents' home, pocketed his keys, walked up the steps to where his father was sitting on the porch, a cigar in one hand. They appeared only in the rarest of occasions, and this one qualified. Both he and his dad had taken some hard hits over the years, but nothing like this. A child victim of horrendous abuse in their midst, and they hadn't seen it to reach out and help. He could see the shared pain in his father's gaze.

"Grace back at her campsite?" his dad asked.

"Yes."

Caleb poured a mug of coffee from the thermos nearby, motioned for Gabriel to help himself. "Your mom went into town to speak with Ann. I've told her."

Gabriel nodded, not surprised, and took a seat on the porch with his own mug. "How did Josh take it?"

"Went very, very quiet."

Gabriel nodded again. He wasn't sure how a person processed the fact that a girl you cared deeply about had suffered so greatly. "One of us needs to update Will."

"I'll go tell him," Caleb offered. "The Thane family faces this together. However we can help Grace, we'll do it as a unit."

"I think Josh will be the major one helping her."

"She has to let him in first. I think she does what she must, then runs as far as she can from this place."

"And he's liable to follow."

"He's got strong convictions. Grace is one of those, I'm thinking."

Gabriel sighed and stretched his legs out, thought about the week ahead. "You think the Dayton girl's remains are out there?"

"She's there. As soon as Ann put up that photo, I knew she would be." Caleb leaned over to pour more coffee. "Invite Grace to dinner tomorrow, let's start putting comfortable friends around her. I don't want her brooding out there, alone and back in Carin where the memories are the strongest."

"I'll mention it to Josh, have him bring her this way when they're done at the farm tomorrow." Gabriel found his sense of time was out of kilter, had to concentrate. "Just four days ago, it was a normal November around here."

Caleb's smile was sad. "Wasn't normal — we just hadn't seen the dark spots yet. Evie strikes me as being a good cop. She's kind of young for the job, but that crime wall on the Florist family shows real progress in a short time, particularly given that she started out getting all banged up."

"Yeah, she's got some ambition in her," Gabe noted. "A good thing, considering what she's tackling. I'll be around, Dad, if something comes to mind I need to know."

Caleb nodded. "Get some rest later. Tomorrow's sure to be a challenging one. For everyone."

Gabriel pushed to his feet, set his mug back on the small table. "No one's out there to arrest for this terrible crime, Dad. Two beautiful little girls . . ." He shook his head. "That's what makes it all so awfully tough. I can't provide the justice Grace should have, needs to have. Or the Daytons . . ."

"God can, though," Caleb said quietly. "Let it go, Son. This isn't yours to carry. It's going to bust you if you try."

"Yeah." Then he said again, "You'll tell Will?"

"I will."

"Ask him about Evie's dogs too — if he's all right with keeping them a few more days. Evie will want to have them around; they'd be a welcome distraction. But she also could benefit from a few more days just reading

236

the files. She's still stiff, and cautious about that back of hers."

"I'm sure he's fine about having them there. You know Will and his animals."

Gabriel smiled. "If it's got four legs — for that matter, two — he'll tend it like a mother hen. I never figured out how he's kept that trait, being as how he grew up with me."

"It's why being a combat medic suited him so well. You guys tumbled over each other on everything, but if someone else tried to come at either you or Will or Josh, you suddenly became the Three Musketeers."

They both laughed. "Get on about the job, Gabriel," Caleb said. "I know it's sitting heavy today, but you'll shift and bear up under this, we both will. Just give it time."

"Yeah. See you, Pop." Gabriel laid a fist lightly on his father's shoulder, headed back to his truck feeling lighter than when he arrived. He'd stop by his place for a shovel and get on with what had to be done.

Joshua Thane

Josh desperately wanted a few hours on the water. He needed the time alone, but it wasn't going to be possible. He gathered up the necessary supplies in town, exchanged a few polite words with those he had to, and pushed down the sick feelings as best he could. There were moments in life when perceptions shattered, and his just had in a way he'd never experienced or expected.

He'd had his idealized image of Grace, and someone had just ripped a curtain back to show what he hadn't seen all those years ago. He mostly wanted to wrap her up in a hug and cry with her, and if that emotion didn't spill over today, he'd be a fortunate man.

Grace wouldn't want it known, surely wouldn't want him to know the truth. Ann had told him only because the cop in her had to alert him to the likelihood that there were other remains out there. He'd searched in this kind of situation with Ann before. He knew that look on her face, the tone in her voice. Ann figured there was a better than even chance his dogs could find the Dayton girl's remains on the farm.

Grace had lived with what had happened to her on that farm for decades now. He'd lived with it for a couple of hours. The best thing he could do was give it time. Without even knowing it, he'd let down a friend, for she'd been that and more to him. He hadn't known she needed help, hadn't been alert enough to catch the signals, and that was going to take some time to grieve and accept. He wasn't going to let her down again if he could possibly help it.

He understood the sad eyes now, but he wasn't going to let her sorrow push him away. She was too important to him to let that darkness stain what he remembered of her. But for the time being he'd have to deal with staying quiet, calm, matter-of-fact, the friend she needed.

He collected his dogs at the house, drove the short distance to the campground, glad Grace was nearby rather than in town. Word would get out eventually that she was back, and he'd do what he could to downplay it as anything more than a short return to visit Carin.

Grace must have seen his truck coming. When he pulled in, she was waiting for him with cooler in hand. He pulled in a deep breath and disciplined his expression. He could do this. He *would* do this.

He smiled as he stepped from the truck. "You're a timely one, Grace. I think that was true of you back in school too."

She approached the truck. "Being late, unless someone is bleeding, is just plain rude."

His smile faltered. *Her uncle used to say that.* Thankfully she didn't see his reaction as she climbed in on the passenger side. *Okay, not so controlled as I thought.* He'd do well to avoid anything that brought up memories of the past. "You may remember my dogs' father. These two boys are Duke and Slim."

They both were looking at her through the back window. She laughed and greeted them by name. "They're wonderful."

"They travel everywhere together, always curious about what the other has found to do. They love a belly rub, and they'll lick you to death if you let them."

Josh settled on the driver's side after finding a place for the cooler. "I'm going to take a few minutes to go hook up a small camper I take out to the field. It's parked at the other end of the campground. If the dogs need a break, or a rain shower comes in, I've got shelter at hand." *And it removes the need to have to go into that farmhouse.*

As they drove up to the camper, Grace asked, "Anything I can do to help?"

"After I get the truck lined up, you can take the driver's seat, tap the brake, test the turn signals so I can check them once I've got everything hitched together."

"I can do that."

He expertly backed in. They both stepped out, and he turned the crank to lift the wheel and settle the camper onto the truck's hitch.

"You must camp a lot," she observed.

"I live on the lake, make my living from it, so I try to camp around it when I've got a few free days. Makes me better appreciate the experience tourists come here to find." He flashed her a quick grin. "It helps that the bugs don't bother me."

"You're lucky. They love me."

"Which reminds me. Sunscreen and bug spray are in the backpack behind the seat. You'll want to make use of both." He connected the wire plug from the truck to the camper. "Okay, let's check the lights and we'll be ready to go."

"That easy?"

He nodded and walked to the back. "I'm a man who keeps things simple," he called as she settled behind the wheel. "I park it with everything locked down, all set to go out again."

The lights worked fine. Josh tossed aside the wood blocks he used to anchor the wheels, took the driver's seat again, and eased the camper out. "We're good to go, Grace. Find us a radio station you like, then tell me something fun you did in Chicago last year. I'm guessing there isn't much grass and trees for camping up there."

"Nope, all this green is wonderful." She reached to the radio.

He'd be asking a lot of questions about Chicago during the hours they walked. Besides it being a safe topic, he wanted to find out about the life she'd carved out for herself there. He needed to understand who Grace was today, and he figured they had a hundred hours or better of conversation ahead of them. He'd start with an easy topic, see what pieces he could discover to fill in a new picture of her.

Josh let his dogs roam the farmhouse yard, stretch their legs after the ride in the truck, get settled into the general scents of the place before he called them over. "Grace, you'll want to watch for uneven ground — moles have been at work out here," he told her, feeling the surface soft under his boots.

"I will." She had on decent tennis shoes, jeans, and she'd worn layers with the jacket so she could adjust to the day's temperatures. He'd find her a pair of boots for tomorrow to better protect against the harsh terrain.

She'd requested something of him, and finding the location of her parents' remains would most likely involve spotting land that had settled around the graves, rather than the dogs picking up the scent. But he didn't bother explaining that to her. He'd had enough experience to know what to look for.

"How will you know if they locate something?" Grace asked.

He knelt and whistled. "They will lie down," he told her as he lavished affection on the dogs, "or if the ground is too uneven, sit down. They'll put their paws and nose where the scent is strongest. They can mostly tell whether it's animal remains to be ignored, but when it gets to a certain age, it's just remains to them. If I don't set a dozen red flags in the next three hours, I'll be surprised." She looked startled at the number, but nodded.

"The dogs and I work with basic voice commands, unique to each dog. They search best as a team, crossing back and forth over a section of land, working scents together."

Josh gave the dogs the forward-search command, and they turned from playful Labradors to focused trackers, tails wagging, eager to please, on-task animals. They trotted out ahead, noses down. He'd take them from here to the clothesline post in the first pass. "See how the dogs are moving? That's work mode. See the difference in their attention?"

"It's noticeable," she said, shaking her head in wonder.

"The key thing is to stay behind them, downwind if possible, and not distract them." He soon whistled to terminate the current search pattern, and the dogs came loping back. He dug out treats, lavished praise on the two again. He let them go exploring on their own for a while. "When they're roaming in search mode, I'm going to be directing them a bit with my voice, watching the ground ahead of them. My job is to keep the dogs out of trouble and on task. I sure don't want to run them into a nest of skunks if I can avoid it."

Grace made a face, then smiled.

"I need you to be the record keeper while I direct the dogs. The GPS reader tells you where you're standing." He turned the small piece of equipment on, called up a reading. Numbers lit the screen in soft blue. "The topology maps" — he handed her one — "are indexed on the sides by the last two digits of these readings." He traced the co-ordinates on the map to where they crossed and pointed to the spot. "See? We're standing right here."

She nodded, looking at the map she was holding.

"What I'd like you to do is mark an X

when we start a search pattern, then approximately every football field in length, do another GPS reading and put a line on the map. Do that until I call 'Search string ended,' and then you mark an X where we stop. We won't walk straight lines — it's more the contours you're tracking. When we're back tomorrow, that map will be my starting plan. I won't repeat ground we've already covered, or I'll intentionally criss-cross the ground from another direction. Any questions?"

"So just tick lines along the route with final X's?"

"You got it."

"I can do that."

He appreciated her confidence. "Just to warn you, it's not as easy as you might think after we've been walking for a while. You'll be watching for obstacles in your path, holding tree branches aside, keeping an eye on the dogs, getting distracted by wildlife and poison ivy. It's not a simple task being on a search. If you find your attention drifting, speak up. We'll take a ten-minute break, drink some water. I can't monitor the dogs, watch where I'm going myself, and correctly judge how you're doing."

Grace smiled. "I won't be a wimp — I'll speak up."

"Good. What did you bring for food?"

"Sandwiches. Peanut butter and jelly."

"Nice. I'll take one to get started."

Grace walked back to the truck and the cooler, and he used the time to send a text to Ann, letting her know they were starting. He had a gut feeling the Dayton child was going to be found near the house, or at a location the uncle could easily see, rather than in an obscure corner of the woods. If his fervent prayer was answered, they'd locate the little girl's body in the first few days, and Grace's parents — *if* they were here — within days after that.

He could keep Grace occupied while they searched the fields and woods, but he'd already seen her quick glances toward the house. He wanted it out of their sight just as rapidly as he could make that happen.

He slid his phone back in his pocket, took the sandwich she offered, smiled his thanks. "Ready?" He whistled for the dogs. "Let's cover some ground."

He called out the search-forward command again, using the clothesline post to steer a straight course. He watched Grace make the starting X on the map, nodded his approval, and set his pace to one comfortable for her. The dogs would surge ahead in the first twenty minutes, overeager

246

to be on the job, but would settle back to a more normal pace after they were on task for a while.

Ten minutes into the walk, one of the dogs dropped to the ground. The other ran over to check it out, dropping immediately to the ground as well. Josh planted a flag, handed out treats and praise, gave the search-forward command again. He caught the motion as Grace sniffed, wiped her eyes. He dug out a package of tissues he'd stuffed in his jacket pocket, offered them to her.

"Thanks," she whispered. "Probably just my cat. I had a few burial ceremonies out here."

He reached over to lightly touch her hand. "I do this for a living, Grace. If you can agree with me that you should be curled up on that couch in the motor home or at Evie's while this gets done by a couple of the Thane brothers, I'm not going to think less of you for it."

"I can't, Josh. I can't leave this question for others."

"Did you look for them . . . your parents, when you lived here?"

"Not consciously, no."

"Good. You were way too young to be doing it then."

She reached for his hand in return,

squeezed it and let go. He directed the dogs to the left. At least once their painful search was done, it would be over one way or another, and she wouldn't have to think about this property any longer.

Before long, the dogs dropped to the ground again, and Josh set another flag marking the spot.

Evie Blackwell

The Florist family crime wall was holding any further secrets to itself. Evie rolled her shoulders, thought about pacing a while. She glanced over at her friend, wondering how long to let the silence go before she interrupted. "You okay, Ann?"

"Just tired."

Evie pushed the last of the breadsticks her way, since Ann hadn't eaten much of her spaghetti. "Did you call Paul?"

She nodded. "One of the better things about being married, Evie, is that there's always someone to call on bad days." Ann picked up the last breadstick, but just nibbled at it.

"We could go out to the farm, search with Grace and Josh."

Ann shook her head. "Tonight is soon enough. Grace has two ways of coping: bury it inside and do the work in front of her, and the more chaotic kind of coping where she relaxes her guard and the memories come roaring back. The evenings are by far the hardest for Grace. She'll take some company tonight — the kind who don't feel the need to talk, who can just hang out."

Evie nodded. "That's the kind of friend I can be, if she'll let me." She looked at the case wall once more but couldn't generate further interest in it. "I could be out there helping with the flags . . ."

"No," Ann said, "the guys are better at the shovel work. They'll recognize animal remains at a glance, while you and I would have to take a photo and ask an expert for an opinion. Besides, you can't be two places at once, and the Florist case desperately needs solving. What are you doing now? I'll help. It'll give me something else to think about."

"The Florist family finances," she replied. "Their banker relative thinks money's missing from the estate."

Ann pointed to the open files. "Send some of them my way. I can give myself a new kind of headache thinking about money."

Evie passed over the checkbook registry pages. "I'm trying to figure out how they might have siphoned money to cash without it being obvious."

"How far back? The month they disappeared? The year it happened?"

"I don't know. And I don't know which of them was doing it or why. I'm not reading this as a couple heading to a divorce, one of them secretly stashing away funds. And I don't think we've got someone who was simply a worrier, setting aside a rainy-day fund. But the banker's pretty insistent that the estate's assets are lighter than they should have been. So maybe it's there, like the counseling was there, hidden away behind other items."

Ann started going through the papers in front of her. "How would you siphon cash from your own income, be able to hide it for any length of time?" she asked idly.

Evie had to think about it. "I shop at a number of flea markets. I could make it look as though I paid more for something than I did, then pocket the cash difference."

"Small amounts, but do that often enough, it adds up," Ann agreed. "Or stop buying that five-dollar cup of coffee every morning and pocket a thousand dollars in a year. I suppose there are dozens of ways to come up with cash. Which one of them handled the family finances, paid the bills?"

"Susan did. Her bank job suggests she

liked numbers and was good at accounting."

"Start with her. Things she bought for herself, not Joe or Scott."

Evie pulled over files she'd pored over the day before, but it was like trying to walk through setting concrete. Her mind wasn't absorbing any of the details. After thirty minutes, she shook her head. "We'd be better off going to see a movie this afternoon, clear Grace out of our heads."

"I'd like to simply go cry," Ann said. "Are there any good teary movies playing right now?"

One of the numbers on Gabriel's phone list was a movie theater in town. Evie pulled out her phone. "You want to go see *Mrs. Rushville*? PG-13, and reviews say it's guaranteed to make you cry. Let's see . . . it starts in twenty minutes."

Ann pushed away the file. "I'll need Milk Duds or something to go with it."

Evie smiled. "I can deliver on that. Come on, I'll drive."

"I'm going to freeze in that car of yours."

"It's got a heater that could melt a glacier. You'll be fine."

Evie sent a text to Gabriel that she and Ann would be at the movies, hoped he wouldn't think it entirely frivolous. "You want to split a large popcorn too?"

"Sure. Maybe I'll eat more of it than the lunch."

Evie nodded. She was on vacation. She wasn't going to feel guilty for helping a friend. If ever someone needed a break, it was Ann. *And I wouldn't mind one either,* she thought as they climbed into the convertible.

Gabriel Thane

Gabriel saw that Josh had brought his camper out to the farm — a place to stretch out, a table for eating, a bathroom and shower if needed. Josh could impose a break on the search when he thought it warranted. *A very smart move. No need for Grace to step foot in that house.*

Gabriel parked beside Josh's truck. He could see Josh and Grace walking a ways behind the house, the dogs roaming ahead of them. It looked like they'd covered the east side of the house. Red flags marked where the dogs had gone on alert. Not many, but enough that the ground was going to be yielding something. If any secrets, that was another question.

Gabriel took a shovel to the first flag and began to turn over the dirt. He found bones down about a foot, cleared aside soil with a

252

gloved hand and recognized a raccoon, surprised it was buried so near the house. He dug another foot around it and two feet further down to confirm it wasn't simply a deceptive covering over something else, then refilled the hole, picked up the flag, and moved to the next one.

He listened as Josh occasionally called out to his dogs, changed their search path, but Gabe didn't disturb their progress, working flags well back of where the dogs were searching. If he found something that might be human, he would quietly refill and back off the location until Grace was no longer on the scene. Then he'd call in the specialists who would carry out the crime-scene work.

He turned over four holes, finding only chicken bones, wiped dirt off the end of the stakes, and took them back to Josh's truck. Before the search was finished, he figured he'd dig up a few hundred spots. He moved toward the garage and the next flag. He needed a long-handled shovel if he was going to be doing a lot of this. He'd stop at Will's for one before he came out again tomorrow.

His phone chimed with a message. Evie and Ann were going to a movie. He smiled. Evie's idea rather than Ann's, he guessed, and a very good one. Someone needed to be able to pull them back from the quicksand they were in. Evie was about the only one still able to stand without being swamped by it all. He sent a text back: *Good. Next time it's you and me. GT.*

Within the hour, he was done with the marked flags. He settled in the passenger seat of his truck to read a book, forcing his mind to disengage from the recent activity while Josh and Grace continued to search. He needed the distraction of a novel to take him out of this place and the weight of the day — his version of a movie.

He didn't remember much of what he read, but it did feel as if the tension came down a notch by the time he heard Josh whistle the dogs in for the day.

Gabriel thought about joining them as Grace and Josh toweled the dogs off and brushed their coats free of accumulated burrs. But he saw they were having a conversation, and Grace looked visibly stressed. The best end of this day was to get it over with and leave.

Once Josh had loaded the dogs in the truck and Grace took the passenger seat, Gabriel walked over. Josh came to meet him. "Any change to the plans?"

"No." Josh glanced back at his truck, offered a low, "She's stubborn about doing this herself. We'll be out tomorrow morning, start sweeping the pasture."

"She knows her own mind on how she feels about everything, what she needs to do."

Josh grimaced. "Yeah. Anyway, I'll try to convince her to get some dinner with me, but at the moment she just wants to go back to the motor home. So that's where we're heading. Then I'll take the dogs back to the house, get them settled."

"The day's over. Consider that a win, Josh."

"Not much of one, but I hear you."

Josh headed back to his truck, and Gabriel waited until they had left before taking a final walk around the search area. He wanted to see if anything in the terrain caught his attention — sometimes a faint depression might have been overlooked.

Satisfied, Gabriel looked at the time, determined he would be back in town shortly after six p.m. He'd find Ann later for a conversation, but for now assumed she would be meeting up with Grace. He'd get himself something to eat, confirm the rest of the county was quiet. Something always needed his attention, but if it was critical, the dispatcher or a deputy would've called.

He'd stop by the office, clear away what couldn't wait until morning, leave the rest.

He took a final glance around the farm. A monster had lived here. That terrible truth hurt deep inside him. He'd deal with it because it was what being sheriff required. But it would never fade entirely, this ache for a different history for Grace, her parents, for what might have been.

EIGHT

Joshua Thane

Josh walked up to Grace's motor home shortly after seven p.m. The evening light was rapidly fading, but he didn't need the flashlight in his pocket yet. He found folding chairs set out, a decent fire going in the ring. Evie and Ann were there. Grace was sitting in the chair nearest the motor home, her feet stretched out in front of her, a brown bottle dangling from her fingers. Root beer, he was relieved to see.

"Grace."

She tipped her head his direction. "That would indeed be me."

He narrowed his eyes at her tone as much as her words, scanned the bottles on the ground under her chair, realized she must have started with a beer before Ann and Evie arrived to shift that choice to something else. Such a slight woman, with not much of a meal today . . . she'd be feeling it. Given he'd watched her tense up as they walked around that house, knew her memories were running dark, he wasn't entirely surprised. He'd had an inkling the day would end badly, and he could sympathize with her reaching for some way to forget. He'd hoped Ann and Evie would be the answer, but it looked as though they were simply cushioning Grace's tumble. He so wanted to help with the pain she was in, yet he didn't know how. "Come watch a movie with me, Grace, share some popcorn."

"I'm good here. Join us, Josh."

"I'm thinking you maybe need some dinner too."

"Marshmallows are around here somewhere."

He hunkered down beside her to be at eye level, smiled. "Maybe not so much the puffed sugar," he replied gently. "How about chicken pasta, with garlic bread?"

Ann, sitting in a folding chair across from Grace, watched them, drinking from a tall insulated cup what likely was coffee. Evie was resting on a blanket on the ground beside the fire, her feet up on a log, staring at the stars beginning to appear. Whatever the ladies had been talking about, Grace still had traces of tears. *Grace's friends are doing what only they can do, crawl inside the pain with her . . . as much as she will let them.*

"Which movie?" Grace said.

"I've got a few dozen of them on the shelf — you'll find something you like."

"Are you feeling sorry for me?"

Grace didn't know Ann had told him about her childhood, so it would take some careful stepping around the question, but this one seemed easy enough. "Yeah."

"That at least makes you an honest man." She tried to tap his chest with her finger and mostly sloshed root beer on him.

He rescued the bottle, mostly full, and set it on the ground with the empties. One beer, he saw in the line of bottles, little food, and a lot of tears added up to a miserable night. "Up, honey. You've been thinking enough, I'm thinking."

She half laughed, half hiccupped, and pushed herself out of the chair. Josh settled his jacket over hers, added crushing fatigue to his guess about what was going on. "The change of scenery will do you good, Grace," he said as he led her toward his truck. Ann tipped her cup his direction in thanks.

Coming back to Carin, Grace had taken a long step off the edge at the deep end of the pool, Josh thought while helping her into the vehicle.

"You shouldn't feel that sorry for me,

Josh. I could have told you back then." She was leaning her head back against the seat as he climbed in the driver's seat, and he knew she said more than she realized.

"Somehow I don't think you had it in you at the time," he said gently. "And *sorry* isn't exactly the word I would use."

He noticed she'd started crying again but put his attention on the road ahead rather than comment. He finally said, "You like chocolate ice cream? I might have some tucked away in the freezer."

"Sure."

She'd cry, eat a bowl of ice cream, watch a movie, probably cry some more. It would be an evening he wouldn't likely forget, but it struck him as what she most needed. The stress of being here had to be monumental for her.

"We'll watch a movie, have supper, then ice cream for dessert, and you'll stop thinking quite so hard. I can hear your mind whirling all the way over here, Grace."

She gave him a weak smile. "What am I thinking?"

"In a minute you're going to be thinking about red rabbits, because I'm going to tell you a story you won't be able to resist — about pink elephants and red rabbits and a great big green circus tent."

Her reply was a bit wobbly when she said, "Really? What happens?"

"The circus comes to town," he began, "and the pink elephants escape by pulling the green circus tent right over on top of them."

"Chased by red rabbits, no, blue rabbits. That's a better story."

"Blue rabbits, there's an image. Then what?"

She sighed. "I don't know." She wiped a hand across her eyes. "It's been a bad, very bad, no good day," she muttered, trying to quote a children's book title. "And I've got a headache."

"I just bet you do," he said in sympathy, his hand reaching over to hers. "How about telling me of a day that was the opposite of this one. A very good, extraordinary day."

"My Angel made me breakfast for my birthday."

The way she smiled satisfied him that whatever she was thinking about was a good memory. He hoped it wasn't a guy she was calling her angel. "What did you have?"

"A blueberry bagel with cream cheese, orange juice, strawberries, and some more blueberries." Grace sighed. "A nice break-fast."

"You want breakfast stuff tonight for our meal?"

"Sugared cereal? Like Cocoa Puffs?"

"Hmm, I've got oatmeal."

She made a face, and he laughed. "You still prefer your oatmeal in oatmeal cookies, I expect."

"I remember your mother made the best cookies," she said wistfully.

"She does. We're invited over there for dinner tomorrow night. She loves company, and I bet she'll fix us a batch of oatmeal cookies if I told her you requested it. You could take some back to the camper with you."

"That sounds nice. I have good memories of your mom."

"We Thanes don't mind sharing her."

They arrived at his home, and he came around to help her from the truck. They followed a ribbon of solar lights up to the front door. Steam rose on the lake in the cool evening. He stopped to show her. "I bet you don't see views like this in Chicago." The water shimmered and caught the moon rising just over the trees.

"Oh, Josh, it's beautiful," she murmured. "Like a picture painted just for me."

"Maybe it is, Grace," he said quietly. "It's easy to imagine our Father saying, 'I think my daughter Grace should see something truly lovely this evening,' and arranging that specifically with you in mind." He didn't know if she thought much about God anymore. That would be another layer of sadness if her childhood had robbed her of that too.

She didn't respond except to whisper, "Thank you."

She took a couple of steps back down the path to where the view of the lake was more expansive, and he followed a step behind her. It was a peaceful night, still and beautiful, the sounds in the moonlight beginning to chorus, an owl calling close by.

Josh wondered if Grace would agree to a visitor once she was back in Chicago. He wasn't about to let her disappear from his life for another dozen years. Not now that he knew what she was dealing with. *If ever a woman needed a safe friend,* he thought, *it's this one.* He would be that, one way or another. He'd nudge his way back into her life and figure out what he could do to help. Christmas was coming, a reason to visit.

Back when she was a kid, had she ever risked telling *anyone* what was happening? Ann had said no when he asked her, but he wondered if Grace might have tried but hadn't been believed. The implications of that possibility cut like a sharp blade through him.

She'll be getting cold. Josh went over and caught her hand. "Come on, Grace." He led her up onto the porch, opened the door, and helped her inside.

"Josh?"

"Hmm?"

"Do you like kids?"

"Love them," he replied promptly as he hung up the jacket she'd worn.

"Truly?"

"What? I can't be good with kids and like the outdoors?"

"Then why aren't you married, raising a family?"

His ability to follow her train of thought wasn't improving. "I've been waiting for you," he quipped, one eyebrow raised over a grin.

She gave him a look he didn't need to interpret.

"Okay, so that was the quick answer-in-the-moment. My brother, Will, probably gets there first with Karen, has a bunch of grandkids for Mom and Dad to enjoy. But I figure Gabriel and I are going to get there eventually. I like kids. I like tossing a ball around, putting worms on hooks, being lifeguard when they splash around in the lake."

"So you'd settle down?"

"It's no doubt in the realm of possibility that I *might* grow up that much someday. Not that I'm in any rush."

She smiled. "Now that sounds more like you."

"I'm the youngest. I've got time to consider matters. But I do like kids. They get to have most of the fun in life."

"You sound like you mean it."

"I do. This house is designed so I can build on another section when I need the room for a family." That was true enough — he actually did plan the design around the idea of having a wife and kids one day, though he'd kept that to himself.

"Where are your dogs?" she wondered, looking around.

He could handle that turn in the conversation. "Probably sleeping in the living room on their sofa. We have a deal — they get one piece of furniture in the house, and I don't complain about how they laze around on it, sometimes with their feet in the air."

Grace laughed — shaky, but it was a laugh.

"Through there." He gestured toward the living room. Sure enough, the dogs were there and stirred themselves enough to check out who it was, then went back to resting their heads on their paws. Grace went over and stroked their backs.

The people couch was still neatly arranged with pillows and his mother's comforter. "Make yourself at home, Grace. There are photos on the walls and movies on the shelf, so feel free to browse while I find us some food."

"I'm not much for eating right now, Josh."

"You can have something simple with me then — take a few bites to be polite. Go wander. I've got some pictures of the lake you'll enjoy."

He deliberately left her on her own and headed into the kitchen. He started coffee, reflected a moment, and heated water for tea in case that would sound better to her. She needed to eat, so something that would tempt her lack of an appetite.

He opened cabinets and considered options, opened the refrigerator, and finally settled on fixings for a simple meal. He listened to Grace moving around the living room, recognized the sound of the floorboards as she walked over to the shelves where he had family photos displayed, movies and books stacked. He heard the fireplace doors swing open. Good. She needed the warmth. He'd left it banked, but it should kick back to a good blaze when he tossed on another log.

When he walked into the living room carrying a tray, Grace was curled up on the couch with a movie cued up to the opening credits, a book in her lap. He recognized one from the library, a retrospective on bridges and how they were engineered. "What did you settle on for a movie?" he asked as he put the tray on the coffee table.

"American Sniper."

"A guy movie? A war movie?"

"It's a lot like Will's experience, isn't it?"

"He refuses to watch it with me, though he's got a copy of the film. From the little he's said, I think his experience was more IEDs and exploding mortar rounds than sniper fire, though I've seen that thousand-yard stare at times when he's lost in a memory. Why this one?"

"Maybe a reminder my days aren't so bad now. No one's shooting at me."

"I suppose it's all relative." He handed her two aspirin and a cup of tea. "Take these if you haven't already had something for the headache."

"I haven't." She swallowed the aspirin, sipped the tea. She looked with mild interest at the tray he set on the table. "What are we having?"

"Chicken salad with grapes and pecans, orange slices, and some kind of white soft cheese on crackers. The cashews are if you don't like the other choices. If you give this a try, I'll fix popcorn for the movie."

"Sounds like a bribe to me." But she picked up a plate, served herself a small helping of the salad.

He added two logs to the fire, stoked it back to life. He dimmed the lights for the movie and to better enjoy the fireplace. He dropped a box of tissues on the table in case she needed them and took a seat beside her. "That headache is killing you," he mentioned kindly, looking into her face.

She rubbed her forehead. "Yeah. I hope the aspirin kicks in soon."

"What were you talking with Ann about that made you cry?"

She shook her head. *Okay. Not going there tonight.* He considered her movie choice. "You sure you wouldn't want something else, like maybe Captain America in a merely fictional war?"

"Nope, this one."

"Okay, let's start the movie," he said, picking up his plate. "It's going to be the oddest date I've ever had."

She picked up the remote. "It's not a date."

He took a bite of the chicken salad, then said, "I invited you over, and you came. You're drinking my tea, eating my food, and hogging the most comfortable pillows on the couch. What else is needed?"

"A date doesn't feel sorry for me."

"Good point." He snagged one of the few pillows she wasn't using, propped his feet on the table. He caught her glance. "We'll try this again tomorrow night. Maybe I won't be feeling sorry for you then."

She smiled slightly. "Okay."

"Mom swears my chicken salad is as good as hers."

"You made it?"

"I'm a surprisingly good cook, and not just for things that are headed to my grill."

He smiled when she went back for another helping a few minutes later. He'd get popcorn in her tonight, maybe a piece of pie. She needed the carbs.

She was silently crying again. Josh leaned over to pull the box of tissues closer to her reach, leaned his head back against the couch cushion. She had so much to be sad about, and the tears surfaced whenever she gave herself a moment to think. It was probably as good a movie to cry through as any. War was depressing, and his brother had volunteered for six years. Josh could appreciate Will's sacrifice while accepting his own choice not to volunteer. He himself didn't carry around such bad memories, something he was grateful for. He'd lived a mostly stress-free life, and he didn't apologize for it. But he could appreciate the fact others didn't get that luxury. Grace, most of all . . .

When he realized Grace wasn't going to stop crying, he reached for her hand, held it lightly in case it made her at all uncomfortable. But she left it there. He could provide food, hold her hand, and think up enough "non-dates" that she might eventually get through an evening without crying. And if his heart didn't break sometime during the process, that would be a good thing too. He was close to thinking he'd rather take a bullet than watch her in pain like this.

"Josh?"

He tipped his head her way. "Yeah?"

"Why are you doing this?"

"I don't know."

"You are a strangely honest man."

"One of my many quirky and likable characteristics."

"Seriously, Josh. Thank you."

He tightened his hand around hers. "I am glad to have you back here, Grace, no matter the circumstances. Never doubt that."

"Okay," she whispered.

He turned back to the movie so she wouldn't see his own tears. She had such sad eyes. She had been the best part of his childhood, yet what he'd had was a mirage of the truth, and his heart ached tonight at the realization.

Evie Blackwell

Evie waited until Josh and Grace had disappeared down the road, until the truck's engine was a faint echo and the night insects were humming again, before she said, "Ann, I'm so sorry about your day. Even sorrier it was Grace's too. If that woman doesn't splinter into pieces in the next few weeks, I'll be stunned."

"I'm afraid I see the same thing. I'll call her doctor tomorrow, get Rachel down here for the weekend."

It was getting colder, but the fire was throwing out enough heat to make it tolerable. "You ever have a more difficult time than today?" Evie asked, curious.

"The day the nation's VP was nearly killed would be right up there. But this one rips my insides more."

"Is she ever going to be okay?"

"Eventually," Ann replied, leaning forward to toss another log onto the fire. "She's got

271

friends around her who won't let it be otherwise. I've known several survivors — Ruth Bazoni, Shannon Bliss are two. It will be even harder for Grace, though, because it was a family member."

"Yeah." Evie sighed. "Some days I hate being a cop, and yet at the same time I'm grateful I can stop guys like this when we can find them."

"Key point being 'when we can find them.' We mostly find their victims first . . . and too often *only* the victim."

"You should call Paul."

"He's on his way — he'll be at the airport in about an hour. Our state attorney general needed some of his time, so Paul flew south with him. They'll drop him off at the airport here, then fly the AG on to Springfield."

"Good."

"Our original plans were to fly down together Friday and spend the weekend here, so he's just moved it forward a few days. And you're right — I do need him."

Evie turned to better see Ann. "You like being married, don't you?"

Ann considered the question for a moment. Evie sat up, arms across her knees. Ann finally answered, "I wouldn't trade it for not being married."

Evie found that response revealing. Ann

had been single into her forties. Evie still had a few more years before she'd be at that point. She didn't feel the emotions, the burden, of this case like Ann did, but Evie knew if she stayed in the job long enough, there were going to be situations that would be just as personal for her. There would be days she, too, needed someone to lean on. She just wasn't sure if Rob Turney was that guy.

She lay back on the blanket, propped her feet up on the log again. It had been a truly miserable day. Guys like Grace's uncle corrupted an entire community. This would echo through the town for years. People would wonder who else the man might have hurt. Evie was glad she wouldn't be living in Carin. Leaks about the case would happen, bits would be put together, and the truth would filter out. If it was proved that Kevin Arnett had abducted and killed the Dayton girl, speculations about Grace would naturally surface as a result. *How would Gabriel handle those questions?* Evie thought her job was hard, but his was brutal by comparison.

Not for the first time, Evie thought about why she'd prefer to marry someone other than a cop. Two cops, both with days like this, there wouldn't be any room to breathe.

She needed someone who didn't carry these kinds of troubles home with him. "Ann?"

"Yeah?"

"Tell me to stop thinking."

Ann chuckled. "You could say the same to me. It's a night for it."

Evie went back to studying the stars. Spread out above her, they filled the night sky. She considered praying, but what was there to say? *God, I don't know what to do with my future?* She'd been having that conversation with Him for the last four years. A few decisions on the edges had been made, but nothing seemed like a certain direction.

She knew God was simply letting her have time to think, to decide what it was she really wanted. That was the pleasure of being His daughter. Within wide boundaries, she could choose the path, and God would be fine with her decision.

"You're still thinking too hard," Ann commented, looking over with a smile.

"Ever been so uncertain about something that you ended up not deciding at all?" Evie asked.

Ann didn't say anything for a long beat. "I'm fine with the future looking like today. That's a decision of its own."

Evie looked over at Ann. "I don't want

things to change."

Ann shrugged. "That's a decision. Don't knock it. Oftentimes it's the right one too."

"Why would I want things to change?" Evie agreed.

"It doesn't eliminate answering the questions, since change keeps coming whether you want it to or not. But if there isn't a reason for a change, why do it? I lived a lot of years content with life, perfectly fine with having the future look like the present."

"And then . . . ?"

"Paul showed up. It's not easy, that transition to being married. It can be a disconcerting shift in day-to-day life, but it becomes an 'at home' place of its own, if it's a wisely chosen marriage."

"Better than single?"

Ann was quiet again, then said, "Not better than single, just different. It has its own dynamics. I wouldn't change being married to be single again because Paul is in the equation. But put any generic guy in the picture, I'd probably be happier being single than married. Paul is the reason this marriage is a success. I got very lucky — very blessed — with the guy who chose me."

"You didn't go looking for him?"

Ann smiled. "I gave him every reason I could come up with for us *not* to be more than friends, and he saw something appealing enough in what the marriage could be that he kept pursuing it. It came down to trusting that he was right, and saying yes even though I knew there was risk involved. It felt like stepping off a cliff when I made it, but I don't regret the decision. Never will."

"I wouldn't have figured there was a struggle," Evie said. "Not looking at you today."

"Some days God smiles at you, and Paul was one of those blessings that just showed up when I wasn't looking for it. God is nice that way."

Evie was pretty sure Rob was not her Paul. The man had a lot going for him, but it didn't feel at all like Ann's experience — not that she was trying for the same journey, but she liked the outcome Ann had found. She'd like, in her own way, to end up with at least something like that one day.

Yeah, she was thinking too hard. She went back to counting stars and wondering if they might be God's brushstrokes tonight to keep her occupied.

Gabriel Thane

Restless, Gabriel drove out to the campground just after eight p.m. and found Ann and Evie sitting by the fire. He looked at the dark motor home behind them. "Grace already turned in for the night?"

"Josh talked her into going his way for popcorn and a movie," Evie said.

Gabriel got himself a cold soda and took one of the extra chairs. "I hope it's a good distraction, helps her sleep tonight."

"She needs to get far away from Carin County," Ann remarked. "When she leaves, when this is done, thankfully she won't be coming back — won't again be facing all the memories lumped together like this."

"Josh will be saying goodbye a second time." Gabe sighed, shook his head. "It'll be as hard on him as it was back then, probably harder." He stretched out his legs, looked over at Evie, smiled at the sight she made on the blanket, feet crossed at the ankles and propped on a log. "Nice camping spot. Great view of the stars tonight."

"Come out to see Grace about anything in particular?" Evie asked.

"Mom would like her to come over for dinner tomorrow. Figured I would invite her, if Josh hasn't already."

"That's very kind of your mom," Ann said. "Evie, maybe you could stay here until Grace is back, tend the fire, make sure she's okay? I can take the convertible to pick up

Paul — and I'm putting the top up. Maybe Gabe can bring you back to your place?"

"Sure," he put in, "no problem."

"I'm not planning to move for a while," Evie said, tossing the car keys from her pocket across to Ann. "I'm still counting stars. I hate to leave a job unfinished. Tell your husband I'd like his pancakes for breakfast," Evie requested. "I'm partial to his cooking over yours or mine."

"A wise choice," Ann agreed as she stood. "Gabriel, you and I need to talk soon about Will and Karen."

He looked her direction, blinked, sighed again. "Don't take this wrong, but I'd actually forgotten about them. Text me when you're turning in. I'll call you when I get home if I haven't heard anything from you before then."

"That works."

Gabriel followed her over to the yellow rental to help with the top. He watched her car lights fade, settled back into his chair, listened to the night sounds and finished his soda, enjoying the peace of the moment.

"You don't need to stay, Gabriel," Evie said. "I'm sure Josh could run me home when he brings Grace back. Wander up to your brother's place, say hello to Grace. Josh might be in dire need of help if she's

278

crying again."

"Josh can handle Grace. The best thing for her would be just that kind of open, honest grief." He reached for a long stick and stirred the fire. "He made her a Valentine's Day card, back when he was in the sixth grade. That's what I remember most about Josh and Grace, that sweet crush he had on her. Made me proud to be his brother, even if I did give him some minor grief about having a girlfriend. I mostly wished I had one too."

She smiled. "Childhood days are the innocent ones. We don't see the evil lurking around us." She studied him across the firelight. "You okay, Gabriel?"

He shook his head. "I've been better."

"I bet your dad is having an equally hard night."

"He's got Mom. She won't let the grief overpower him. He didn't know any of this, but it doesn't lessen the pain of it now."

"Your father would have stepped in front of a train for that little girl — both Ashley and Grace. He would have dealt with this hard and fast, if he'd known."

Gabriel nodded and watched the fire. He was grateful that nothing else was needed of him tonight. He felt at his limit.

"Grace *couldn't* talk about it." Evie looked

over at him. "You know that, don't you, more than just the theory of it? She couldn't talk about it or she would have. He'd destroyed her world, her sense of self, so completely that telling someone wasn't possible. She was only six years old. She buried it in order to keep breathing, simply to survive."

"I know it, Evie." He blew out a breath, put the empty soda can on the ground. "My head knows it, but my emotions can't yet accept the fact." He looked over at her. "You have any secrets buried this deep?" he asked idly. "No need to answer that — simply curious."

She lifted the bottle she held, moved it out to arm's length, using it to block stars to make it easier to count a line of them. "I killed my brother." She said it so softly, he almost didn't hear her.

He felt like he'd been hit by a fastball. "You . . . ?"

"I was seven. I gave him my toy plane to play with because I didn't want him to play with my dolls, undo their ribbons, mess up their hair. He ate one of the wheels and choked to death. Our babysitter from that night committed suicide six months later."

"Oh, Evie, I am so sorry. I — I can't . . ." But he couldn't finish.

She tipped the bottle back and forth. "I slit my wrist a year later. It was too painful for me to do the job properly, so here I am."

"Talk about the wrong question to have asked. Have you . . . ?" There wasn't any good way to word the question. "You've been able to deal with it?"

"I don't know. My brother's name was Sam. I called him Sammy. Some days it's tolerable, realizing he's not here, and other days it just aches. They tell you it gets better with time, but mostly it just *is*. 'Accidents happen' doesn't change the fact he's not here. And I caused it."

"How are your parents?"

"Terrified I will die on them too. They abhor the fact I became a cop. They think I have a death wish."

"Do you?"

In the dim firelight he saw her shrug. "I don't know. That a deep enough secret for you, Gabriel?"

"Feeling guilty about something so catastrophic is pretty normal."

"I know."

"Have you told Rob about Sammy?"

"He knows I once had a brother, but no."

"Why not?"

"He hasn't asked about my secrets."

"You're not going to marry him, are you?"

He punched a stick into the fire to have something to do. "Sorry, I shouldn't be prying on that topic. Ann's concerned."

"I know she is." Evie set down the root-beer bottle. "I do fine not answering when I think someone is prying, Gabriel." She was silent for a while. "I don't know. Rob has his flaws. He can be arrogant, and blind to it. He can be overly impressed by people who have money. But he can also be generous to a fault. He remembers names of the janitors, he likes my jokes for the most part, and he puts up with my crazy work schedule with good humor."

She sat up, wrapped her arms around her knees. "I like the fact he doesn't have the details of a single crime to discuss while we're having a meal together. It's nice not dating a cop. He's got generations of solid family behind him, no divorces, a confidence about himself, he's sincere about religion, even if he's — how should I put it? — more showy about it than I am. And he's good to me. There would be much worse husbands to have." She smiled at her own list. "But I'm not sure I want to quit being a cop for the sake of peace with my mother-in-law. His parents think marrying a cop is a bit too downscale for them — you know, blue collar. I don't think they'd ever met a cop before Rob brought me to their brownstone on Chicago's Lake Shore Drive."

Gabriel smiled at the way she said it. "Do you love him?"

"Hmm . . . I can say I *like* him. And for now, that's been enough."

"Is he going to propose, you think?"

She thought about it. "He probably will," she guessed. "He likes to present something as a *fait accompli,* let others adjust to the idea it's been decided, rather than let things develop outside his control. He won't ask as much as presume it's a yes, until he's certain what I will say. He's big into knowing the outcome, saving face. Then he'll want to have that elaborate engagement party, public wedding, make it a big social event."

"Do you want to be married?"

She shrugged. "Some days I do. Like this one — the last thing I want is to be alone, churning through the memories of this day. But being married means big changes, probably kids. I'm not much on making changes." She stirred the fire. "Tit for tat, Gabriel. You have something you consider a deep secret?"

He thought about how to answer, finally said, "I was engaged once."

She turned her head on her folded arms

283

to better see him. "Really?"

"Really. Didn't tell my folks. Eventually told my brothers."

"I'm thinking I might not want to know this story."

"Your choice."

She considered it, then said, "Tell me."

"Elizabeth Sara Doevelly, a literature major, born in Paris, raised in London. I met her in Chicago when she was a graduate student at the same college as me."

"Why the secret, Gabriel?"

"Her parents were divorced, her father a diplomat. He gave his blessing to us marrying, but asked for my word that we would tell her mother first before we told my parents. We made arrangements to fly to London to meet her mom.

"We wanted ceremonies in both America and England" — he gestured with a hand — "wanted to hang the marriage certificates side by side. So we got on the flight to tell her mom, were planning a garden ceremony at her parents' home for that weekend. After a honeymoon in Europe, we'd come back to the States and tell my folks, have a church wedding here in Carin with family and friends. I know that sounds over the top, but we were young, Elizabeth was very creative, and it solved a stack of problems for how to honor her father's request. My parents liked her, they were going to approve of our getting married, so it was a logistics kind of thing. Elizabeth was close to her mother, and it was a big deal for her to have a wedding in London."

"What happened?" Evie asked when he stopped.

"Our taxicab in London got hit by a truck. Two doctors in a restaurant nearby came running. There was nothing that could be done. She was gone nearly instantly." He had thought he could tell it without the pain, but he was startled at how it washed over him once more.

"That's an awful way to lose someone you love, and so close to her becoming your wife," Evie whispered.

His sigh was long. "Yeah, not good. I didn't tell my family we were engaged and that close to being married — they already knew how important Elizabeth was to me. It would have added another layer to their grief for me, and I didn't think either they or I could carry that. I came back, focused on being a good cop, became sheriff of Carin County."

"Is that why you've never married?"

He honestly didn't know. He tried his own shrug. "I am marriage-minded. I like the

285

thought of it. But practicalities have pushed it to the background. I like my work. I don't mind the hours, though some disruptions can begin to irritate. I want to have what I have now, plus something more, and it's not a simple thing to figure out."

"Paul and Ann are interesting to watch together," Evie said thoughtfully. "She still travels a lot, more than you realize at first. But their marriage works. Works well, I would say. There's no sense of distance in their relationship when you see them together."

Gabriel smiled. "Nothing happens in Ann's life that she doesn't tell Paul. That's part of it."

"The other part?" Evie asked, sounding curious.

"Paul has created a safe place for her in his world. She can still be herself inside the marriage. She's understood and welcomed for who she is; he went into the marriage having figured that out before he asked her to marry him. He was smart that way."

"He does that all very, very well — accepting, customizing, loving Ann as Ann."

"Envious, Evie?"

She sighed. "Green with it."

Gabriel chuckled. "Yeah. I can relate."

■ ■ ■

It was eleven p.m. before Grace and Josh returned. Evie went inside with Grace to make sure she was settled in the motor home for the night, Gabriel quietly suggesting she stay until Grace had fallen asleep. He needed a few minutes of conversation with his brother.

"Josh, you want to talk?" Gabriel asked.

"About which part of this horrific day?"

He nodded toward the road. "Let's walk for a while."

Josh shoved his hands into his pockets and matched his stride to his brother's. "She cried much of the evening. The whole thing is killing her."

"She needed to do this, Josh, or she wouldn't have come."

"Yeah. Got that." Josh sighed. "What's a guy suppose to do? Nearly as long as I knew her, this was going on. I didn't have a clue. To care about someone, yet not catch on . . ."

"We were kids, Josh. I have to keep telling myself that."

"So was she."

"Her tears are probably the best thing that could happen."

Josh shook his head. "You didn't see Grace out in those woods this morning, staring at the lake, wondering if a car could be driven over one of those bluffs and not be seen again. There's an anger in Grace that feels . . . well, feels almost physical, and it's an emotion she has nowhere to direct for some closure. It's eating her alive. And this afternoon, just walking that land around the house, she's stretched beyond anything I can imagine with those memories. She can put on an appearance that she's okay, but she's dying inside."

"She's talking with a doctor, with Ann. She's come back here. She's dealing with it, Josh."

"Not very well. I should insist that she not be part of the search. I can tell her I can do it better, faster without her there. Which is true."

"Do that if you need to," Gabriel agreed, "but it doesn't help the inevitable, Josh. If you find an answer — or don't — regarding her parents, she'll have to face it then. Same with any information about the Dayton girl. Grace will have to find a way to come to terms with all of it. We can help, but ultimately it's her journey, one step at a time."

Josh blew out a breath. "There's no way I'll find her parents after twenty-five years

— not unless we trip over the car itself, which isn't entirely out of the question. Otherwise it's finding where the ground has shifted, the graves have worked back toward the surface as trees fall and roots push up the ground. Only under the very best of conditions will the dogs trigger on remains that old."

"You'll do what can be done, and that's what Grace needs. Even if we can't find the remains, I think we talk to her about a small funeral service for her parents, one that she'll remember and will provide some closure. She was two when the first memorial service was held," Gabriel said, "I think she needs another fixed day to say, 'Goodbye, I'll see you in heaven.' "

"That would help," Josh agreed. "Dad said he'd be out at the farm tomorrow morning, take up a shovel for a while. I think he wants to see the place again now that he knows the truth. I'll ask him to take a walk through the house and barns once Grace and I are working the pastureland where she can't see him."

"Good. Anything you need from me, Josh?"

"Prayer for good weather. I don't want to have to stop until we're done."

"Let's do that now." Gabriel put an arm

across Josh's shoulders, asked God for a reasonably good day tomorrow, especially for Grace.

"Amen," Josh echoed.

Gabriel turned to the motor home as Josh headed back to his truck. They would get through this as a family. But it was going to get heavier as it went on.

He smothered the fire in the ring, collected the bottles to recycle, folded up the blanket Evie had used, and stored the chairs. Evie stepped out just as Gabriel finished scanning the area with a flashlight to confirm all was secure for the night.

"She's asleep. I waited a bit to be sure, prayed for her and for the rest of us."

"Josh and I prayed too before he left. There are so many questions, so much grief and anger that's being dug up along with this search, Evie. It's hard to know exactly what to ask the Almighty to do."

"I know," Evie said. "It's a good thing our prayers don't require instructions for God — He knows what each one of us needs."

Gabriel smiled. "Probably better than we can put them into words anyway." He helped Evie settle in his truck for the ride to her place, circled around to climb in himself, hoping the truck's engine wouldn't disturb Grace for more than a brief moment. "Why don't you tip that seat back and close your eyes, Evie? You've earned a few minutes of quiet."

"You don't need to offer twice. I'm exhausted." She did as he suggested, and if she didn't doze, she at least rested. Gabriel caught glimpses of her face in the lights of occasional passing cars. She was turning off her mind, getting some needed shut-eye. If only he could do the same when he got home.

As they drove up to the house, Gabriel saw the convertible in the driveway, a few lights on in the house. Ann and Paul had returned from the airport. He pulled into the drive, and Evie pushed the seat upright, waved him off walking her to the door. He waited until she stepped inside, then pulled out.

Gabriel figured his letter to God tonight would be a short one. He'd already composed it: *God, please heal a lot of broken hearts. GT.* Grace, Ann, Josh, himself, his parents, the Dayton girl's parents — the list of people still in pain tonight, even after many years, was long. *And don't forget Evie. She's carried an unimaginable burden for an awfully long time.*

Gabriel didn't have a text from Ann that she was calling it a night, so he made a call as he drove through the sleeping town. "Ann," he said when she picked up, "I've mentally jarred myself from thinking 'Josh and Grace' to thinking about 'Will and Karen.' I can't say I'm at my best at the moment, but let's talk, if now is okay with you."

"Now's fine. Karen said we could tell Will the story about Tom Lander and the trial."

"I was hoping she'd agree. When do you want to do it?"

"Time doesn't help this, Gabe. Josh finds something out at the farm, the media shows up in town, we can't risk Karen being caught on film in the background of a reporter's statement. Let's get the conversation over with. Wednesday morning?"

"You mean like tomorrow, which starts in about ten minutes?"

"I'm thinking we go see Will first thing. But we begin with what's going on with Grace. You, Josh, and your father knowing what's coming, Will not being in the loop isn't going to work."

"Dad already had a word with him about Grace. We'll go talk with him about Karen. I'll pick you up at the house at seven — if that's not too early."

"Paul will be flipping pancakes by then. Eat with us."

"Works for me. We'll tell Will about this guy Karen is trying to shake, make sure Will stays level-headed, doesn't take off to Chicago to get a look at him. One crisis at a time is enough right now."

"Let's hope."

Gabriel smiled at Ann's tone. "Something has to break our way one of these days, Ann. You okay?"

"Better, now that Paul's around asking me the same question. I'll see you in a few hours, Gabriel."

"Done." He put his phone away. Ann had been smart to get married. He would prefer not to be going home to an empty house tonight. *God, do you have a marriage in my future? Because tonight the idea rather appeals.*

NINE

Gabriel Thane

Dragging a bit from lack of sleep, Gabriel arrived at the house on Kearns Road at seven o'clock the next morning. He noted the security team's car in the drive, traded nods as he was recognized. If he'd had any questions about Paul Falcon being on-site, he had his confirmation. As head of the FBI's Chicago office, the man had no choice about the security that traveled with him.

Paul opened the door, wearing dress slacks and a white shirt — no jacket yet, but the cuff links were in place, his shoes polished. Paul wore authority comfortably and it showed. "Come on in, Gabriel. I'm in the kitchen following instructions I got from the women last night." The two men chuckled, and Paul glanced at the stairs. "They aren't down yet."

"Ann fall asleep again?"

"I made sure her feet touched the floor before I came down. It's more likely there's a caucus going on that doesn't involve us guys."

They moved into the kitchen, where Gabriel accepted the mug Paul offered, drank the coffee with appreciation. "You're looking good, Paul. Marriage and running the Chicago office appear to agree with you."

Paul turned the heat up under the skillet, poured in pancake batter. "I'm helping Matthew Dane train for the Boston Marathon, and it's got me in the best shape of my life. You, on the other hand, look a bit . . . rough," he decided after a scan, but his grin softened the words.

"Bad day yesterday," Gabriel said.

"I heard." Paul flipped the pancakes, got out another plate, stacked them, and pushed it over. "Not a thing you could have done about it, Gabe, nor your father."

He chose blueberry syrup and selected several pieces of crisp bacon from another plate. "We both know there are men like Arnett out there, with victims left in their wake. But you don't expect them to be next door. We were childhood friends with Grace. It's overwhelming to me — to all of us — that we didn't see it, didn't help her. Even worse is not knowing how to help her now."

Paul slid a glass of orange juice Gabriel's way. "Ann and I didn't see it either, not at first. Rachel knew something was back there, would have said it was likely since her training picks up on that kind of trauma. But until Grace wanted to talk, it wasn't a secret that was going to surface. Grace started trusting her doctor four years ago, let Ann in two years ago. She's made progress, but I'm with Ann — I don't think Grace is ready to face head on what she's decided to do. This is going to be brutally hard on her."

"Josh said she cried most of the evening with him."

"That's probably the best thing she could do at this point. She stops letting those tears show, then it's time to get worried." Paul picked up a piece of bacon. "Ann said you're heading over this morning to see Will, tell him about Karen."

"That's the plan," Gabriel replied as he switched focus, equally concerned about how that conversation was going to go. "We'll tell him about Tom Lander, talk about the plan if and when the guy shows up around here."

"Now that's a man I'd like to see tossed in jail with the key dropped in the Chicago River," Paul said. "He's slick, smooth, dangerous, and deceptive clear down to the core. A chameleon who appears innocent of everything until you peel back the skin and see the viper underneath. He enjoys his rage-driven violence and the destruction he leaves behind."

Gabriel listened to the summary, knew that coming from Paul it was, if anything, understated. "My goal is to avoid a day Tom Lander and Will Thane come face-to-face."

"A reasonable goal," Paul agreed. "Maybe Lander never locates her, and this problem is theoretical. But if he does learn she's in Carin, your best defense is probably a strong proactive offense. Circulate a photo of Tom Lander, let it be known he's a person of interest. Gas stations, hotels, campgrounds — he'll get here sooner or later, and you've got contacts and friends you can use in a home-court advantage. Put some Thane money on sightings of him. Set it up before it's needed. He comes to Carin, he has to drive here, fly, he has to stay somewhere. Covering airport and rental cars should be relatively easy. Lodging is broader, but he'll likely stay at a hotel. He's not an outdoor camping kind of guy. He shows up, you promptly hear about it."

"An interesting suggestion, Paul," Gabriel said, visualizing how just such a campaign across the county might function.

"I've been thinking about this for a while. Chicago PD will eventually get enough to prove Tom Lander murdered his ex-wife. On our side, we're trying to build a case related to his past business dealings — I don't care if we put him in jail for tax fraud so long as we get him behind bars. In the long term, eventually, inevitably, he'll do something we can arrest him for and get a conviction. Time should help this problem get resolved. My concern is whether that will come soon enough for Karen.

"But for now, the Chicago PD is keeping an eye on him. He leaves Chicago, I'll hear about it, and you'll hear about it immediately. I figure even if he shows up in Carin, it's not catastrophic if you can get Karen out of sight. He might believe she's in town, might even have her working at the café. But if he can't see her, can't find her, she's still safe. You just have to keep her hidden away until he gives up. I'm certain there are places all over this county you can hide her comfortably."

Gabriel agreed. Hiding someone was relatively simple around here. Given the number of family friends he could tap, Karen could stay on any number of properties where no one could approach without being tagged long before they reached the house.

Paul leaned back against the counter. "You can get even more creative, Gabe. Tom hires a local PI, turns out the guy's rather slow and not very good at his job — as he also happens to be working for the Thane family. And while Tom Lander is occupied here, Chicago can get very inconvenient for him. I happen to know the person buying the building he's leasing for a new business — he's hung out a shingle to enter the exterminator business. We can give Lander reasons he has to be back in Chicago. A problem with the building. License issues. Employees quit on him for greener pastures."

Gabriel smiled. "I like the way you think, Paul."

"He got away with a double murder, he terrorized a witness, he killed his ex-wife — between Chicago PD and FBI, there are a lot of people motivated to see Tom Lander shut down. You won't be fighting this alone."

Gabriel considered that, finished the orange juice, studied Paul. "Ann's given the impression there's very little to be done if Tom Lander finds Karen here, except to move her far away."

"I make a point never to disagree with my

wife, and in this case, I actually don't," Paul responded. "I just think there are some things to be tried before that outcome. You don't leave Karen open to his attack. You keep her out of sight, keep those she cares about beyond reach. But within those parameters, there are options."

"I'm realizing that, Paul. I'm glad you came down for the day." Gabriel heard footsteps on the stairs and turned as Ann and Evie joined them, both looking a lot more alert than he felt.

Ann greeted Paul with a kiss, a whispered word. Evie tactfully looked away, caught his gaze. Gabriel smiled, and her answering one was tentative, maybe a bit flustered, as she glanced away from him.

Ann picked up a glass of orange juice. "Sorry I'm late, Gabriel. I'll take breakfast to go. I can eat while you drive."

"We can spare ten minutes so you can eat a civilized breakfast."

Ann filled her insulated cup, rolled up bacon in a pancake, waved toward the door. "This is how I enjoy Paul's breakfasts more mornings than I'll admit. Let's go deal with Will, get this day started. Who's with Josh and Grace today?"

"Dad's handling the shovel this morning, Will after that. Evie and I are heading to

Decatur to have lunch with the Florist family doctor at noon."

Ann nodded. "A packed day all around. Evie, while we're talking with Will, how about taking Paul by the post office, get him up to speed on the Florist case, see what he notices? He's good at finances."

Her husband winced, and Ann laughed, gave him a hug. "You really are, it's just geeky grunt work. Gabriel will drop me off there, and you can pay me back by explaining — in copious detail — what you've found."

"Now that sounds like a deal," Paul said. "Gabriel, take care of my girl."

"Plan to. Come on, Ann. For some odd reason, Will tends to be an early riser."

"Yeah." Ann grabbed her jacket. "We should be about an hour."

Gabriel nodded goodbye to Paul and Evie and followed Ann out. He was hoping nothing else in the county needed his attention today — no car wrecks, domestic calls, farm accidents during the last of the harvest, school fire alarms pulled in jest. It would already be a long, intense day without the normal problems of being sheriff crowding in.

Will Thane

Sitting on the steps of his back porch, Will Thane broke a strip of bacon in half and held the pieces out to the dogs on either side of him. Apollo nipped the snack from his fingers, swallowed it in one gulp. Zeus sniffed first, bit the top edge, tugged it free, and swallowed it. Will looked at him with amusement. "Took you long enough, young man." He reached over and scratched the animal behind the ears, got a thank-you lick to the face. Evie's dogs were getting comfortable with him.

Apollo subsided to watchful resting, his attention on the barn cats leaping over each other in the backyard, if you could call three acres of open prairie a backyard. Will kept the walks neatly trimmed, but the rest of it was native grasses. He could do without the snakes, but the chipmunks and mice, rabbits and possums, the ground-nesting birds all making their home in the grass attracted eager four-footed and winged prey and kept the snakes' numbers under control.

Apollo leaped from the porch to the ground, took off like a dart. A rabbit burst from cover, slipping underneath the shed just in time. "I'd say those bruises are healing," Will said under his breath, watching Apollo lope back to the porch. His own two

302

dogs were likely down at the pond, pointing birds even though Will wasn't there to appreciate their skill. The four animals had been enjoying each other's company.

Will heard the car before it turned onto the crushed gravel of his long drive, watched it crest the rise and saw its distinct squad-car markings. *Probably Gabe bringing Evie out to collect her dogs,* he thought, with not a little regret. They were war dogs trained to search out explosives, he'd realized after trying the handful of Dutch words he learned from dog handlers in Iraq. That they were retired while still relatively middle-aged suggested they'd lived through some close explosions and been medically discharged. They seemed calm enough, though he wouldn't want to be shooting off a firearm near the two. For a cop to have adopted two of them made it likely they were war buddies, accustomed to being together. He was glad they had each other in civilian life.

A combat medic for a lot of years, he still missed the guys in his battalion. He'd done a solid job over his six years, had the medals to prove it. He'd left because it was time, but he missed his buddies. He hugged the two animals on either side of him, affection for them running deep. Dogs had been part of those years overseas, mostly German shepherds like these two. "That your mom coming to get you, fellas?"

The car pulled around to the front of the house where he kept a neatly mowed patch of grass and flowers alongside the walk. He heard car doors slam, said *go ahead* in Dutch, and both dogs bolted from the back porch. He followed them around the corner.

The dogs were leaping up to greet Gabriel. But it wasn't Evie Blackwell with him. Will paused, held out his hand with a smile. "Ann. Hello. I heard you were in town." She'd become an important friend to his brothers while he was away. The news about Grace his father had told him the night before likely explained her visit now. A hard thing, what his father had told him, and a harder thing yet, what Grace was asking Josh to do.

"Will, good morning," Ann said. "We need to talk with you about something. It's related to Karen Lewis."

The way Ann said it had him narrowing his eyes at her, then looking to Gabriel. He recognized the expression on his brother's face — sheriff's resolve crossed with a large slice of empathy. Will had promised his mom to clean up his language now that he was home or he would have expressed his feelings in the words first to mind. Will sighed instead and walked up the front steps to open the door for his guests. "Come on in. Coffee is hot."

He'd made a deal with himself that he'd make no major decisions in the first three years back in the States — a homecoming gift to himself, and so far he was honoring it. Come year four, he planned to build a larger master bedroom onto this place, ask Karen to marry him. Then he'd start blue-prints for a few more bedrooms. The land was spacious enough to raise half a dozen kids, with room for outdoor forts, golf carts, bikes, horses, some sheep and cattle. Karen wanted kids too, he'd already discovered.

Karen Joy Lewis had a way with her smile that reminded a man of what was good in life, and a joyful woman was high on his wish list. He figured he'd fallen for the crepes coming out of the restaurant kitchen, then spied the woman making them, and tumbled a bit further the first time he was able to catch her eye and get that flash of a smile before she looked away. Karen would be a delight to have sitting at his table for the next fifty-plus years. He'd rival his dad for being a contented married man.

Whatever Gabriel and Ann wanted to talk about concerning Karen, he needed coffee in hand first. "Watch the construction zone." He was getting ready to gut the living room and dining room to redo the electrical and put up new drywall. "The kitchen half is finished. Come on through."

The updated kitchen had counters long enough to make a professional chef envious, with double ovens, a large range, and a wide-screen TV to keep him company while he worked at the center island.

Will pulled out a chair for Ann, let his brother get them coffee, pulled out another chair so he could see the back porch and open the patio door if the dogs wanted to come in. "What do we need to discuss about Karen?"

"Do you remember a trial up in Chicago," Gabriel began, "a few months after you came back home . . . restaurant owners, a couple, stabbed to death?"

Will shook his head. "It wouldn't have stuck with me even if I'd seen something in the news about it." He accepted the mug of coffee Gabriel handed him.

Ann laid a folder on the table in front of him. "I pulled three articles from the *Chicago Tribune.* The first report is on the crime, then the trial in progress, its verdict. Take your time reading. It's easier this way."

"Easier for who?"

"Me mostly."

Will pulled out the articles, found them in chronological order, and began to read, assuming it related to Karen. Given the look he saw pass between Ann and Gabe, he wondered if Karen was maybe the daughter of the victims.

She'd come to town with some kind of trouble in her past, he knew. He'd seen soldiers who had lived through years of war and recognized a similar look in her eyes at times. Given that sadness, he was careful in how he asked about the past so as not to stir the pain. He was content to enjoy the present he had with her and let her talk, or not talk, as she preferred.

He got his first real surprise in the second article, reading about the trial. As he made the connection, he said in a low voice, "She's the witness."

"Yes."

He glanced over as he heard Evie's dogs return to the back porch, settle back into a watchful waiting. He turned the page in the article, kept reading. "Karen Josephine Spencer," he said. "Now, that's a nice name." Karen Joy captured her personality, but her birth name was pretty cool too. Nice and regal, that Josephine. He smiled at the thought and moved to the final article.

He scowled at the headline. *"Not guilty? Are they nuts?"*

He read through to the conclusion, looked up at his guests. "The jury agrees he probably did it, but they let him walk on two violent murders because they didn't think Karen's testimony was enough to make it beyond a reasonable doubt. Did they *listen* to her? She's like the nitpicker of precision in everything she says. She won't say white when its cream, won't say a few hours when she means two and a quarter. She's so precise, I joke about it just to get that smile of hers."

"They didn't believe her," Ann said softly, watching him. "She found that bewildering, Will. Devastating. She's become even more cautious and precise in what she says because of it."

Will dropped the articles back on the table. "Okay, you've showed me stuff about the trial. Karen obviously decided to wash her hands of Chicago and find somewhere else to settle, use her skills as a chef elsewhere. What's the problem? I get the name change. That's common sense. Why bring gossip with you when you can change your name and not have people asking you lame questions about what happened?"

"Tom Lander."

"He's here giving her trouble?" He was on his feet before he finished the question. "Where is she now?"

Ann cast a look at Gabriel, already blocking his brother's path.

"What? Come on, guys, spill it!"

"Karen's likely working the first shift at the Fast Café as she does most Wednesdays," Gabriel replied easily. "Lander is in Chicago. He doesn't know she's in Carin County. Sit down, Will, we need you to listen."

Will dropped back into the seat, picked up the coffee mug to have something in his hands. "Fine. Just make it the Cliffs-Notes version."

Ann nodded. "He's an extremely violent man who terrorized Karen for the sport of it, then stabbed to death his ex-wife. Maybe simply to send a message."

Will closed his eyes and rolled the mug between his hands. "Okay. Got it." He looked from Ann to his brother. "You're still the sheriff, right? You're carrying a gun? What's the problem? He shows up, you deal with him."

"You know it's not that simple, Will."

"Of course it is. You're the one who makes the law difficult, Gabriel. I'm like, that's a *good guy,* that's the *bad guy,* now let's go deal with business."

"Yeah." Gabriel smiled, and it was a look Will remembered from their childhood.

"What?"

"I don't need a soldier messing up my town."

Will snorted. "I'm retired. Am I not up to my armpits in house construction, barn construction, baby animals, and Mom's fussy pansies?"

Gabriel laughed. "Mostly, yes. You've also got a shooting range out back, and don't bother telling me those illegal M-80 fireworks I hear go off occasionally aren't you blowing up coffee cans to see how high they'll fly."

"Those were legal when I bought them a decade ago. You should have confiscated the leftover spare box."

"Boys."

Will and Gabriel both looked over at Ann.

"Back to the problem at hand. Karen Joy."

"Did you come up with her new name?" Will asked. "Nice job, if that was you."

"It was her idea, but I like it too. She's worried about you, Will."

"Karen? Why?" He groaned. "Oh, I was teasing her a bit about being a soldier guy. She'd been ragging on me that, as a medic, I was more nurse than soldier. And I protested it was more like Rambo with a first-aid kit. Did she take that the wrong way? I didn't mean to spook her, Ann. It wasn't —"

"Will, shut up," Gabriel said, but his tone was kind.

He stopped talking, not because of his brother but because his gut was churning. He'd scared the girl he liked more than anyone he'd met in his life, and she was wondering if he was a violent man like this Chicago guy. He'd often complimented her that she was a really good chef, but occasionally jested that he was good with a knife too. What an *idiotic* thing to have said. He was feeling sicker by the minute.

Ann's hand came over to rest on his arm, and she squeezed, tight enough to force him to look at her. "Chill out, Will. *Please.* She likes you, more than a little. I'd say she's halfway toward being in love with you."

He sucked in a breath, let it out. A smile then spread across his face. "Really?"

Ann looked at him with a humor that went back years. "What is it with you Thane men? You're hung up on Karen, Josh is still hung up on Grace, and Gabriel would be hung up on someone around here if he'd let himself, and you're all stunned that it might be reciprocated. My advice, Will? Put a ring on the woman's finger, settle down, have some kids. Life would be so much easier on the females around here to not have you three all still available."

"Ann, I thought we were here to talk about some cautions," Gabriel said, stepping on her statement to pull it back a bit.

Ann smiled. "I'm changing my mind. Do you see Tom Lander causing problems for anyone Will cares about, that between the three of you brothers and your dad, you can't effectively halt in its tracks? Look at this place." She gestured toward the backyard. "Tom Lander hasn't seen more than a patch of manicured grass and a few neatly kept trees in his life. He couldn't get near here without being bit by a few snakes, find some dogs sniffing around him with bared fangs, or finding an M-80 tossed at his feet to move him along. It would be a collision of worlds so far apart he'd be lucky to leave the county in one piece. Although what Karen would think of living out here is a mystery, but that's another question."

"She's coming around to the view that a town with a couple of stoplights is too much traffic for her; country life sounds more appealing," Will calmly replied.

Ann laughed, then turned somber again. "Seriously, Will, you need to know Tom

Lander is a nasty, dangerous man, and life stays better for everyone if he never learns Karen is living in this county. If he figures it out, if he comes this direction, you *don't* attempt to handle it alone. You call every family member and friend you have, we create a little war council of our own to convince Tom Lander he doesn't want to be here or have anything to do with Karen in the future. Promise me that? No handling it on your own?"

Will held out his hand. "I'm retired."

She accepted the handshake, and Will smiled, rather than let go of her hand. "Of course, I hear you are too."

She smiled back, tipped her head. "I was afraid you'd mention that."

Will nodded and gently let go. "Ann, I appreciate you telling me all this. It explains a lot of things Karen hasn't said. But we Thanes have a long history of taking care of our own within the law. That's not going to change if Tom Lander shows his face in Carin County." He paused and grinned. "Mostly because Mom wouldn't like it, Karen might not either, and life is more pleasant when a guy is in good graces with his mother and his girl."

Ann leaned over and kissed his cheek. "Thank you, Will."

He felt himself turning red and went for a change of subject. "Does Evie want her dogs back? Because they're comfortable here and welcome to stay another week, if that would help."

"I can tell." Ann nodded toward the back porch, where Evie's two dogs and his own two were now lined up in their own pack, studying the backyard for interesting movements. "If you can keep them for now, it's appreciated."

"They're fine here," Will repeated, pushing back his chair. He had a place to be and it wasn't here. "Karen was worried what I was going to think?"

"Some, yes."

"She didn't flinch when I told her I tumbled out of a helicopter once on purpose, so why does she think this was going to bother me?"

"She's a woman. We tend to let such things bother us."

Will laughed at the way Ann said it. "I'll set her mind at rest on this topic, you can be sure of that. Gabe, I want a photo of Tom Lander, along with his bio. It needs to be spread around town that I'm looking for the guy and paying a nice reward to anybody who calls me with a sighting. I've got a few favors to call in. He won't be showing up without me hearing about it."

"I'll get you the photo," Gabriel promised. "We'll be talking more, Will."

"I expect so. I'm going to stop by the café for a late breakfast and a Karen coffee break. Anything you want me tell her, Ann? Not tell her?"

"Tell her to enjoy the day and not to worry about the past, present, or future."

He smiled. "I can do that. For both of us."

Gabriel Thane

Gabriel looked over at Ann as he pulled out of Will's driveway. "That did not go as I expected. You caved, Ann, like two minutes into the discussion. I thought we were going to head him off —"

"I forgot who Will is," Ann cut in with a shake of her head. "And wisely, I think, changed my mind." She turned reflective. "Seriously, Gabe, are you worried about Will meeting up with Tom Lander?"

Gabriel thought about it. "Not really, no. That guy has been terrorizing civilians who don't know how to fight back. He'd get the shock of his life if he tried to threaten Will or someone he cares about. You don't take the soldier out of a man once you've trained it into him. You might temper it a bit, but it's still there."

"He's a good, capable man," Ann agreed.

"If it didn't sound like Karen was headed toward marrying Will, shifting to a life out here, it would worry me a bit more," Gabriel said. "Being in town on her own makes her much more vulnerable. She's a lot safer once she's married and her life is in the middle of us Thanes. We've a tradition of moving in and out of each other's lives. We'd all naturally be able to keep an eye out for her safety."

"Exactly," Ann said. "I'm thinking the best place for Karen is where she can have a good life and good future, and I couldn't draw up a better solution than the one she has here. We make it work. Whatever it takes, we adapt, draw the line here, and make Carin work for Karen." She smiled at the rhyme of her words.

"Suits me fine," Gabriel said with a smile. "But if Tom Lander steps one foot outside Chicago, I need to be the second call."

"I'll make that happen," Ann said. She shifted her seat back, closed her eyes against the morning sun.

Gabriel thought about his conversation with Evie the night before, his own thoughts on the drive home, and shifted the subject. "Grace had a hard night."

Ann murmured her agreement.

"I know you're keeping her confidences, Ann. I'm not looking to trespass there, but anything Josh can do — the rest of us in the family can do — to help Grace, you're the bridge. We're floundering right now."

She was quiet for a long moment before she said, "You already know what to do, Gabe. Don't treat Grace differently from others. If you can smile without sadness, hug without a hesitation, joke about Josh's crush on her in grade school without thinking twice about the remark, you'll do more toward helping her heal than anything else you could do or say."

She turned her head toward him. "I don't know how you do that, but you all need to figure it out and give her that. Be yourself. Treat her as if she can and will be normal again. Give her the gift of seeing past this and treat her accordingly. She can't imagine that for herself yet. It has to be friends who paint that picture for her, give her permission and space to recover, to reaffirm she will heal, that the past doesn't have to come forward into the future a day further than it has. She's going to be beyond these crying waves when she's done the unpacking of the memories, but it's a three- or four-year process, and she's pretty much in the middle of it now."

"This is nearly as hard on you as it is on her."

"Being friends of a victim is its own particular kind of weight. I wouldn't ever want to be left in the dark, not know, not be that friend. I know we'll survive, Grace and I, because I've done this journey before. But sometimes that knowledge just makes the days heavier. I can anticipate the coming terrain and the mountains and valleys ahead, which sometimes only makes it worse."

"I can understand that, Ann."

"Do you? You need to know something else. Grace really hasn't let me in that far. I know she's in great pain, processing unimaginable grief. I know she's facing some first memories, her mind bringing up fresh ones like toxic bubbles rising in a hot spring. I know she's getting struck by painful emotions striking her in unexpected ways. The smell of an aftershave making her vomit is the latest one. But I know that only because I've seen the signs rather than her telling me." She shifted in the seat with a sigh.

"After the abuse ended," Ann said, "Grace got seven years of a surface kind of peace, and then the past washed up like a tidal wave. She's getting badly buffeted right

318

now. She'll survive it, she'll get back to an authentic rest, but it's going to be years of work. She's dealing with the past the hard way, pushing way too fast through it. I ache watching her make the attempt. As I've said, this isn't how I would have had this unfold. And if we find the Dayton girl's remains on that land, I honestly don't know how Grace will keep breathing through it."

"If you can't ease her away, you help hold her together. You help her crumble in a controlled and safe way."

Ann nodded. "Yes. Mostly. I just don't know what day and time Josh plants that flag, one of you turns over that dirt, and we see what we fear is there."

"Do you want the Dayton girl to be found?"

Ann shook her head. "No. And that's sad, because as an officer of the law, it's the thing I should most want — closure for the Dayton family. But for Grace . . . if she could walk the farmland with Josh, they discover nothing, she sells the land and moves on, that's probably a better outcome. She needs hours of sharing trivial things with him, sharing memories from child-hood, talking about life in the decade since they last saw each other. The interaction with Josh about their shared past will maybe give Grace a new layer of memories that can be useful. When she thinks of Carin, it isn't just the devastation of life with her uncle."

"I see what you mean, Ann. The memories have to be made more manageable, and Josh providing other memories from their childhood might help with that."

"I think it will." Ann looked his way again. "How's Josh doing? He's bearing the brunt of this. I should have called him last night."

"He's shaken but determined. He wants, *needs,* to help her. Like the rest of us, only more for him, I think. It's eating him alive that he didn't see the signs of trouble."

Ann nodded. "If there were any to be seen — that's what you should tell each other. You need to caution Josh about something. She has to be willing to risk talking with a guy about this. So far she's only told women. She has to risk a small comment, get a reply, and find out a man can get through it without viewing her as damaged beyond repair. I don't know if she'll choose Josh to be that guy, or she may first turn to Paul, but she'll eventually decide on someone.

"I can't coach Josh on what those words should be, because I don't know them," she said after a moment. "It's a guy's reaction she needs. It may be anger over what happened, or kindness towards her, or a hand touching her arm when she tells him something awful. I don't know what she needs. I just know it's something she can't get from the women in her life. When it's the authentic reply of a male who cares about her, it's going to matter. Warn Josh so that if she ever does say something about it, his best move is not a nod and then silence."

"He'd be relieved that she opened a difficult subject, and he'll handle it okay. But I'll talk with him about it anyway."

Ann nodded, accepting Gabriel's reassurances.

"Paul's staying in town for the day?" Gabriel asked as they turned into Carin.

"Yes. We'll fly back tonight late, return this weekend with Rachel — at least that's the current plan."

"Come to dinner tonight at my parents' place. It'd be nice to have everyone there."

"I'll ask him," Ann said. "You're doing okay with Evie?"

He was surprised by her question. "Sure. The doctor thing at lunch today, we wouldn't have that if she weren't so curious about matters and dug it out. I'd given up on the Florist case having an answer, but maybe Evie is right. The person who did it can still be found. She's got me hoping again we can catch a break in the case."

Ann smiled at his answer. "Not exactly what I was after, but it'll do for now." He pulled up to the building where they were working. Ann stepped out and then leaned back into the vehicle. "Let's assemble here after dinner with your family, talk the case through with Paul before we leave," she said. "You, me, Evie, your dad. We'll have whatever your lunch appointment turns up, and maybe Paul will have something from their finances."

Gabriel agreed. "I'll have most of the interviews done by end of the day too. We'll do that, Ann. Thanks for your help with Will. The conversation went better than I hoped."

Ann smiled. "He's going to be fine — he's a Thane. See you later, Gabe."

Karen Joy Lewis

The familiar sounds of the restaurant were soothing to Karen — the clatter of dishes and pans, the called-out order tickets, the two others working with her prepping soups for the lunch menu and watching over the fryers as fresh donuts were turned. She worked in the rhythm of it, not having to think about specifics, simply cook and pull

322

together great-looking plates of food. It was her domain, if only for this shift. It felt like home.

"There's a gentleman at the counter who would like to say hi when you have a moment."

Karen nodded her acknowledgment and flipped a perfectly cooked second crepe onto a plate. It was out to the customer just seconds later, filled with strawberries and topped with freshly whipped cream. *Nothing from a spray can in this restaurant,* she thought, satisfied. She peered into the dining area and saw Will Thane sitting at the end of the counter, opening a packet of sugar to go in his coffee, scanning the menu.

She felt herself stiffen a bit — not because she wasn't glad to see him, but because she couldn't tell if he'd had a conversation with Gabriel and Ann yet. When she'd agreed to let them speak with him about why she was in Carin, she'd taken a very big risk. Will was going to have something to say about why, for over a year, she hadn't told him herself. She didn't want to lose him right now . . . or ever.

She felt her hands turning sweaty and slippery on the skillet handle, forced her attention back to the next order. She filled orders for another twenty minutes before handing off the kitchen to Jimmy while she took her break. She washed her hands, hung up her apron, took a quick glance in the restroom mirror, tucked a strand of hair under her cap, and forced herself to walk out into the dining area. She greeted several regular customers at nearby tables, then took a seat on the stool next to Will.

He was working his way through an omelet. "There's a good cook working here," he said around a bite, the familiar grin helping her insides to relax a bit.

She smiled back at his teasing comment. He liked her cooking, and she appreciated the compliment. That was how he'd first introduced himself, offering a sincere compliment for a good meal. The café was not the big-city Italian restaurant where she'd been able to showcase her skills, but in its own way it was a comfortable setting and nice change of pace.

Will held out another fork and slid the plate toward her. "Eat some of this omelet. You don't get to sit and enjoy your own cooking that often."

She'd been too nervous to eat breakfast that morning, worrying about this first encounter with Will after he learned the truth. She ate a few bites, braced for his voice to drop, to tell her quietly that they had to talk.

But Will was signaling the server, ordering a cup of tea, doctoring it the way she preferred, placing it in front of her. "Want to go fishing with me this afternoon? I can pick you up after you get off work. Josh says the bass are fattening up for winter and snapping at anything that moves on the surface."

He doesn't know yet. No way he'd sit here this casually if he knew. She struggled to keep her voice even. "I could do that."

"Good." He leaned over and lightly kissed her. "Pick you up at three at your place, unless you call to say you're somewhere else."

"You're in a good mood today," she commented, forcing herself to keep the tone light as she turned to face him.

He smiled that slow smile of his. "It's been a nice day — actually, a very nice day — and it's just getting started. Gabriel and Ann gave me some news. About time you let me in on those secrets of yours, Karen. Here I was wasting worries that you had a former boyfriend someplace you preferred over me. You're cooking any fish we catch after I clean them, but a bakery stop I can handle. You want me to pick up apple pie or cherry?"

She blinked, tried to think, went with the

last item because that was the only one she could remember. "Cherry."

He leaned over to say next to her ear, "Don't worry so much. I think you're by far the most interesting catch in all of Carin County — maybe throw in Chicago too." He kissed her again, slid off the stool, and dropped a twenty on the counter. "Back at three."

Eyes damp with tears, she nodded, watched the blurred figure walk to the door, wave goodbye. *No shadows with this man.* It hadn't changed what he thought about her. She felt a quiver inside and fought back the tears that threatened to overflow.

She was sure they would talk more while they fished, *though not much, knowing Will,* she concluded with a little smile. Ann wouldn't have sugarcoated matters. Gabriel certainly would have understood all the implications, been blunt about what it meant for her . . . for him. But Will had heard the news, come to find her, mostly to tease a smile out of her. He was confident in who he was and what he could do. Where she saw life-threatening danger, he saw an obstacle that could be overcome. She felt her heart quiver again. She was a lucky woman.

She surreptitiously wiped her eyes, slid off

the stool, and took her tea with her, feeling nearly dizzy with relief. She'd been braced for a breakup, for Will to pull back and say they had to talk, that this news changed things for them. But he hadn't drawn back, not even a little. *That is so like the Will I've come to know . . . and love.*

She could have offered to meet him at the lake, but he'd explained early on that when it was a date, he'd come to get her. He would always take her home, walk her to the door. He didn't want her thinking she wasn't worth the effort. He'd arrive with flowers too, sometimes picked from his own property. But mostly he overpaid at the florist to get them presented properly. She let him do it because it said something between them that might not yet be ready for words. He was telling her she was important, and when she accepted the bouquet, she acknowledged that his interest was welcome. *A nice courtship in small gestures,* she exulted as she tied her apron and turned back to the kitchen. She had gotten so very lucky — *some would say blessed* — when Will Thane walked into the Fast Café looking for a meal and spotted her.

"You doin' okay, Karen?" Jimmy asked as he stepped back from the grill.

"Oh, yes, thanks — I'm good." She

pointed to the next order slip, and he passed it her way.

A great guy was coming to pick her up in a few hours. The day had gone from her being braced for bad news to as carefree a one as she could remember in years. It was indeed turning into a *very* nice day.

TEN

Gabriel Thane

Gabe had planned to use their drive to Decatur to get his mind shifted firmly back onto the Florist case, but he was finding it difficult to concentrate. Evie was doing a better job of it, working down a lined notepad with a list of questions they should cover during the luncheon.

"Read me the ones you have so far," Gabriel said. Evie did so. "You'll be the one asking them," he recommended.

Evie shook her head. "No, he's going to respond better to interactions with you. You're Sheriff Thane, the authority in the room."

"He's a psychiatrist with experience working with cops. He counsels couples and families, Evie. I'm thinking he'll expect to give facts to me, and the 'why' of something to you, assuming a woman cares more about the emotional side of a situation. He'll be more inclined to give you at least hypothetically speaking answers, rather than 'I can't comment' statements."

"A decent point, but I'd still rather you ask the questions." She grinned over at him. "Rock, paper, scissors?"

"Not while I'm driving. Flip a coin."

She found a quarter in the center cubbyhole. "Heads or tails?"

"Tails," Gabriel called while the coin spun in the air and landed on the floor at Evie's feet.

"Tails."

"You ask the questions," Gabriel replied, pleased.

"Then you'll have to take notes."

Gabriel winced, wondering if his version of shorthand was up for it. "I hate taking notes — I make my deputies do it." He looked over at her. "Okay, this time I'll take the notes."

She studied the directions and pointed to the next exit. "It will be the second light, a right, and then we look for a gray, stone building about a block down on the left. Parking is just past the building, his assistant told me."

Gabriel nodded. "Give me the CliffsNotes on the doctor again, please."

"Doctor Richard Wales, twenty-three years

in practice, married, two grown children. Gets good reviews from other doctors I know. A level-headed, commonsense guy is the gist of it." She turned her phone so he could see a photo.

"Useful to hear about a psychiatrist." The photo showed enough gray hair, the doctor wasn't vain about his image, and he wasn't so fit he lived on a golf course. Gabriel spotted the building and pulled into its parking lot.

"Don't get your hopes too high," Evie cautioned as they walked toward the building.

He smiled at her. "Now who's being a pessimist?"

"I can identify lots of ideas. Finding the one that goes somewhere means wading through promising leads that turn into dead ends. I don't hit a home run without first hitting a few fouls along the way."

He held the door open for her. "Point taken."

They found the office on the second floor, a receptionist stationed in front of a hallway with several offices to each side and a rather large waiting room with couches and child-sized tables with toys to their left. Gabriel took notice of the inquiry in the woman's expression. Since they were both in civilian attire, maybe a couple here for counseling?

"Sheriff Gabriel Thane and Lieutenant Evie Blackwell. We have an appointment with Dr. Wales."

The woman smiled, rose, pushed a button on her phone console to hold calls. "Of course. I hope you enjoy chicken parmesan — we ordered from a nearby restaurant for your lunch meeting. Please, follow me. He's on schedule today, for a change," she added over her shoulder as she led the way to an office at the end of the hall. They stepped into what could only be his private office, the desk cluttered with files and reading material, a round table at the window cleared and set for lunch. The receptionist motioned toward it. "Please, have a seat, Lieutenant, Sheriff. I'll let him know you're here. I have coffee, iced tea, or maybe a soft drink?"

"Tea would be fine," Evie said.

"For both of us," Gabriel added.

"I'll bring it in. Lunch should arrive in about ten minutes." The door closed behind her.

"A friendly receptionist," Gabriel remarked, holding a chair for Evie.

"No doubt useful when the practice has families with kids coming and going."

The door opened minutes later, and a

casually dressed man matching the doctor's photo walked in, carrying a tray with a pitcher of tea and ice-filled glasses. Gabriel rose to his feet.

"Welcome, welcome, let me get this put down before I spill it." The doctor eased the tray onto the table and held out his hand. "Sheriff. We haven't met, but I admit to having heard your name from clients over the years . . . well, your father's name as often as your own." He turned to Evie and offered a hand. "Lieutenant, I'm told you are the one who called." He pulled out a seat for himself. "Lunch should be here momentarily. My schedule is clear for the next hour and a half — only paperwork awaits when we have concluded our discussion, so we should not be rushed. Would you mind if we have this conversation using first names? I'd rather be called Richard than Doctor."

Gabriel poured the tea and let Evie handle the opening.

"Informal is fine," she assured him. "You're making an effort at welcoming us. I'll admit, it's a bit unusual in my experience with others in your profession."

Richard smiled. "I don't want you to have wasted a journey, and the courtesy of a welcome is the least I can do."

Evie reached for her glass of tea. "We're

here to talk about some previous clients of yours, the Florist family."

"My scheduler mentioned that was the reason for your call." He looked from one to the other. "The Florist name is one that has come up many times over the last twelve years, if only in my own mind," he replied, "as I'm aware of the unresolved search to locate the family. You are welcome to record this interview if you would find it helpful. My only request is that if you do so, you provide a copy of it for my files."

Evie glanced over at Gabriel. He had no difficulty reading her reaction to the doctor's opening remarks — heading toward unsettling. But she nodded to the doctor, dug in her bag, set a recorder on the table.

Gabriel was glad for it. He'd take notes as a precaution if the tape had technical problems, but it saved him the effort of getting the nuances right.

Richard reached for his tea. "Some ground rules, so you understand my position. You both realize I can't reveal what was discussed with a patient. While I would like to help you, and will endeavor to do so, my answers will be limited to what the law permits me to say. I shall try to be tactful when I say no and will apologize for the fact it may have to be said a great many times." He offered an engaging smile. "With that on the table, shall we begin?"

Evie simply smiled back. "Would you confirm you saw the Florists, individually and as a family, for a period of approximately two years, and that they were still clients who had a standing Wednesday night appointment when they disappeared?"

The doctor nodded. "Yes, I'll confirm that. I'll also mention that family dynamics often require sessions with all members present, even if they are themselves not the actual client. But in this case, Scott, Susan, and Joe Florist were each my clients. I had at least one individual session with each member of the family during the time in question, and at least one family session with all three present. The Florist family had a two-hour block of time on my calendar every Wednesday evening, which would occasionally go longer since they were the last appointment on my schedule. I would add too that the time frame is broader than two years."

"Would you confirm Mrs. Florist sought counseling for a miscarriage?" Evie asked.

His expression turned grave. "I can't answer that. But, hypothetically, it's an area in which I have years of clinical experience. My wife and I have suffered three miscarriages during our marriage, so she'll occasionally join me for a conversation should that be helpful in a particular situation."

"Did Susan and Scott Florist ever meet your wife?"

A slight smile. "I'm afraid I can't answer that either."

"Did Joe Florist ever play video games while here, using one of the computers on these premises?"

Richard looked surprised at the question, but nodded. "Yes, both as a reward for his participation and as a diversion when one or both parents needed to be otherwise engaged."

"In your twenty-plus years as a counselor, you have met with numerous couples. Would you consider Scott and Susan to have had a solid marriage? Communication was good between them, the marriage stable enough to go the distance?"

"I can't answer that in particular, although I can say in general I found them less in need of counseling for marriage issues than most."

A tap on the door heralded lunch. Evie pressed the pause button on the recorder and didn't resume questions until they had begun the meal and pleasantries about the food were behind them.

Evie turned on the recorder again and asked a softball question. "When did they first come to you as clients?"

"Scott Florist had been a client since considering a job change to become a police officer, and he saw me on various occasions for other matters. Some of those visits were in accordance with the professional requirements of his workplace, as you would be aware, Sheriff. Susan Florist was a client since shortly before they were married and seeing me on various occasions for matters mostly of a personal nature. Their son, Joe, was a client since age four, seeing me also on various occasions for a variety of matters. I believe I can say without violating patient privilege that death is hard for a child to understand, and that his grandmother, as a matter of public record, passed away when he was four."

Evie nodded at the lengthy answer, gave Gabriel a look he easily interpreted. Too much information could be as informative to a cop as hearing a "no comment."

"Will you confirm all three family members were here at your office the Wednesday before they disappeared?"

The doctor hesitated briefly. "Yes. And before you ask the next question regarding why I didn't call the police with that information, let me first add a caveat and a caution.

"Please don't assume that on any particular night when they were at my office that they were necessarily here for a session themselves. The Florist family had friends among others who are also my clients. The partner of a cop, a best friend, even an ex-wife are all relationships that can have clinical significance. It's not uncommon for such individuals to be invited to join a conversation. One or more of the Florist family were here when it was not specifically an appointment for them."

Evie smiled, nodded. "Right, understood and appreciated. And now, why didn't you inform the police they were here the evening before they disappeared?"

He spun his fork a couple of times, watching it turn, then looked back at her and answered with obvious care, "I believed at the time of their disappearance the information about this appointment was listed in both Scott and Susan's calendar, and the authorities would be in touch in due course during their investigation. When time passed and I was not contacted, I came to believe Scott and Susan had concealed these sessions and the trail was not apparent in their records. It was a dilemma I chose to resolve

338

by honoring my clients' wishes as defined by their own actions. If they didn't choose to tell someone about the sessions, they had reasons, which I had to deem valid. I admit to having wrestled with that decision many times since."

Gabriel decided to ask the next obvious question himself. "Do you believe you have information relevant to the Florist family's disappearance?"

The doctor looked over at him, laid down his silverware, and steepled his fingers. In a rather overdramatic way, the man could convey significant *gravitas* merely with his body language. Gabriel found it useful also to realize the man couldn't lie any better than a child. For an instant it looked like the doctor was going to attempt to sell them a no, but he clearly changed his mind and simply thought for a while before proceeding.

He gave a rueful smile, then replied, "Patient confidentiality severely restricts my answer, but I do wish to be as helpful as I can. It won't do either of us any good if I say no at this point. Allow me to attempt a reply in a broad way. I know of events that occurred, which affected this family and caused them to seek my help. I don't know if those events had any bearing on their disappearance. I want to say they did not, but the fact is I would not be surprised to learn they did." Like a professor in a lecture hall, he held up a restraining finger when Evie started to respond.

"I'm willing to say this: I have closely followed the news regarding the search to locate the Florist family. I have read newspaper articles and seen television coverage. I can say with some certainty that the names of individuals which came up in conversations with the Florist family are known to the police. Names I heard referred to during our sessions I have read about in the newspaper." Another pause. "A caveat that this would be adult individuals. Names of children which might have come up, friends of Joe, for example, would be more . . . nebulous, shall we say?" He turned to Evie. "Now, please, your question."

She cleared her throat. "Are the events they discussed with you — which led to them coming to see you, or which they otherwise brought to your attention as being of concern to them — also known to the police?"

He considered her question for a good long while before answering. "In broad parameters, based on newspaper accounts, I would say yes. The details discussed might be different from the news account, or might not have been mentioned in the news account, but the events themselves were in the news. The private matters I am aware of affecting this family have not become public, and I am severely restricted in what I can say about those."

"A two-hour-plus session every week seems like a significant amount of time, even for a family. Wouldn't one hour be more standard?"

"They traveled a distance. If it's not practical to see a patient two or three times a week, then adding time to a single session is more efficient than trying to make clinical progress in simply one hour a week."

Evie tilted her head slightly, pondered that, and began to lead him with how she worded her next question. "You believed clinical treatment in this instance required a two-hour block of time every week?"

"Yes."

"In your clinical opinion, was two hours a week still necessary after two years?"

"Yes."

She looked over her list of questions, then at the doctor. "Did you then, or do you now when looking back in light of events, consider any member of the Florist family a danger to themselves or to others?"

He hesitated. "Let me answer it this way. The law requires I report someone who is a present danger to himself or to others. I did not report anyone."

"Do you have knowledge of a member of the Florist family committing a crime?"

His body recoiled slightly as he said firmly, "I can't answer that question."

"Do you believe Scott Florist killed his family?"

His eyes flared with heat, and he leaned forward and replied in a hardened voice, "No. The same answer to the question for Susan or Joe."

She quickly threw in another one. "During that final Wednesday session, a day before they disappeared, did you become aware of anything that had recently occurred or recently changed, which raised a concern in your mind or suggested to you in any way that a member of the family was in crisis?"

"I'm sorry, I can't answer that."

Evie set down her pen and changed tactics. "Were you surprised when the Florist family disappeared?"

"Very."

"What do *you* think happened to the family?"

"I think they were going on vacation to

give themselves space and breathing room for three days, and something tragic occurred, about which I have not an iota of information."

"Where were you on the night they disappeared?"

He visibly relaxed. "Right, I know you must ask that. I have a rotation at Decatur Mercy Hospital every Thursday that ends at midnight. I'm the specialist on call and was in the ER during part of the particular evening in question. When I was originally waiting for a visit from police investigators, I checked my calendar to confirm this. I've kept that assigned slot for going on twenty years, since my wife works the same shift in the neonatal ward. From Thursday midnight to Sunday midnight, we both go off duty, off call, and have a personal life."

"Did one of your other clients in any way harm the Florist family?"

He winced. "I can't say, though it's an interesting question for you to have thought to ask. Hypothetically, I would answer it as a no."

"Thank you, Richard. Those were my key questions."

The doctor relaxed, but Gabriel wasn't finished yet. "Tell me, Richard," he said with a disarming smile, "what *should* we have asked, hypothetically speaking or otherwise?"

Evie picked up her fork to finish her lunch and signal the formal interview was over. Then she gave Gabriel a look that told him the actual interview was just starting. They still had forty minutes to get something useful from the doctor without being obvious they were on a fishing expedition.

The doctor first offered a comment to Evie. "Your list, Lieutenant, seemed very well-thought-out to me, if aggressive, in its assumptions about the family."

"If I don't ask, I won't know," she replied with a smile.

The doctor smiled back. "Yes, I can see your point."

"Was Joe good at playing that video game . . . DDM?" Gabriel asked, looking for something innocuous to start the conversation moving again.

Richard looked perplexed that they knew which game it was, then nodded. "He had a competitive streak. He'd come with notes and a plan of attack, do a victory dance when he made another level. I can appreciate a young man's enthusiasm for competition," the doctor replied.

"Did he like playing baseball?"

"Sure."

"Swimming?"

"At times."

"I've been trying to understand him," Gabriel said, "to figure out how he might have reacted to trouble happening to his parents. Was he the type to try to intervene, to freeze, to try to run, hide, or — ?"

"Hypothetically?"

Gabriel shrugged. "Sure."

"I would say if he were a typical boy with a desire to be a cop like his father, he would act in ways he thought his father would approve. Of those choices you gave, he'd intervene before he thought about what might be better or wiser to do given his age and size. He should run and hide, but that would not be what his father would do, so he wouldn't consider it for himself at first."

"That's useful. Thanks."

The doctor nodded.

"Would you say Scott Florist was a good cop?" Gabriel idly posed.

The doctor grimaced. "To not answer that is to imply something I wouldn't want to convey. He worked for your father, you saw him on the job. You would be more able to judge his abilities as a cop than I would, as all I would have to go on would be statements he made about his own performance."

"I'll accept that." Gabriel rephrased his question. "Did he consider himself to be a good cop?"

"I can't answer that."

"Did he consider himself to be a good father?" Evie asked, curious about the doctor's reluctance on a seemingly innocuous subject.

The doctor hesitated. "I'd say that everything Scott Florist did in life could be captured in his desire to be a good father, a good husband, a good cop. He might not live up to his expectations for himself, but he made a sincere effort to do so. He was a deliberative man."

Gabriel picked up on that choice of words. "Deliberative, you say . . . as in thoughtful about what he would do? Or he planned in advance what he would do?"

Small hesitation, then, "Both."

"I'm guessing you also saw them around the holidays, birthdays, that kind of thing," Evie mentioned.

"Yes."

"Would you consider them a frugal family or a generous one?"

The doctor smiled. "Hypothetically speaking, they were like any typical family — presents went on credit and got paid off afterwards with a touch of regret about the amounts. That's not based on specifics, just a sense."

"Did they ever discuss with you stopping the weekly sessions, go to every other week, once a month, that kind of thing?" Evie asked.

"No."

"The events that brought them to your office, would you say the family was in crisis when they initially came to see you?"

He paused again, seemed to come to a decision. He nodded. "Yes. *Crisis* is an appropriate word."

Evie shot Gabriel another meaningful look. Here was where they needed to press. Gabriel lobbed the next question to the doctor. "Did the events that brought them to your office affect each person equally, or was one the center of the crisis and the others supportive?"

"I can't answer that."

"Do you feel family members were honest with you during those two-hour sessions?" Gabriel asked.

The doctor gave a small smile, even as he sighed. "That's a powerful question. I'm sorry, I can't answer that. I wish I could."

"The disappearance of the Florist family shocked the community and led to a massive search and investigation," Gabriel went on. "You have decades of experience in this job. Looking back, do you think the events that brought them to your office left a person out there angry enough to have killed the Florist family?"

"I can't answer that."

"Hypothetically, if you *could* answer it."

"People are affected by events — the person involved, but also their family and friends. How much something matters to a person not involved in the actual event is always a matter of degree."

"Someone with a degree of separation from the event might have a reason to kill the Florist family," Gabriel said, making it a statement. "Would you agree?"

"In a general sense, that would be true, yes. In this specific instance, I don't know. The person involved in the initial event is dead and is not the one you would be looking to find."

Gabriel caught Evie's quick glance.

The doctor rubbed his eyes. "And since you just recorded that, let me add that as far as I know, there is no family or friends of the deceased who would have taken up the cause on his behalf against the Florist family. Believe me, I've considered the matter carefully. If I thought this was your solution, I would have been in touch with the authorities many years ago."

The doctor looked at Evie, then over to Gabriel. "You know I deal with the police on a routine basis. I'm not naïve about violent crimes and those who are likely to commit them. But I can tell you there is no line I can draw from the events I know about to someone killing the Florist family. There is no person I know about or suspect might still be out there angry enough to kill the Florist family."

"Richard, please. They're gone. Give us what we need," Evie said quietly.

He considered her for a long moment, nodded. "Joe and Scott told me different stories regarding the same event, told me consistently the same contradictory stories for two years. Scott believed Joe did something. Joe believed Scott did something. I ended up believing both of them. They were both telling me the truth as they knew it."

"Did Joe or Scott kill someone?" Evie asked.

"No."

"No question in your mind?"

"None."

"Were they worried the other one had?" Gabriel asked, picking up the thread Evie was tugging.

"Yes."

"Who's dead?"

"I can't answer that."

"Do the police know the person is dead or are they just missing?"

"There's been a funeral."

"The father thinks his son killed someone, the son thinks his father did. Who did kill the person?" Gabriel asked.

"As far as I know, that question remains open."

"We're talking about Frank Ash, aren't we?" Evie asked.

The doctor merely shook his head. "I can't answer that."

Gabriel looked at Evie, got a slight shake of her head in reply to his unspoken question. "I appreciate you telling us what you did in confidence, Richard," he said to the doctor. "We've looked at the Frank Ash murder and believe a family member of one of his victims likely shot him. There are two boys who have admitted to being molested by him after he was released from prison."

The doctor nodded, looking tired. "Joe wasn't one of them, based on what he said. He might have been had things turned out differently. He had a close call with Frank Ash, but he wasn't lying to me about something that crucial. He was younger than Frank Ash would have preferred, given that age-preferential offenders are often rather selective. I believed Joe at the time. Nothing since has changed that assessment."

"Scott didn't kill Frank Ash?"

"No."

"Joe didn't kill Frank Ash?"

"No."

"Susan?"

The doctor smiled. "Thank you for that. No, she did not."

"Did they know anything about who did kill Frank Ash?" Evie asked.

"No. Which is why the son and father were at an impasse, not able to believe each other. Not knowing who killed Frank Ash, just that he was missing, they each believed it of the other. The discovery of Frank Ash's body was a huge deal that final week. The fact his remains were found behind the truck stop convinced Scott his son wasn't involved. The fact he had been shot three times surprised them both. No one wanted the results regarding the Frank Ash investigation more than these two. They both thought there would be answers by the time they came to see me the following week. Concrete information about who killed Frank Ash was going to be a breakthrough for their family, would solve the tangle the father and son had gotten themselves into.

The plan to go away for a weekend camping trip was a relief valve while they waited for results, for the cops to come up with the one who had done it."

Evie said, "If no one in the Florist family killed Frank Ash, regardless of what they had suspected of each other over the years, there would be no one associated with Frank Ash who would have reason to take revenge and kill the Florist family."

The doctor nodded. "Which is why I never contacted the authorities. There is no person out there angry enough over what happened to Frank Ash to take the huge risk of murdering the Florist family. Their involvement existed only in what Joe and Scott thought the other had done. I'm sorry. I've basically given you a rabbit trail down a hole that goes nowhere."

"Nothing in that final Wednesday session raised a concern with you?" Gabriel asked, letting his doubts show. "Scott and Joe were both relieved Frank Ash's body had been recovered? Both were looking forward to seeing you the following week with whatever the investigation would have found?"

"Scott was visibly relieved," Richard assured Gabriel. "That the body was found behind the truck stop some distance from their home convinced Scott his son couldn't have been involved. And that Ash was shot rather wildly three times in the chest, and it appeared to be with a .22, got Joe to agree that such a shooting would be very unlike his dad, who was trained to shoot in tight groupings and only owned large-caliber handguns. Scott expected forensics to run the slugs, match up with a gun, and find another case that would put a name to who had killed Frank Ash. They needed that name.

"Scott was the one to suggest the camping trip. He wanted Joe to be assured his dad wouldn't be near the autopsy or the recovered bullets, wouldn't be around to taint the evidence, so his son would believe him when that evidence confirmed it hadn't been him. It was important for the father and son to start rebuilding trust between them, and that was the point of the camping trip, to start that process in earnest."

Gabriel was willing to accept that the doctor had talked himself into this version of the final Wednesday session with the Florist family. Gabriel also thought the whole thing was at best a major headache in the making. However this proceeded — figuring out who killed Frank Ash — would now be on the must-solve board. He shot a look at Evie and could tell she agreed they had all they were going to get.

Evie stood and offered her hand. "Richard, I want to thank you for the conversation. It has been helpful, if only to understand what was on their minds that final week."

He smiled and rose, shook her hand, obviously trying to regroup, no doubt mentally rewinding the tape on all he'd shared. "I do wish you all the best in finding out what happened to the Florist family. Frank Ash is what brought them to my office and why they continued to see me until they disappeared. But I can't figure out a reason they were killed that could link to Frank Ash. Whatever did happen, it is truly a tragedy."

"It is that," Gabriel agreed, shaking the man's hand. "We both appreciate your time."

Evie clicked off the recorder and slipped it into her bag with her notepad of questions.

"Do you have a headache?" Gabriel asked, pocketing his wallet after paying the parking fee.

Evie looked over and laughed. "I was about to ask you the same question. Please tell me there are effective pain-killers in our near future."

"I'm in desperate need of them. Lunch was good, but that spider web of an interview left me spinning like a trapped fly. I'll find a pharmacy."

"We passed a 7-Eleven at the first stoplight."

He nodded and soon pulled in. Evie unfastened her seat belt. "Back soon. Caffeine or decaf for your soda?"

"Make it caffeine — it's a fairly long drive."

She returned and generously passed over the first two Tylenol from the bottle before she palmed a couple for herself. "Please protect me from doctors who don't want to say too much, who know a lot more and are bursting to say what they actually know."

He laughed because he actually followed her description. He swallowed the two Tylenol with a drink of orange soda. She sipped at a grape one for herself. "Sum it up for me please, Evie."

"Joe has a bad encounter with Frank Ash, he's not molested, but it's too close. His dad learns what happened. Frank Ash goes missing. The son, horrified, thinks the father killed him. The father, knowing he did not, thinks the son did. Classic impasse, each scared witless that the other one is the culprit. Hence the counseling the father seeks for the son, and the son's willingness to stay mum about that weekly counseling to protect the father."

Gabriel nodded. "Thanks. If only the doctor had been willing to give us that summary when we sat down with him, we could have enjoyed lunch and pondered the next two obvious questions."

"And those are . . . ?"

"Who *did* kill Frank Ash, and does that have any bearing on what happened to the Florist family? And back to the top we go. What *did* happen to the Florist family?"

She didn't answer right away, but she finally said, "Their disappearance probably had nothing to do with Frank Ash."

Gabriel reached over and tapped her soda bottle with his. "But what a tangle we will have to unravel to prove that fact. You need a new crime wall, Evie. We have to solve who killed Frank Ash."

She shook her head. "Only if I get stuck on other ideas will I go down *that* rabbit hole. I'd rather prove they hit a deer."

"You've already disproved that."

"They could have hauled the animal with them, stopped for repairs somewhere, been carjacked, or truck-jacked, to be more accurate —"

356

"Evie . . ."

Big sigh. "Fine. If unraveling the Florist case means first solving the Frank Ash case, we'll go there. But think about it, Gabriel. Two boys who admitted to being molested, the working assumption was someone in one of their families likely killed Ash. That gives you . . . what, about ten names as candidates, going out to their cousins? Unless one of those ten names also had a problem with the Florist family, we've already reached a dead end. It doesn't matter which of the ten people killed Frank Ash. It doesn't help solve the Florist case. It's an unrelated crime."

Gabriel reluctantly agreed. "We just had lunch and a fascinating interview and insight into the Florist family's internal workings, and it has nothing at all to do with their disappearance."

Evie raised her soda in agreement. "It *was* a great idea on my part. But zip for payout." She shifted in the seat and got out her sunglasses. "I think we could solve the Frank Ash murder, but no matter what name you put on it from the candidate pool, that doesn't do anything for the Florist family. And regarding their disappearance, we're still talking murder?"

"It fits what evidence we've got."

"Okay. Say a vigilante-type kills Frank Ash for molesting a boy. He doesn't then kill a deputy and his family. It goes entirely against type. Unless you think Scott Florist knew what was going on with the boys and did nothing about it?"

"He was a straight cop," Gabriel said, shaking his head. "If he even *suspected* something, he'd be all over that."

"So . . ." Evie shrugged. "We have unrelated crimes. Which is what Ann told us yesterday. A pedophile who likes young boys is murdered. A pedophile who likes young girls dies in a hunting accident. And the Florist family disappears. Three years, different victim sets, different MOs. All unrelated events."

Gabriel sighed. "I'm simply tired of thinking about it right now."

Evie smiled. "Want to stop and see a movie on the way back to Carin?"

"Don't tempt me. Technically I'm on duty until six p.m. — not that I ever get to *not* be sheriff and ignore the calls."

"Whereas I'm actually on vacation — no one will care if I go see a movie when we get back."

"Don't rub it in," Gabriel suggested, amused.

Evie laughed.

"Tell me another joke or two." He wanted something other than this case to think about, and Evie providing reasons to laugh suited him just fine.

Evie settled back in her seat and spun out her first joke. They passed the time sharing humorous stories and reasons for a chuckle or two.

Gabriel let himself relax. *Paul was right, Evie can shift the weight of the day to the side and embrace laughter with ease.* It was one more thing to admire about her, and he was grateful he was on the receiving end of that today.

ELEVEN

Evie Blackwell

Evie slid the package of Oreos down the table to Ann, passing them right under the Nerf football being tossed from Gabriel to Paul with an occasional lob to Gabriel's dad, Caleb. The guys "thought better" while in motion, or so they claimed. The dinner with the Thane family had been relaxing, and for Grace's sake no one had talked work. But now they had regrouped at the post office to end the evening.

It was coming up on eight p.m. Wednesday night, late enough that Evie was mentally following longer strands of ideas, growing less cautious about which of them she decided to share with the group. The Florist case had turned into a concrete wall. *Painful.* "Review for me again, what did we learn today?" she asked over the minor din.

Gabriel answered as he caught the football from Paul, shot it over to Caleb. "Father and son spent two years tying themselves into knots over the fear the other had been involved in Frank Ash's murder. The discovery of the body at the truck stop seems to have relieved that stress. Scott hadn't done it, and given where the body was found, he no longer thought his son, Joe, could have done it. So knowing he had a relationship to rebuild with his son, he suggested they go camping for a few days. That fact itself is useful to know. Up until now, we thought the camping trip had been planned further in advance. Turns out the decision to go camping was made that week. So there's even less opportunity for someone to hear about it, and come up with a plan to harm to the family."

Evie nodded. "Good point."

Paul hustled over to catch a bad throw, added, "We also know cash was being squirreled away for the last two years." The ball sailed back to Caleb. "Which makes sense now we know Scott thought for those two years that his son had killed Ash. They were making contingency plans to leave town rather than let their son be questioned by the police should that day ever come."

"You've earned another hat tip for finding proof," Evie remarked. Ann was right — Paul was good at finances.

"It was a challenge," Paul said with a smile. "Susan hid it well. To retire the house debt early, they were making double mortgage payments up until two years before their disappearance. Their checkbook still records the double payment, but the mortgage loan itself was only credited for a single payment. Susan was withdrawing half of it as cash — easy enough with her bank job. Over two years, Susan pulled twenty-eight thousand out of their accounts. If she got that creative, she probably found another couple of opportunities to slip cash out without being obvious. So, say they had pulled out forty thousand in cash. Who knows where they had that money stored? Most likely it was in the house safe, but it didn't hold any cash when the police opened it."

"They could have been killed by someone who wanted the money," Caleb suggested. "Put a gun on the boy, ask the dad what the safe combination is. That would work."

Gabriel was shaking his head. "No sign of violence at the house," he replied, "and that requires someone to know what Susan had been doing. It took our financial guru here to identify the withdrawals twelve years later."

"Also, anyone reconciling the bank cash

drawer at the end of the day would see the regular withdrawals to cash each month," Paul said.

"Any co-worker could see it," Ann agreed, "but wouldn't they assume it was cash for that month? They wouldn't have reason to add up twenty to forty thousand piling up."

"True. It would have to be someone Scott would trust to see inside the house safe, see the money was there," Gabriel said.

"It's family then," Evie said.

Gabriel looked over at her with a frown.

"What?" Evie protested. "It's the obvious answer to who would be around when Scott opened the safe — family, someone he wouldn't think to worry about. Did a Florist family member have serious money problems, then all of a sudden get themselves out of debt? With no signs of violence at the house, it's gotta be somebody who can get next to the Florist family without raising any flags, and who better than an extended family member who needs the money that's sitting right there?"

Those who knew the Florists didn't want to go there, but Evie realized it was the obvious answer. This could have been a family thing — most murders were. Someone wanted that cash and took it.

"No one comes to mind," Caleb said

slowly, "but we'll think on it, Evie. If family came into that kind of money, it's going to leave a trail."

"What about the doctor?" Ann asked.

Evie glanced her way, interested. "Keep going."

"You've got to figure Scott at least had dropped hints he would protect Joe if it came to that. The doctor maybe figures the family's making plans to leave. The family's paying his fees in cash — no checks to him are in the records. He would have reason to suspect they're putting money in the mattress in preparation. And," she said, holding up her Oreo cookie, "one person who did know about the camping trip is the doctor."

Evie smiled. "I do like this thread."

"What does he have to gain from harming the Florist family other than money?" Gabriel asked.

"It might be enough," Ann replied. "If his own marriage was in trouble, or he needed bailing out of a financial problem. It's worth another look at our doc."

"It's worth a closer look," Caleb said. "I like it if only because it's not someone from this county." He threw the football back to Paul, who in a single motion caught it and shot it over to Gabriel.

Evie ducked and held up her cookie in

protest when Gabriel considered sending the ball her way. She wasn't giving up an Oreo to play ball. She decided to lay yet another possibility on the table. "The Florist family disappears. Their bodies are not found. In twelve years of searching, no one has turned up even a trace of their remains, their belongings, or their vehicles. Or the possible forty thousand in cash. At some point it means they aren't out there to find. So let's assume for a moment that they're still alive."

Paul stopped mid-throw. "A big assumption."

"Add to that an even bigger assumption — they left of their own volition. No criminal intervention, no bad guy shows up. The family told their friends they'd meet them at the campground for three days of camping, and then deliberately they don't arrive that weekend."

"They intentionally disappear . . ."

Evie nodded. "We've only got the doctor's word that everything was settling down that week after the discovery of Frank Ash's body. I agree it doesn't seem likely the son was involved, given where the body was found, and the shooting itself — three scattered shots from a .22 doesn't sound like a cop. But maybe something else was in the mix that week that they didn't tell the doctor." Evie pointed at Ann. "You're the storyteller, Ann. They're alive, and they disappeared by their own choice. Run with that narrative. Where does it go?"

Ann leaned back in her chair, thought for a long moment, then slowly nodded. "The family packs to go camping, leaves their home, takes the cash, and deliberately abandons their lives. For now we'll grant they had good reason to do so, tied to the convoluted mess they thought about each other related to the Ash murder. Maybe they ran to avoid an interview, to keep someone from falling under suspicion as a person of interest, to keep someone out of jail. Whatever the reason, it was serious enough to compel this drastic action. The fact the body was found could be the trigger. They'd been making contingency plans for a couple of years, things like the cash. Maybe they had time to prepare last details, maybe it's a rush job on the fly to get away, but the decision is made.

"To establish a new life elsewhere, they'd need new IDs, new jobs. A way to settle in somewhere, blend in. But in the initial days, it's narrower than that. They need a destination that can be reached overnight — the manhunt to locate them will be swift and frantic once they're reported missing, and their faces will be all over state and national news, social media. They won't be able to travel past, say, eight a.m. Friday without taking a huge risk, unless they change their appearances in radical ways and split up. Better to hunker down and wait out the media storm. And it's going to be weeks or months before they're out of range for a possible news story with their photos."

Ann paused, and Evie put in, "Given how smooth and error-free this seems to have gone, I think they had time to prepare those details. To plan how to disappear, and with two years to prepare, what would they be doing during that time?"

"Accumulating cash," Ann said, ticking the items off on her fingers. "Arranging new IDs. Getting copies of school records and doctors' immunization records. Making preventative visits to the dentist and eye doctor. Securing at least three months of prescriptions they regularly take. Seeing family and friends . . . and while they can't say goodbye, they do see them a final time. Probably securing a new firearm or two. They would need new phones; they couldn't use their current ones anymore. New computers too — they can't touch an existing account or online profile. And they can't make it obvious they took stuff with them that wouldn't be unusual to pack for a camping trip. The dad would probably be researching the trip and destination, planning the travel, with the mom handling their clothes and food. My guess is the son wouldn't be in the loop until they were on the road and leaving town. They couldn't risk telling him they're leaving for good. He might slip up, tell a friend or a relative," Ann finished.

"So, what on that list did the three of them actually do?" Evie asked. "There should be evidence if they were taking these kinds of steps."

"Forty thousand is sizable," Gabriel observed, "but it only gets them a year or two, even with careful planning. But since they left behind every asset they had — bank accounts, retirement funds, life-insurance policies, the home and land — that tells me they didn't run. They even left their pets behind. Given they were hauling a camper, if they were leaving for good, they could easily have taken the pets along too."

"Not if they were planning to travel far and fast, didn't want that complication. Not if they were getting on a plane to somewhere like Alaska," Evie speculated.

Paul smiled, and Evie realized she now

had the family leaving town abruptly, leaving behind everything they owned, and catching a plane to Alaska. It was a bit of a stretch even for her.

But Caleb gave her some credit for even that far-out possibility. "Makes sense, Evie, in that it explains why the family or their vehicles haven't surfaced somewhere. Knowing Scott Florist, though, I sure don't think it *sounds* like something he would do."

"It would mean Susan left her mother, who was fighting cancer," Gabriel pointed out. "Scott walked away from a job he was good at, left behind numerous family members. Joe would have had to be trusted not to give anything away in order to keep them hidden. Given all that, wouldn't they have waited for the evidence to develop, to confirm there was a good enough *reason* they needed to leave? They ran too early for all they were giving up."

"A very good point," Evie conceded.

"What if Scott Florist covered up the murder of Frank Ash?" Ann asked. "Hadn't shot him, but moved his body, disposed of it behind the truck stop, that kind of thing? The father thinks he's protecting his son by corrupting the crime scene. Would they maybe have run in that situation? The nice thing about the truck-stop location is that the land behind it is state land. It changes who investigates the murder."

"Okay . . ." Caleb nodded slowly. "I buy that as possible. Scott learns what happened to Joe, goes out to confront Frank Ash, finds him dead of three gun shots, fears his son killed him, so he moves the body to try to protect his son. I could see Scott doing that."

"If either Scott or Joe murdered Frank Ash," Gabriel said, "they had a good reason to run. But short of that, even if Scott moved the body, why take off? He knew about evidence collection, so he's not going to make an obvious mistake. Wait a few days before taking off, but only if the evidence points in your direction. It doesn't make any sense to go before then. They stayed put for two years after Frank Ash disappeared, and then they leave when his body is discovered, but before any evidence is analyzed? Just doesn't add up. No, Scott would wait it out. And Susan would insist they wait because of her mother. They would go camping, get out of easy reach, keep their ear to the ground on details of the investigation, and leave *only* if there was cause."

"What were the dates on the Ash autopsy, the bullet comparison at the lab, those sorts of results?" Ann asked.

Evie looked it up in the files they had brought over on the Frank Ash case. "The autopsy was . . . the Monday after the Florist family disappeared. A look at the recovered slugs happened Tuesday but didn't generate a match in the database. There's nothing in the notes, the investigation, to raise an issue. You're right, Gabriel, why leave before the evidence is analyzed? If you did want to take precautions, why not say you're going on a vacation, then keep an eye on things. Come back if everything looks fine, or keep going only if there's a question. Why run first? They were about to be free of this."

Gabriel nodded. "Say they took off, thinking the Frank Ash investigation would incriminate one of them. They ran before the evidence had been analyzed. A couple of weeks pass, there's nothing that points to them. The Frank Ash case went nowhere. Why not come back to town with a plausible story, return to their lives? 'We went camping, and Scott got sick and gave it to me, so we took another week to recover before driving home.' Keep it vague but consistent, and just return to their lives." Gabriel looked around the little group, saw a couple of nods to that scenario.

"That would make more sense than staying away all this time over something they didn't need to worry about," Ann agreed. "If they're still alive, they let a lot of people they love and who love them remain worried and, finally, devastated thinking they're dead. That doesn't seem like either Susan or Scott."

"We only have the word of family that they haven't been in touch. Who knows who might be lying to us," Caleb said, laying that fact on the table.

"True." Gabriel turned to his father. "But can you really see Scott letting cops do the level of search for the family that occurred here? He'd know what happens if he just disappears. He had options for how they could have left. He could have announced a sabbatical, that they were taking Joe traveling for a few months. Sounds sudden, but he could say 'Susan and I have been talking about it, and we've decided after the recent miscarriage we need that break now.' So they go rather abruptly, then over the following weeks and months give excuses about finding the perfect new place and decide not to come back here. If they wanted to leave town, they could do it in a way that wouldn't leave their extended family in the dark and the cops searching for

372

them. Think about it just in practical terms. If you want to disappear for some reason, the last thing you want is your photos all over the Midwest with overlapping law-enforcement agencies tracking you down. Instead, you'd come up with a reason to leave, as tenuous as it was, and slowly cut ties — a phone number changed, the address is old, that kind of thing."

Evie could see Gabriel's point. "You don't make it so everyone's urgently searching for you if your hope is to slip away," she said. "So . . . they didn't disappear on their own. And they're not out there alive somewhere."

"I'm willing to entertain both those ideas," Gabriel said, "if you can figure out how we look for them. Their being alive certainly is a direction we haven't pursued yet. But realistically, no. I think it's a lot less likely than that the family was murdered."

"Which brings us back to the possibility someone needed the money they'd accumulated," Caleb suggested. "It's at least a new suspect pool to consider, since we didn't know about the money before."

"That's true," Ann said.

Evie got up to stretch. Susan had been close to her mom, had left when she was sick, and she hadn't returned for the funeral. Gabriel was right. It would take an awfully good reason for them to cut those ties so completely. "Maybe there's a way we can *prove* they didn't leave of their own choice," Evie offered. "If they were raising cash, it's likely Scott had secured in advance fake IDs for them. Who in this county or surrounding counties would he have gone to for that? We find the person he paid, we learn the names they would have been using. If we find those names were never used, we can rule out they left of their own choice."

Gabriel looked over with interest. "That's smart thinking, Evie." He then asked his father, "Who made good fake IDs in your day?"

"I'll have to think on it, but Robert Light comes to mind. He might be a place to start, or maybe Chesapeake Bob. They would have done the quality of work Scott would look for. If they didn't make the IDs themselves, they would know others who could have. They'll talk to me."

"Thanks, Caleb." Evie picked up a marker, added the item to the work list.

"All right, Evie," Ann said, "you can eliminate that they left of their own accord if the IDs they acquired were never used. Or if they did go on their own, you'll know what names they planned to travel under. Any other ideas floating out there?" Ann

374

scanned the group.

Gabriel shook his head. Caleb did as well. Evie felt like she was burned out just coming up with this one. "I'm fried." She put down the marker. Ann and Paul needed to be heading to the airport. Caleb needed to get home. Gabriel too. For the fifth day of her working vacation, it wasn't so bad an ending for the day.

"I wish you luck with this tomorrow," Ann said as she stood, gathered up her jacket and briefcase. "Paul and I will be back Friday evening. Rachel is coming down with us to stay the weekend with Grace."

"Sounds like a plan," Evie said. She could see a long Thursday and Friday ahead of her as she tried to put some details to what had been discussed tonight. If they could figure out what new names Scott had arranged to use, prove those names had never been used, it would confirm their murders, with the missing cash as a probable motive. If the names *had* been used, it would indicate the Florist family had left of their own accord, the money with them.

Either way, it would be critically useful toward solving the case. Evie would gladly take it. She said good-night to Gabriel and Caleb, then headed out with Ann and Paul. The vacation house would be quiet tonight with just Evie there, but she was okay with that. She was ready to crash and get some much-needed sleep.

TWELVE

Evie Blackwell

It was already Friday, and Evie didn't look up from the report she was reading as a chair scraped across the floor and Gabriel sat down. He thankfully had stopped whistling that song fragment, though he still made sure she was aware he was coming through the door. "Eat something, Evie. You've been nose to the grindstone for the last day and a half."

She marked her place in the report and glanced up as a plate stacked with tacos slid onto the table. Gabriel looked less put together than usual, his hair windblown, a couple of burrs caught on his shirtsleeve, his jeans dirt-stained. She hadn't seen much of him since Wednesday night. He'd been spending most of his time out at the farm. Evie reached for napkins and a taco. "How's the search going?"

"Josh has the dogs working the animal

trails now. Grace mostly gives a polite smile and stays quiet. She loses her train of thought when she tries to have a conversation. Josh is keeping her moving, which is probably for the best, and making sure to put something to eat in front of her when they do take a break. Consider me doing the same. Eat." He unwrapped a taco for himself. "So, you're still working on the possibility the Florist family left of their own volition?"

Evie accepted that he didn't want to talk about the farm and went with the change of subject. She nodded. "The money withdrawals say they were making contingency plans. They would have had a plan — for the new names, new job references, everything. Scott's a detail guy, you can see that in the reports he wrote, and the doctor described him as 'deliberative.' Scott would want to leave here and establish the family in a new place as quickly as possible. New job, new apartment, new school for Joe. He would have figured out exactly how to do that. He had two years to get the plan in place."

"Dad will find you names for the fake IDs Scott arranged — if they are out there."

"He's trying," Evie said. It didn't follow that the Florists would have squirreled away cash without arranging new IDs. So far, the people Caleb had spoken with were adamant Scott hadn't approached them about the matter. It was likely, though, that Scott would have gone outside the county, even beyond the adjacent counties, to get them made. Scott might have tapped someone as far away as Chicago. It could take some time, but Evie was certain Caleb would find the person Scott had approached.

Gabriel tapped his knuckles lightly on the table. "You need to come at the case from another direction, Evie. This idea is interesting to speculate on, but you've gotten yourself hung up in the weeds."

She raised an eyebrow. "You think so?"

"Lay out how you might look for them once you have the names they arranged, add that to the wall of things to do, then start looking for new possibilities again. You found the counseling connection, Paul found the money trail, you'll find something else. At least until Dad comes back with names you can search. My opinion is they prepared to run, but in the end had no reason to do so."

She ate another taco while she pondered that. She almost agreed with him. She'd given her idea a day and a half and it was losing momentum. "I'll give it a few more hours, then change tactics, see what else I can find," she said.

"It comes back to the basic question, Why go?"

Evie had come up with only one new answer that made sense to her. "A .22 sounds like a lady's gun. Did Susan shoot Frank Ash?"

Gabriel made a face between a wince and a frown.

Evie understood the sentiment, but it was worth considering. "Owning a .22, being comfortable firing it, sounds like something a cop's wife might have for her own protection. There's no gun permit on file for her, but maybe it got slipped out of the records. Her son comes home very upset, Scott goes to confront Frank Ash, maybe can't find him that day, goes home and tells his wife what happened, then has to go to work because he's on shift that night. Susan waits until Scott has left the house and Joe is settled. She heads out to find Frank Ash, figuring there aren't all that many places he might be. She finds him by chance at the truck stop when she stops to fill up the car with gas. She shoots him, never says a word to her family or to the doctor. Everyone around her has plausible deniability."

"It would be a reason they ran two years

later when the body's found," Gabriel said. "Susan finally tells Scott what she's done. And Scott makes the decision to run . . . probably fly out of an airport somewhere that night as they got clean away."

Evie nodded. "It's a long shot, Gabe, and I don't see how Susan stays calm and level-headed for the two years they were in counseling, but it's the only thing that would explain their leaving when they did that doesn't have the doctor lying to us." She moved to the next problem. "When your dad gets me the names Scott arranged for new IDs, it's still going to be a challenge to find them. I doubt they used those names for more than a few months, a year at most, before they changed them again."

"Start in Alaska, Hawaii, Guam, as far as you can go and still be in a U.S. territory," Gabriel suggested. "Their photos were plastered everywhere around the Midwest. They can't afford to be recognized. If they were preparing to run, odds are good the location was studied carefully. They may have made a flight to that destination early in their planning to make arrangements, or maybe just one of them flies there to set up bank accounts, look at housing options, schools. We can't find the cash because some of it has already been transferred ahead under the new IDs. But something will still be out there."

"You're willing to head down this rabbit trail," Evie noted, wiping her mouth with a napkin.

"I'm a realist. You've come up with ideas we haven't considered before. I need that new thinking. Eventually, one of them will pan out. Dad comes up with new IDs, has names, that's the time to explore this one further. I'd like you looking at the overall case to find the next possibility."

"Okay." Evie leaned back, the last of her soda in hand. "I did have one rather interesting thought last night. Assume the family is still alive. What are the odds the son managed to become a cop when he grew up?"

Once again Gabriel looked at her, intrigued. "I like that, Evie. He certainly had his focus on that when he was a boy."

"He'd be old enough now to be out of a police academy. Choose your state. I think we could find him if we look at police academy graduating class pictures. He surely looks something like his dad. And I've got photos of his dad at age twenty."

"Put that on the board. It's an interesting question to follow up on." He rapped his knuckles on the table again. "Keep at it, Evie." He pushed back his chair. "I'll be

382

down at the office for an hour, then back here. Anything you need? Dessert?"

"I'm good."

He smiled, nodded, and left.

Evie picked up the roll of sweet-tarts that had appeared beside her plate. She knew this case and the Dayton one, along with his job as sheriff, was running Gabriel in circles, and yet he still found the energy to take care of others. She smiled and popped in a sweet-tart from the roll.

She turned to study the crime wall. *Come on, Florist family. Did you leave on your own? Did someone kill you? Which way does this case fork? I need a way to locate you, even if it's simply your remains.*

She went back to reading a report by Phil Peters, the officer Scott Florist most often partnered with on the job. She needed to sit down and talk with the retired officer. If someone had known about the counseling, if someone had known Scott Florist was taking a particular interest in the disappearance of Frank Ash, that person was most likely Phil Peters. But before she had that conversation, she needed to know enough about him to have a sense of the man — what kind of cop he was, his background, and connections within the county. Would he be about protecting Scott even after this many years, or would he be willing to offer details if he knew them? It was the next logical place for her to dig.

Gabriel Thane

Gabriel could feel a tension headache starting and swallowed two Tylenol before rejoining Evie. This week felt like it had been going on for a month.

Evie gave an absent-minded thanks when she reached for the drink he set beside her, but looked up in surprise when she realized it was a milk shake. She was reading police reports, he noticed, a stack of them.

"Tell me about Phil Peters," Evie said, leaning back in her chair.

"What might you be looking for?" he asked around the straw of his own chocolate milk shake.

"He's the next interview we need to have. Is he a good cop? A fussy one? A live-and-let-live type about the rules? What would he have noticed about Scott Florist?"

Gabriel smiled at the questions. "I'll start by mentioning Susan Florist introduced Phil Peters to his future wife, so there was in general a good vibe between the two couples. Susan and Jenna were friends, often seen together around town, shopping or grabbing a coffee. The guys were friendly, and not just as partners on the job. I don't think they hung out at each other's place, not as close as that, but still, friendly."

"Okay. That's useful."

"Scott and Phil were very different individuals. Phil was a former Navy investigator, came from a strict and disciplined world. He liked to control things in a rather nitpicking kind of way, though that was fine. If you keep the small things under control, the big ones are more manageable. Scott Florist liked that about him, actually. It's why they most often partnered together. They liked each other's style. Different ways of getting there, but the same intensity to get the job done right. They worked well together, no friction in that relationship."

"Think Phil will talk about Scott?"

"He'll talk to us," Gabriel assured her. "He's retired now, lives over in Indiana, about a two-hour drive if you want to talk in person. This case has always mattered to him. Phil and Jenna's wedding was that Sunday, and Scott Florist was to stand up as the best man. Scott and his family go missing Friday morning. The wedding almost got postponed. In fact, his fiancée, Jenna, said that would be best. But my dad talked them into going ahead as planned — the honeymoon cruise was already paid for, and it was non-refundable.

"Looking back, that was probably a mistake, not delaying things. While on his honeymoon, Phil was calling in at least three times a day, offering ideas and asking questions. As soon as they got back to town, Phil started right in, working the case around the clock. That caused problems in the new marriage. I seem to remember them living apart for a time. But they've been back together for the last . . . what, eight years? Jenna might be as helpful to talk with as Phil. Jenna and Susan were good friends long before Phil entered the picture."

"They have any children?" Evie asked.

"No. I know Jenna likes kids — she worked for the school district here. So it surprises me they don't have three or four by now. That may have been part of the marriage tension for all I know, not being able to have children for some reason." Gabriel's cellphone rang. He checked the readout and tensed. "Josh," he told Evie. "Yes, Josh," he said into the phone.

"You need to come right away. Will just gave me the signal to get Grace out of here."

Gabriel flinched. "We're on our way." He met Evie's gaze as he pushed back his chair. "Human remains at the farm."

She closed up the file. "Adult or child?"

she asked as she stood.

"Don't know yet." He saw a massive sequence of events coming at him in the next few hours and shifted into triage mode. "I'm calling state crime-scene folks next, but until I know what we're dealing with, the lid stays on. I'm not bringing in my own deputies yet."

"It has to be that way, Gabriel. You'll know more in a couple hours."

He nodded, already speed-dialing his dad's number. He got his voicemail, left a message for his dad to call Evie. "When he checks in with you, tell him what's going on. What time are Ann and Paul due in with Rachel?"

"Six."

"Josh will have Grace at his place, or he will have taken her to our parents' house."

"I'll make sure they know. Head on out to the farm, Gabriel. I'll get locked up, post security here, make sure Grace is settled with Rachel before we drive out. We can talk then about what we tell Grace, if tonight or tomorrow morning makes the most sense for when to do so."

"Thanks, Evie."

"We knew this day was coming. Go ahead and work the scene. You'll deal with it because you have to."

He nodded. "I'll call you as soon as I have details." He headed out to the farm, speaking to the crime-scene personnel as he drove. He hoped the remains were that of Grace's parents, but realistically he knew the odds favored the Dayton girl. He could only hope it wasn't someone else they didn't even have on their radar yet.

Gabriel parked behind Will, shut off his truck, and bowed his head over the wheel. "God, you know how I get when I'm dealing with death. Don't let me puke." He sighed, got out, pulled a couple of water bottles out of the cooler behind the seat. He made another call. "Will, I'm here. How do I find you?"

"Second deer blind, then east. You'll see red flags I haven't cleared yet."

Gabriel slung the evidence-collection bag across his shoulder, picked up the camera bag, moved to the back of the truck and got his shovel. He walked at a good clip across the pastureland, then into the woods.

Will was sitting on a fallen tree trunk, shovel beside him, legs outstretched, boots crossed, seeming relaxed until you saw his grim expression. Will simply nodded to an oval patch of ground on the other side of the faint animal trail.

A wild blackberry bush had tried to grow, and a red flag was planted at the east side of it. A small tree had come down, its branches spread in a tangled mess across the ground. Will had scraped away fallen leaves with his boot and shovel, so the ground was moist dirt with traces of crushed mushrooms. He'd dug a hole alongside the fallen tree.

"The bone is about eight inches down, pretty much right at the flag," Will said. "Either the femur bone of a child or the radius arm bone of a woman — they'd be similar dimensions just looking at the center few inches. It's old skeletal remains. I'm guessing it's a child, feet about here" — Will pointed — "lying that direction."

Gabriel handed his brother one of the water bottles, pulled out the camera from the bag, pulled on a pair of gloves, and went to kneel by the flag and the hole. He used his gloved hand to gently move aside the dirt. It was human bone. Hard to tell if it was a child or a woman, but it definitely was human.

He studied the area. "State crime-scene people are going to be an hour getting here. But they were already packed for this possibility, as I'd given them a heads-up a search was in progress. Have you seen anything on the surface that suggests this is anything other than an old gravesite?"

"I've walked it in a spiral outward and I'm finding only vegetation," Will replied.

"I'll take some photos. Then we'll get that tree moved and the area cleared." Gabriel took his shovel and skimmed away a wider circle of leaves. "It's still somewhat wet ground — that will make it easier getting to the rest of the bones."

"It would be worth getting the other flags cleared while we wait for people, confirm this is the only site we need them to work for now," Will suggested.

Gabriel nodded his agreement. "I'm sorry it was you who turned this shovel of dirt, Will."

"Someone was going to do it. I'm glad it wasn't Dad. Are they bringing in generators and lights or should I make arrangements?"

"They'll have what they need, I'm sure of it." Gabriel began snapping photographs of the scene. "You need to tell Karen what you've been doing out here. Go spend some time with her tonight."

"Yeah. What do you figure? A few hours we'll know child or adult?"

"I think I can convince them to clear dirt back from the visible bone before they start the rest of the excavation, get us that basic answer. How this bone is positioned will tell them how the body is resting." Gabriel could feel himself building an emotional distance from the reality of the scene. "Dad's going to be out here soon. We need something for him to do."

"He's good at coordinating people," Will said. "Word is going to get out soon. You and I need to be elsewhere, let Dad manage this scene. He can be the gatekeeper, controlling who has access. We don't want freelancers deciding to walk around these woods looking for more . . ." He didn't finish.

Gabriel grimaced. "Yeah, you're right about that." He set aside the camera and nodded at the fallen tree. "Let's move it to the north. Once it's out of the way, we can break through the roots of the blackberry bush with a shovel, get it out of the way too."

Will slid on his work gloves as he walked over to the tree. "When are you planning to tell Grace?"

"Ask me that in a few hours." Gabriel heaved with his brother, and they got the tree to shift a few inches, pulling its branches out of the tangled brush. *Should've been working out more,* Gabriel told himself as they struggled to yank it free. They might need to wait for help.

Will said, "Lift with your legs, not your back."

Gabriel barked out a laugh. "Shut up, Will," he replied good-naturedly. At least the tree was an inanimate thing, and he could direct his frustration without mercy. On the third attempt, with Will generating most of the lift, they managed to haul the tree out of the way. They picked up shovels and set to work on the underbrush, clearing it back.

Gabriel rested against his shovel, breathing hard. An eight-by-ten-foot piece of land, a simple red flag marking the spot where the bone was. In about five hours this would be a pit, with more than just a fragment of bone to see. He wiped the back of his wrist across his eyes.

Will knelt to say a silent prayer, and his brother wasn't a religious man by any stretch of the definition. It was a powerful gesture. Gabriel doubted the remains had gone in the ground with any kind of recognition or ceremony. Most likely it had been Kevin Arnett hiding what he'd done. He said a quiet prayer of his own. They'd get the truth unearthed. Grant a proper burial.

Will stood and reached for his shovel. "Let's clear the rest of the flags while we wait for the crime-scene people."

Gabriel nodded. Will took the right while he himself moved to the left, heading toward the other flags. If this was Ashley Dayton, he'd call her parents, tell his father, his officers, then tell Grace. If this was her parents, he'd end up with a shorter but similar list. It was going to be a long, miserable day, no matter how he looked at it.

He felt a raindrop strike his face and glanced up at the sky. *God, we don't need rain right now, but I share your sadness.* He put his shovel into the ground at the base of a flag. It would take a steady rain to become a real problem this deep in the woods. Likely it was just a passing drizzle, he thought, recalling the forecast. He had a rain slicker in the truck. The work wasn't going to suspend tonight no matter how much rain came in.

Evie Blackwell

Three crime-scene vehicles could be seen in the headlights of the rental Paul had parked beside the Thane family's vehicles. Evie stepped out. The light rain earlier had brought a deeper chill to the air. Lights set up to deal with the coming night illuminated the general area in the woods, but from this distance details were indistinct. Evie sent a text to Gabriel to let him know they'd arrived.

"What do you think, Ann, can it stay quiet another day before the rumors begin?" Evie asked as her friend stopped beside her.

"They'll be circulating by morning. The folks working the scene have to get coffee, sleep somewhere. State crime-lab folks don't come to town unless something's up."

Evie saw a figure start across the pasture toward them. "That's Gabriel, I think, or maybe Will."

"Looks like Gabriel," Paul replied.

They waited in silence. Evie easily read the strain on Gabriel's face as he drew nearer, knew the answer before he spoke.

"It's a child. And from what's in the grave, it looks to be Ashley Dayton. The shoes are a match — she had beads tied into her shoelaces. And there's a bracelet that was made for her with her name on it."

"I'm so sorry, Gabriel," Evie said softly.

He rubbed a hand across the back of his neck. "I'll be calling her family once the medical examiner concludes his initial exam. He's offered to make the dental assessment right here with the portable X-ray so we can give the family the confirmation ASAP."

"You will not be surprising them," Ann

said quietly. "The place will be a shock, but her death is not a surprise."

"I know," Gabriel said heavily. "It's a relatively shallow grave, three feet down, off to the side of one of the animal trails and within sight of the second hunting blind. I don't think the location is an accident. I think the man wanted to look down on where she was buried." His voice cracked on the last words, but he drew a ragged breath and went on, "Will's still back there, and I've got Dad coordinating the scene. I need to get my guys informed, get security posted out here."

"When the family arrives, the media will follow. We need to tell Grace," Ann said.

"We'll tell her," Gabriel said. "Whether tonight or tomorrow morning is the only question."

"I'm not one for delaying hard news. Let's get it done. Rachel is with her now — that's going to help."

Gabriel nodded. "I need to give Josh a call, fill him in. I didn't want to do that until we were sure."

Evie bit her lip. "Gabriel, I don't mean to be tactless with this question, but the fact the grave was shallow and within sight of a place the uncle would often go, do you think the same might also be the case with Grace's parents if they are buried out here? Would he want to pass the site regularly?"

He shook his head. "I doubt it gives us that much direction. The child mattered to him. Grace's parents were simply an obstacle. I'm inclined toward his burying them somewhere convenient, getting rid of the car."

"It might be easier on Grace if we could also tell her we found her parents."

"We'll push on clearing the rest of the farm once the remains are removed, and that's going to happen within a day at the pace they're working. Let's see what Josh wants to do. I'm going to have the crime-scene personnel focus on the house, outbuildings on the property. Once they finish with the remains, we'll get that locked down. Then it'll be up to Josh and the dogs."

"Gabriel, why don't you and Evie head into town, brief your officers on what's been found," Ann suggested. "Paul and I can go talk with Grace. Rachel is there, and Josh. She'll be okay with us."

He hesitated.

Evie reached out a hand and nudged his arm. "You look pretty grim, Sheriff," she said with a little smile. "Your dad and Will can handle what's going on here. Go clean up, talk to your guys, prepare what you will tell the Daytons. I'll help put together a press statement for when you need to go public, get ahead of what's coming. It's going to be a long twenty-four hours."

Gabriel shook his head. "Some things you don't delegate, and this is one of them. Grace deserves to hear it first from me. I'm the authority here."

Paul nodded. "She'll appreciate that, Gabriel."

"Will you do it now or talk with your guys first?" Ann asked. "It's not going to shift things that much for Grace. Do whatever works best for you, Gabriel."

"I'm going to call Josh, alert him I'm coming, and talk with her now. Evie, how about you ride with me?" Gabriel said. "I'll have dispatch start alerting officers that we'll meet at the post office in an hour. They know what you've come to town to do. We'll update on the Dayton girl and hopefully slide past any ties to Grace. I'm thinking something like 'Grace was preparing to sell the land, Josh was walking the property with her, they were checking out the condition of the hunting blinds before the wooded section of the property is listed for sale when his dogs pointed on a location.' "

Evie considered it, nodded. "I can finesse that since the core of it is fact."

Ann offered an additional refinement. "You need to allow for the fact Grace's parents might still be found, so maybe add 'There are no other missing children from this area. The rest of the land is going to be swept as a precaution, but we don't expect to find other child remains. We're not sure who buried the Dayton girl on this land, but the location now suggests the crime has a local connection, and it will be investigated as such.' "

"Better," Gabriel said. "I don't mind destroying Arnett's reputation after the fact, but I don't want to put Grace out there in the center of everything. Knowing who did it and proving it are two different things. For now, Grace was preparing to sell the land, Josh was walking the farm with her, this looks like a convenient burial site for someone who knows the area, and we'll be investigating it as a local crime."

"Once the recovery of remains becomes public," Paul suggested, "you should mention there's a viable person of interest in the case, and the State Police in coordination with the FBI are reviewing those findings. This is a case you are pleased to have resolved for the sake of the Dayton family, but it is an old case, and given the current information, there's no present concern for the community's safety."

"Good," Gabriel agreed as Evie took notes.

"Once you have the sheriff's statement," Evie said, "I can have a variation of it issued from the State Police. The fact I'm in town looking at two cold cases, and the Dayton case happens to be one of them, is going to get noticed. I can pull a fair amount of attention away from Grace simply by talking about the new governor's proposed task force and what I'm doing here. If it becomes necessary, throw me to the media wolves. I can handle it. They'll latch on to the Florist case if I point them in the right direction. The recovered remains of a child is news, but new theories in the case of a missing deputy and his family would be bigger news if it's handled properly."

Gabriel smiled. "Let's hope I don't need to resort to 'tossing you to the media wolves,' Evie, but thank you. I'm going to take you up on that if I need a distraction away from Grace."

"Evie does well in front of a camera," Ann told them. "It's part of her charm." Ann laughed at the look Evie gave her. "Gabriel, the media will come to town because of this. We need to get Tom Lander's photo distributed, get Karen somewhere out of sight so she isn't on the B-roll of a reporter's broadcast. If you shut down access to the farm and frontage road, some reporters are going to default to the most convenient place in town to interview people for comments, and that's the Fast Café."

"Good point. I've already suggested when Will gets free from here tonight that he should find Karen and tell her what's going on. He's feeling the weight of being the one to turn over that shovel of dirt, and he could use an hour with Karen to decompress. I'll alert him about the media concerns."

"I'll coordinate with Will," Paul offered, "make sure Tom Lander's photo gets distributed widely, and get word out that Will wants to hear it if the guy shows up."

"Thanks," Gabriel said. "Paul, if you and Ann could also pick up where Caleb was working today on the Florist case, that would be useful. He has a lead on where Scott might have secured new IDs. If we can lock down the new names they had arranged to use, it could move Evie's board a long way forward. Maybe movement on the Florist case can shift some of the media interest off the farm."

"I'll talk with your father," Paul said. "I'm all for splitting the media's attention with other news whenever you can do so."

Evie looked around the group. Gabriel looked less grim just having a chance to talk out the plan for the next few hours. Once Grace heard the news, the worst of this evening would be over for him.

He glanced in her direction. "Anything else before we go?"

"You might ask your parents to invite Grace to stay with them should the media discover she's at the campground," Evie suggested. "I'd offer my place, but I'm going to get tracked down too easily. My sense is Grace isn't going to wish to return to Chicago so long as Josh is making progress on locating her parents' bodies."

Gabriel nodded. "A good precaution. I'll talk to my folks." He looked a final time around the group. "I'll tell Grace and leave it to you to help her through it. Evie and I will then go tell my deputies what's happening."

Ann said, "Let's plan to meet for breakfast early tomorrow at the house, or Josh's place, depending on how this evening goes. We'll sort out how to handle the next few days then."

Evie nodded, grateful that Ann and Paul would be here for the weekend. They all needed to get through these few days in as careful a sequence as possible, and Paul and Ann were both good at strategy. Evie followed Gabriel to his truck, glad she wasn't the one in charge. She liked her job, but no one ever got used to having to break this kind of news.

Grace Arnett

Grace turned as she heard the front door of Josh's home open and close, heard voices. *Paul and Ann, Gabriel and Evie . . .* She watched as the four of them came in together, saw the serious expressions, and pushed aside the comforter across her lap. She recognized the look on the sheriff's face. "This isn't going to be good," she whispered to herself.

Rachel pushed pause on the movie. Grace had been watching a DVD chosen at random while Josh fussed in the kitchen over a dinner she wasn't sure she could eat. They had stopped their search early today because Josh said the dogs needed a break, but she'd known it was more than that. The arrival of these four confirmed it.

"Grace, we've got difficult news."

She simply nodded at Gabriel's statement. Something related to her parents would have been that, but still positive. This wasn't going to be.

Gabriel moved to sit on the coffee table facing her, and Grace idly wondered if the furniture was going to hold him. His hand came over and covered hers, and he felt cold to her, even though she still felt chilled from the day spent outside.

"Grace . . ." He waited until her eyes lifted from his hand covering hers. "Human remains were found at your uncle's farm. Those of a child named Ashley Dayton. She went missing when she was six."

She heard him, heard the words, and she felt . . . numb. Not surprised. Why should she be with news that the monster she already believed killed her parents had also killed a child? *A child.* Panic suddenly overcame the numbness. She felt her heart begin to race. *How many children?*

"Grace, are you okay?" She felt someone ease her head down. Josh, she realized, as the smell of his shirt got through her muddled senses. *Wow.* She had absorbed some shocks before and thought she knew every way her body could react, but this was a first. The world spun dizzily sideways as if she'd gotten slammed on her head. "How many children?" she whispered.

Gabriel's hand on hers tightened. "She is the only one missing in this area . . . the only one we know of."

Grace tried to nod. One was too many, but more? She carefully straightened to see if the room was still spinning. "Tell me the name again. How old she was."

"Ashley Dayton. She was six, Grace."

She felt something burning in her heart, an ache so intense it was like an ember bursting into flame. She knew what a six-year-old child looked like, and it didn't take a leap to guess that Ashley was blue-eyed and blond. "I'm okay, Gabriel," she said. Seeing his worried expression somehow forced a steadiness back into her voice. "Are her parents from around here?" she asked.

"They live in Florida. I'll be talking with them tonight, and expect them to fly into town tomorrow."

She needed to stand up, to pace the room. She leaned forward to rise, caught Rachel's gaze, the tension telling her what she must look like. She stayed seated. She couldn't think. "What do you need from me?"

Gabriel gave a slight smile as he rubbed her hand. "You'll do, Grace. Listen to Josh, my folks, Ann. We're going to keep the media away from you."

She tried to moisten her lips. "You'll have to tell people, the press."

"Let us speak for you regarding all this. We've got some thoughts on how to do it.

Those woods are known to many in the community, and we can keep you out of the spotlight for now."

She was intensely grateful. "What about my parents?"

He shook his head. "We don't know. Josh will be back on his search in a day or two. I promise you, if your parents are out there, we will do everything we can to find them before the weather closes the door. But I need you to stay put while the press is around."

"I can do that."

"Any questions you have for me at this point?"

She really couldn't think. She tried, shook her head, but stopped quickly when the room started to whirl again.

"I'll be around if you need to see me — just let Josh know. If you want to return to Chicago while this plays out, Rachel and Ann are your traveling companions. They can make that happen for you."

"I'll be all right here." She took a deep breath. "I will."

He nodded. "Then I'll head out." He released her hand.

"Ann, have you and Paul eaten?" Rachel asked, rising from her seat. "Let's get some dinner on the table. Josh has got a pizza in the oven, and there's potato soup simmering on the stove." Grace smiled her thanks at Rachel for diverting the moment. She gratefully watched the others leave the room with Gabriel.

She felt as if she'd taken a punch, followed by a shot of Novocain to deaden any feeling. Her body didn't feel like her own. She felt the couch beside her shift. A mug was tucked into her hands. *Josh. Of course, Josh.*

"I'll be okay," she repeated, pushing aside the tea. "I just got a little light-headed."

"You went sheet-white and were about to hit the deck," he countered and pushed the tea back into her hands.

She wrapped both hands around the mug. "It's not like I didn't know something more was going on, even if I was mostly hiding behind the decision not to know the details. I've heard Ann and Evie talking about the two cases they hoped to resolve. Even I can put together the description of Ashley Dayton and the odds that my . . . that he was involved. Not wanting to face it isn't the same as being blind to the possibility."

"You shouldn't have been out there during the search, Grace. It's hard enough on someone who isn't tied —"

"My parents are out there, Josh," she interrupted. "I'm certain of that." She closed her eyes and let herself say something she hadn't told even Rachel. "Until I have that closure, I'm left with this awful hole inside that whispers to me: 'They didn't love you. They left you behind with that monster. That's how much your parents cared about you.' It isn't true, I know that now, but my childhood was lived with that running around in my mind. I need to prove that it's false, if it can be proven. I *need* that, Josh."

Josh sighed, and his hand covered hers as his brother's had. "Then we will find out, Grace. However we have to tear apart that property, we will find out if they are there."

She realized when he handed her a tissue that she'd begun to cry again. The tears had become so common lately, she didn't even realize it most of the time. "Thank you," she said, wiping at her eyes. "I'd like a funeral for my parents. Then I want to get back to Chicago and resume my life. I want to lay to rest these ghosts, so the past won't keep dragging me down."

"We'll have that funeral one way or another. And I'll get you safely back home," Josh promised. "Come eat something, Grace. If you're here another week, I'd like you not to blow away on me."

She forced a smile she didn't feel and sipped at the sweetened tea. She rose slowly, found her balance again. "I might try some of your soup."

"I make great soup," he said immediately, and she was able to laugh.

Oh, she needed this old friend, and the way Josh went out of his way to make her laugh was like he'd done years ago, getting her to smile as if that was the reward he was after when he kept her company. He'd been a friend she had shared the good moments of her childhood with, and she couldn't put into words how valuable that was to her now. *Something from the past was good,* she silently reminded herself.

She let Josh guide her toward the kitchen and didn't resist when an old sweatshirt of his dropped around her shoulders. She wasn't sure she'd ever be warm again.

THIRTEEN

Evie Blackwell

A radio station's upbeat music filled the room. Evie knew it didn't compensate for her sadness, but it gave her some distraction while she worked. She was deconstructing the crime wall for Ashley Dayton, taking pieces down one at a time, putting the case to rest once more in its boxes. The only thing left to do for Ashley was to add the final report on her remains.

"Want some help?"

She looked over as Ann walked in. "Sure."

"Caleb is escorting the Dayton family out to the farm," Ann said. "The medical examiner is going to release the remains for burial in Chicago. Ashley Dayton died of a blow to the head. The answers to other questions her parents have are unfortunately lost to history."

That the medical examiner had put in overtime to complete the autopsy was what

Evie would expect in a case like this. The week was ending as she thought it might, with the case itself as closed as they could make it, given the years that had passed.

"The media is camped out at the Fast Café, so Karen is taking a few days off," Ann continued. "I think Will has her helping him tear out drywall or some such demolition project."

Evie smiled. "I've been meaning to go pick up my dogs the last two days, and I keep getting interrupted."

"Will would've let you know if they're in the way. I'd say they're enjoying their stay in the country, and his own two appreciate the company." Ann helped her box photographs. "Do you want to suspend this, Evie? Take the last week of your vacation as a true holiday somewhere? Go sit on a beach, find some movies, read a book? No one would blame you. You've made significant progress on the Florist case, and it will still be here in January when the task force officially launches. You can come back and work it then — on more than vacation pay," she added with a smile.

Evie had been considering just that, but didn't answer. She took down the large pieces of paper from the wall, stacked them, rolled them tightly, and secured it with rubber bands. "Is Grace going to stick around or go to Chicago with you tonight?" she asked instead.

"Josh goes back to searching the farm tomorrow, so she's planning to stay a few more days. At Marie's invitation, Paul and I are coming down for Thanksgiving and returning home that night. Grace will probably return to Chicago with us then. I want a few minutes with Gabriel once things have settled down around here."

"That would be helpful." Other than in passing, Evie hadn't seen Gabriel since Friday night. The number of people needing a slice of his time right now would fill a phone book. She glanced over at the other wall, at the Florist case, made a decision.

"I think I'll stay on the Florist case. I don't need to report back to work until December first. I can give it this final week. I want to know, Ann, if it can be solved, if I can solve it. It's not my usual ambition in play here — more a need to have that basic question answered. I think the town needs it after all this turmoil."

"The new IDs go anywhere?" Ann asked. Caleb had narrowed things down to a forger now in federal prison, and Paul had managed to get information from him in exchange for some considerations on the man's prison-work detail.

"Nothing so far," Evie answered. "Paul's been running the three names through the national databases for me, and I also sent them over to a state researcher. If the FBI can't lock in on the names, they probably weren't used. The fact the new IDs exist tells us the Florist family planned to leave if it became necessary. If they were never used, that will confirm they were likely murdered that night."

"Which goes back to the possible motive for the murders — the large amount of money the Florist family had with them," Ann said. "Do you want to take another look at the doctor?"

"He's on my list." Evie perched on one of the tables, noted that Gabriel hadn't been by with a new sweet-tarts roll, had to settle for a piece of hard candy from a bowl on the table. "I think I might take the case back to the beginning, start over, see what might show up if I clear the slate."

Ann paused. "That's got merit, Evie. The Florist case has gone so many directions, it's like a spider web that has collapsed and is just a sticky mess now."

"That's exactly what it feels like," Evie agreed. "We know who Ashley Dayton's killer was, whether or not it can ever be proven. The search to find Grace's parents will go where it's going to go. But the Florist case I can still maybe move to the next step. I'm just not sure what we accomplished on it this last week. We know more, we're inside the dynamics of the family for the first time, but I'm not sure we've really changed what we know about the crime."

Ann nodded. "Then start over, Evie. That gut instinct is probably telling you something important. Use this bare wall to take it apart again."

"Yeah." She could fill it once more with blank sheets, begin again on the Florist case. "Ann, do you think being a cop is a choice, or is it something God wires into a person? I'm spending what could be a vacation week to wade through a messy case again, and I honestly can't say I mind the idea. I'm doing it by choice. That's just weird when I think about it."

Ann laughed, lowered the box she held onto the table. "I think you're young, Evie, and part of what you enjoy about real-life puzzles is that satisfaction you feel at learning the ending. To have true justice, people need answers, so God gave you important work to do. If you weren't a cop, you'd be curious about other mysteries. You'd be a good research chemist, a scientist, you'd find other puzzles to figure out. When the weight of this job gets to where you need to step away from the blood and violence, you'll find a new avenue for solving things. That won't ever leave you. But the impulse to solve crimes, that you can let go when it becomes necessary."

"That's one reason you retired, Ann? The amount of violence you had seen across your career?"

"It was a significant factor, yes. I shifted my interest in solving matters into writing, where I can both create the problem and figure out how to solve it. I'm breathing again, according to Paul. I still enjoy the occasional real-life puzzle, the cold cases Paul and I work together, but when something touches on the personal like this Dayton one did with Grace . . ." She shook her head, then added, "I used to be able to handle these moments better than I did today. I absorb the grief at a much deeper level now."

"That's not such a bad thing," Evie replied. "I know I seem cold to Gabriel at times, with my curiosity and not much pain showing when I talk about a case. Looking at the photos on the walls, he sees people he knows, while I see strangers. I care about what happened to them, but more in the context of their place in the puzzle."

"If you couldn't retain that curiosity and equilibrium, you couldn't solve the problem, Evie. The longer you two are friends, Gabriel will adjust to the fact you'll always have a natural detachment about you. You see puzzles. He sees people. God wired you both as He intended. You've got a gift Gabriel doesn't have. And he's got connections you could never manage. Gabriel is knit into the people and fabric of this community. He'll be buttonholed for conversations by hundreds of people during the next month. You would smother to death if even just five cops wanted to come help you work the Florist case. You need space, solitude, to think. Gabriel needs to take what happened with Grace and her uncle and figure out how to learn from it. There won't be another child abused in Carin County if Gabriel can possibly figure out how to apply the lessons taken away from this case."

Evie took a moment to absorb that. "I hadn't thought about what Gabriel does next with all this. For me, the case is finished. It goes back in the box and I move on. But Gabriel's job is to deal with the impact on the community, try to prevent another child from being hurt."

"Different jobs, different roles. Gabriel's

job is to be watchful, aware of what's going on, and protect the people who live here. You're more wired to be a detective, to look closely at a case, solve it, and then move to the next one."

Evie nodded, looked at Ann, and turned the conversation personal. "I've also been thinking if I stay here this week, stay here over Thanksgiving, that I can be sure Rob will wonder again about my priorities when I won't even take a day off from the job for the holiday. He's decided I'm pretty much a workaholic since I'm spending my vacation time doing this. He's probably right. That's a bad trait for a cop to develop, being that single-minded about work."

Ann didn't give her a quick answer, but instead perched herself on the table beside the box and studied her. "Evie, it's possible that you use work and the time it demands to ensure you stay single. Not that you love work so much, but that you're scared of what kind of life you might have if you built something outside of work, and failed at it. So rather than feel the stress of your potentially less-than-great personal life, you shift more hours over into work. Does that make sense?"

Evie considered that and sighed. "That's

just sad, Ann. That you can analyze me so easily."

Ann smiled. "Enjoy the job, Evie. Don't ever apologize for appreciating these puzzles and solving them. It's important work — what you do matters. But when your 'Paul' starts nudging you to give him room in your life, be willing to let him have that slice of you. You may be less than deft at building a personal life by yourself, but you'd probably do fine building one with someone else. Rob might be that right guy for you. Or it may be someone even more ambitious than you about work — I think you'd make an interesting politician's wife. But when it's time, let yourself enjoy that next chapter."

"Ann, I find it interesting that you are the most relaxed I ever see you when you're with Paul."

Ann's smile grew wide. "I've noticed the same. I don't have to think as much about life when I'm with him. We're just doing life together, and he has things flowing in a nice direction."

"Would you take this the right way when I say I envy you?" Evie remarked lightly.

"I'm glad you do. It means you don't have your head in the sand about the decisions you need to make for your own life. It's fine to decide you are comfortable with the present, Evie, to decide a future looking like today is something you're content with. Just look at the options with your eyes open. That's where wisdom comes from."

"I'll try and do that."

"Paul and I will be back for Thanksgiving," Ann told her again. "You may have the Florist case solved by then. If you do, that ice cream reward is still on the table."

Evie grinned. "I'll take you up on it. Pumpkin pie and ice cream suits me fine. And I never did get my flight overview of Carin County you promised. Maybe we can fit that in over Thanksgiving too."

"I'd like that," Ann said. "You'll figure this out, Evie. The answer is here somewhere."

Evie appreciated the support, both personally and professionally. "Tell Paul thanks for coming down this weekend."

Ann nodded and headed out. Evie turned to consider the present Florist crime wall. She'd solve this case if she could, for her own sake and because it would help Gabriel to have it answered. He was having a miserable week, and figuring out what happened to the Florist family would be welcome news. She'd like to leave with that outcome behind her, rather than just pack up and go.

She locked the door behind Ann, picked up a root beer, and went to studying the board, then moved to the blank wall. It was time to go back to the beginning.

Evie propped her feet on a chair, idly eating pretzels, thinking about the Florist case, sorting how she wanted to approach it. A couple of dangling threads were worth pursuing.

She needed the list Gabriel had put together of the county's violent residents. She'd like to look at those names with an eye for those with boys in their families. Joe Florist had a close call with Frank Ash. Two other boys had admitted being molested by Ash — three they could name, and no doubt there were others. A pool of people, both boys and adults, had reason to want Frank Ash gone. And most of them also didn't like cops very much.

Interesting. Maybe the Frank Ash murder and the Florist family disappearance were connected, if she put her finger on the right family that harbored violence. She wrote the idea down at the top of a new pad of paper.

She wanted to talk with Phil Peters and his wife, Jenna. The wedding that had nearly not taken place was on the Florist family calendar for that Sunday, the event noted in a hot-pink marker. Susan and Jenna were good friends. They would have been confirming wedding preparations that week — flowers and cake, decorations and invitations. A lot of time spent together. If a problem was brewing, Susan likely would have let something slip — maybe not significant at the time, but what about from the perspective of looking back? Evie made a note to see Phil and Jenna in person.

What else? Evie began cataloging what she knew.

The Florist family had been accumulating cash and storing it somewhere. Could she trace where it had gone? *Where was the money now?*

Scott had purchased new IDs for the family as Simon and May Carnoff — using their middle names — their son Joseph Carnoff. The accompanying birth certificates, the social security numbers, would pass a cursory check. So far, none of the alternate names appeared to have ever been used. *Keep pushing to confirm the IDs were never used.*

The father and son had feared the other had murdered Ash. They both seemed to be innocent of any involvement. But plenty of others likely had a motive to want Frank Ash out of the way. *Who did kill Frank Ash?*

The Florist family disappeared sometime

between Thursday night and Friday morning. Had she ever pursued an interview with the friends they were meeting at the campground? Evie was stunned to realize she hadn't even thought of them beyond that they had called the authorities to report the Florist family hadn't arrived. *Who are they?*

"Dublin," she muttered as she shuffled quickly through the file . . . no, there it was. "Durbin." William and Nancy Durbin, family on Scott's side. Nancy was Scott's younger cousin, the notes indicated.

The Durbins certainly knew the Florist family's travel plans. Evie felt a hot spark of interest. *Any reason they could have been involved?* That was a new direction — a nice big *maybe.*

Evie circled it on her new page of notes. What better way to get away with a crime than to control when and how it was discovered? The Durbins would have been able to make sure everything was tucked away nice and neat before the cops were even called. It felt promising. Evie was relieved just at the thought. There *were* new avenues to explore.

All right . . . She leaned back, clasped her hands behind her head. *What better place to hide a camper and truck than in a campground full of campers and trucks?* Maybe camouflage the camper — old decal stickers, dirty it up, swap it with another camper set in among the weeds so it looked as if it had been parked for months. The truck could simply have plates swapped, be left sitting at the lake's boat launch in a row of parked vehicles. The first day or two of the search had focused south around the Florist house. Cops wouldn't have been looking at campgrounds north of where the family had been traveling. That first night, drive the truck and camper another thirty minutes or so north, tuck the camper and truck into a campground full of other campers, leave those parts of the mystery hidden in plain sight. The bodies were still a problem, but Carin Lake is right there. Go out at night, weight them down, drop them over the side of the boat. The Florist family arrive at their destination, were murdered, vehicles moved, their bodies dumped — all taken care of before you call the cops at seven o'clock Friday morning to say your friends haven't arrived. And you're a whole bunch of cash wealthier if you knew about that money. . . .

Evie whispered "Eureka," wondering if she just might have it.

She ran that thought out. *This case maybe isn't that complicated.* They simply hadn't looked in the right direction. Like Grace's uncle being well-known in town but hiding his true colors, maybe these killers had done the same. William and Nancy Durbin . . . family, where she had gone so many times before in her thinking. Were they having money issues, and then suddenly had none?

She picked up her pad and added more notes.

How hard would it be to make a camper disappear, a truck? If William Durbin left the keys in the truck, the truck unlocked, how many hours would it remain at the boat launch before someone stole it? An hour maybe? It could have been driven away before cops were even looking for the truck. Park the camper on a weed-filled lot, it would be equally invisible.

Evie felt a cold certainty as she wrote, for this was not only possible, it fit with the facts of the case. She needed to know a great deal more about William and Nancy Durbin, and fast. They might be good, salt-of-the-earth people, and this was a flight of fancy that would crash into a wall . . . or they might be the desperate people who had spotted a quick answer to all their troubles and murdered three people to acquire a lot of cash.

Evie glanced at the time. Ann and Paul might not have taken off from the airport yet. She grabbed her phone and made the call. "Paul, I need a favor."

"Name it, Evie."

"Everything you can tell me about a local couple without Gabriel finding out I'm asking."

"Names?"

"William and Nancy Durbin. She's a cousin of Scott Florist."

"I'll get back to you."

Evie put down her phone, feeling another surge of confidence. He didn't even ask — it was there in his voice. This might be the answer, and he'd get her the information she needed. Knowing Paul, she'd probably get a call back later this evening.

She wasn't going to do a victory dance yet, but she felt like celebrating just the same. She should order in some supper. There were only so many pretzels that qualified as a meal, she told herself as she set them back on the table.

"God, calm me down, please," she whispered. "I want so *badly* to have this solved, I'm grasping at this idea. It *could* be the one, it feels promising and possible and right, but I need the facts to support it before I upset and maybe taint an innocent couple. Please don't let me say anything to Gabriel about this until I know for certain.

But I know something about you — the truth matters — and maybe you've led me to find it. If that's the case, *thank you,* profoundly. If this isn't it, move me off this idea and on to others." She thought about something else to say, realized just whispering the prayer had begun to calm her. "Thanks again, God, that at least there's hope an answer is here. I'm going back to work now. Thanks for this idea."

This could turn out to be like the counseling and the doctor — something that fit, but wasn't the answer. Evie accepted that. Paul was the guy with the ability to get her concrete information. She'd have something in a few hours, a day at most, and she'd know. One of these ideas would pan out to be the right one sooner or later.

She pulled out her phone to order something from the pizza parlor, studying the crime wall while she waited for her order to be taken. What else? William and Nancy Durbin seemed to be a brilliant possibility. Experience had taught her if there was one idea left to find, there were two. There would be something else here. *What else?* She started thinking again about the night the family disappeared.

"Evie."

She looked around as the door pushed open. "Hi there, Gabriel." The man looked like he'd aged years in the week she had known him.

"It's one a.m." he told her, voice rough with exhaustion. She was surprised at the time. No wonder she was beginning to get bleary-eyed. "Finding something?" Gabriel asked.

She bit her tongue so as not to tell him. She *wanted* to tell him it could be William and Nancy Durbin, but she didn't have word back from Paul, and she refused to let herself give Gabriel a roller coaster of an idea that turned into a dead end, not after the week he'd had. So she went with what she was working on now — maybe it would cheer him up.

She broke a breadstick in two and held out half. "I'm on a roll of sorts. I think I've located who did kill Frank Ash, so I'm going to push on that for a bit to clear that question." She gestured to the pages spread out on the table as he walked over. "Names appearing on your violent list who have boys in their family, age fourteen to seventeen."

"Find the motive, find the person who did it," he said, sinking into a chair beside her.

"Exactly. It might not have been the two boys' families we know about. If there were two, there likely were more. Your list of violent people in the county fits who could also murder Frank Ash." She used a napkin to wipe a smear off her laptop screen. "A .22 is rather an odd gun of choice for this group. I've got gun permits for every type of weapon you can imagine for people on the list, but no .22 so far. But I figure someone had access to a .22 even if he didn't own it."

"Yeah, I can imagine that."

"Anyway, I'm going on the assumption someone on the list did the crime and wouldn't want to throw away a perfectly good gun. He might have used it again or at least still have it. The Ash murder is still open, the evidence on file, so I've sent the slugs through the lab again. Maybe we get a match to a later crime."

"An obvious step — one I wish I'd thought of first." He tried to smile, but he was so tired it didn't come off that well.

She patted his arm resting on the table beside her. "You've had a few other things on your mind. Eat something." She pushed the pizza box his way, took another slice out for herself to encourage him to do the same. "I'm going to go see Phil Peters and his wife on Friday. They already have family in town for Thanksgiving, but they'll send the last ones off to the airport Friday morning. I told them I'd be over their way about one o'clock. Want to come along?"

He pushed up the pizza box lid, took a slice. "If things are quiet here, sure."

"I want to have that conversation in person rather than on the phone. Not just because Scott and Phil partnered together. Susan and Jenna were friends. I think Jenna would have known about Decatur — maybe not the specifics, but about the counseling. I'm curious why she never said anything about it. Or if she told Phil, why he didn't say anything. And if she never told Phil, why not?"

"Good questions to ask them both."

Evie decided it was time to change the subject. Gabriel needed to sleep, but he also looked like he needed to talk. "How's Grace?" she asked gently.

He sighed. "I left her watching a movie with Josh at my parents' place. The media — thankfully — haven't bothered her. Maybe they've heard my dad would run them off. Having Rachel around for the weekend helped — you can tell Grace and Rachel and Ann click well together. Grace was lighter in mood than I thought she'd be."

"I'm glad. The weather looks good for this

coming week. Clear skies, windy, but not too cold."

Gabriel nodded. "Josh will be out there with the dogs in the morning. Grace still wants to be the one doing the map work, and so far none of us have been able to talk her out of it."

"For her own reasons, Grace knows what she needs to do."

"I get that . . . it's just so painful to watch. I've got a press conference tomorrow at one p.m. Hopefully it will satisfy the last of the lingering media. You're welcome to attend. We aren't naming the person of interest in the Dayton girl case, so speculation is all over the place. But the questions about Kevin Arnett have been minimal. The Dayton family has agreed to stay quiet about what we've told them in order to give Grace breathing room."

"That's kind of them."

"They understand better than most what she's going through." Gabriel pushed his chair back. "Don't work too late, Evie. Well, I guess it's already beyond late," he said after a glance at his watch.

"Just until I get through these names," she promised. "I've left the top up on the convertible, so I won't freeze going to the house."

He smiled. "I saw that. Call if you need me in the morning. I'll be around."

"Thanks, Gabriel."

She'd tell him to get some sleep, but it would sound too much like his mother. Gabriel had family, and they were going to provide that support and strength he needed to get through this. She saw him off, then locked the door.

God, I'll mention what you already know. That is one man carrying more weight than is good for him. Help me give him answers. It's not much, but it's what I can do.

Not for the first time she felt like she was in the middle of having that prayer answered tonight. William and Nancy Durbin might be the key to the Florist family disappearance. Evie stretched her arms back, looked again at the names spread across the pages, thought she was looking at solving the Frank Ash murder, a case she hadn't even come here to work. It felt good, being useful. She pulled over the list of names and went back to work.

While Evie ate breakfast Monday morning — after a very short night — she perused the report on William and Nancy Durbin, which Paul had emailed to her. The report was still preliminary, more info was coming, but already it proved useful.

The Durbins had been married for four years at the time the Florist family went missing. Longtime residents of Carin County, both had attended the local high school. They made a respectable living farming, he also worked as a notary and did earth-moving jobs with his backhoe to bring in extra cash, and she tutored in math and gave piano lessons, had won awards for her pies. No debt on the property — the mortgage paid off the year before the Florist family disappeared, Evie noted from the date.

William had a long string of DUI arrests going back to his teens. Nancy had been arrested twice on minor drug violations. They were divorced now. An unusual distribution of assets had occurred. The cash and investments had been split, but they still jointly owned farmland, cattle, and horses, and lived on the same property but in separate houses on opposite sides of the land. There had been two domestic-disturbance calls since the divorce, both involving a shotgun being fired at the pet of the other.

It was the kind of acrimonious split suggesting each would be of a mind to implicate the other in a crime if given the chance. Evie wanted to interview them both as soon

431

as possible. But her night of restless sleep had raised some questions she was mulling over now, and it was cooling her certainty that this was the answer.

Why had Scott arranged to go camping with the Durbins, of all people, on a last-minute vacation when the focus of the trip was to repair the relationship with his son? There weren't boys the same age in both families. To go camping beside a huge lake and not go out on the water didn't seem likely. So maybe the Durbins had the boat? Or had Scott been planning to rent a boat once they arrived? That seemed equally as likely. If not for a boat, why plan to meet up with the Durbins? Maybe a social thing, a family thing that just sort of happened? *You're going camping? Oh, so are we, let's park together and share meals.* Good luck getting out of that when it was a family relationship. Evie could see a scenario like that playing out.

The Durbin marriage couldn't have been too rocky back then. If they were heading toward a nasty divorce, they wouldn't have been going camping, staying together in a twenty-some-foot camper. So the marriage was probably okay at the time. No doubt volatile on occasion, but reasonably peaceable.

Ample assets were in play when the couple divorced, suggesting forty thousand wouldn't have seemed like a life-changing amount. *But maybe that amount in cash was significant at the time of the camping trip?* She needed the rest of the report from Paul's researchers to answer that question. Money was often a motivator for murder, but three killings, one of them a child? The need would've had to be acute.

The Durbins fit the crime. They could control when the police were informed, they had the means and the time to get rid of the car, camper, and bodies. But she shook her head as she tried to picture them taking it as far as a triple homicide. If there was trouble between the relatives, Scott would not have agreed to the camping trip. He was a cop, so he wouldn't have been blind to tension that acute. If money had been that strained, Scott would likely as not have made them a loan. *And my biggest problem with this report,* she told herself, tapping the page of notes, *the Durbins divorced in acrimony.* If there was a murder in their past, one of them would have tried to frame the other to get the entire estate.

With that realization her solid idea felt like it died.

She'd interview them. She'd find out how

tight money had been for them back then. But on a second look, her hot lead of the night before was turning cold. The Durbins had no obvious reason to murder the entire Florist family. Killing a child truly changed the equation. The DUIs William Durbin had racked up were as much a reason for her doubts now as the acrimonious divorce. A drunk couldn't keep this kind of secret for thirteen years, nor could a bitter ex-wife.

Monday morning was turning out the way she feared her week was headed. She would spend the next few days interviewing people on Gabriel's list who had kids, see if she could firm up something about the Frank Ash murder. She'd see if the doctor would talk to her once more. She wanted to pursue further the new IDs Scott had acquired. She'd interview the Durbins, and later in the week, Phil and Jenna Peters. But she might not find her answer, she had to admit to herself.

Killing a family of three — and one of them a kid — requires something unique as the trigger, Evie acknowledged, reading the report again, and she knew in her gut she didn't have it yet. She'd convinced herself this was solid, and now the roller coaster headed back to reality. She'd push on the Durbins, but it was beginning to wobble. The interviews would be interesting, though. She'd head that way first. Maybe the idea would turn hot again when she met William and Nancy Durbin in person. She could always hope.

She smiled to herself and poured coffee to go, headed out to the car. She'd take hope wherever she could find it, knowing it would be a long week. Luck was mostly perspiration. She'd keep digging until there were no more questions to push and something gave. It usually did.

Gabriel Thane

Gabriel pushed aside another branch threatening to slap his face as he followed his brother back to the vehicles. Tuesday's search was over, another dozen flags had been set, and Gabriel — once Josh and Grace were safely out of sight — had dug up the ground to check what the dogs had found, but had discovered only animal remains. He watched Grace striding ahead of them, carrying the maps, while the dogs, happy to be free from further responsibility, circled around her.

"How's it going, Josh?" he asked.

His brother grimaced. "She stands looking out at the lake a lot, or silently crying as she walks behind me, marking the map. She

435

won't talk about much of anything. She's sometimes got headphones on, listening to music while we trail the dogs."

"Want me to come up with a solid reason she can't come out here for a few days?" Gabriel asked.

Josh shook his head. "It won't change things for her, Gabriel. Every day we clear more of this land and don't find anything, her sadness goes deeper. She'd convinced herself her parents were here, that we could find them. She's letting that go now. She'll go back with Ann and Paul Thursday evening, let me finish the search without her. Later in the week, the weather looks like it's going to turn, slow the search down."

"She'll be at your place this evening?"

"Dinner and a movie, then I'll take her over to our folks to sleep. It helps that she's not trying to stay at the campground — I don't have to worry about a reporter or former neighbor showing up. Why don't you bring Evie over and join us? Or at least take Evie out to a movie or something. She's been doing nothing but work too. It can't be what she planned when she thought about coming to Carin for a working vacation."

"She's got a guy, Josh. Name of Rob Turney. And the more I think about it, the more

I think he might be good for her. Evie's like Ann. She gets her head into a case, she just keeps turning it until something gives. She needs a life with someone other than a cop. The work never shuts off otherwise."

"All the more reason she needs to take a break. Frankly, you need the break more than any of us. You're looking pretty low, Gabriel, and it's not just the day-old stubble on your chin."

Gabriel rubbed his jaw, knew the tension he felt was visible, looked ahead at the farmhouse as they approached it. "This place does that to me."

"Yeah, we're both feeling a hint of what Grace is going through."

Josh pushed aside a low-hanging branch. "Grace hasn't said anything directly about her uncle. She's alluded to it, if you know what to listen for, but that's all. She did mention she's been going to church with Ann and Paul. I find it interesting that she's been able to face her pain with God easier than she's been able to talk with people."

"A little at a time," Gabriel replied. "How about you — you're going to be okay if she does mention it?"

Josh nodded. "I think so, if only because there are a few things I would like to say that I can't bring up until she opens that door. I think at times she is the saddest person I know, but then her gaze will clear and there's the Grace I remember."

"She's cracked a window, coming back here, letting herself remember."

"I think so," Josh agreed. "She's doing this alone, and that's the part that's so troubling."

"You're there for her. She can't fall that far down into her memories when friends like you are around."

"That's mostly what Ann and Rachel were doing, just being there. Anyway, food and a movie tonight. Come by if you change your mind, bring Evie," Josh mentioned again as the two caught up with Grace and the dogs.

"I'll see," Gabriel said. He went and said goodbye to Grace, then turned toward his truck. He wasn't sure he wanted to knock on that door. He'd found some kind of footing with Evie — task-focused, a friendship forming, not unlike the early days with Ann. Evie didn't want anything else right now. Another week, the Florist case solved or not, Evie wasn't even going to be here. He was careful to keep that in mind, for her sake as well as his.

Gabriel pushed open the post-office door, held his hand palm down behind him in the silent command Will had taught him.

"Do you know what the weather was like the night they disappeared?" Evie called over to him without looking up. "Full moon and bright, cloudy and dark, or . . . ?"

"Quarter moon, clear skies, but relatively dark," he replied. "And good evening to you too."

She looked up then, smiled, yet all she said was "Thanks," and then turned back to her notes.

"How does pizza sound for dinner again, shared with your dogs?"

That got her attention. He whispered a Dutch word Will had taught him as he stepped aside, and the dogs both barked. Evie was up in a flash. The dogs raced across the concrete floor to join her. She laughed and crouched down to give them a double hug. "Oh, you adorable guys, you look wonderful!"

Gabriel smiled at the warm greeting. "While you've been working, at least these two have been having a real vacation."

"Yeah, I saw the photos of them on the course Will had built for his own dogs, the teeter-totter and the hurdles to jump. I felt guilty even considering bringing them into town after I saw what they were enjoying with their two new friends."

Gabriel handed over the tug-of-war rope Will had made for them. "Apollo, Zeus, here you go," and the dogs leaped over to pick up either end, showing off for Evie. She laughed, watching them.

"What kind of pizza do you want? I'm going to order a medium meat-lovers just for them."

Evie's grin lit her face. "Canadian bacon and pineapple, if you don't mind being weird."

"I can handle it." He nodded at the second wall she was now filling in. It was, surprisingly, mostly artwork. "I'll order us dinner to be delivered and then you can talk to me about what you're doing. Does that work for you?"

"That would be great."

Gabriel offered her the sack of other dog toys Will had sent with him. Evie sent a couple of tennis balls sailing down the length of the post office, and the dogs gave an excited bark and surged after them. Gabriel pulled out his phone and ordered dinner with an extra twenty-minute delay. She needed the time to play with her dogs.

Gabriel pulled another tasty piece of pizza from the box, glad he'd ordered the thick crust. He picked up his root beer. For having dinner with a lady, it was as comfortable a date as most he'd had, which was either a sad fact or an acknowledgment that he didn't mind an evening with good food and work mixed in . . . *along with an intriguing woman,* he added silently, watching Evie over the lip of the bottle.

Evie had settled on a chair with her feet propped on another one, the dogs on either side of her. The dogs were content, having eaten well, played hard. Evie gestured at the second wall. "The sketches show the most likely routes the Florist family took that night from the house to the campground. If they needed to stop for gas, they went this way" — she pointed — "if they were interested in scenery along the route, they went that way. I started putting Xs on the routes, trying to figure out if that was where the crime happened, what was the most likely scenario. At the house, someone wants the cash they've got stored in the safe. At the gas station, someone wants the truck they're driving. That kind of thing. Just plotting where possible events might have taken place, seeing what makes the most sense."

"Okay, I follow. Anything new pop out?"

"A couple of things." She drank the last of her root beer. "What if they were killed in a car accident, three people dead? A truck

441

and camper accident, in this case. We see that all the time. A family gets killed in a bad vehicle accident. Only someone covers up the crash. Someone with multiple DUIs. Someone hauling a drug shipment. Driving a stolen semi. Someone with a reason to hide the accident from the authorities decides to cover it up."

He leaned forward, finding the idea interesting. "A bad accident that kills people is possible," he agreed. He'd worked a few horrific crashes during his career. "And I agree there could be a motive to hide a wreck, but the means to do so? If the truck could still be driven well enough to haul the camper, it probably wasn't a serious enough wreck to kill three people. And you're talking major moving equipment to clear vehicles off a road that were damaged enough for deaths. A tow truck. A tractor. You couldn't haul them much of a distance unless you could get them on a flatbed. If they went over the side of a bridge, down a ravine, smashed into a cornfield, or were moved there, the vehicles eventually get found. Maybe not in first few days, but the first week or two they'd get spotted from the air."

Evie considered that, nodded. "A wreck is the cleanest answer, and not finding them means someone wanted to cover it up. But I'll go along with you that it isn't easy to hide a wreck of this magnitude."

She leaned over to pat each dog. "Here's another idea. Say they arrived at the campground as planned, got parked, and settled in. Since the whole idea of the trip was family time, they get up early and rent a boat to go fishing, get out on the lake at dawn. Did the family get killed on the lake?"

Gabriel found the question equally intriguing. "A boating accident?"

"Could be," Evie said. "The boat flips suddenly, the water's really cold, three people drown. It happens. The problem is the truck and camper. Again, someone would have to have a reason to cover up what happened and move their truck and camper out of the park."

"State parks after hours use an honor system," Gabriel said. "You choose a place to park, the next morning park staff comes by and collects the lot fees, signs you in. You could figure out quickly who was a recent arrival by seeing who didn't have a check-in card lying on the vehicle dashboard. It's possible they could have arrived at the park and there's no record of it — if the vehicles were moved before staff came around."

"That's good to know. But it doesn't fit that it was a stranger crime. Someone recognizes the Florist family, kills them on the lake, knows what their truck and camper look like, finds the vehicles in the campground, and moves the vehicles before their friends call the cops to report they hadn't arrived," she summarized.

Gabriel liked the clean lines of it. The family was killed on the lake, the vehicles were moved, and all before the cops began the search. But he could see problems. "Bodies float," he pointed out, "unless they're weighted down. And gunshots on the water echo — a violent crime would have been heard by someone. I can see choppy water and a speedboat wake causing a smaller boat to flip over, I can see a near collision between boats, I can see an accident that puts the Florist family into the water, and maybe the son panics — it's cold water, trying to save each other, the family drowns. I can even see it being unnoticed — other boaters a distance away don't realize what's happened, especially if there's fog early in the morning. But the bodies would have been found. Maybe not that morning, but a day or two underwater, a body comes back to the surface. Three people drown — they get found unless deliberately held down somehow."

Evie thought about it, then said, "The family is killed on the lake. Someone had a reason to kill them and the time to cover it up, weigh down the bodies. They were out on the lake at dawn. Did anyone else disappear that weekend? Did the Florists see a body dumped in the lake, and someone had to kill the family to keep what they saw under wraps?"

Gabriel had to smile. "Now you're really getting out there, Evie."

"Yeah, I'm getting out there," she conceded. "But the idea of something happening to them after they arrived at their destination seems like a possibility. That lake is the perfect place to make bodies disappear."

She glanced over at him. "I've been looking at the Durbins — I was sure it was them for part of a day — but as volatile as they are, it's mostly petty stuff. I didn't get any particular hostile vibes from my interviews with them, and the money as a motive just doesn't work. They simply weren't broke enough to justify killing an entire family."

"I could have told you that had you asked," Gabriel said mildly.

"It would have been a family thing if it was them, and I didn't want to drag you in that direction again."

Gabriel chuckled. "I appreciate it. They're mostly nice people, who direct their annoyances and frustrations at each other. The rest of the world gets a pass."

"I concluded the same. Something happening at the campground, after the Florist family arrived — that idea still resonates as interesting to me." She studied the sketches again. "And I come back to the initial question. Where did this happen, Gabriel? At the house? During the drive? At the campground? Or is this a case where the family decided to run, and they vanished because they chose to?"

"Evie, those are questions we've been asking about this case on and off for twelve years. You need to accept that it may not be solvable, at least not with what we know today. You've given us a lot more information to consider than we had before, but the missing piece may not be here."

He could see from the stubborn set of her jaw that she didn't want to accept that. He felt an odd tenderness at the fact she didn't want to let this go. He'd admit they were finished before she did, but she'd get there. "What are the checkmarks on the aerial maps? Those are new."

She shifted to look at where he pointed.

"I've been checking off properties where I can document an interview took place. It's another way to look at the same basic question — the most likely routes they might have traveled that night and where something might have happened. Thirty miles is a lot of territory. I wanted to make sure everyone living along those routes was interviewed, that there weren't gaps in the coverage asking the basic questions — did you see anything, hear anything, notice something unusual that Thursday night or Friday morning? There are a few gaps as you get farther north toward the campground, a few stretches where it's four miles between interviews, but it's not out of line with the number of homes in the area. It was an interesting question, except it didn't take me anywhere particularly useful."

Gabriel studied that map. "Trying to fill in those gaps after this many years is a long shot, but it's something to consider."

"If someone had noticed something, I'm guessing they would have made a point to call and mention it at the time," Evie replied. "Putting out a new reward for information might help, though, give someone with a sliver of a memory a reason to call you."

"Let's give that some thought. So the new

IDs haven't gone anywhere?" he asked.

Rather absently, she shook her head. "They don't appear to have ever been used, not for a driver's license, for tax returns, to register a PO box, take out a business license, buy real estate or a vehicle. The state databases don't have the names, and the FBI is about done looking at national records."

"What about the idea of the son becoming a cop?"

"I've been looking through police academy class photos, because I like that idea, looking for someone who resembles Scott's photo when he was twenty. So far it's not led anywhere."

He studied the work she'd done and nodded. "Evie, let's call it a night. Ride with me out to Will's with the dogs, they might as well stay with him the last few days rather than be stuck in town. We'll find something to talk about that isn't work. At some point you have to accept this case has pushed as far as it's going to move, and let it go."

Evie looked at the two dogs stretched out beside her, ran her foot over Apollo's back. "They have been enjoying their stay with Will and his dogs."

He smiled. "Why don't you let me help you pack this case away tomorrow, you can have Thanksgiving with us on Thursday, and then you should get yourself home, have Friday through Sunday as a true vacation before you're back at work with the State Police on Monday. I'm feeling rather guilty you haven't watched more than one movie since you've been on this so-called vacation, haven't enjoyed that nice house you rented. You've only worked. Rob would enjoy seeing you this weekend, I'm sure, and there's probably stuff you need to do in Springfield."

Evie faintly smiled back. "Kicking me out, Gabriel?"

"Just trying to be fair-minded. I really do appreciate what you've done here, Evie. These people are my friends, and I want to know what happened to them. But there's a point you put it back in the box and go on with life. I think we're there."

She nodded. "I'll think about it, Gabriel. There's a place where I'm content to say I've done what I can do, but I don't think I'm quite there yet. Let's take the dogs out to Will's. You can find me some ice cream for dessert if there's a place still open this late."

"I imagine there is," he replied, mildly amused. *As stubborn as Ann,* he thought, but really didn't mind. Evie did this job until there was nothing else to do. That determination was apparently bedrock to her personality.

Evie slipped her shoes on, the dogs crowding around her. She laughed. "I'm coming with you, guys." She glanced over and smiled. "I've missed running with them. They do a couple of miles with me most days."

He tried to imagine doing that for fun, couldn't picture it. "I'll settle for tossing a tennis ball for them to chase." He held the door open, and the dogs maneuvered Evie outside ahead of them. Gabriel looked between Zeus and Apollo, thought the two animals had her figured out. *They shepherd her around as the third member of their pack without her even realizing it. Smart dogs.* He held the back door of the truck open, and they scrambled in behind the front seats. "Think they would like ice cream? We could get them both basic sundaes."

Evie clicked her seat belt in place. "They'd love it."

Gabriel wouldn't mind another hour with the dogs around. Evie relaxed when they were with her. He'd take full advantage of that.

FOURTEEN

Evie Blackwell

Evie heard Gabriel's whistle as the door opened, noted he'd taken it up again, and had to admit the song fragment was growing on her. She could almost whistle it in harmony now.

"Thanksgiving, Evie. Shut it down for a couple hours for some good food."

"Almost there," she replied. She added another date to her timeline. "What are the odds you could park a camper someplace for twelve years and no one would mention it?"

"If the lot fees are paid on time, who cares how long a camper sits there?"

"That's what I'm thinking. Like an old bank box. So long as the fee is paid, and the automatic transfer from a savings or checking account clears, the box can go dormant and no one would know."

"Are you thinking the cash is sitting in a

451

bank box?"

She turned at the remark, startled. "What did you say?"

"The cash they were accumulating. Susan could have been storing it in one of the larger safe-deposit boxes rather than carrying it home. Forty thousand would fit."

She beamed. "Yes!" She spun back to the wall, grabbed the green marker, and wrote *Bank box!* on the first open area of white paper.

Gabriel chuckled. "I think we just cross-communicated. What were *you* talking about?"

"I think they unhitched the camper and left it at the campground — either at their destination or farther north, away from where the search would have started. Or maybe they parked it at a storage lot. But my gut says they just parked it at a campground. Swap it with one that hasn't been moved for a couple months, has grass growing up around it, slap on some bumper stickers, swap license plates, and hide the camper in plain sight. One camper basically looks the same as the next."

"Who?"

"Either the Florist family making a clean getaway or whoever killed them." She picked up her root beer from the table. "Or maybe someone else who followed the Florist family to the campground. I do lean toward the fact they arrived at their destination before trouble happened. Anyway, that bank-box comment of yours is brilliant. What do you want to bet there's a bank account and safe-deposit box in the name of Simon or May Carnoff? Susan could have opened an account once they had the false IDs. She opened new accounts as a routine part of her job. Seed the account with five hundred dollars and pay the box rent automatically as an account transfer. She handled accessing the safe-deposit box room too as part of her job. The money is still sitting in the bank here. Why carry that much cash home when she could just store it in a bank box?"

"A great question," Gabriel said, "but the bank is closed on Thanksgiving. You won't get an answer until tomorrow."

"The banker in the family — is he high enough up the chain to have keys? All we need is a check on the name to know if it's something to pursue."

"I'll make a call. Now come on, Evie, close it down. Good turkey waits for no person, and I'm not giving up the wishbone without good cause — it's my year to claim it."

Evie laughed and closed the files. "Tell security to come on over. I'm done for

453

now." She had leads to tug on and that felt good. She was also in favor of a good meal that wasn't pizza.

Joshua Thane

Josh closed the grill, satisfied the turkey was coming along. His phone chimed a message, and he glanced at it. "Ann's here. I'll walk down and meet her, Mom, see if she needs help carrying anything."

"If you can carry it along with her stuff, bring me another bag of ice from the bait shop. Or if you see your father, he can bring it."

"Will do." Josh headed down the path toward the pier to meet Ann, figuring he could share a quick update with her and ask about the Dayton family.

He heard the ice cream truck's jingle before he saw the vehicle in the parking lot. The campgrounds were full this holiday weekend with those who preferred a less traditional Thanksgiving celebration.

Josh saw Ann walking toward the pier, eating an ice cream cone. It was a nice sunny day, probably one of the last this warm for the year. He bought himself a vanilla cone and headed after Ann, looking forward to a few private minutes. A small group of people were on the pier, an older couple getting situated in a boat, one of his staff helping them out, and a girl probably six or seven, who was peering over the edge of the dock at the water, a chocolate ice cream cone dripping onto her hand.

Ann stopped beside her and said something to the girl, handed over extra napkins. Their laughter rippled out over the water. Josh stopped and watched. Ann hadn't come here alone. He walked across the dock to join them, Ann glancing back over her shoulder as she felt the gentle sway of the boards. Her smile was calm and quiet and quintessential Ann. *Another secret unfolding,* he thought as he stopped beside the two. The child's attention was on a sunfish just below the surface, producing an occasional bubble and flip of fin that caught the light.

"Hello."

She looked up at him. *Six years old,* he thought, *without a doubt.* He struggled for words after hello. To give himself a moment, he settled to her height and looked down into the water with her. "Nice fish." There were half a dozen small sunfish in the group.

"I don't want to catch them, just look."

"Okay."

He considered the little girl, saw her lick at her melting cone. "Try vanilla." He held out his cone for her. She smiled and did so.

"You'd be Little Grace. You're adorable, like your mom."

"Yes, I am."

He grinned. "Like to swim?"

"Will the fish nibble at my toes? Andy says they will."

He thought about how to answer. "Andy must like you a lot to tell you that secret."

"He gave me a valentine. I didn't give him one."

"Maybe next year, if he's still a friend, you can."

The fish moved toward the end of the dock, and she went with them, back to licking her chocolate cone before it was a puddle on the dock.

"Major secret, Ann," he whispered as he rose.

"Yes."

They stood watching as the child finished her cone, then knelt down to watch the fish dart around the post of the dock. The boat was loaded with guests now and finally left the dock, its small motor sputtering away. The girl watched it go with interest.

"Single mom," Ann said softly.

"A dad in the picture?"

"No. Never will be."

Josh nodded, handed Ann his cone, and walked down the dock to join the girl.

"Little Grace, come meet my mom. She's fixing a feast, and we can sample if we're quick about it."

She giggled. "My name's Angel."

"Of course it is," he said with a smile. "You can ride up top." He swung her up to sit on his shoulders.

She held on to his hands rather than his hair — someone had given the child lessons in how to be a good passenger. *Paul probably,* he thought, seeing the comfortable look Ann shared with the child.

"Don't forget to tell Josh about your vacation."

The girl leaned over to see his face. "Do you like horses?"

"Yes."

"I rode on one that belongs to a real cowboy."

"Did you now, really?"

"I flew in a big plane with lots of people, and Quinn taught me to laugh from my belly and throw a lasso at a post, and I ran around with old Blue, he's their dog, and chased a cow back into the corral, and Lisa fit me with chaps for my jeans so I could be official and everything, and my cowboy boots are beautiful like me, 'cause Quinn agreed it was okay for them to be pink 'cause I'm a girl."

He grinned as he followed that report to interesting places. "Did you see any lambs while you were out there? My brother Will has a couple of those."

"Can you show me?"

"Sure."

"Do you have lots of brothers? 'Cause I've only got me and Mom, and I want brothers, lots of them, so they can be my posse when we go after bad guys and gold and stuff."

"Are you a treasure hunter?"

"Well, not yet, but I want to be."

"What else do you want to be?"

"Oh, chipmunks!" Her slender body twitched around as he stopped and she watched two of them chase each other. When they had disappeared, he set out walking again.

"I want to have adventures and see the sea, but I don't think I want to go in caves, 'cause they're creepy and dark and might have snakes, and the really old mines are grimy and might fall down on you, so I won't go in those either, but old cellars and barns and dried riverbeds often hide stuff so I could look there for treasure."

"That would be smart for an adventurer."

She leaned over to look at him again. "I might want to go into space like Bishop, but you can't tell Mom because she's like 'Keep your feet on the ground, Angel,' " she mimicked in a singsong voice, "but I think floating around without gravity would be a lot of fun."

"That's a big secret to keep. What do I get in return if I do?"

"What do you want?"

He thought about it. "Could you make me a valentine?" he asked.

"Yes."

"Then we have our first secret that I won't tell your mom. Though maybe we can only have three or four of those, because I like talking to your mom about stuff."

"Okay. I only have a couple I could tell you."

"What's another one?"

"She thinks I don't know her uncle made her sad."

He gently rubbed her knee and tried to swallow the lump growing in his throat. "Yeah. That would be an okay secret not to tell your mom." He shifted his grip to her tennis shoes as they reached the level ground. "Do you like turkey?"

"Yes. Is that what smells good?"

He smiled. "I cooked it."

"You did? Really?"

He swung her down from his shoulders.

459

"Come and see." He took her over to the grill. "Hold your breath, it's going to shoot out smoke at you," he warned and lifted the lid. She waved her hand and giggled.

"Okay, what do you think?" He lifted her up so she could see the browning bird.

She studied it. "It looks really good," she declared.

He kissed her cheek and set her back on the ground. "Compliments are accepted." His mother, seated at the patio table, was watching them with great curiosity. "Angel, this is my mother, Marie."

Angel turned shy, keeping a hand on his jeans as she greeted the woman. "Hello."

His mom leaned forward and offered her hand. "Hello back to you."

They carefully shook. The girl tipped her head to look up at Josh. "She's tiny," she whispered. "How did she have you?"

His mother laughed. "I have lots of photos of him and his brothers when they were small. Would you like to see some of them?"

"Smaller than me?"

"A lot smaller."

"Yes, please — then I can believe it."

Marie offered her hand. "Some of the pictures are on the walls inside. And I need to check pumpkin pies in the oven. Would you like to help me do that?"

"Sure. Do you have that white stuff for on top of the pie? Because ice cream is okay, but that fluffy white is better."

"If I don't, I will send Josh to get us some."

"That would be good." The little girl slid her hand into his mother's and they disappeared into the house together.

Josh could think of a dozen questions, but he cleared up a fairly major one first. "Space?" he queried Ann, glancing over as she took a seat at the patio table.

Ann smiled. "She's spent time this last year over at Bishop Space Repair, Inc. with Jim Bishop. Grace works there on occasion when they need small hands to build one of their space bots. Angel hangs out in the workshop, helping out Jim, or Kelly Gold, his number two."

He knew astronaut Jim Bishop had retired after the last shuttle launch, but he hadn't heard about the company. "They're going to make it back into space as a private venture?"

"Gina Bishop figured out how to 3-D print a rocket made of solid rocket fuels. They've been launching small-scale versions of it for months in all kinds of weather and wind conditions. You'll see a big one launch into space next month on a test flight with the Navy. It's dropped the costs from several million for a space launch to about two hundred thousand."

"That sounds like Gina."

Ann laughed. "It does. The Bishop brothers are going into business to repair satellites that otherwise would enter orbital decay, tumble into the atmosphere, and burn up. A satellite costs three to four hundred million to build, minimum; they'll charge five or six million to go fix it. They plan to send up a couple of spider-like robots and a repair box of supplies, catch up to the satellite in question, use the bots to replace gyroscopes, swap out electronic boards and instruments, add more fuel so the maneuvering thrusters can keep the satellite in position, then lift the satellite back to its normal orbit. To listen to Bryce and Jim Bishop talk, it's going to be a viable business doing four to six repair flights a year within three years. When Mark Bishop retires from the Navy, he's going to join them as president of the company."

"The things being done in secret . . ."

Ann smiled. "It won't be a secret much longer once the big rocket flies. I figure they're going to pour the profits of the satellite repairs into building a capsule so that Jim can go back into space himself as a privately funded astronaut. Give it a decade and it's likely Angel's going to have astronaut friends coming to her high school graduation party. If she really wants to dream of space, there's going to be a door waiting wide open for her to walk through."

"A little girl should dream big," he agreed. "I'm glad those dreams are being encouraged, Ann, rather than knocked down by events. Where's Grace?"

Ann's smile faded. "She's talking with Paul. He's going to bring her out this way when she's ready. I told her not to hurry. If she needs a few hours on her own, I've got Angel here with me, and a plate from Thanksgiving will heat up fine."

"Thanks, Ann, for giving her what she needs."

"It's what I can do. She's wrapping this up, Josh. I don't think she'll be here after today. Angel wanted to see the lake her mom talks about, and I think Grace needed to give you the rest of the story, which is why she asked me to bring her daughter here. Grace didn't have it in her to explain all this. Don't think less of her for that."

"I'm glad she let me in on the full picture. It doesn't change things or push us apart. Probably the opposite."

"I thought it might. She's a good kid."

463

"Grace without the shadows," Josh murmured.

"Exactly," Ann said.

He smiled. "It's going to be easy to love both of them."

"Those around her already do. You're welcome to be part of that circle if you want in."

He listened to the girl laughing inside with his mom. "I want in."

Gabriel Thane

Gabriel watched the little girl laughing with Josh, and he thought Angel had transformed this Thanksgiving Day. Karen and Will looked quite content too, sharing an outdoor lounge chair and watching eagles soar over the lake. He saw Evie disappear down the hall with Ann, heard the two of them chuckling over something. The stress of the last two weeks was easing away, that was apparent. He didn't see his father, Paul, or Grace, so the complete group had yet to arrive.

The shock of learning that Grace had a daughter had worn off rather abruptly with a simple introduction from Josh and a meaningful brother-to-brother glance. Since Gabriel rarely met a kid he didn't like, and the girl had a smile that could make a stone heart smile back, he thought he'd done fine with the introductions.

He checked out the appetizers, picked up a cucumber slice with a green pepper mustache, red pepper lips, and black olive eyes. A spreadable cheese held the vegetables together. It was the first time he could remember laughing before he ate vegetables. Karen's contribution, he was sure. He helped himself to a second one. *Remarkably good,* he decided.

Evie returned, and Gabriel blinked at the color splash. She'd changed her shirt to match Ann and Angel. They were now a vibrant neon yellow, hand-painted with what might be turkeys.

Evie plopped a shirt in his hands. "You're messing up the dress code."

He simply grinned. *Why not?* He stepped into Josh's room and changed, looked in the mirror and winced. At least he wouldn't have to look at himself. He found his mother in the kitchen, filling an ice bucket, sporting one of the yellow shirts, only this one had lots of feathers painted on it. Or maybe it was ears of corn.

Casserole dishes were in the oven keeping warm, three crock-pots were lined up on the counter, the stove top held pans with noodles, corn on the cob, potatoes and gravy, and, on the far counter, pies were cooling. *A true Thane Thanksgiving Day feast.* As soon as Josh declared the bird done, this meal would be ready. "Mom, what's left?"

She glanced around. "You can set the tables, inside and out."

He opened the cupboard to get down plates. Evie offered to help, and he handed her the plates and gathered glasses together. He smiled at the two coming into the kitchen. "Your vegetables are good enough to eat, Karen."

"Thanks." She saw what he was doing. "Will, you do the silverware."

Will obliged while Karen got out napkins and holders for the corn on the cob.

His mom nodded her approval. "Karen."

"Yes, ma'am."

"I've got something I'd like to say."

Karen looked over at Marie with a cautious smile. "I'd like to hear it. I think."

"I appreciate you bringing those cute vegetables even my sons are eating without a fuss. It shows you put some time and effort into the dish, but didn't want to show up other cooks in the house. You've got a nice, tactful side to you, given I know you're the best cook to ever step into a Thane house."

Karen blushed.

"I've got three sons," Marie went on, "and it's wonderful to see one of them settling down." Will was turning red. "You don't need to be cooking great meals and inviting family over on holidays, Karen. You just show up here hungry and bring whatever suits your fancy and you'll fit in this family fine. But just remember one thing. You want peace with a man's mother, you bring him to church every Sunday, and when the kids come along, you bring them too."

"Mom —"

Karen sent Will a quelling look. "I can do that, Mrs. Thane," she replied promptly.

Marie laughed. "You'll be good for my son. He gives you trouble, you just tell me. And it's 'Marie' from now on."

Karen's blush covered her face now, but her smile was real. "I can do that too, Marie."

Gabriel watched the exchange, gave Will a glance, saw relief under the embarrassment. Mom's approval would matter for so many reasons, just as his father's would. He hadn't expected her to be quite so forward about matters, but it was clear Karen had just been welcomed to the family in more than a passing manner.

"Gabriel, there's your father," Marie was saying. "He's got more ice. Fill those glasses

467

before you put them around." Paul and Grace came in, both already in the yellow shirts. Gabriel saw his mom give Angel the job of carrying the salad bowls to the table and smiled at the girl's concentration. Get assigned a job, you had a place in this family.

He waited at the door for Grace to bring through the hot bread basket and the salad dressing options, softly said, "Your daughter has stolen Mom's heart. She's been hoping for a decade for some grandkids to enjoy."

Grace met his gaze and seemed to understand the deeper meaning. "I like your mom, I always have."

"She's always wanted to see Chicago at Christmastime — all those decorations and places to shop," he added.

Grace smiled. "One holiday at a time, Gabriel."

Josh joined them with a questioning look, but Grace moved on to the table with the bread. Gabriel thought it likely their family Christmas was going to be spread out this year. He worked Christmas Day so that his deputies could be with their families, just as his dad had always done, so the Thane family was used to getting together a day or two early or late. Some would find a reason to go north this year, he expected, to stop and see Grace and her daughter.

"Angel, come tell me if you think the turkey is done," Josh called. He waited until the girl joined him before lifting the lid. He boosted her up to see, poked a long fork into it, watched the juice run clear. "What do you think, Angel?"

She nodded decisively. "It's done."

"Then I need you to bring me that big silver tray on the kitchen counter, the one with the turkey picture on it."

She went to get it as Josh shut down the grill. Josh lifted the bird onto the plate, brought it over to the table, and handed the carving knife to Caleb. Dad said grace, a particularly meaningful one, sliced the turkey, and the feast officially began.

Gabriel wrapped the wishbone ends in two napkins and went to find Evie. She was sitting at the table on the deck with a piece of pumpkin pie, whipped cream on top, along with a side scoop of vanilla ice cream. Her conversation with Grace was mostly laughter. Gabriel almost hated to interrupt, but some things were important. He hunkered down beside her. "Make a wish."

Evie considered the offer and took a good competitive hold of her end. She closed her eyes. "Okay."

He tugged quick, having learned if he wanted to win, it took a swift break. But she must have had some experience in the matter too, and she twisted her wrist, grinning as she came up with the winning piece.

"A good wish?"

"One of the best," she assured him.

"Better be. I don't get the wishbone for another four years."

She laughed.

"I got a call from the banker in the Florist family," he said quietly. "There's a bank account in the name Simon Carnoff and a safe-deposit box. We'll have to drill the box, which requires a court order and a locksmith. I'm getting it arranged for eight a.m. tomorrow. There will be time to see what's there before we head over to interview Phil Peters and his wife."

Her sudden hug nearly toppled him. "Yes!" She grinned at him. "Have you told Paul? Your dad? They're the ones who found the names."

"I'll tell them next." He realized he was wearing some of the whipped cream from her fork.

"Oops," she giggled as he wiped it off his shirt and licked his finger.

"Enjoy the rest of your pie."

"It really is great news," she told him

again, her face alight.

"It is." But he wasn't letting work intrude any further into the day, so he simply smiled and left to get a piece of pie of his own.

Evie Blackwell

Evie noticed Ann on the pier and headed down to join her. Josh had taken Grace and Angel along with Karen out for a boat ride, and it didn't take much to interpret the child's laughter over the water. Josh was letting the child steer the boat as they came back toward the pier.

"I'll be sad to see Grace leave," Evie said, watching the boat head in. Grace and her daughter would be flying back to Chicago with Ann and Paul later tonight.

Ann waved at the little girl. "Grace handled her time here better than I thought she would. But she's ready to go home, be with Angel, focus on Christmas plans. Josh will get the search of the land finished in another week, depending on the weather. Either way, I think Grace will be able to accept the news, whichever way it goes."

Evie agreed with that assessment. "I'll call you if the bank box yields anything interesting. If the Florist family ran, the box is empty, and if they didn't, the box has something in it. I can't decide which answer

I want."

"You're making progress, Evie. You've still got three more days."

Evie smiled. "Hope springs eternal that a cold case can get solved."

"The task force is going to face a lot of days like this one," Ann noted.

"I just wanted to impress him, you know? Pick the one. Governor Bliss, Gabriel, the other cops who are going to be on the task force. Solving the disappearance of a deputy and his family — my ambition has never been a problem."

"You've still got the interview with the Peters tomorrow. I can come down this weekend to do a last review of the case if you like."

Evie shook her head. "That's okay, Ann. The Dayton case is solved, and I can live with one out of two. Gabriel and I will talk over the Florist case one more time during the drive back from the interview tomorrow, and I'll be ready to let it go. If we don't get a break and solve it now, it's time to put it back in the box."

"Has it been fun, Evie? The last couple of weeks?" Ann asked. "And I use the word *fun* deliberately."

She thought about it and nodded. "It's been a wide open case, where you can consider whatever you can come up with, and I've needed that, Ann. I wasn't standing over a bloodstained dead body in a bedroom, trying to figure out if the husband did it or the son. As serious as this case is — a family of three missing — it didn't have the weight that something more immediate would have. I needed the freedom a cold case gave me just to explore what might be answers without having to worry about what the idea sounded like in a daily progress report."

Ann nodded. "That's one reason I didn't try very hard to talk you out of using your vacation time for this. The pace of your job, the immediacy of cases, has a different tempo than this kind of work. I think you'll enjoy being on the task force, going after these unsolved cases. Some of them can be miserable, as the Dayton one became, but some of them can be like the Florists, a challenging puzzle to solve. And you will solve any number of them, Evie."

"I'm becoming resigned to the fact that someone else is going to locate the missing piece of this one. I know it's there. I also know I don't have it yet. Maybe we get lucky with the safe-deposit box tomorrow, or the partner interview, but I'm probably clutching at straws."

"I'd like to have lunch with you and debrief these two weeks sometime later in December, after you've gotten some distance from the work, both in time and space."

"We'll do that, Ann," Evie said, pleased at the suggestion. She was having a hard time imagining life back on the job, being home in Springfield, and that was going to be her reality in just a few days. This working vacation had been a true break for her in that respect — it had pushed normal so far into the background, it was no longer a clear picture in her mind.

Gabriel's life will get back to normal too, she realized, once their temporary work area was cleared and the cases boxed away again. She'd turn in her yellow convertible, pick up keys to her now-repaired car, and collect the dogs. Life was moving back toward its normal routine again. She'd adjust — a day or two back on the job and this would seem like a distant memory. But she'd miss Carin County, the people, and especially the Thanes.

She watched Gabriel and Will walk out of the bait shop with their father, talking with Paul. *An interesting family, the Thanes.* Saying she was going to miss them didn't quite fit the emotions she was feeling.

"Friends don't cease being friends," Ann commented softly. Evie glanced over, realized Ann had noticed her gaze.

"You collect friends this way, don't you?" Evie said. "A day or two in a place, put down a marker, come back again and fill in more of the picture with another day or two." She was beginning to understand what had puzzled her about Ann.

"Sure." Ann tipped her head toward Josh, who was getting ready to tie up the boat. "You didn't spend much time with Josh the last couple of weeks, but I bet you have a pretty good sense of him. The same with Will."

"I do. Mostly through what Gabriel has said, or times I've seen them as a family."

"Just take that knowledge and start adding layers to it. People who know them mention something, adding to comments you hear about what's going on in their lives. The Thanes are an easy family in which to form friendships because there isn't tension within its members. You come in the door with one person and end up knowing the group if you pay attention to the details."

"You do that so easily, Ann," Evie remarked.

"It's just practice, and listening," Ann replied. "Gabriel isn't sure how he wants things left with you. That was obvious today. He's aware you've got a life away from here, don't plan to come back this way, but he's not inclined to simply accept a goodbye. I have a feeling he'll let you decide that. That's his way. For his brothers, Josh and Grace are renewing a childhood friendship that mattered to both of them. Will and Karen are falling in love. Back to Gabe — he would make room for you in his life, if you want that. He can be a good friend. If you see that in your future, or something more than that one day, he's a safe and comfortable guy, Evie."

"The 'something more' part, I don't know that I do, at least not right now."

Ann thoughtfully nodded. "Then accept some advice, friend, no matter what you conclude about Gabriel. Make a point to stop this way when business has you in the area, start layering in friendships with Marie, with Karen. They're the kind of women who can appreciate who you are as a cop and yet give you room to breathe. You'll never regret that kind of relationship."

It made sense what Ann was suggesting, staying tied into the dynamic here, and for so many reasons. Evie wanted the circles of friends Ann seemed to naturally form around her, and she was seeing how they could be built. She could start a circle of her own here in Carin. She'd be welcome, understood, and she was beginning to grasp the significance of having that in her life.

Paul strolled down to the dock to join them, and Ann went to meet him, slipping her arms under his for a hug. Evie watched them together, let herself consider that picture. Ann was a good cop who had decided a guy mattered. Evie knew her own world might be better off if she decided to go that way one day. *But it isn't today,* she concluded. She looked back as Josh helped Angel hop out of the boat onto the dock, her smile turned up to his face. A child's delight without shadows. Evie wished the world was all such joy.

Okay, it was time to get back to work, finish what she'd come here to do, and then pack to go home. Whatever Carin County was going to be to her in the future would sort itself out. She had a final three days, and she was determined to make the most of them.

Joshua Thane

"Grace has a daughter."

Josh turned with a smile at the quiet words of his mother, patted the seat on the bench beside him. The evening was wrapping up as most holidays did, with leftovers boxed and distributed for family to take home, and with a few spare moments of time just to sit and think.

Marie took the seat beside him. "I thought for a moment I was seeing things, when you walked up the path with Angel riding on your shoulders, and I saw that smile she has, that joy. I remember Grace when she was five, when she still had that same smile. It was like being transported back in time."

"I saw that in your expression, that fleeting sense of shock. Thanks for making the shift so quickly so Angel felt your welcome."

"It's impossible not to welcome that little girl," his mom answered with a smile. "Are you doing okay, honey?"

"The news was a punch, I'll admit that, but yeah, I'm good," Josh replied. "In a way it's easier, knowing Grace went on with her life, made some mistakes of her own, but at least let a guy love her once. She has a daughter. I was afraid she was going to be so off men after what she'd been through, no one would ever get close. As painful as it must be to have a relationship fail, to be a single mom, she at least was willing to let someone in."

"Looking for love."

Josh nodded his agreement with her quiet

statement. "Yeah." He didn't try to sort out the rest of what he was feeling. Grace was working her way back from the pain of what had happened to her, the pain of what she'd done to herself, but she was facing it and dealing with it. He understood what courage looked like. "Angel is fascinating — has such a big view of life and loves her mom. She's a wonderful girl. You see the two of them together and it's a great picture."

Marie patted his knee. "Which is one reason why I keep waiting for my sons to marry, give me grandkids. There's a lifetime of those memories when you have children around."

Josh smiled. "I'm thinking Will and Karen will give you those grandchildren in the next few years. Gabriel and I . . . we're going to remain your problem sons for a while yet."

Marie laughed. "My sons keep me young, which is as it should be." She rested her hands on either side of his face, studied him closely, nodded at what she saw in his expression. "Grace returns to Chicago, and you finish the search she's asked of you. That's what a Thane does, for the girl he had a crush on in grade school. Then you call her, you talk, and this time she isn't the girl who leaves and is gone. Yes?"

Josh had to smile at the way she worded

it. "Yes."

She rose to her feet. "Time will solve the rest. Don't sit out so late tonight you catch yourself a cold."

"Mom —"

She laughed at his protest that could make two syllables out of *mom*, waved goodbye.

Josh watched her walk down the path around the house and thought he was a most blessed son to have her as his mother. Wherever matters went with Grace and Angel, he'd have family around to share that journey.

He turned back to studying the fading sunset, content to have a stunning day of surprises now end quietly. *Grace has a daughter.* The world had tilted on its axis today and become a different shape. The door had now opened for him to get to know Angel too. He suspected Angel would share her life easily, while Grace would still hold on to layers of reserve for a considerable amount of time. He'd learned patience watching Will. He'd adapt. He had two good reasons to do so now.

He pushed his hands into his pockets, admitted to himself he was beginning to get chilled. Trust Mom to always be right. He gave himself a few more minutes, then rose to go inside. Grace and Angel would be arriving back in Chicago soon, and Grace had promised a text to say they were safely home. After that came through, he'd call it an early night himself. This day had taken enough turns, and it was time to have it behind him.

Fifteen

Evie Blackwell

Evie had never witnessed a safe-deposit box's lock being drilled out before. She found it fascinating even if rather swiftly over. The long drill bit cut through with ease, and then the man cut the power and lifted his goggles. "There you go," the locksmith said. He gathered up his tools. "I'll send my bill to the bank."

"Thank you, Kyle."

"Anytime, Sheriff, anytime."

Gabriel turned to the bank manager. "Mr. Nelson, I appreciate you arranging this for us. Now it's police business, and I'll need to ask you to step outside." With notable reluctance, the manager left with the locksmith.

Evie stepped over to the safe-deposit box, twelve by ten inches and quite deep. Gabriel pulled the box from its slot. "It doesn't feel empty," he said as he set it on a roll-cart table. They had the room to themselves, so he didn't suggest the privacy booth but merely stepped back. "Want to do the honors, Evie?"

She'd hoped he would ask. "Sure." She moved to the end of the box, feeling a mixture of anticipation and dread. She lifted the lid, braced to find it mostly empty. Instead, neat stacks of deposit envelopes at one end reached nearly to the top of the box. At the other end were wrapped pieces of fabric — *from a cut-up pillowcase,* she thought after a moment's study.

Gabriel opened one of the envelopes. "Cash." He quickly counted up the bills. "Looks to be the duplicate mortgage payment Susan was withdrawing. So twenty-four envelopes like this one will give us about twenty-eight thousand total. The rest of the envelopes . . ." He chose one at random to open. "There's three hundred dollars in this one." He did a quick count of envelopes in the sacks. "If that's representative, say another ten thousand in cash."

"So the money has been here all along," Evie said.

"What's the cloth about?"

Evie picked up the top item, unfolded it, found several watches and bracelets. "Easy items to pawn, I think, probably worth a thousand."

She set it aside and picked up the next one, recognized it by the feel. "Gabriel, this is a gun." She unfolded the fabric, carefully cleared the weapon to confirm it wasn't loaded. "It's a .22." It didn't smell of either gunpowder or the cleaning solvent commonly used, but then it had been stored for a long time.

Gabriel sucked in a breath. "The gun that killed Frank Ash?"

She nodded. "We put a rush on the request. We'll know in a day if you can have a deputy run it over to the lab."

"I'll get that arranged."

She wrapped the gun back in the cloth and handed it to him. "The Florists don't strike me as the type to knowingly keep a murder weapon."

"I'd agree." Gabriel opened the evidence box he had brought and stored the gun inside.

Evie leaned against the wall as she watched Gabriel transfer the rest of the contents of the safe-deposit box over to the evidence box. "We found their money. And we just hit another dead end."

He glanced over at her.

She elaborated. "Scott purchased new IDs for them. Susan used that new name to open an account and safe-deposit box. They were squirreling away cash. The gun — they probably secured a weapon that wouldn't be traced to the family for security, as Scott would be leaving behind any gun known to be his. The fact this box is full, and that it's all still here, says they didn't run. Someone murdered them, probably that night, and my best new motive for why — the money — just went up in smoke. The money is right here."

"I can hear your disappointment," Gabriel said with a smile. "But look at it the other way. You've managed to prove they were in counseling, had acquired new IDs, were stashing away money, and you've found that money. Enjoy this discovery, Evie. It's confirmation of what they planned."

"But I haven't found *them*. And as far as I can tell, I'm nowhere closer to the Florist family's whereabouts than I was when this started."

"The gun may go somewhere we can follow." He closed up the evidence box. "Let me get this logged into evidence and locked away in the property room, get a deputy on the way to the lab with the .22. Then we'll regroup, get on the road. Let's go talk with Phil Peters and his wife."

She nodded, wondering what it was going

to feel like if the gun led nowhere and this interview also turned into a dead end. She'd have to put everything back in the boxes, store it back in the archives, and accept it was still a cold case. She didn't like that kind of finish, not one bit, but she could see it coming at her like a train without brakes.

Phil Peters looked like the retired Navy guy and deputy he was. He had the size for it, both height and strength, and a bluntness that fit, though nothing about him was harsh or intimidating. Evie appreciated that kind of directness. Jenna was a petite woman, cheerful yet quiet. They were a nice couple — that was Evie's first impression. When they were comfortably seated, cold drinks in hand, pleasantries exchanged, Phil, in his down-to-business style, turned the conversation to the Florist family.

"I saw Scott that Wednesday night about ten p.m., took over charcoal and my traveling grill he wanted to borrow for camping. Everything seemed fine to me. Joe was casting fishing rods in the side yard to see if any needed respooling. Susan was around too; I saw her carrying out jackets and towels to the camper. They were looking forward to the three days away, it looked to me.

"I was butting heads a bit with Scott

about them going with the Durbins, figuring they would be having anything but a restful weekend. But Scott was like, 'Family is family, and it won't be so bad.' This was at a time when the Durbins were starting to squabble with each other, even in public — you'd hear them four tables away at the Fast Café. The wife had a yen to travel, and William's solution was to go camping, which wasn't exactly what Nancy had in mind.

"Scott mostly wanted to see me that night to go over reminders for my wedding on Sunday. I had the ring, the tux fit, even remembered the mints for my pocket. He was more uptight about the wedding than I was. Jenna and Susan had every detail planned in triplicate. I just wanted him to go camping, get out of my hair for a few hours."

Jenna, shy as she seemed, laughed. "That's about all Susan and I talked about that last month — flowers and decorations, invitations and seating arrangements. There was a wedding planner in charge of the final seventy-two hours, and even volunteers backing up the ones doing the decorating. She made sure I wouldn't set foot in the church until the wedding march. I was supposed to stop thinking *wedding* and go enjoy a spa outing with my college roommates. It was a treat being at that point — there really was nothing left that was my responsibility, except getting my gown on." Jenna laughed again. "We were already packed for the honeymoon cruise. Even our driver to the airport, another deputy, had a backup in case he got called into work. That was what Susan and I talked about that day they were leaving, the honeymoon cruise we had planned. Life was chaotic but normal, happy."

Phil nodded. "Chaotic and happy, that about sums it up," he agreed.

"You said you went over about ten p.m. Wednesday," Evie mentioned to Phil. "That's late for a weekday evening. Were you aware of where the family went on Wednesday nights?"

"If you're asking did I know they were doing some counseling with a doctor in Decatur, I'll say I had my suspicions," Phil replied. "Scott had asked around about the doctor, was making plans to shift things when he was assigned a Wednesday evening rotation. You spend hours every day with a guy on the job, you know if there's family trouble, marriage trouble. They were a content couple. A bit stressed at times, but normal. Scott had talked about having more kids, then stopped bringing up the topic. I figured, knowing who the doctor was, Susan was having some issues."

Jenna said, "She never told me she miscarried, but you get a sense of things when a stroller goes by and she turns emotional. Babies were at least part of the equation for whatever was going on that needed counseling."

Evie looked over at Gabriel. This wasn't going as she had expected. Either Phil was clueless about his partner or he was covering for Scott.

"Did you know they were raising cash?" Gabriel asked.

Phil and Jenna shared a look. Jenna shrugged. "They were talking about remodeling the kitchen. Susan was collecting cabinet door samples, tile samples, color charts and sketches for how they might relocate appliances. I know they were conserving cash any way they could for the project, selling some furniture they had decided to switch, that kind of thing."

Gabriel shifted in his chair. "Can you think of any reason the Florist family might have left here on their own, not under duress?"

"What?" Phil asked, looking genuinely surprised.

"Have you heard from Scott or Susan or

their son, Joe, since they went missing?"

Phil's blood pressure was rising — Evie could see it in his posture as he sat forward. "Come on, Gabriel. What are you implying? You're crazy if you think that family left town on their own accord, or that I might have known and kept it under wraps!"

"There's no reason you can think of they might have left? Would it surprise you to realize the family owned a .22 and Frank Ash was killed with a .22?"

"Who's Frank — ?" Jenna started to ask.

"A lowlife who got himself killed," Phil interrupted. "Now you're just smearing the name of a good cop, Sheriff. Scott worked that Ash case, we both did, the disappearance, and we worked that initial scene behind the truck stop when his body was discovered. But you're barking up the wrong tree if you think Scott had anything to do with that death."

"No question in your mind, Scott was a good cop."

"No question in my mind," Phil said firmly. "Scott was careful on the details, doing it proper — it's why I chose to work with him. He didn't cut corners on getting something right. Now, why are you asking these questions?" he demanded.

"Scott believed his son, Joe, killed Frank Ash."

"Little Joe?" Phil looked stunned. "I can see the kid shooting a burglar coming in the house. The kid knew how to safely handle a gun — Scott saw to that. And Joe had a protective streak about him for his parents . . . but to shoot a guy like Frank Ash? The body is at a truck stop just off the Interstate, shot three times in the chest. That doesn't sound like Joe. Angles were all wrong, for one thing. There's like a four-foot height distance. Unless Joe was standing on a lot of boxes, no way he shoots Frank Ash straight on in the chest. And the location isn't somewhere Joe's going to be, then get himself back home." He stared at Gabriel, frowned. "That's why they were in counseling?"

"One of the reasons."

Phil shook his head. "Scott must have been blindsided to think Joe could have been involved. I can see a question until the body was found, but after that? It's not Joe, no way. And before you ask, it's not Scott either. For one thing, he was too serious about being a careful cop and good role model for his son. The man would toss a guy in jail for life where punishment meant something before he'd just shoot him dead

— there wasn't much justice in that."

"Would you have done it?"

The two men stared at each other for a moment. But Phil must have seen in Gabe's face that it was an honest question. "Probably," he said, "if I knew there was a problem going on. Joe had a problem with Frank Ash — I'm gathering that from what you're saying. But Scott would have handled it proper. Had Joe told me, I'd have handled it for the boy — maybe not so properly at first — I'd likely run the scoundrel out of town. But I would've believed Joe. He didn't say anything to me. Neither Scott nor Joe ever made a comment regarding Frank Ash that I could put together toward what you're suggesting."

Gabriel nodded. "We don't know why they disappeared, Phil. You're willing to state you've never heard from Scott or Susan, from Joe, since they disappeared? No cryptic phone call, postcard, anything odd?"

"They haven't been in touch. Until you sat here today and asked that question, I've never considered the fact they might be alive. They didn't leave, Sheriff. Whatever is the answer, you can trust that."

"Jenna?"

"I wish they had. I wish Susan was still

out there . . . someplace." Her eyes filled with tears. "They haven't been in touch, in any way," she added, her voice shaky. "I'd tell you in the hopes of finding them alive. They were good friends. They died that week. Whatever happened, they wouldn't have walked out on their family, their friends."

Gabriel nodded. "Okay. I appreciate your time."

"It was a normal week," Phil repeated. "I saw the family that Wednesday evening. They were going camping. We had the wedding coming on Sunday. There wasn't tension in them — or between them — when I last saw them. It was a normal night. But something happened. They didn't intend to disappear, Sheriff. No way, no how, was that family getting ready to disappear."

"Sheriff, you can't believe that of them either," Jenna pressed. "You knew them. You've been looking at the case. What do you think happened to them?"

"I don't know. I could give you as many reasons that say they were murdered as I can they planned to leave on their own accord. I just don't know."

Evie caught the look Gabriel gave her, but merely gave a brief headshake. She had nothing left to ask. This interview only confirmed where the case had begun. The Florist family had gone camping, and something had happened. Where the search began was where it was ending.

Gabriel Thane

Gabriel liked the house Evie had rented, with its tall windows and polished hardwood floors. He wondered how many hours she'd actually spent here, other than sleeping, during the last fourteen days. She had barely touched the food Trina had stocked for the visit. He put together a sandwich for himself, paused to stir the soup Evie had chosen.

His phone rang, and he listened while he wiped off the counter. "Thanks. If you could fax over the paperwork to the office, that would be helpful." He finished his sandwich, considering matters. The soup was beginning to steam. He turned it to low and walked back into the living room. "Evie."

She had stretched out on the couch and reluctantly opened her eyes.

"I heard back from the lab. The gun in the safe-deposit box didn't kill Frank Ash, ballistics aren't a match. It's a cold .22, not in any database. The serial number isn't registered."

She grimaced. "Somehow that figures."

494

Gabe walked over to the tall windows to watch a storm coming in — lightning flashes, trees beginning to sway in the wind.

"You should be getting home," she murmured.

He nodded.

"I'm sorry today was a bust," she said, swinging her feet to the floor.

He turned, smiled. "Don't be. It was helpful to see Phil's reaction."

"You think he could have had something to do with whatever happened to Frank Ash." She was now standing beside him as the rain began pelting the panes.

He realized he'd better work some more on his poker face. Gabriel shrugged. "This many years later, I think he remembered the details of the Frank Ash shooting with more precision than I would expect. The angle of the shots being too high for a kid like Joe? The way he said it didn't sound like a guess."

"Did Phil have a .22 registered?"

"I checked. He didn't. But Jenna did. She reported it stolen a few years ago."

"Jenna worked at the school district, liked kids, could have heard a rumor about Frank Ash. She's dating a cop, so she'd probably mention it to Phil."

Gabriel nodded. "He wouldn't use a gun

traceable to himself, but maybe use hers, then destroy the gun, trust she wouldn't notice for a long while that it was missing."

"Is it worth pursuing?" Evie asked.

"I'm going to stew on it for a bit, then decide."

"I'm still stewing on whether Grace's uncle had a hunting accident."

"I haven't forgotten that question either."

Evie sighed as she turned toward the kitchen. "Old ghosts, Gabriel. Some of them can be laid to rest, while others are lost to history." Another crack of thunder had her turning back to the window and the rain now coming down in sheets. "This is going to slow Josh getting the search finished."

"A few days," Gabriel guessed. "He's not looking forward to that call to Grace that says he can't find anything."

"She's resigned to it, you know, Gabriel. One could see that in her face before she left yesterday. She's got her daughter and a future to build. I'd say she's making a strong effort to close this door."

They were quiet for a moment, simply gazing out at the storm together.

"You made any decisions, Evie?"

His voice was quiet, and she knew this was a new topic, a personal question. She didn't bother to try to skirt it. "I'll be going back to work on Monday. Beyond that," she said with a wave of her hand, "a personal life is a complicated thing. I can't put it in a box on a shelf and move on. The only thing for sure is that I'm not sure yet what I want." She looked up at him with a little smile, then back at the storm.

Gabriel's tone remained thoughtful. "I decided years ago I wanted to be the sheriff of this county, call it home, build a life around my family, some good friends. That hasn't changed much. But I'd like to add more faces to that friend circle — namely, yours."

She smiled again. "Thanks, Gabriel. That was a nice invitation, and I'd like that too." She turned toward the kitchen. "There's enough soup for both of us. Come have a bowl while the rain lets up."

Gabriel followed her. "Do you want help boxing up the Florist case tomorrow?"

Evie got down two bowls from a cupboard. "I appreciate the offer, but no thanks. I'll rethink the details of it one last time as I put it away. That can be useful, at least to me. I figure the whole task force might be back in a year or two, to look at it again."

"I just realized we've decided it can't be solved."

"It needs a major break, Gabriel, and as

hard as we tried, we didn't find one." She ladled out the soup. "Although . . . I was thinking last night about those gaps in the interviews along their likely routes. Over the next few months, would you have the resources to do a phone survey? Maybe tie it in with news about a new reward offer: 'The police are generating a list of things that happened in Carin County the week the Florist family disappeared. Call with your memories. Anyone who calls with a new item for our list will receive a check for fifty dollars.' Something like that. Maybe it gets us that major break, the one useful fact we didn't know."

"It's worth a try. I'll work on the budget and schedule, get something put together." He pulled two sodas out of the refrigerator and took a seat at the table with her, looked around the cozy kitchen. "Next time you're going to have to be around this house enough to enjoy it. You should have some people over, a little party, actually have a day or two of vacation."

"The car was fully appreciated, especially with the top down. So the days weren't a total bust. And my dogs have never been happier."

"True enough. You didn't get your flight over Carin, though."

"Something else to put on my list for the future," Evie said.

Evie got out a loaf of fresh bakery bread and sliced a thick piece for herself, offered him the knife and the loaf. "So how should we say goodbye?"

"That tends to be such a *forever* word." He gestured to the soup. "I do enjoy sharing a meal with you, Evie. We've done it more than a few times the last couple of weeks."

"I could say the same."

"I figure you're going to put more than the case in a box. You'll put the last two weeks in a comfortable box of your personal life, put this place called Carin on the shelf until you happen to travel through the area again. You'll find I don't mind. You and I . . . well, it won't be as easy a friendship as the one I have with Ann. Sorry, but you're not quite as comfortable as she is to be around." He smiled to take the sting out of the words. "But she and I have known each other a lot longer. It will sort itself out, Evie. I'm good for a meal when you happen to be around. When you have stopped running circles in your mind and decide what you want, you'll settle somewhere. Maybe it's planting roots up north with your guy, or maybe it's in Springfield around your job, or maybe you decide it's fine to let someone else determine the patch of ground. In time you'll figure it out."

"You're an odd man. See, I can do left-handed compliments too."

They both laughed, and he said, "Now *that* was comfortable," and they laughed some more. After a moment, he added, "I'm a long ways toward being a settled man. I'm beginning to appreciate what that means. I think you don't have many 'settled things' in your life yet, Evie. It sounds like Rob does, which is why you're uncertain about what to do there. He's got a life and a place for you in his world if you want that. You're just not sure you do.

"On my side of things, there are some similarities here in Carin," he continued. "You've pretty much seen my life. You'll eventually decide if you want something like this. I'll stick as a friend, because I figure you need someone to ground you occasionally, same as Ann does. She sees a lot of herself in you. And I'm curious where you do end up one day."

"In case you're wondering, I'm not going to marry Rob Turney," she said, toying with her soup.

"I know." She glanced up, and he smiled. "Listen to yourself, Evie. You don't want to marry anyone yet. You sure don't want to think of being old and alone, but you're not ready to attach yourself to someone, make the effort necessary to make it work. You like being single. Why not just accept that . . . at least for now?"

"I've already told you I really don't like going home to an empty house either, Gabe. Springfield is many things, but not much of me. I'm mostly the work I do."

He split his slice of bread in half, buttered it. "It's a season in life. You're proving yourself on the job, wanting to do the same with the task force. Ambition is fine. It doesn't have to preclude a personal life. Look at Ann. She's built a lot of friendships while being good at the job. She's good at being married too. Open your eyes to what is around you as you work. You can box up the cases and move on, but there's no reason you need to box up the people too."

"You wouldn't mind if I stopped in to see the Thane family, particularly your mom, on occasion? Maybe even you?" She grinned.

"Not at all." He grinned back.

She nodded thoughtfully. "I like you, Gabriel. Probably a lot. But you'll understand if I say I don't know what to do about that right now."

"Evie, that answer doesn't surprise me a bit."

She nodded again and gathered up their empty bowls. "Trina makes good soup."

And thus endeth the conversation, he thought with a little smile at his formal wording. He didn't mind. "You'd be smart to take Trina's cookies with you for the drive home. No one does chocolate macadamia better." He finished his bread. "When you pick up the dogs at Will's on Sunday, give yourself an extra hour. The family is going to be out there helping him hang new drywall after church. Karen offered to put together lunch. You don't want to miss that."

"Four sweaty guys with hammers? I definitely don't want to miss it," she joked. "What about the yellow shirts?"

He gave her an amused smile. "Hopefully they're deep-sixed."

"Oh, I'm keeping mine for next year," she said, tipping her head to watch his reaction. He looked pleased. She had no idea where she would be next year, but she'd keep her options open.

"Dad does the measuring," he said, back to the remodeling discussion, "I handle the power saw. The hauling and hammering are for Josh and Will."

"Keeping Josh busy so he's not pining for

Grace and Angel?"

"Something like that."

"I'll leave time," Evie promised.

Gabriel accepted his coffee from the server with a thanks, cut into the omelet Karen had prepared. The Fast Café was busy this Saturday morning, but it was local folks, no reporters in sight. It felt normal, and that was a very good thing.

His brother reached across for the pancake syrup. "The ground's too muddy to get any useful searching done today," Josh said. "I figure I'll take the boat into the inlet, scope out the shoreline and those bluffs. After the rain and wind last night, there's likely more washout. If there's anything worth finding there, it may show up."

"Want company?" Will offered, working on his third waffle. It wasn't often the three met for breakfast, but they had the routine down. The breakfast orders didn't change, and the first one at the table put it in for all.

"I could use another set or two of eyes," Josh agreed. "I'll be busy enough trying to keep the bottom of the boat from snaring on debris."

"We'll all go," Gabriel decided, "so we'll only have to do this once. Between us maybe we get back out of that inlet in one piece. I remember strong currents, wicked underwater obstacles."

"We'll take it slow, be thorough," Josh said.

Will picked up his orange juice. "I saw Evie on my way in — she's at the post office."

Gabriel nodded. "She's doing a final review of the Florist case, boxing up what's on the wall."

"Karen wants to invite her to dinner tonight at my place, unless you've got an objection."

Gabriel wasn't going to touch that one. "Invite away. I already mentioned Sunday at your place for a late lunch." He shifted the conversation by pulling out his phone and passing it to Josh. "Grace's daughter sent me her official portrait since I'm the sheriff and need good luck, she says." She was wearing angel wings, a halo, and smiling just like one.

Josh grinned. "That looks like our Angel." He laid his own phone on the table. "Mine's better." Angel was wearing her cowboy outfit, chaps, pink boots and cowboy hat.

"Yeah, that's our girl."

Will nodded toward Josh's phone. "Forward it, I'm feeling left out."

"I saw you showing Angel photos of your

lambs and dogs, doing just fine making friends yourself. You were all she wanted to talk about when I was saying goodbye to Grace — she wants to visit 'that brother with the baby lambs.' As soon as she wears Grace down, she'll be back for a visit."

Will smiled, finished his waffle. "I'm good with kids." He glanced at the time. "What do you think, five hours on the water, give or take? I'll tell Karen I'll be back to pick her up at four."

"That'll work."

Will nodded. "Give me a few minutes." He took his coffee with him and sauntered through the employee door.

"You can practically hear him making plans for them," Josh remarked.

"Will does go after what matters to him," Gabriel agreed.

"You think Tom Lander is going to be a concern around here?"

Gabriel had been pondering it. "I think it's time we hired someone of our own to watch what he's doing, see if we can't collect enough evidence to put him in jail for something. I'll feel a lot better when he's not walking around thinking he's not got a care in the world."

Josh nodded. "Thought I might go put eyes on him while I'm visiting Grace in

Chicago, just to get a firsthand look."

"Will's probably thinking the same." Gabriel had accepted the inevitable, knowing Will. "I'm thinking it would be a nice wedding present for Karen to have word that Tom Lander is no longer a concern. It would take a top-notch PI, but we can afford to pay a guy for a few months. I'm certain Paul knows the name of someone worth hiring."

"Arrange something," Josh said. "I'll help with the cost."

Gabriel nodded. "How are things with Grace?"

"It's in an odd place," Josh replied, folding his napkin, then his hands. "She's in too much inner turmoil to figure out how to handle even a friendship right now, so I'm just leaving the end of each conversation with a reason I'll be in touch again. Angel helps. A more happy, normal, full-of-life kid I've never met. She likes me enough it makes it easy for me."

"Grace is doing a good job with her."

"The father isn't around. Grace didn't say more than that. Ann said the same."

"Grace has a lot of hurt to work through," Gabriel said, "all that's been inflicted on her, and some she did to herself. And I see a woman who's willing to deal with it. She has a daughter, she finds the courage to talk about the past with a doctor, she tells Ann, she comes back here. I'd say she's determined to lay the past to rest, however that road has to be traveled."

"I'd say the same," Josh said. "I still care about her, Gabe. More than I thought I would. Even crying all over me, she was at times the Grace I remember. You look at her daughter, and like I told Ann, it's Grace without the shadows. She'll be clear of this one day. I want to be there to see that. I want to find out what we might have then."

Gabriel smiled. "You're a fortunate man, Josh. You have the time to put into what matters to you. That book you've been mentally writing, a friendship with Grace — they're both mostly time and attention, and you've got the freedom to give both. I'd say enjoy it. You'll be helping Grace, however that story turns out."

Josh looked at him a while. "Odd that you aren't doing a little more considering yourself, Gabe."

He accepted the jab with good humor. "I see what's in front of me, Josh. Green eyes and a nice smile and a good sense of humor and a curiosity I admire." Gabriel could visualize Evie clearly enough as he described her. "You ever go chasing one of those birds you like to watch, know there's no way you're going to get that photo you're looking for, so you just have to stop the chase and let it go?"

"Yeah."

"Evie is like that. Try to catch her, she bangs her wings against your hands because she's caught. I'm noticing that guy up north isn't calling her this week, tagging her, checking in, and if that isn't deliberate strategy on his part, I'll eat my paycheck. He knows if he closes his hand on her, she's gone. She'll enjoy Christmas with him, clip her own wings, maybe let it go on with him a few more months because she wants to have it be a fit. Maybe it will be. But you won't catch her by wanting it. Evie has to decide to land, and right now she's mostly seeing how close the walls are getting, and taking off before they can shut her in."

"I'd say you've mostly got her figured out," Josh kidded. "But let me ask this, would you like to be married to a cop?"

Gabriel smiled. "Detective. There's a difference. I imagine Paul looked at Ann, decided she was the one, and the rest he would work out. I sincerely doubt he's ever regretted that decision. I like the person I see in Evie. But I'm not as flexible on the details. I was born here and I plan to die

508

here. And I like being Carin's sheriff."

Josh nodded. "You tell her about Elizabeth?"

"I did."

"Okay." Josh pushed back his plate. "Ann's going to teach Evie to fly, not that that changes matters, but it's going to put a thumb down on the geographical problem. A Christmas gift from Ann and Paul. You might be thinking something practical — or not so practical — to make a statement of your own."

"Already done," Gabriel replied. The yellow convertible Evie had been driving around would title in his name and get parked in Will's barn. It wasn't worth much, given its accident history, but she liked the fun of it. She needed an excuse to come visit Marie and the rest of the Thanes, enjoy a drive. He'd give her that excuse by mailing her a set of car keys and an invitation to bring her dogs to visit their new buddies at Will's.

Will returned from the kitchen. Josh, eyebrows raised, gave him a long look. "You've got lipstick where a guy just looks funny wearing it." Will rubbed the heel of his hand across his face as Josh laughed. "A good shade on you, though."

His brothers would rag on each other for

the next hour if he didn't divert matters. Gabriel paid for the meal and added a sizable tip. "Let's go get a boat and get out on the water, guys."

The wind was stronger than Gabriel would like, but it was blowing them straight into the inlet. He looked back at Josh, efficiently controlling the shallow-bottom boat with the trolling motor. Too much debris below the surface made even thinking about using the more powerful engine impossible. "Watch that you don't get pushed into either bank," he called back. "Straight in, then straight back out. As slow as you can."

"Got it," Josh called back.

They'd have to do this strategically — it wasn't worth trying to come back in with the dangerous mix of debris and current. "Will, the first pass, just look for whatever appears out of place. Think about those animal trails in the woods above here. If he was bringing a car through the woods to the lake to dump it, he had to maneuver all the way to the bluff. I'm thinking the center section of that shoreline" — Gabriel pointed — "is the only place it could have been done."

Will nodded. "See how that cliff face has been undercut," he called, "and then it sheered off and dropped into the lake?" He too pointed. "Trees as well as a huge amount of dirt and rock have gone down with it. Whatever this inlet looked like when Grace's parents disappeared, it wasn't anything like what we now see."

Gabriel knew that was a big part of their challenge. "The inlet has been cutting further into the shore and woods with each passing year. So look down, as well as at the cliff face. If a car got sent over the cliff and buried under a falling slide behind it, it's spent years being hammered by winds, water, and tides."

"It wouldn't have been pulled into Carin Lake itself," Josh said. "Feel those gusts? Everything flows *into* here, not out. Trees, debris, wind. Look at the erosion at the waterline. What was buried gets unburied over time. Graves do it on land, water will do the same."

Gabriel gave a nod. "I'll take those field glasses, Will. My eyesight isn't as good as yours." His brother passed them over. "Take us in, Josh, as slow as you can while holding control."

They searched the inlet for over an hour, Josh moving them slowly into the narrowing channel, maneuvering across massive trees now underwater and showing only the tips of a branch or two above the surface.

"I see something back there." Will pointed. "Let me have the binoculars. There's something there at the shoreline."

Gabriel passed them over. Will adjusted the magnification to his eyes, found the spot again. "Yeah. There's something. Rust. I think it's a rusty piece of metal. Josh, bring me in close so I can get to that fallen tree. I can pick my way along its trunk. A good third of it is still on land; it won't shift under me."

Motor idling, Josh studied the log. "There's got to be something better than you trying to climb your way in there," he argued. "That dirt on the east side is fresh — you can see where part of the cliff face came down in the rain last night. The rest could slide down with only the wind triggering it."

"Do we, or do we not, need to know?" Will passed the binoculars back to Gabriel. "East side of the fallen oak, about two feet up on the bank."

Gabriel stared through the lenses. Dull. Square. Rusted. Not natural. The edges disappeared into the mud. He studied the fresh earth slide that was all too near that spot for his comfort, looked up the cliff face to where the dirt had dislodged. Maybe the rest would hold for now, but he wouldn't want to bet it would stay in place with any further rain. "Josh, get us closer. Will, you get yourself soaked in water this cold, Mom's going to have all our hides. Can we get to it from above?"

"You mean slide down that crumbling slope on a couple of ropes? No, thank you. The whole face will go if you disturb the wrong spot."

Gabriel focused the binoculars on the hollowed-out earth under the cliff ledge, conceded Will's point. No foundation, just air and a fifty-foot drop. Coming down from above wasn't an option.

Gabriel shook his head, blew out a long breath. "If he drove the car off the bluff above here, and half a ton of rock and dirt followed and dropped on the car, buried it whole, the lake has been washing away the layers of that grave for years. That rusty metal is what it might look like. Yeah, this could be it. I agree we need to know."

Will carefully stood up. "Go in soft, Josh, like you're moving explosives. I don't want you hitting that tree. Just come alongside it, let me reach over to it."

He stepped cleanly from the boat onto the log, and Gabriel echoed Josh's relieved sigh. Josh backed them away from the tree while

Will carefully made his way across the log to the shore and climbed up and over to what he'd seen.

He knelt and used his gloved hands to push away more dirt. "Metal, all right," he called. "Could be old sheet metal from a corn silo that's forty-year-old junk, but I'm thinking roof of a car, maybe trunk. It's got that original smooth finish under the rust."

He moved away, studying the landslide under his feet. "Look at the trees trying to grow out of this slide. We're talking ten years or more since this area shifted. It's being washed over when the inlet water rises, carved into, but the slide itself has been here a long while." He pointed to the new earth from the recent rains. "That's going to be growing a few new trees of its own soon, while this stretch gets buried again."

"What do you want to do?" Gabriel asked.

"I want a shovel is what I want," Will decided. "Go get me one."

"We're not leaving you sitting there while we're gone for an hour."

"You want answers?"

"Will, come on. Think this through."

His brother studied the area, found a solid piece of driftwood. "I'll improvise for twenty minutes, and then you're going to go get

514

me a shovel when this doesn't work."

He started clearing, using the wood as a scraping tool. For ten minutes they watched him labor in the mud. When he stopped and leaned back on his heels, he pointed at the water. "I need a wave washing over this area. Use the paddles, see if you can't kick up something."

Gabriel slapped a paddle against the water's surface — also got Will a couple of times — but it was enough to do the job. Will used his hands to clear the area where the water was pooling. "It's the roof of a car, all right. I'm sitting on it, Josh. At least two feet by three feet of smooth metal."

"What do you want to do?" Gabriel asked again.

"Gotta have a shovel."

"Tell me you've got phone service and a full charge on that phone."

Will took it out of his pocket, checked, nodded.

Gabriel picked up the backpack of water bottles, towels, extra gloves they had brought, took off his jacket and pushed it inside, zipped the backpack up, and gave it his best swing to Will on the shore. "We'll be back ASAP."

Before long they returned with two shovels, hot coffee, and more gear to keep warm when wet.

"You should let me beach the boat," Josh argued quietly as they trolled into the inlet.

"Not going to happen," Gabriel replied. "Push out once I'm with Will, get GPS readings on any landmarks you can see above us. I agree with Will. That cliff face is one minor jolt away from sliding down on top of this. If we have to dig the car out, I'd like to know exactly where we found it."

"We need to sort out something more substantial than us and a fishing boat."

"One problem at a time," Gabriel replied. "Ease in by the log and set me off as neatly as you did Will. First we determine with certainty what we're looking at." Cold lake water in November would be more than merely uncomfortable, but he knew it had to be done. He stood in the boat, made the same long step he'd watched Will do, balanced his way across the log over to the shoreline, such as it was — mostly rocks, underbrush, and mud with a steep embankment towering above.

"You made good time."

"Josh is tense," Gabriel said, leaving it at that as he handed over the shovels and slipped off his backpack.

Will pointed to the sizable hole he'd punched through the metal with his knife, held out his flashlight.

Gabriel took a breath, set his jaw, and accepted the light. He stretched out, getting his face close to the hole. He was feeling a bit queasy when he leaned back. "No way we're letting Josh beach that boat. See this," he muttered. "One of us gets to go through life without images like this seared into his mind."

"No disagreement from me," Will said. "We get the remains out of here before we tell Grace. She doesn't need to know they've basically been in a rock, mud, and water grave for years, still resting in their car. We just say we found them near the lake."

"She'll need to know some details," Gabriel replied, sitting back on his heels and shifting that conclusion to one he could live with, "but she doesn't need to see this. We definitely get her parents out of here before we tell her we've found them. I don't want her to see this scene." Gabriel took a minute to get his breathing level. "Just for argument's sake, how do we know this is them? Dig out the license plate? Try to find a wallet and ID? DNA will confirm it, but that's days away. I'm thinking maybe we recover something that leaves no question the remains are theirs — wedding bands, a watch, a piece of jewelry — so we can tell her it's certain."

Will held out his hand. "It was hanging on the rearview mirror."

A silver chain, a locket, the photos inside long since decayed, but the names engraved on the back still clear: Aaron, Shelley, Grace. That would help Grace, that simple proof.

"Call Josh," Gabriel said softly. "Describe the locket."

Will pulled out his phone and made the call.

Grace's parents had been discovered. Relief and sadness both dominated the moment. Gabriel said a quiet prayer while Will finished talking with Josh.

Will pocketed his phone, said quietly, "I'm thinking we can clear mud and rock, pull the roof open, lift the remains out, and leave the car where it is, bury it again under a ton of rock and dirt just by punching that cliff edge above us into coming down once more."

Gabriel absorbed the suggestion. Leaving the vehicle in place would eliminate the risk of injury to one of his deputies or crime-scene personnel. If he could somehow conclusively prove Grace's uncle had done the murders, the case could close without the vehicle in evidence. Depending on how her parents had been killed, that might be possible, if confirmation had survived. "One problem at a time," he said. They wouldn't be moving the car today. "I agree we need to get the remains out of here. Right now I'm worried about the next rain bringing down the rest of that earth and burying them again. And I'd like to do it without the press hearing what's going on. So . . . you and me?"

Will nodded. "Tell Josh to get us body bags. An hour on the shovel work, an hour to punch through the metal, a couple more hours once we're inside the car, another hour to figure out how to transport what we recover safely away from this place — it will be close, but there's enough daylight. I'll call Karen to cancel our date. Have Josh tell Dad to bring a bigger boat to the opening of the inlet and drop the anchor. He can be our security on this, keep an eye on matters while we work, make sure we don't get curious boaters. We wait for others, we'll burn more daylight than we have and risk word getting out."

Gabriel agreed with Will's unspoken subtext. If someone got killed in a sudden slide of rock and dirt, they would both prefer that person have a last name Thane rather than be some twenty-something crime-scene staffer. Gabriel called Josh to describe what they needed. The Thane brothers would be the only ones put at risk retrieving the remains of Aaron and Shelley Arnett.

It took more effort than Gabriel had ever expended, but it was finished as dusk was setting in. He was wet, tired, chilled to the bone, and had images in his head that wouldn't easily leave. They had the car roof opened up, the remains gathered with bullets still embedded in bones, and carefully laid in the all-too-familiar black bags. Gabriel had collected a meager but telling group of personal effects — a man's watch and wallet, wedding rings, a bracelet and necklace, all safely stowed in evidence bags in his backpack. As best they could, they would be leaving the wreck cleared of personal effects. Will had worked beside him with the shovel and a light, taking turns down inside the car. It wasn't as awful as picking up body parts on a battlefield, it wasn't the first time for either of them dealing with remains, but it wasn't something they would ever be able to forget.

Gabriel passed Will the last of the coffee. "What do you think? Josh beaches the boat near the opening of the inlet, we carry the body bags down the shore to him? Or do we try to bring them out the way we came in, across that fallen tree?"

"I'm thinking if Dad moves the big boat about ten degrees farther south, and Josh puts the rubber dinghy over the side, the wind will carry it into the shore near about there." Will pointed farther down the shoreline. "We load a body bag, and they haul it back with a rope. So long as the dinghy doesn't capsize in a wind gust or get punctured, it's stable enough. We can have him send over a couple of marking buoys so that if the craft does go down, the body bag will still be attached by rope to the floating buoy."

Gabriel pulled out his phone. The battery was running down, but the need for the phone connection was about done. "What do you think, four trips? Two for the body bags, two for us?" he asked as he dialed Josh.

Will nodded. Gabriel described to Josh what they wanted, pocketed his phone.

Will stood and moved to the foot of the first body bag. Gabriel picked up the front strap, and between them they carefully carried the remains of Shelley Arnett toward the spot where the dinghy would land. He had been a pallbearer many times. Never had he carried a more heartrending funeral shroud.

"Josh, you should be the one to tell Grace we were able to locate her parents' remains," Gabriel said, having thought through the formality of hearing from the sheriff or receiving a personal call from someone who had cared about her for a long time — and the one she'd selected to do the searching. "I'll call her after you speak with her, give her the official notification." Josh, drinking hot coffee their mother was handing around, merely nodded, his expression unreadable.

Gabriel finished toweling his hair, looked over as Will joined them. A light rain had begun as they came back across the lake. Will looked less drawn after taking a hot shower. They had assembled at Josh's home, the nearest place to anchor the boat. The remains were still onboard.

"I'm for Josh telling Grace in person, all things being equal," Will put in. "Ask Ann to fly down and pick you up, Josh. And I'm thinking the State Police should handle the remains. Let's push this out of Carin County, limit any speculation."

Their father nodded. "There's good sense to that. And thinking ahead, Grace would be better off if the funeral takes place in Chicago, which she now considers home, so she can visit her parents' graves when she likes without stirring up other memories."

Gabriel agreed with both of them. He wanted to also avoid giving the media any photo ops. "I'll drive the remains to the state lab tonight, formally report the recovery of Aaron and Shelley Arnett. Sufficient personal effects are here for IDs without DNA testing, but we'll arrange for that to be done for Grace's benefit. Ballistics can be run — maybe they'll find a match with one of the uncle's firearms. He left behind quite a few when he was killed. I wouldn't expect him to have kept the handgun he used, but there's a chance."

"Pursue those questions first. If there's a way to avoid pulling out that car, it would be for the best," Caleb said.

"I'm guessing by morning there isn't going to be much of a decision left on that," Gabriel noted. "This rain is going to bring down the rest of that bluff and bury the car again." They had pulled over fallen branches so there weren't visible signs of the wreck or their work, but water would wash away that short-term solution in a few days. If by some chance the car didn't get buried in a new slide, he'd determine what to do after he knew the ballistics test outcome. He'd intentionally bring down that cliff face and bury the vehicle for good if he had a choice in the matter.

Caleb finished his coffee. "Let's get the remains moved to our sheriff's vehicle" — he gave a quick smile to Gabriel — "and you can write up the report you'll need." He turned to his wife. "Would you call Karen and ask her to join us here? I want to say a few words, read Psalm twenty-three over the remains before they're transported. This is a family matter, and she's family."

Gabriel appreciated the way his dad said it. Will had seen enough today that having Karen here would help. He wasn't doing that well himself. "I'll give Evie a call, have her come with me to the lab." He tried not to feel anything other than simple duty with that decision. "I'm going to hold off calling my deputies. I've got more to explain than I'm inclined to do at the moment. Better to have the day finished first. I trust their discretion, but I'm carrying enough for tonight. Tomorrow will be soon enough."

Caleb nodded. "That's wisdom, Son."

They retrieved jackets and headed outside to move the remains from the boat to the sheriff's vehicle.

"God's rest upon the dead . . . and the living," Marie said softly as the task was finished. She turned around. "Josh."

"Yes, ma'am."

"You'll tell Grace her parents loved her, didn't leave her behind, and would be so proud of their first granddaughter. Tell her I'd like to help her plan their funeral if she would allow me the honor."

"I will, Mom."

"Gabriel, tell Evie the full truth tonight during the drive, not just the easy version you gave me. It strikes me as important, what she thinks about today."

"Yes, ma'am."

Marie patted his chest. "You're a fan of annoying your mother with that 'ma'am.' "

"Josh just said it," he protested.

"He says it nice. You have that bit of 'humoring your mother' in your voice."

He sighed. "Yes, ma'am."

He got a hug, then was pushed away with a chuckle. "Go help your father refuel and secure the boat for the night. You know he drives it like a lumberjack."

Gabriel willingly complied, walking back to join his father. He wasn't surprised to see him light a cigar as they approached the pier. Each dealt with hard days in his own way, and his dad was mocking death with that smoke he'd occasionally enjoy.

"The tombstone could read, 'Beloved Parents and Grandparents of Grace and

Angel,' " Caleb suggested over his shoulder as he stepped onto the boat.

Gabriel thought it the right sentiment. "I'll mention it to Josh." He was aware the entire family was shifting to make sure Josh could carry matters for Grace. He'd add his official help to that so Josh could also handle matters for Grace with the medical examiner. The remains should be ready for transport to Chicago and burial in about a week. Better to get it done early in December, not too near Christmas.

Josh joined them and set to work securing the dinghy they had used. Gabriel had something of his own he wanted passed on. "Josh, mention to Grace for me that closure sometimes doesn't feel like what you want or expect, but it's still the milestone that over time will be what she needs."

"I'm no good at funerals."

"You will be at this one," Gabriel assured him, draping an arm around his brother's shoulders. "She came to you with her request. Close it out now with honor. Mom's offered to help with the details, and you'll see to it they get carried out so Grace and her daughter find the solace they need."

Josh nodded. "You should've let me help today onshore."

Gabriel shook his head. "Will and I do

526

things I hope you never have to see, Josh. Someone in the family needs to know what peace is like. You're the one who can assure Angel that life doesn't have to be marred by tragedy."

Cutting drywall needed more rest than he'd been able to grab the night before. So Gabriel drank a root beer and enjoyed Will's back porch, listening to Karen and his mother working companionably in the kitchen. Will and Josh were enjoying a spirited game of tag with the four dogs. The work planned for today would get done another time.

"I came to say goodbye."

Gabriel leaned back from his perch on the steps to see Evie standing behind him. For having been dropped off at her rented Victorian only about five hours ago, he thought she looked remarkably alert. He couldn't say their talking about bones had made for the most enjoyable last conversation, but it had been illuminating. Evie had wondered why he didn't ask her to help them out there on the lake since she was a fraction of the size of him or Will, could have worked without nearly the strain in the wrecked automobile's small area. Her only other significant comment on their decision to do the recovery themselves had been the risks the living were willing to take to recover the dead.

"The Florist case boxes are marked, ready to be put back into the archives. There's an index of sorts in the first box," Evie told him now as she joined him on the steps.

"Iris will appreciate that."

She had her own root beer. He turned his attention back to the game of tag going on.

"You solved yours. I didn't solve mine," she mentioned.

He smiled. "You gave it a good effort. It'll still be here when the task force decides to take another look. Will you come back, Evie?"

"Probably."

"It's been a personal and professional pleasure having you in my county," he offered, sincerely meaning the words.

She smiled. "Can't say I enjoyed the deer, but the rest of it was an experience." She handed him the phone from her pocket. "Thank you for the loan."

"Anytime."

"Have my personal number?"

"I know who has it," he replied. "Have mine?"

"You were only a speed dial on that one. But I know who has it."

They smiled at each other, and he said, "I'm going to miss that quick wit of yours."

"I'll miss the sweet-tarts."

The dogs spotted her. Evie darted off the steps to join the game of tag, and Gabriel lifted an eyebrow as he saw how fast she cut a turn. The next time they played flag football with the Thane tribe, he'd make sure she was on his team. *A year or two,* he thought, *a few more cold cases under her belt, she'll realize what I already know — the extraordinary job she's done the last two weeks, even if it didn't end as we'd hoped.* She had nothing to feel apologetic about. Gabriel smiled when her dogs got Evie cornered. He figured the odds were good he'd still be sheriff when the Florist disappearance eventually did get solved — maybe by Evie.

He wasn't inclined to say goodbye. When Evie got ready to drive out, he'd simply say, "See you around," and find a reason to make that happen. He might be a small county sheriff in an otherwise big state, but he was resourceful. He'd track her down if necessary.

Ann would be here this afternoon to fly Josh to Chicago to talk with Grace in person. He'd be working over Christmas, but there would be opportunities around then he could fit in a visit to Springfield. Evie built a snowman in February when she was tired of the winter, he remembered. There wasn't a need to say goodbye today. He finished his root beer, watching her laugh with the dogs, fully relaxed for the first time since they'd met. Evie was as interesting a woman as he'd thought she would be. He wasn't going to regret how this had to transition now. Life went on.

Evie Blackwell

Evie didn't have to glance at the map for the route home to Springfield. She set the cruise control, shifted in the seat, finding it familiar but different from the convertible she'd been driving. She looked in the rearview mirror at the dogs, already half dozing and tucked around each other.

She opened the center console for sunglasses. Saw the plastic sack resting there and had to laugh. Gabriel had tucked in a bag of sweet-tarts. She picked up a roll, opened it, ate the first one. He was good at subtleties. *Subtle, yes, but clear in its message.* She rather liked that about him.

She wasn't a banker's wife — *probably same for the wife of a sheriff* — she mulled over as she drove. But it was a worthwhile debate to decide if she could be. She found some music and turned up the volume, not so high it would bother the dogs. She'd return home, go to work in the morning at her State Police job, and when asked, say it had been an interesting vacation. It certainly wasn't one she was likely to forget.

SIXTEEN

Evie Blackwell

Evie spotted Ann easily enough. She simply looked for a woman willing to stand in a parking lot on a winter day. Not that Ann looked cold — she was dressed in a black cashmere coat, gloves, plus earmuffs in a soft, white rabbit fur. Nor would many stand near a crime scene, not be put off by the fluttering police tape, the cops coming and going.

"Evie, thanks for making the time," Ann said as Evie walked over.

"You make it easy for me, Ann, showing up right where I'm working for the day."

"There's a good place that does gyros over on MacArthur Avenue. Ride with me, we'll order to go, and take a walk on the bike path."

"You want to take a walk on December twenty-two when there's six inches of snow on the ground," Evie felt compelled to ask, "not to mention a wind freezing whatever it can touch?"

"It will wake us up, and only one direction of the walk will we feel the wind."

Evie laughed at that image. "Sure, why not?" It would be a couple of hours before the medical examiner would hand the crime scene back to her. She had time. She tossed her backpack on the backseat of Ann's airport rental, slid into the passenger seat, glad for the warmth.

"Your current case — serious trouble?" Ann asked as she swung out of the lot.

"A lawyer committed suicide — at first glance, at least. State got the case because he once sued the current police chief, and no one in that office was going to touch this investigation."

"Smart of them."

They stopped to get their lunch to go and then found the bike path easily enough. Ann parked at a nearby church's lot, and they pulled up their collars and walked across the footbridge connecting with an asphalt path that followed a former railroad line. They had walked here before in the distant past. The wind wasn't bad with the trees on either side, but the smooth snow was more like ten inches. Both were wearing boots — as functional as they were fashionable —

and the snow wasn't that much of a problem. Evie appreciated the stillness, and the lunch was as good as advertised. She kept it mostly wrapped in the foil to keep it warm, and they ate as they walked. She'd forgotten how nice it was to share a meal with a good friend, especially one that wasn't rushed.

"I came to ask you something," Ann said.

Evie nodded. "Ask me what?"

"I'll get to that in a minute. But first . . . you haven't heard from Gabriel recently, have you?"

"No. Didn't expect to."

"And you haven't thought about calling him?"

Evie gave Ann a curious glance. "No, should I have? Something going on I haven't heard about?"

"Nothing in particular. Grace's parents — ballistics were a match to a handgun Kevin Arnett once owned, so that case has officially closed. The Thane brothers triggered a slide along that entire bluff to make the area safer before the land was sold and reburied the car, hopefully for good."

"I'm very glad to hear that."

"Yeah," Ann said. "Grace appreciated the flowers you sent for her parents' funeral, and the gift you sent for Angel — it was a thoughtful gesture, Evie."

"It seemed appropriate." The plastic horses had been hers as a child, and she remembered what it had been like opening that Christmas gift box and finding her wish list fulfilled. She'd kept them neatly boxed in her spare room for a child she still didn't have. It was time to pass them on so that another could enjoy them.

"Grace is doing well," Ann added. "She's enjoying planning for Christmas. Baking up a storm. Her tears have passed, for the most part. I wanted to mention that because you saw so many of them over those two weeks."

"She arranged her daughter's vacation," Evie said, "returned to Carin with all its terrible memories, and then gave herself two weeks where she could safely cry because that's what she needed to do. You think I didn't see that, Ann? That planning on Grace's part to handle a personal crisis well? She's got guts, that friend of yours."

"Thanks for noticing. May I tell her that observation?"

Evie nodded.

"Josh is going to take them skating, build a snowman with Angel, generally find reasons for Grace to let him into her life this winter. His work gets busy come March and April, but he's got some time now, and he's planning to use it well. When you next come to Chicago, Josh would like to meet up with you, take you to dinner with Grace and Angel. I think he figures having Grace comfortable with a few cops would be a good thing. I can wave him off, though, if you prefer not to get that invitation."

"No, it's fine, Ann. I'd like to be more than passing acquaintances with Grace and her daughter."

"She will appreciate that. I do too."

"Sure. Will and Karen are doing okay?"

"I haven't heard anything since we were there, but I expect so. Tom Lander got himself a summons to appear in tax court, so that saga continues. He started hiding money from his creditors and underreporting his income when his businesses began to fail — someone good in finance happened to notice that fact."

"Paul's pretty good with numbers," Evie noted with a knowing grin.

"Super geeky grunt work, but he's willing to dive in when it's for a good cause," Ann said with an answering smile.

Evie finished her lunch, tucked the foil in the bag. "I appreciate the updates, Ann. But that isn't why you came to find me. What's on your mind?"

"A formal invitation for the task force is

536

coming from the governor-elect unless you want to decline it. A two-year deal, you keep the same title and desk you have now, time-share between your current boss and Sharon Noble, keep your hands on some current cases while primarily working cold cases with the task force."

Evie had thought about the differences of her day job and what those two weeks in Carin had been like. The depths a cold case would require that a current one didn't often need. "I'm excited about the challenge, Ann. I want in."

"He'll call you."

"The governor-elect will call me," Evie repeated with a smile. "Have to admit — that statement's got a 'wow factor' to it."

Ann laughed. "Been there. The first time the vice-president called me from DC, it took my breath away." Ann neatly folded up the napkins and foil wrapper of her lunch, pocketed it. "All right. That was just the preliminaries. I'm retiring in a more formal way, Evie. And over the next couple of years I'll be passing what has been falling on me over to you."

"Ann . . ." Evie stopped to look at her friend.

"You're ready for it."

Evie felt her heart stutter. "Not particularly. What I know you do is already way deeper than I want to even think about, let alone what you haven't told me."

Ann simply smiled. "Flying lessons are your Christmas gift from Paul and me. And you'll get comfortable with the governor calling you. I'll open the door gradually to what is going on, Evie. But you're made for more than you've considered for yourself, both personally and professionally. When the governor asks you to call him Jeffery, do so. Or stay with 'sir' if it's impossible to make that step. But I think you'll get there."

"Okay." Evie felt like the earth had just shifted under her, tried to find her sense of balance. "Why me, Ann?"

"I see a lot of myself in you. The personal questions you keep wrestling with as much as the work. God has a good path in mind for you, Evie. There's a rich life ahead of you, and it's got so many facets. Work, certainly. But I'm also certain He has a rich personal life in mind for you too. Don't be afraid of that. Wary about taking a wrong step, sure, and patience is a good thing. But don't be scared of where He leads.

"I want you to enjoy the task force work, learn to fly, and begin to figure out how to take a deep breath and let important people lean on your expertise. They're going to start doing so. The governor is likely in office for eight years. I predict over the next three years, his wife will become someone you'll think of as a friend, his daughter will call you by name and not be surprised to find you at the breakfast table. The governor will hand you hard things to do because he'll learn to trust what you tell him. When those days come, say yes, do your best work, and let the outcome go where it will."

"Can I ask you something?" Evie asked.

"Sure."

"You do that for people now, solve problems?"

Ann thought about it. "I have a friend gifted at solving problems. Like you're gifted at being a detective, she can look at a situation and see what needs to happen. I think I mostly sort out how to help, as a friend. Sometimes it's what I can do, sometimes it's the resources I can bring to bear, but most of the time it's knowing who I can ask for a favor.

"The calls I get are often a situation that requires discretion, occasionally secrecy, and probably has a security concern. That's the circle of influence I walk in — my own and Paul's. I don't regret laying down the badge, not being the one dispatch will call to a scene. There's still interesting work that needs to be done. But I can tell it's shifting again, what God has in mind for me. I'm retiring in a more complete way and making sure people are there to deal with matters — passing the mantle, so to speak. You're one of those people — not the only one, but an important one. If you're married, single, retired, still on the job, the surface can look like many things, and it's not going to be an issue, Evie. I want you to see the role, try it on for size. That's part of the next few years if you want it." Ann gave her a long, considering look. "You'll take the flying lessons, think about it for a year?"

"I can do that, but I can't imagine stepping into the role you fill."

"You'll adapt. He's a nice guy, the governor. Adorable daughter. Great wife. His sister Shannon is a stitch, likes jokes like you do. We're having a late holiday party on the twenty-ninth, Paul and I, seven o'clock at our place, and they'll be there. Come with Rob if you wish, if he can get free for the evening. Matthew Dane will be there too if the weather cooperates. A few other people as well. Dress is jeans and some kind of holiday-decorated sweater, or dress slacks and a jacket if you're not comfortable going casual."

"A few other people would be who?"

"Mostly cops, or those who spend their lives around them. If a third of the guests aren't children and dogs, I haven't thrown a good party."

Evie appreciated the image. "Thank you. I'm delighted to be invited."

They turned back the way they had come. Ann offered a cherry candy from her pocket, and Evie unwrapped it with a thanks.

"I want to mention one other thing," Ann said, "compliments of Paul."

"Oh?"

"He said it's the first time Gabriel had ever asked him for a read on a woman, that first day when he called to ask about you."

"Did he now?" Evie asked, intrigued.

"Rob will grow on me," Ann said, "if you like him enough to stick with him. I'll figure out what you see in him and start to appreciate him more. But for what it's worth, I think there's somebody who's a better fit for you, Evie. I think you know that."

"I'm aware. You've been tactful, but not silent on the subject. I'm not sheriff's wife material either, Ann."

"Maybe not. But I would suggest you insert a *maybe* in your statement."

"I'm aware of the fact that I'm waiting. I'm single because that's the step I'm on. But it's not the step I'll stay on. I'm aware of that too." Evie glanced over. "Gabriel Thane is not a small county sheriff, no matter what his job title says. Just as you're not a retired cop. He just happens to inhabit that space for now, and he's comfortable there. It's where God has placed him. I like that about him. Gabriel's got excellence in mind for the job he does now, and he's not pushing out the walls of it on the assumption a bigger turf is more important."

"He's ambitious in the right ways," Ann agreed. "It's why Paul likes him."

Evie got it. She nodded, glanced at her friend. "Flying lessons, huh?"

Ann smiled. "Wait till you learn how to take off on a runway packed with snow. It's not something you do every day, but in the right situation where it's necessary, those are some good skills to have in your tool kit. Flying at night around a storm is another one."

"Okay, I vote for summer flying lessons . . . in something that flies about the speed of a bicycle," Evie replied.

Ann laughed. "You'll love it, Evie."

"It's a really nice gift. The truth is, I've been thinking about it for a while."

"I know you have, hence the offer. It's time."

Evie nodded and repeated, "It's time."

They were back in sight of the car and warmth. "I've got a lawyer who needs an official ruling of suicide or murder. That's my afternoon."

"I'm picking up a state congressman, flying him to Chicago so he can apologize to his daughter for forgetting her birthday."

"Ouch."

"The divorce was messy, but he honestly didn't intend to hurt his daughter. He's beginning to realize why his life ran so smoothly before, and it wasn't because of his staff. He had an organized wife who loved him."

"Playing matchmaker, Ann?"

"I'm all for people admitting they made a mistake. A second marriage to his ex-wife would probably go better than the first attempt. I like them both, so I don't mind playing Cupid."

Evie laughed at the way Ann described it. "Yeah. I can see why you'd spend an afternoon doing that favor."

Ann drove back to the crime scene and parked past the police tape. Evie got out, picked up her backpack. "Thanks for lunch. I'll call you about the party."

"No need. Show up with a guest if you're free, no big deal if you're late or alone. You have other plans that night, I'll invite you to the next one."

"Okay. Thanks again, Ann." Evie ducked under the tape, headed back to work. She felt a bit like she'd been walloped with a fastball. Evie glanced up toward heaven for a brief moment. She'd never been so grateful for a day job and a case to work as she was right now. This was something she was comfortable concentrating on for the next several hours. She'd think about Ann's visit and its implications later tonight. She knocked snow off her boots and stepped into the building. "Where are we, Bill?"

The officer pointed to the service elevator. "Body's on its way down. Think he had help, Lieutenant?"

"I'm going to find out." Based on what she'd learned so far, she figured it was a coin toss, suicide or murder. That would tip in the next few hours because she was good at the job.

A fat cardboard tube with a red bow on top sat on her desk. Evie walked over to check the attached card while she unbuttoned her coat. The gift hadn't been there when she left yesterday evening for the shooting range. The parking lot had been mostly cars she recognized when she eventually left for home. Ann, she guessed, as she had been in town the day before and liked to arrange things like this.

She picked up the card. *Merry Christmas, Evie.* She recognized Gabriel's handwriting even before she saw the initials GT. She removed the bow and lifted the rather heavy tube. A map of some sort? No, the tube was too short for that. She reached inside and felt metal, flexible but strong, and eased the coil out.

Precision-cut metal letters in Calibri font. *I am not a wo . . .* She didn't need to see more and laughed out loud. *I am not a woman of small ambitions.* He'd remembered the stencil she suggested for her office, had the sign made for her. She glanced at the wall over the window and thought it would be perfect there. She unrolled the gift and saw it hooked with wire loops at the top and either end. A small plastic bag with picture nails had been taped to the first letter. *Oh yeah, he does thoughtful, all right.*

She opened the top left drawer of her desk, pulled out a blank stationery card embossed with her name at the top. *Gabriel, you hit a home run with your Christmas gift. Thank you. Evie.* She slipped the card in its matching envelope, found his work address in her files, and put the card in her outgoing mail. She hadn't gotten him anything but wasn't going to sweat it. When she saw something that reminded her of him, she'd buy him a gift.

This was turning out to be a very nice end to the year.

January arrived and stomped on her cheerful mood. Normally, Evie didn't mind working weekends, but right now half the support staff were still vacationing somewhere warm and she didn't get paid enough for the reality of working crime scenes in the cold and blowing snow. She'd pulled a body out of the semi-frozen Illinois River today and still smelled like it, even after washing her hair twice in the locker room shower and changing clothes down to the new tennis shoes she wore. It seemed like the odor had invaded her skin, or at least her nose, and Evie was tempted to find some Vicks ointment to combat it. She did pull a rarely used bottle of perfume from her desk drawer and sprayed it more liberally than she otherwise might. She'd have to ID the man before she could figure out how he ended up in the river. But at least this one still had his hands — the last body pulled from the river didn't.

A new folder had landed in her inbox. Lab results on the dead lawyer, sent to her from the medical examiner. The official cause of death was determined to be suicide, yet Evie found it odd the lawyer had overdosed on his cousin's prescription rather than his wife's. A good defense lawyer with an ego to match didn't go the suicide route easily. She wanted a solid reason for his taking the pills, one that made some sense to her before she closed the case. She could imagine a suicide note: *Blackmail drove me to kill myself . . .* She'd find more time to analyze the case before she moved it off her desk.

The light was blinking on her phone. She entered her password to play back messages. "Lieutenant, it's Sheriff Thane. This is an official call. Please call me back at your first opportunity." Gabriel gave her a number. There was a long pause during the recording. It was the first she'd heard his voice since she left Carin. He went on, "Evie, we've found a property of interest out on County Road 33 — the phone canvas turned up the lead. I'm working on a warrant and hope to search there in the morning. Feel free to just show up if you can join us. Anyway, you can reach me at that number anytime. Either way, I'll let you know how it goes."

He sounded like the same Gabriel, but terribly sad. She picked up the phone and hit the speed dial for her boss. Someone else would have to ID the guy from the river. She needed a couple of personal days.

The state and federal flags in front of the Carin County sheriff's office hung heavy with moisture, but the metal ringlets rang like a bell as they struck the pole in the wind. Evie turned up the collar of her coat as she walked the shoveled sidewalks and was glad to step into the heated building. She greeted the officers she recognized. Iris was at the front desk and on the phone. Evie pointed toward the hall, and Iris nodded for her to go on back.

Evie found the sheriff in his office just putting down his phone, so she tapped on the doorframe. "You called."

Gabriel merely nodded and reached for his hat and coat. "Come with me." No *Hello* or *Nice to see you.* She wondered if she could see more gray hairs than before. Looking grim, he headed outside and over to the truck he favored, paused to open the passenger door for her. "You'll want to buckle in."

Something really, really bad. Evie didn't know what to brace for, icy roads or dreadful news, but she prepared for both. The snow had come down heavy in the county over the New Year's weekend. The roads were packed with it and showing ice in places. They headed out of town, and she soon recognized the route the Florist family might have taken the night they disappeared.

"Sorry for the terse welcome."

Evie glanced over at him. She knew pain when she heard it. "Tired of talking about it?"

"I understand what Grace means when she says talking about it is like ripping her guts out. We'll get to it, Evie, in about thirty minutes when I show you why I called. The warrant came through an hour ago. We're just waiting on the crime-scene people to arrive before I serve it. How's Springfield?"

He obviously wanted a change in subject. "I'd say the job is much the same as it's been," she responded, "mostly messy crime scenes to wade into and try to solve. I had a nice Christmas with Rob and his family. Even his mother was mostly kind in her remarks about my being a cop. It probably helped that Governor-elect Bliss called while I was sitting down to dinner with them, to formally invite me to his inauguration in Springfield and the press conference the next day when he plans to announce the new task force."

"That's next week?"

"The twelfth for the inauguration, one p.m. the following day for the announcement."

Gabriel nodded. "I figured it would get some press. I'm glad you're taking the job. You'll solve a lot of cases over the next couple of years, I'm sure of it. Can I get an invite?"

"Of course. If I can't get you in, Ann can." They shared a chuckle. "Seriously, Gabriel, I'd like to show you my place if you have time for a meal. I built the dogs two large doghouses, and after seeing Will's creations, I added a few more items to their backyard playground as their Christmas presents. You'll enjoy seeing it, even in the winter."

"I'm sure I will. Who looks after the dogs when you travel?"

"Two people in my neighborhood, both recently retired vets. They've got some post-deployment problems they're working through, and the dogs are good therapy. Apollo and Zeus enjoy their company. If I'm not home, one or both of the guys will be around."

"I'm glad you've got that arrangement."

"Anything new with you?"

"I bought myself a new snowblower."

She laughed. "Please tell me Christmas

was more interesting than that."

"The county mostly behaved itself. There were a few home burglaries while people were at the Christmas Eve church services. We had our share of domestic-disturbance calls with family grievances escalating at holiday gatherings. We had two suicides and a probable murder-suicide. As you know, the season can be extra stressful for people with ongoing problems in their lives."

"I'm sorry to hear that."

"It's the job, Evie." He looked over, smiled. "More cop work than detective work, I'll admit."

"I can handle mine easier than yours," she said.

A comfortable silence settled as Gabriel drove them north for thirty minutes. The woods grew thicker and the snowfall more even. Traffic dwindled to only the occasional vehicle.

Gabriel began to decelerate, and Evie sat up straighter, knowing from the tension in him they were nearing their destination. They took a curve, and Evie saw sheriff vehicles parked along the roadside. Gabriel pulled in behind them but didn't shut off the engine. He pointed to a driveway up ahead. "Elliot Fray owns that property. It's a decent-sized place — he raises horses, cattle, leases out his farmland for a share of the crops. He's not on any of our lists, no priors of any kind. A good guy, according to those who know him. Been in this county all his life. He's married, father of two. His wife died of cancer about fifteen years ago. Sons are married now, each living on opposite coasts. Elliot is an old man now, not as active, but he's still a hands-on owner with a good business sense. My father knows him better than I do.

"That phone canvas you suggested turned up a postman who remembers a mailbox post being shattered and replaced." Gabriel nodded to the end of the driveway. "That mailbox. Elliot doesn't remember the specifics, only grimaced at the reminder and said he's replaced it at least four times now, as delivery trucks coming into the property misjudge the turn. Probably true enough; it's a common problem along these country roads, especially in the winter. But one of my deputies took some initiative and walked the roadside before the first snow came down and found some items of interest.

"We've got dried blood on the underside of an almost-buried rock found near that replaced mailbox, blood that matches by type with Scott. And a fragment of front headlight plastic that matches the model of truck he was driving. That was enough to put several deputies walking this road, and they located a few more small pieces of debris that match the Florist truck.

"Back twelve years ago, four employees worked for Elliot Fray, handling a dozen horses and a hundred-plus head of cattle. They've all moved on since, and there's new staff now, but we tracked the former four down. There's nothing I've discovered about them that would cause concern. The staff worked daylight hours, mucking out the stalls, exercising the horses, feeding the cattle, cutting the hay. Elliot was considered a good boss, not one to say much, concise on what needed done, one who did the work alongside them.

"What I've got are two odd facts those employees mentioned. Elliot nearly drank himself to death back a dozen years ago. He had never been much of a drinker until that year. And there's a barn on the property that has been locked for years. He told staff the floor was buckling. He didn't want an accident, to be paying a workman's comp claim. They vaguely remember the concrete was buckling some in the freeze and thaw. It's the oldest of the barns on the property. The building was padlocked the same calendar year the Florist family disappeared.

With the dried blood, the headlight fragment and other debris, a locked barn, and a very sympathetic judge, it's enough for a warrant to search the property."

"You think the Florists were involved in an accident here, and it was covered up?"

"I don't know what to think, Evie. I've spoken to Elliot twice. When he says he doesn't remember anything unusual happening back then, he's convincing. If the deputy hadn't found what he did, I would have written up the note about the mailbox and moved on."

"What did Elliot say about the barn?"

"The same as what his past employees told me. I asked if I could see inside, and he said the padlock key had been lost for years. He's mostly polite, but turns grouchy with the conversation going on for a while. He wasn't interested in having me buy him a new lock." Two vehicles pulled in behind them. "There's crime-scene personnel now. I'm going to serve the warrant to look around, get this search started." He held out the keys. "It's likely to be a long day. Come back to the vehicle and kick on the heater to warm up occasionally."

"Thanks." Evie pocketed the keys.

Evie hung back as Gabriel served the warrant, catching only a quick glimpse of the man inside his doorway before he closed it again. Gabriel organized his men, his deputies spread out to walk the property, the current employees going along to handle the gates, move horses and cattle out of the way as required.

Evie walked beside Gabriel as they trailed down the slope to the old barn, fighting through heavy snowdrifts. The drive this direction hadn't been plowed. The owner had joined them in cold-weather jacket and boots, now walking beside them — elderly but not particularly frail, a man accustomed to hard work. He wasn't saying much, but he wasn't as angry as Evie would have expected, given the warrant to search his property.

The barn showed the neglect of years, paint flaking off weathered boards, weeds tall enough that a few poked through the deep snow. The deputy with them had brought along bolt cutters. The rusted padlock hanging from the barn door showed its age.

"Elliot, you could give us the key."

"Haven't had it in over a decade. I told you that when you asked me to open this place before."

"Then I'll be buying you a new lock." Gabriel nodded to his deputy.

He cut the padlock, then pushed away the snow to get the door to swing outward. The smells of dust and hay hung in the air. The light from the doorway was enough to reveal the interior as they stepped inside.

They were staring at a damaged truck and camper.

Gabriel's face turned to flint. He swung around. "Where are they, Elliot?"

Evie had to walk away from where the bones were being excavated. Officers standing at the perimeter watching the crime-scene team work had their badges covered with strips of black tape as a sign of respect for one of their own. Thankfully, the frozen earth was cooperating, as the Florists' bodies had been buried deep, well below the frost line.

Gabriel was still doing the interview at the house. The DA had joined him, and the story had mostly come out now. She felt more than slightly sick and gratefully sipped the coffee someone had handed her. She'd push this one away — she would have to — but it would take some time. Gabriel wouldn't be able to do so.

She strode over to the vehicles, considered knocking the snow off her boots to sit inside for a bit, but the wind was dying down and she was bundled up. Instead, she leaned against the vehicle and closed her eyes, breathed deeply and let the time pass.

Minutes later she saw Gabriel leaving the house, gave him time to talk with his deputies and the crime-scene supervisor before joining him. His face was etched with a grief beyond words. Evie understood it better than he realized. It was like another boulder had crashed down.

"I can't do this with the smoothness you do, Gabriel." She held out a sweet-tarts roll.

He looked at it, blinked, then managed a smile. "Thanks." He thumbed out the first one, offered it to her. She took it. He slid the next two into his mouth. "I can get a deputy to drive you back to town or you're welcome to take my truck. I can catch a ride with one of the guys. There will be a press statement to release, questions to answer, but that won't be today. This is going to take some time."

"I'll leave here when you do. I asked my boss for a few days off."

"I appreciate that."

She reached over and squeezed his arm. "Tell me the details, just dump them and get them out of your head. You'll drown in them otherwise. You've got to talk to someone, Gabriel. If not me, go talk to your father."

His gaze met hers for a long moment. Then he gave a nod and said, "Let's walk, Evie."

He pushed his hands into his pockets as they moved down the driveway, didn't speak for a long time, and when he did his voice sounded tired. "The accident happened at the end of the driveway. Scott was driving north, as we did, doing about forty miles an hour, the truck pulling the camper. It was dark that night, but road surfaces were good, there wasn't much traffic, and he was driving safely for what this was. He hit a horse."

Evie flinched. Even knowing that was coming, the image hurt.

"The impact shattered the horse's ribs, the animal went under the truck rather than over it, crushed its legs. The truck stopped mostly on the road, the camper swung to the maximum movement of the hitch, came to rest against the back of the truck." Gabriel rubbed his eyes. "The horse was alive, but dying, screaming in pain, trapped under the truck. Scott shot it to put the animal out of its misery. It's pretty much chaos. Scott's hurting from the impact of the crash, the airbags deploying. Susan's nearly hysterical, and Joe's throwing up. The accident scene, it was . . . bad.

"Elliot had been trying to corral his prized horse, which had jumped the gate after being spooked by a wolf. He was carrying his hunting rifle and a side arm, hoping to spot the wolf. He got to the foot of the drive just as Scott shot the horse. Elliot goes crazy, shoots Scott. Scott shoots back, but he's dying. Susan runs to her fallen husband. Joe scrambles to get his father's gun that had fallen on the roadside, tries to kill Fray. It's not clear yet who killed Susan, whether a stray bullet from Elliot or Joe, but she was hit in the side. Joe died there beside his mom. Fray survived it mostly by luck — two bullets passed through his arm without hitting bone.

"It was a hellish accident that shifted to a multiple murder in less than thirty seconds. And I believe Elliot when he said it was the heat of the moment — the screams of his horse, the blood, the adrenaline, the gunfire — that he reacted to. He never thought until it was too late to think, and by then it was all over.

"It takes a sizable forklift to move a dead horse, but it wasn't the first large animal to die on the property. Elliot had the equipment. He buried them and then buried the horse. Drove the truck and trailer into the first barn, padlocked it, and threw away the key. The horse's bones — they'll tell the story, as will the bullets in the bodies. The truck still has the impact damage, and there's horsehair and traces of blood on the vehicle's undercarriage. The tires have rotted, the food inside the camper has petrified, but it's otherwise as it was that night it all happened. The crime-scene folks are going to excavate everything. We'll have our answers confirmed." His voice became rough. "It should never have happened, not that kind of accident, that collision of gunfire. . . ."

She tightened her grip on his arm for a brief moment. "Another tragedy pulled from the ground. You've had too many of those, Gabriel."

"This will go down as one of the saddest cases I've ever closed."

"What about the employees?"

"They worked days, didn't live on the property. Never knew a thing. It was a strong stallion and a beautiful animal, the man's pride and joy. He told his employees the horse had gotten free of its paddock, broken its legs, that he'd been forced to put the animal down. Most of them used the back entrance to the property that comes in at the stables, rather than this road that runs around the house. Whatever was left at the crash site, Fray had resolved it enough that it wasn't obvious to anyone there had been a collision like what took place there. A broken mailbox was about all that was left to see. He told us he handled the blood by dumping a load of feed, using his tractor's scoop to shove it off the road as if a spill had happened during a turn into the farm. The birds would have cleared it away for him in a day or so. The underside of a rock with dried blood on it and the small debris left behind from the damaged vehicle are the only lingering pieces of evidence."

"Elliot Fray wasn't on our list of names," Evie said. "He's nowhere in the case file."

"Your deer accident was one of your first hunches; the actual truth was so close it rhymed. You had mapped out who it was cops had interviewed along the routes, where there were gaps. The phone survey was targeted off that data, and it gave us the broken mailbox. If not that, we would have found this eventually — the right phone call, the right question. Someone would've remembered a horse died that week."

She smiled at the pep talk Gabriel was giving her. "The owner would have said nothing unusual happened that week; he wouldn't have confessed simply because he received a phone call. And the odds one of his former staff would remember a horse dying that particular week would be slim. This was an accident that turned into a crime scene, and someone had time to cover it up. If there's a reason it was missed originally, blame the lack of traffic on this roadway late on a Thursday night when it happened. You got lucky with the mail carrier remembering the mailbox. I'm okay, Gabriel, with the new piece of information turning up mostly by luck. The case is solved. That's the point of all this effort, however it comes."

"Yeah, you take the win however it comes."

"What's going to happen to Elliot?"

"He'll die from his pancreatic cancer long before the DA is able to bring formal charges and take the case to trial. His doctor confirmed it's in the late stages. That's the only reason he was willing to talk with us today. There's no specific punishment he'll face, and this way he doesn't leave to his sons the discovery in that barn."

"Not so much justice in this case either," Evie said with a sigh.

"Not so much. Reality is what it is. The DA suggested we seal his interview, the forensic findings, rather than let them go public. The Florists' relatives deserve what privacy we can give them, even if the funeral is going to be attended by hundreds of friends and neighbors and cops from everywhere."

Evie smiled at the remark, knowing that was an understatement. People would come to pay their respects, to honor the fallen deputy and his family. "How else can I help, Gabriel?"

He squeezed her gloved hand. "You just did."

"Have you spoken with your father?"

Gabriel nodded. "He's coming out."

"The Thanes will get through this together."

Gabriel faintly smiled. "We always do."

"When will you tell the Florist family?"

"Calls are already going out, asking people to come to town in the morning. They've previously asked me to tell them any news as a group, and a few have to travel some distance. The medical examiner will have dental confirmations for me by then. I'll be able to make an official notification."

"Good that they'll be together. And that you'll only have to do it once."

"A small mercy I'll gladly take."

"Being sheriff is not an easy calling."

"The hard days are brutal, and the good days are mostly quiet and occasionally boring," Gabriel agreed.

Evie smiled. "You wouldn't have it any other way."

"There are days . . ." he began, then stopped and offered her a smile instead of completing the sentence. "I'm a good sheriff, I know it. And on days like this, no one else wants the job. I'm likely to keep getting elected until I stop putting my name on the ballot."

"Its own form of job security," she quipped to further lighten the moment.

"Something like that." They turned to walk back. He offered another sweet-tart from the roll. "I'm glad you came, Evie."

"So am I. It's good to end together what we started . . . what seems like ages ago now."

Evie took off her gloves and held her hands to the warm air pouring from the heater, grateful Gabriel was the one driving as they headed back toward town. She was pretty much freezing from her fingertips to her toes and looking forward to Marie's offer of hot chocolate.

"Mind if I mention something?" Gabriel asked.

She glanced over. "Depends on what it is." He didn't look as grim now — the hours of routine work had helped. She was glad to see the change as he smiled.

"That task force you're taking on? I hope you find more than an occasional missing person who's still alive — like Shannon Bliss. Those cases that still can provide a happy ending. But all too many of the cases will be closed with a death. When you remember Carin County and the Florist family, Ashley Dayton, the Arnetts, when you think of the funerals, I hope you can keep this in mind, Evie — they may be sad moments, but families and friends are finally having the memorial service they and their loved ones deserve. It's not such a bad outcome. The cases are now solved rather than left in those 'unknown' folders. Accept that as a win in its own right."

"We made an effort to unearth the truth and eventually got answers." Evie nodded. "I can live with that, Gabriel. Can you?"

"I'm working on it."

"How's your father doing with this?" Evie asked. She'd seen Caleb speaking with Gabriel at the excavation site in the hour before they left the scene.

"He's in better shape than I am. We knew they were dead, Evie, have lived with that likelihood for years. But the *how* of it has been hard to absorb."

"Sad doesn't cover it."

Gabriel nodded. "You unearth the truth, you deal with what comes into the light. Nothing says the truth isn't going be painful, but at least it's known now. Twelve years of wondering what happened finally gets laid to rest." He glanced over. "That's why you're a detective, Evie. If you ever wonder if it's worth it or not, it is. I now know what happened to my friends."

She heard the strong emotion along with the sadness and finally understood what closure really meant when she saw it in Gabriel. Acceptance could come now. "The Thanes are going to get through this together," she reminded him once more.

Gabriel smiled, reached over to squeeze her hand. "Yeah. That matters."

She deliberately steered the conversation away from the events of the day. "I envy you for that, the family you have."

"Nothing says you can't have the same, Evie. You choose someone, you build a family together, you slide into his. The process isn't hard, it simply takes time."

"I'm sitting on a marriage proposal."

"Are you now?" he asked, looking over at her with more than some interest.

"One of those kind where he's not going to officially ask unless he's sure I'm going to say yes, but it's got a nice ring attached and a five-year plan."

Gabriel chuckled. "Admit it, that five-year plan is a relief — a picture of the future painted by someone else, something you struggle so hard to see yourself."

"The banker in him can't resist painting in the future."

"Do you like the picture?"

"Mostly. I'm not a detective, though, in his view of things."

"Just a point of reference here, Evie? You're like a good baseball pitcher — your career does have an end date. There will be a day you stop being a detective. There's no reason why you can't make that decision, the *when* that best fits with what you want in your personal life. It doesn't always have to be work that wins. Acting in favor of your personal life is perfectly acceptable. Even smart. So there it is. What do you want, Evie?"

"I still don't know." Evie turned to give him a long look. "You know what you want. Your picture is so clear, you can lay it out with ease. I want to solve real-life puzzles, and along with that figure out how to have a personal life that I consider successful.

But I don't see what that looks like yet."

"Then wait," Gabriel said. "It hasn't aged enough yet, the answer you're looking for. Just put it away for now, Evie, and let it be. Focus on solving the next crime you're handed, the next cold cases your new task force has to deal with. Play with your dogs, make more friends, and just live. You'll be fine. Like stinky bait, you catch more interesting things if you just let it sit there."

Evie laughed. "I'm not sure I shouldn't be highly insulted, Gabe. We're talking catfish here?"

He grinned, then turned serious again. "You're after an interesting life. Why not just admit that to yourself? You're ambitious for your personal life, you want a great relationship, like Ann and Paul have, and you haven't figured out where to find it yet. So just let that soak for a while and see what happens. You like Rob?"

"I do."

"Does he make you laugh?"

"On occasion."

"Then consider his proposal, see if it grows on you. I always figured he would propose around Christmastime — seemed a logical move from what I've heard of him. Much like the fact you're not sure you're ready to answer him seems like you. There's nothing at all wrong with that picture, which time isn't going to resolve."

"I can't forget those three near misses —"

"When you say yes," Gabriel said firmly, "I expect you'll make it to 'I do' this time." He glanced at her again. "We're at the Fast Café for a late dinner, whoever in the family is free and available. You have time to stay another hour? Karen's cooking isn't to be missed."

"I've got time," Evie said.

Life was going on, and for now she'd be content with where the days led her. Gabriel was good for her in that respect. He was willing to be a friend, to tell her the truth as he saw it. And she *did* need time. Her professional life was about to take a significant turn. She could afford to give her personal life the space it still needed. She looked over at Gabriel. "I heard a joke last week."

She waited to see if he was ready for something that light. He nodded. "Tell me."

She told him her joke, careful on the timing, and got the full smile she was hoping for. She produced a second roll of sweet-tarts and dropped them into his dashboard change collection.

"Hey, you're stealing my MO," he quipped.

"You taught me well," she said and grinned back. "A good friendship needs the give-and-take, and also something sweet."

Gabe shot her another smile. "It does. All candy is accepted."

He parked at the café. She let him come around and open her door, stepped out into the snowy evening.

She'd picked up another friend in the process of working toward the launch of the task force. It was a beginning. A good beginning for whatever came next in her life.

ABOUT THE AUTHOR

Dee Henderson is the author of numerous novels, including *Taken, Undetected, Unspoken, Jennifer: An O'Malley Love Story, Full Disclosure,* and the acclaimed O'MALLEY series. Her books have won or been nominated for several prestigious industry awards, such as the RITA Award, the Christy Award, and the ECPA Gold Medallion. Dee is a lifelong resident of Illinois. Learn more at DeeHenderson.com or facebook.com/DeeHendersonBooks.